GRAND CENTRAL
PUBLISHING

LARGE
PRINT

ROSES

Leila Meacham

GRAND CENTRAL
PUBLISHING

LARGE PRINT

Grand Central Publishing
Hachette Book Group
237 Park Avenue
New York, NY 10017

www.HachetteBookGroup.com.

Printed in the United States of America

First Edition: January 2010
10 9 8 7 6 5 4 3 2 1

Grand Central Publishing is a division of Hachette Book Group, Inc. The Grand Central Publishing name and logo is a trademark of Hachette Book Group, Inc.

Library of Congress Cataloging-in-Publication Data

Meacham, Leila
   Roses / Leila Meacham.
      p. cm.
Summary: "Spanning the 20th century, the story of Roses takes place in a small East Texas town against the backdrop of the powerful timber and cotton industries, industries controlled by the scions of the town's founding families."—Provided by publisher.
   ISBN 978-0-446-55998-0 (large print)   ISBN 0-446-55998-9
   1. Cities and towns—Texas—Fiction.   2. City and town life—Texas—Fiction.   3. Lumber trade—Texas—Fiction.   4. Cotton trade—Texas—Fiction.   I. Title.
   PS3563.E163R67 2009
   813'.54—dc22

                                                     2009007026

For Janice Jenning Thomson...
a friend for all seasons

And here I prophesy: this brawl today,
Grown to this faction in the Temple garden,
Shall send, between the red rose and the white,
A thousand souls to death and deadly night.
> —Earl of Warwick in
> William Shakespeare's *Henry VI*,
> part I, Act II, scene iv

ACKNOWLEDGMENTS

My thanks, first, to Louise Scherr for bringing the novel to the attention of David McCormick, superb literary agent, who, with his fine staff, made wonderful things happen for me. Among them was placing the book in the hands of Deb Futter, editor in chief of Grand Central Publishing, and her assistant, Dianne Choie. Deb led me through the revisions and Dianne the maze of publishing wickets with such humor and courtesy and understanding that those usually dreaded tasks turned into a happy experience for me.

Thanks, too, to Nancy Johanson, freelance copy editor extraordinaire, whose keen editorial eye and generous assistance were invaluable to me early on, and to Clint Rodgers, computer whiz, who answered my every (and frequent) SOS cheerfully.

And, as always, thanks to my loving husband for the many years of being there for me.

Finally—from the place where my everlasting awe resides—I give thanks for and to the friends who lined the road and cheered me on. Because of you, I reached the finish line. You know who you are.

PART I

Chapter One

At his desk, Amos Hines turned over the last sheet of the two-page legal document he'd been instructed to read. His mouth had gone dry as wheat chaff, and for a moment he could only blink in dazed disbelief at his client and longtime friend seated before his desk, a woman he had admired—revered—for forty years and had thought he knew. He searched her expression for indications that age had finally affected her faculties, but she stared back with all the clear-eyed acuity for which she was renowned. Working saliva into his mouth, he asked, "Is this codicil for real, Mary? You've sold the farms and changed your will?"

Mary Toliver DuMont nodded, the waves of her coiffed white head catching the light from the French windows. "Yes to both, Amos. I know you're shocked, and this isn't a nice way to repay all your years of service and devotion, but you'd have been deeply hurt if I'd put this business in the hands of another attorney."

"Indeed I would have," he said. "Another attorney would not have tried to talk you into rethinking this codicil—at least the part that can be revised." There was no rescuing Toliver Farms, Mary's enormous cotton holdings that she'd sold in secret negotiations the past month, a fact concealed from her great-niece sitting in ignorance out in Lubbock, Texas, as manager of Toliver Farms West.

"There's nothing to revise, Amos," Mary said with a trace of asperity. "What's done is done, and there's no changing my mind. You'd waste your time and mine by trying."

"Has Rachel done something to offend you?" he asked evenly, swiveling his chair around to a credenza. He reached for a carafe and noticed his hand shook as he poured two glasses of water. He would have preferred something stronger, but Mary never touched alcohol. "Is that why you sold the farms and amended your will?"

"Oh, good Lord, no," Mary said, sounding horrified. "You must never believe that. My great-niece has done nothing but be who she is—a Toliver through and through."

He found beverage napkins and rotated to hand Mary her glass. She'd lost weight, he decided. Her couture suit hung on her somewhat, and her coddled face—still striking at eighty-five—looked thinner.

"This business" had taken a toll on her, as it damn well should, he thought, a shaft of anger shooting through him. How could she do this to her great-niece—dispossess her of everything she'd expected to inherit—the land and house of her forebears, her right to live in the town they'd helped to found? He took a long swallow of the water and tried to keep the outrage from his voice when he observed, "You make that sound like a flaw."

"It is, and I'm correcting it." She turned up her glass and drank thirstily, patting the napkin to her lips afterward. "That's the purpose of the codicil. I don't expect you to have a clue as to what that purpose is, Amos, but Percy will when the time comes. So will Rachel once I've explained it."

"And when do you plan to do that?"

"I'm flying to Lubbock tomorrow in the company plane to meet with her. She doesn't know I'm coming. I'll tell her about the sale and the codicil then and hope that my arguments convince her I've done what's best for her."

Best for her? Amos peered over his glasses at her in incredulous wonder. Mary would have better luck selling celibacy to a sailor. Rachel would never forgive her for what she'd done, of that he was certain. He leaned forward and held her with a determined eye. "How about trying your arguments on me first, Mary? Why would you sell Toliver Farms, which you've worked most of your life to build? Why leave

Somerset to Percy Warwick, of all people? What use is a *cotton* plantation to him? Percy is a *lumberman,* for God's sake. He's ninety years old! And bequeathing the Toliver mansion to the Conservation Society is...well, it's the final slap. You know that Rachel has always regarded that house as her home. She's planning on spending the rest of her life in it."

"I know. That's why I've deprived her of it." She appeared unmoved, sitting ramrod straight with her hand curved over the crook of her anchored cane, looking for all the world like a queen on her throne and the cane her scepter. "I want her to make her own home somewhere else, start over on new ground," she said. "I don't want her staying here and living out her life according to the gospel of the Tolivers."

"But...but I don't understand." Amos spread his hands in frustration. "I thought that's what you'd prepared her for all these years."

"It was a mistake—a very selfish mistake. Thank God I realized the tragedy of my error before it was too late and had the gumption and...*wisdom* to correct it." She waved a dismissive hand. "Save your energy and mine in trying to convince me to explain, Amos. It's a puzzle, I know, but keep your faith in me. My motives could not be purer."

Bewildered, he tried another tack. "You haven't done this out of some misguided notion of what you feel you owe her father, William, have you?"

"Absolutely not!" A spark of temper flashed in her

eyes. They were known as the "Toliver eyes"—green as rare emeralds, a feature inherited from her father's side of the family along with her once black hair and the dimple in the center of her chin. "I'm sure my nephew might see it that way—or rather, that wife of his will," she said. "To her mind, I've done what's right and proper by giving William what has justly been his all along." She gave a little snort. "Let Alice Toliver have her illusion that I sold the farms out of guilt over what I owe her husband. I didn't do any of this for him, but for his daughter. I believe he'll realize that." She paused, her finely lined face pensive, doubtful, and added in a less confident tone, "I wish I could be as sure of Rachel...."

"Mary..." Amos strove for his most persuasive timbre. "Rachel's a swatch from the same cloth as you. Do you think that *you* would have understood if your father had deprived you of your legacy—the plantation, the house, the town that owes its birth to your family—no matter how justified his reasons?"

Her jaw tightened beneath the slight droop of her jowls. "No, but I wish he had. I wish to God he'd never left me Somerset."

He gaped at her, truly shocked. "But *why*? You've had a marvelous life—a life that I thought you wished to bequeath to Rachel to perpetuate your family's heritage. This codicil is so"—he swept the back of his hand over the document—"*averse* to everything I thought you'd hoped for her—that you led her to believe you *wanted* for her."

She slackened in her chair, a proud schooner with the wind suddenly sucked from her sails. She laid the cane across her lap. "Oh, Amos, it's such a long story, far too long to go into here. Percy will have to explain it all to you someday."

"Explain what, Mary? What's there to explain?" *And why someday, and why Percy?* He would not be put off by a stab of concern for her. The lines about her eyes and mouth had deepened, and her flawless complexion had paled beneath its olive skin tone. Insistently, he leaned farther over the desk. "What *story* don't I know, Mary? I've read everything ever printed about the Tolivers and Warwicks and DuMonts, not to mention having *lived* among you for forty years. I've been privy to everything affecting each of you since I came to Howbutker. Whatever *secrets* you may have harbored would have come out. I *know* you."

She lowered her lids briefly, fatigue clearly evident in their sepia-tinged folds. When she raised them again, her gaze was soft with affection. "Amos, dear, you came into our lives when our stories were done. You have known us at our best, when all our sad and tragic deeds were behind us and we were living with their consequences. Well, I want to spare Rachel from making the same mistakes I made and suffering the same, inevitable consequences. I don't intend to leave her under the Toliver curse."

"The Toliver curse?" Amos blinked in alarm. Such eccentric language was unlike her. He wondered if age *had* affected her brain. "I never heard of or read anything about a Toliver curse."

"My point exactly," she said, giving him her typical smile, a mere lifting of the lips over teeth that remarkably—unlike those of her contemporaries, unlike his—had not yellowed to the hue of old piano keys.

He refused to be dismissed. "Well, what about *these* consequences?" he demanded. "You owned—or did—a cotton empire stretching across the country. Your husband, Ollie DuMont, possessed one of the finest department stores in Texas, and Percy Warwick's company has been in the Fortune 500 for decades. What 'sad and tragic deeds' led to consequences like *those,* I'd like to know."

"You must believe me," she said, straightening her shoulders. "There *is* a Toliver curse, and it has affected us all. Percy is well aware of it. Rachel will be, too, when I show her evidence of its indisputable existence."

"You've left her a ton of money," he pursued, unwilling to give up. "Suppose she buys land somewhere else, builds another Somerset, roots a new dynasty of Tolivers all over again. Wouldn't this...curse you speak of still hold?"

Her eyes flashed with something indecipherable. Her lip curled with a secret bitterness. "*Dynasty* implies sons and daughters to pass on the ancestral torch. In that respect, the Tolivers have never been a dynasty, a point you may have missed in your history books." Her drawl was heavy with irony. "No, the curse won't hold. Once the umbilical cord is cut to the plantation, the curse will die. No land anywhere else will have the power to extract from us what Somerset has. Rachel will never sell her soul as I have for the sake of family soil."

"You sold your soul for Somerset?"

"Yes, many times. Rachel has, too. I'm breaking her of that tendency."

He slumped in defeat. He was beginning to think that indeed he'd missed a few chapters in the history books. He attempted one final argument. "Mary, this codicil represents your last regards to those you love. Think of how its provisions might affect not only Rachel's memory of you, but also the relationship between her and Percy when he's in possession of her birthright. Are those the regards by which you wish to be remembered?"

"I'll risk their misinterpretation," she said, but her look mellowed. "I know how very fond you are of Rachel and that you think I've betrayed her. I haven't, Amos. I've saved her. I wish there were time today to explain what I mean by that, but there simply isn't. You must trust that I know what I'm doing."

He laced his hands over the codicil. "I have the rest of the day. Susan has rescheduled my afternoon appointments. I have all the time in the world for you to explain to me what this is all about."

She reached over the desk and covered the gnarl of his rawboned hands with her slim, blue-veined one. "You may have, my dear, but I do not. I believe now would be a good time for you to read the letter in the other envelope."

He glanced at the white envelope he'd withdrawn facedown from the one containing the codicil. "Save that one for last to read," she'd instructed, and suddenly—with a sharp flash of intuition—he understood why. His heartbeat arrested, he turned over the envelope and read the sender's address. "A medical clinic in Dallas," he muttered, aware that Mary had turned her head away and was fingering the famed string of pearls around her neck that her husband, Ollie, had presented her, one pearl on each of their wedding anniversaries until the year of his death. There were fifty-two of them now, large as humming-bird eggs, the strand falling perfectly in the collarless opening of her green linen suit. It was on these pearls that he fastened his eyes when he'd finished reading the letter, unable to bring them to her face.

"Metastatic renal cancer," he croaked, his prominent Adam's apple jouncing. "And there's nothing to be done?"

"Oh, the usual," she said, reaching for her water glass. "Surgery and chemo and radiation. But all that would simply prolong my days, not my life. I decided against treatment."

Burning grief, like acid, spilled through him. He

removed his glasses and squeezed his eyes shut, pinching the bridge of his nose to hold back tears. Mary did not like sloppy displays of emotion. Now he knew what she'd been about in Dallas last month besides arranging for the sale of Toliver Farms. They'd had no idea—not her great-niece or her longest friend, Percy, or Sassie, her housekeeper for over forty years, or her devoted old lawyer...all those who loved her. How like Mary to play her last cards so close to the vest.

He reset his glasses and forced himself to meet her eyes—eyes that still, despite their lined settings, reminded him of the color of spring leaves shimmering through raindrops. "How long?" he asked.

"They give me three more weeks...maybe."

Losing the battle to his grief, Amos opened a drawer where he kept a supply of clean handkerchiefs. "I'm sorry, Mary," he said, pressing the voluminous square of white lawn to his eyes, "but too much is coming at me all at once...."

"I know, Amos," she said, and with surprising nimbleness, she hooked the cane on her chair and came around the desk to him. Gently, she drew his head against her linen front. "This day had to come, you know...when we had to say good-bye. After all, I'm fifteen years your senior...."

He pressed her hand, so thin and fragile-boned. When had it become an old woman's hand? He remembered when it had been smooth and unblemished. "Do you know that I still remember the first time I saw you?" he said, keeping his eyes tightly closed. "It was in the DuMont Department Store. You came down the stairs in a royal blue dress, and your hair shone like black satin under the chandeliers."

He could feel her smile above his bald pate. "I remember. You were still in your army serge. By then you'd learned who William was and had come to check on the sort of people who would cause a boy like him to run away from home. I must say you did seem rather dazzled."

"I was bowled over."

She kissed the top of his head and released him. "I've always been grateful for our friendship, Amos. I want you to know that," she said, returning to her chair. "I'm not one to emote, as you know, but the day you wandered into our little East Texas community was one of the more fortunate ones of my life."

Amos honked into his handkerchief. "Thank you, Mary. Now I must ask you, does Percy know about...your condition?"

"Not yet. I'll tell him and Sassie when I get back from Lubbock. I'll make my funeral arrangements at that time as well. If I'd planned them earlier, news of my coming demise would be all over town by the time I left the parking lot. Hospice has been engaged to come a week after I return. Until then, I'd like my illness to remain our secret." She slipped the strap of her handbag over her shoulder. "And now I must be going."

"No, no!" he protested, vaulting up from his chair. "It's early yet."

"No, Amos, it's late." She reached behind her neck and unclasped the pearls. "These are for Rachel," she said, laying the strand on his desk. "I'd like you to give them to her for me. You'll know the proper time."

"Why not give them to her yourself when you see her?" he asked, his throat on fire. She seemed diminished without the pearls, her flesh old and exposed. Since Ollie's death twelve years ago, she was rarely seen without them. She wore them everywhere, with everything.

"She may not accept them after our talk, Amos, and then what would I do with them? They mustn't be left to the discretion of the docents. You keep them until she's ready. They are all she will have from me of the life she was expecting."

He bumped around the desk, his heart thudding. "Let me go with you to Lubbock," he pleaded. "Let me be with you when you tell her."

"No, dear friend. Your presence there might make things awkward for the two of you afterward if things go wrong. Rachel must believe you're impartial. She'll need you. Whatever happens, either way, she'll need you."

"I understand," he said, his voice cracking. She held out her hand, and he understood that she wished them to express their farewells now. In the days to come, they might not be afforded this opportunity to say good-bye in private. He sandwiched her cool palm between his bony slabs, his eyes filling in spite of his determination to keep this moment on the dignified plane she'd lived all her life. "Good-bye, Mary," he said.

She took up her cane. "Good-bye, Amos. See after Rachel and Percy for me."

"You know I will."

She nodded, and he watched her tap her way to the door, back straining for the regal posture so typically Mary. Opening it, she did not look back but gave him a small wave over her shoulder as she stepped out and closed the door behind her.

Chapter Two

Amos stood in the silence, staring numbly into space, letting the tears trickle unchecked down his face. After a moment, he drew in a ragged breath, locked his office door, and returned to his desk, where he carefully wrapped the pearls in a clean handkerchief. They felt cool and fresh. Mary must have had them cleaned recently. There was no oil, no feel of her, to his touch. He would take them home at the end of the day and keep them for Rachel in a hand-carved letter box, the only memento of his mother's he'd chosen to keep. He removed his tie, unbuttoned his collar, and went into an adjoining bathroom to wash his face. After toweling it dry, he administered eyedrops prescribed for ocular fatigue.

Back at his desk, he punched an intercom button. "Susan, take the afternoon off. Hang out the CLOSED sign and hook us up to the answering machine."

"Are you all right, Amos?"

"I'm fine."

"Miss Mary—is she okay?"

"She's fine, too." She didn't believe him, of course, but he trusted his secretary of twenty years to say nothing of her suspicions that all was not fine with her employer and Miss Mary. "Go and enjoy your afternoon."

"Well...until tomorrow, then."

"Yes, until tomorrow."

Tomorrow. He felt sick at what that day would bring to Rachel, who right now was no doubt surveying cotton fields she thought would one day be hers. Tomorrow it would all be over—everything she'd given her adult life to. She was only twenty-nine and soon to be rich. She could start over—if she wasn't too shattered to begin again—but it would be beyond Howbutker, beyond the future he'd envisioned for himself when Percy was gone, the last of the three friends who'd constituted the only family he'd ever known. He regarded Matt, Percy's grandson, like a nephew, but when he married, his wife might have something to say about her family filling the void left by Ollie and Mary and Percy. Rachel, now, would have been another story. She adored him as he did her, and her house would have always been open to him. His old bachelor heart had so looked forward to her coming to live in Howbutker, residing in the Toliver mansion, keeping Mary's spirit alive, marrying and raising kids for him to love and spoil in his declining years. Tomorrow all that would be over for him, too.

He heaved a sigh and opened a door in the credenza. Never did he take a drink before six o'clock in the evening, and then his limit was two shots of Scotch mellowed with twice as much soda. Today he took a bottle from the cabinet, dumped the water from his glass, and unhesitatingly poured it half-full of Johnnie Walker Red.

Glass in hand, he crossed to the French windows overlooking a small courtyard rife with the summer flowers of East Texas—pink primroses and blue plumbago, violet lantana and yellow nasturtium, all climbing the rock fence. The garden had been designed by Charles Waithe, son of the founder of the firm, to serve as a mental retreat from the heartsick duties of his office. Today the therapy didn't work, but it evoked memories that Mary's visit had already jogged to the surface. He remembered the day Charles, then a man of fifty, had turned from this window and asked if he'd be interested in a junior partner position. He'd been stunned, elated. The offer had come within the forty-eight hours he'd given William Toliver his train ticket, seen Mary on the stairs, and met her locally prominent husband and the equally powerful Percy Warwick. It had all happened so fast, his head still spun when he thought of how fate had been kind and parlayed his decision to part with his ticket into the fulfillment of his dreams—a job in his field, a place to call home, and friends to take him to their bosoms.

It had all come about one early October morning in 1945. Just discharged from the army, with no job on the horizon and nowhere to hang his hat, he was on his way to Houston to see a sister he barely knew when the train stopped briefly outside a little burg with a sign over the station house that read: *WELCOME TO HOWBUTKER, HEART OF THE PINEY WOODS OF TEXAS.* He'd gotten off to stretch his legs when a teenage boy with green eyes and hair as black as a cornfield crow ran up to the conductor hollering, "Hold the train! Hold the train!"

"Got a ticket, son?"

"No, sir, I—"

"Well, then, you'll have to wait for the next train. This one's full to capacity from here to Houston."

Amos had looked at the flushed face of the boy, his breath coming out in fast, chilled puffs, and recognized the desperation of a boy running away from home. He's taking too much with him, he'd thought, recalling his own experience as a boy of fifteen on the lam from his parents. He hadn't made it. That's when he'd handed the boy his ticket. "Here. Take mine," he'd said. "I'll wait for the next train."

The boy—whom he later discovered to be the seventeen-year-old nephew of Mary Toliver DuMont—had rushed out on the platform to wave at him as the train bore him away, never to return to Howbutker to live. And Amos had never left. He'd hoisted his duffel and started into town with the idea of staying only one night, but the morning train had taken off without him. He'd often reflected on the irony of it…how William's exit out of Howbutker had been his entrance in, and he'd never regretted a single day of it. Until now.

He took a fiery swallow of the Scotch, feeling it go down like broken razor blades. *Dammit, Mary, what in the world possessed you to do such a deplorable thing?* He ran a hand over his bald scalp. What in God's name had he missed that would explain—*excuse*—what she had done? He'd thought he knew her history and those of Ollie DuMont and Percy Warwick inside out. What he hadn't read, he had heard from their own mouths. Naturally, he had arrived too late to witness the beginning of their stories, but he'd made a point to fill in the gaps. Nowhere had he come across anything—not a scrap of gossip, newspaper clipping, journal, not a word from people who had known them all their lives—that would explain why Mary had severed Rachel's ties to her birthright and destroyed her lifelong dream.

A sudden thought drove him to a bookshelf. He sought and found a volume that he took to his desk. *Could the answer be here?* He'd not read the history of the founding families of Howbutker since that October morning he'd helped William escape. Later in town, he'd learned that a search was on for the runaway, son of the late Miles Toliver, brother of Mary Toliver DuMont, who'd subsequently adopted the boy and given him everything. Bitterly recalling his own mistreatment when he'd been dragged back to his parents, he'd gone to the library seeking information about the rich DuMonts that would help him decide whether he should alert the authorities to the boy's destination or keep his silence. There a librarian had handed him a copy of this book written by Jessica Toliver, Mary's great-grandmother. Now that he was looking, a clue to Mary's motives might pop out that he'd missed forty years ago. The title of the book was *Roses*.

The narrative began with the immigration of Silas William Toliver and Jeremy Matthew Warwick to Texas in the fall of 1836. As the youngest sons of two of South Carolina's most prominent plantation families, they stood little chance of becoming masters of their fathers' estates and thus set out together to establish plantations of their own in a loam-rich area they'd been told existed in the eastern part of the new republic of Texas. Both were blue-blooded descendants of English royalty, though they sprang from warring houses—the Lancasters and the Yorks. In the middle of the 1600s, descendants of their families, who had been enemies during the War of the Roses, found themselves settling cheek by jowl on plantations in the New World near the future site of Charleston, which they helped to establish in 1670. Out of mutual dependence, the two families had buried their ancestral differences, retaining only the emblems by which their allegiance to their respective houses in England were known—their roses. The Warwicks, descended from the House of York, grew only white roses in their gardens, while the Tolivers cultivated exclusively red roses, the symbol of the House of Lancaster.

By 1830, cotton was king in the South, and the two youngest sons yearned for plantations of their own in a place where they might establish a town that reflected the noblest ideals of their English and southern culture. Joining their wagon train were families of lesser breeding and education who nonetheless shared the same dreams, and regard for hard work, God, and their southern heritage. Included also were the slaves—men, women, and children—upon whose backs these dreams were to be made possible. They started west, taking the southern route along the trails that had lured men like Davy Crockett and Jim Bowie. Near New Orleans, a Frenchman, tall and slim in the saddle, rode out to meet them. He introduced himself as Henri DuMont and asked if he could join the train. He was dressed in a suit of the finest cut and cloth and exuded charm and sophistication. He, too, was an aristocrat, a descendant of King Louis VI, whose family had immigrated to Louisiana to escape the horrors of the French Revolution. Owing to a falling-out with his father over how to run their exclusive mercantile store in New Orleans, it was now his intention to establish his own emporium in Texas, without paternal interference. Silas and Jeremy welcomed him.

Had they continued a bit farther west toward a town now called Corsicana, so Jessica Toliver informed the reader, they would have reached the land they were seeking, an area rich in a soil known as "black waxy" that was to yield huge crops of corn and cotton to future landowners. As it was, horses and travelers were tired by the time the wagon train crossed the Sabine River from Louisiana into Texas, and a weary Silas William Toliver surveyed the pine-covered hillsides and drawled, "How about here?"

The question was passed and repeated among the settlers, though with less refined tongues, and by the end of the line it had become: "How 'bout cher?" Thus it was that the town came to be called after the question to which the colonizers unanimously answered yes. The founding fathers gave in to the consensus that the town be so named only on the condition that the *ch* be hardened to a *k* and spelled and pronounced as "How-but-ker."

Despite its rather yokelish name, the first inhabitants were determined to set a cultured tone for the community not unlike the gracious way of life they'd known, or wanted to know. They were in accord that here among the pine trees, life would be lived in the traditional southern fashion. As it turned out, few became plantation owners. There were too many trees to clear from the land, and the hillsides were difficult to work. There were other vocations to which a man could turn his hands if he was able and willing. Some settled for smaller farms, others chose cattle raising, a few went into dairy farming. A number opened businesses built to the exact specifications laid out by the city planning commission and agreed upon by the voting citizens of the young community. Jeremy Warwick saw his financial future assured in the cutting and selling of timber. His eye was on the markets to be found in Dallas and Galveston and other cities springing up in the new republic.

Henri DuMont opened a dry-goods store in the center of town that in time surpassed the elegance of his father's in New Orleans. In addition, he bought and developed property for commercial purposes, renting his buildings to shopkeepers lured to Howbutker by its reputation for civic-mindedness, law and order, and the sobriety of its citizens. But Silas William Toliver had not been willing to turn his hands to another occupation. Convinced that man's only vocation was land, he set about with his slaves to cultivate and plant his acres in cotton, using his profits to expand his holdings. Within a few years, he owned the largest tract of land along the Sabine River, which afforded easy transport of his cotton by raft to the Gulf of Mexico.

He permitted only one alteration to the life he had envisioned when he left South Carolina. Rather than constructing the plantation manor on the land he cleared, he built it in town as a concession to his wife. She preferred to reside among her friends dwelling in other mansions of southern inspiration on a street named Houston Avenue. Along this street, known locally as Founders Row, lived the DuMonts and Warwicks.

Silas called his plantation Somerset, after the English duke from whom he was descended.

Not surprisingly, at the first meeting to discuss the creation of the town, its layout and design, the reins of leadership were voted over to Silas and Jeremy and Henri. As a student of world history, Henri was familiar with the War of the Roses in England and the part his colleagues' families had played in the thirty-two-year conflict. He had noted the root-wrapped rose-bushes each family had labored to bring from South Carolina and understood their significance. After the meeting, he made a private suggestion to the two family heads. Why not grow both colors of roses in their gardens, plant the white and red to mingle equally as a show of unity?

An uncomfortable silence met this proposal. Henri placed a hand on the shoulder of each man and said quietly, "There are bound to be differences between you. You have brought them with you in the guise of your roses."

"They are the symbols of our lineage, of who we are," protested Silas Toliver.

"That is so," agreed Henri. "They are symbols of

what you are *individually,* but they must also represent what you are *collectively.* You are men of responsibility. Responsible men reason out their differences. They do not make war to solve them. As long as your gardens boast only the symbol of your own house to the exclusion of the other, there will be the suggestion of war—at best, estrangement—as an alternate course, the course your forebears chose in England."

"What about you?" one of them asked. "You are with us in this enterprise. What will you grow in your garden?"

"Why…" The Frenchman spread his hands in the manner of his countrymen. "The red and white rose, what else? They will be a reminder of my duty to our friendship, to our joint endeavors. And if ever I should offend you, I will send a red rose to ask forgiveness. And if ever I receive one tendered for that purpose, I will return a white rose to say that all is forgiven."

The two men mused over the suggestion. "We are men of great pride," Jeremy Warwick finally conceded. "It is difficult for men like us to admit our mistakes to those we offend."

"And as hard to give voice to forgiveness," offered Silas Toliver. "Having in our gardens the pick of both roses would allow us to ask for and grant pardon without words." He reflected a moment. "What if…pardon is not granted? What then? Do we grow pink roses as well?"

"*Pink* roses?" Henri scoffed. "What a pithless color

for such a noble flower. No, gentlemen, I would suggest white and red only. The presence of any other implies the possibility of the unthinkable. Among men of honest intentions and goodwill, there is no mistake, no error of human judgment, no faux pas, that cannot be forgiven. Come now, what do you say?"

For answer, Jeremy lifted his champagne glass, and Silas followed suit. "Hear! Hear!" they chorused. "Here's to the red and white. May they grow in our gardens forever!"

Amos let out a sigh and closed the book. Fascinating reading, but no use continuing. The volume ended with an optimistic listing of the progeny expected to carry on in the illustrious tradition of its patriarchs and descendants, namely Percy Warwick, Ollie DuMont, and Miles and Mary Toliver. Since the book was published in 1901, Mary would have been one year old, the boys only five. The answers he sought lay in their later lives. *Roses* would contain nothing of Mary's hint of a tragedy the families had shared that would account for her actions. But what?

It was a well-known fact that while they lived in one another's pockets socially, they worked and prospered separately. It was a rule established at the beginning that each man's enterprise must rise and fall by his own merits—without financial aid or assistance from the others. Amos thought "Neither a lender nor a borrower be" an unneighborly maxim among friends, but as far as he knew, the policy had never been breached. The Tolivers grew cotton, the Warwicks mined timber, the DuMonts sold luxury dry goods, and never—even when Mary Toliver had married Ollie DuMont—had they mingled their entities or relied on one another's resources.

Then why would Mary leave Somerset to Percy?

You came into our lives when our stories were done, Mary had said, and he was now willing to believe that he had. Only one man could supply the missing chapters. He longed to storm to Warwick Hall, pound on the door, and demand that Percy tell him what had led Mary to sell Toliver Farms, bequeath him her family's 160-year-old plantation, and disenfranchise the great-niece she loved from her heritage. What in the name of all that was holy had driven her to draw up this unthinkable, irrevocable codicil in the last weeks of her life?

But as Mary's attorney, he had no choice but to choke on his silence and hope the fallout from this unexpected turn of events would not be as explosive as he feared. He wished Mary luck tomorrow when she dropped her bomb on her great-niece. It broke his heart to think it, but he would not be one bit surprised if Rachel ordered pink roses for her grave. What a sad mantle to Mary's memory. What a tragic ending to the special relationship they had shared.

Wagging his head and a little drunk, Amos heaved

himself up from his chair and slipped the codicil and letter back into their envelopes. For a second he considered the wastebasket, then shrugged and weaved to the documents cabinet, where he filed away in its proper place the last regards of Mary DuMont.

Chapter Three

Relying heavily on her cane, Mary paused on the sidewalk outside Amos's office to draw breath. Her throat and eyes burned. Her lungs felt squeezed. It had been almost too much, that. Dear, faithful, devoted Amos. They hadn't deserved him. Forty years... Had it really been that long since she'd come down the stairs in the department store—worried out of her mind over William's disappearance—to find a young captain of the 101st Airborne Division gawping up at her?

That moment was as fresh to her recollection as if it had happened a few turns of the calendar back. God must have a Machiavellian turn of mind to devise the cruelties inherent with growing old. At the very least, the elderly ought to be allowed an accurate perception of time... to see the years as the stretch they really were, not be made to feel they had all gone in a flash and the beginning was no more than a short distance back. At the end, the old and dying ought to be spared the feeling that life had just begun.

Oh, well, people in hell would like a cold glass of water, too, she thought, shrugging, and reflected again on Amos. She was a dreadful ingrate to leave him with such a task, but he was brave and scrupulous. He would not flinch from his professional duty. Some family lawyers, believing they knew best, would throw the codicil into the wastebasket with no one being the wiser, but not Amos. He would carry out her instructions to the letter, thank God.

Her breathing coming easier, she put on her sunglasses and looked down the sidewalk for a glimpse of Henry returning to drive her home. She'd sent her chauffeur to have a cup of coffee at the Courthouse Café while she visited with Amos, but he was probably still flirting with Ruby, a waitress of his age. Good enough, she thought. It had been her plan to complete one more task at home before lunch, and then all her affairs would be in order. But that could wait, she decided, drawing herself erect. She felt well enough to take a stroll first, her last in the town her family had helped to found.

It had been a long while since she had walked all the way around Courthouse Circle, gazing in shop windows and visiting with proprietors, most of them longtime friends of hers. She was not as visible as she had once been. For years, she had made a point of keeping in touch with the folks who made their East Texas community the pleasant town it was—hardworking storekeepers and clerks, bank tellers, and secretaries, as well as those who ran the place...the City Hall gang, as she referred to them fondly. She was a Toliver, and it was her duty to be seen occasionally, one of the reasons she always dressed to the nines when she came to town, the other being in honor of Ollie's memory.

And she'd have done him proud today, she thought, glancing down at her Albert Nipon suit and reptile pumps and handbag. She felt slightly undressed without the pearls—vulnerable somehow—but that was her imagination, and she hadn't long to miss them anyway.

As expected, she found Henry, her chauffeur of twenty years and the nephew of her housekeeper, at the counter of the Courthouse Café, chatting with Ruby. There was a bit of a flurry when she entered. Her appearance was always cause for notice. A farmer in overalls scooted out of his booth to hold the door open for her, and she had to wave several businessmen back to their lunch specials when she passed their tables.

"How do, Miss Mary," Ruby greeted her. "You come to get this here rascal off my hands?"

"Not for a while, Ruby." Mary indicated that Henry remain on his stool. "Hope you can put up with him a little longer. I want to walk a bit, see some folks. Order yourself another cup, Henry. I won't be long."

Henry's face showed dismay. It was time for Sassie's noonday meal. "You goin' for a walk in this heat, Miss Mary? Sure that's wise?"

"No, but at my age, I'm entitled to a little foolishness."

Outside on the sidewalk, Mary paused to consider her destination, her gaze drifting around the circle to note the number of new businesses that had gone up in the last few years. She eyed them with mixed emotions. Howbutker had become a tourist attraction. Discovered by such magazines as *Southern Living* and *Texas Monthly* that extolled its Greek Revivalist charm, regional cuisine, and clean restrooms, it had become a favorite of the yuppie crowd seeking a weekend retreat from urban hordes and noise. There was a constant clamor from outside interests for permits to renovate period homes into bed-and-breakfasts and to build the commercial eyesores that would detract from its antebellum character. The city council on which Amos served and Percy and Mary sat as members emeriti had managed to restrict all motels, fastfood chains, and discount stores to the city limits.

That won't last long, Mary thought with regret, glancing across the circle at a recently erected boutique owned and run by a stylish New Yorker. The woman's brash manner and accent stuck out like a nose wart, but Mary realized that the town would inevitably draw more like her. Once the old guard disappeared, the preservation of Howbutker would be left to the likes of Gilda Castoni and Max Warner, the rather likable Chicagoan who owned the new and very popular sing-along bar up the street.

Her lips twisted ruefully. She ought to be thankful that these invaders who had fled pollution, crime, and traffic would guard Howbutker's way of life more zealously than the descendants of the original inhabitants. Matt Warwick was one of the remaining few of those. As was Rachel....

There now, no point in harping on that.

She redirected her thoughts. She'd said a final good-bye to Rene Taylor, the postmistress, when she'd dropped off a package at the post office earlier, though her old friend hadn't known it, but it would also be pleasant to visit one last time with Annie Castor, the florist, and James Wilson, president of the First State Bank. Unfortunately, the florist shop and bank were on opposite turns of the circle, and she wasn't strong enough to walk to both. She still had to climb to the attic when she got home and dig to the bottom of Ollie's army trunk. The bank, she decided, tapping forward. Once there, she might as well look through her safe-deposit box. Nothing much was in it, but she may have forgotten something best removed.

She passed the barbershop and nodded through the glass to Bubba Speer, the proprietor. His eyes widened in surprise when he saw her, and he left his draped customer to hurry to the door and call after her, "Well, hello there, Miss Mary! Good to see you. What brings you to town?"

Mary stopped to acknowledge him. Bubba wore a

short-sleeved white barber's smock, and she noticed a faded blue tattoo on his arm. A memento of the war, she'd guess. Was it Korea or Vietnam? How old was Bubba, anyway? She blinked rapidly in a moment of helpless confusion. She had known Bubba Speer all his life and had never noticed a tattoo. Her powers of observation had sharpened lately. She saw things she'd missed, but recently she'd also had trouble with the chronological placement of events and people. "A few legal matters to discuss with Amos," she answered. "How're you, Bubba? Family all right?"

"That boy of mine's been accepted at Texas University. Thanks for remembering his graduation. He can sure use that check you sent. It's going to buy books come September."

"So he said in his thank-you note. He writes a fine hand, that boy of yours. We're proud of him." Vietnam, Mary decided. It had to be Vietnam.

"Well...he's got a lot of folks round here to live up to, Miss Mary," the barber said.

She smiled. "Take care of yourself, Bubba. Tell the family...bye for me." She continued down the street, feeling Bubba's puzzled stare. Now that was a bit melodramatic, but Bubba would feel a sense of importance later when he repeated what she'd said. *She knew,* he'd say. *Miss Mary knew she was dying. Otherwise, why did she say what she did?* It would add to her legend, which would eventually die out as Ollie's had with him, and once the generation of

Bubba's children was gone, there would be no one to remember the Tolivers and who they were.

Well, so be it! Mary thought, pressing her lips together firmly. Only Percy would be leaving a descendant to carry on in the family tradition. And what a chip off his grandfather's block he was! Matt Warwick reminded her of her Matthew in so many ways, though her son had inherited her Toliver features, and Matt, his grandfather's. Even so, sometimes looking at Matt as a man, she saw her own son grown.

She stepped down from the sidewalk onto the street. Motorists wishing to turn right were momentarily held up, but Mary did not hurry, and no one honked. This was Howbutker. People had manners here.

Safely across, she stopped and stared in startled interest at a gigantic elm whose branches shaded an entire side of the courthouse common. She could remember when the tree had been a sapling. In July 1914, that was, the year the courthouse was finished, seventy-one years ago. A tall statue of Saint Francis stood under its branches, the saint's famous prayer chiseled around its stone base.

Mary put a halting step forward, staring at the bench where she'd sat in the elm's patchy shade, listening to her father deliver the dedication speech. It was happening once more, this sense of being young again, new blood running through her veins. It was not "In life we are dying" that she minded so much. It

was that in dying, she should feel so alive, so new, so
fresh, the whole future before her. She remembered—
felt!—being fourteen again, coming down the stairs
that morning in her white eyelet dress with its green
satin trim, a ribbon of the same satin holding back her
hair, its ends as long as the black curls that bounced
off her shoulders. Below, her father had looked up at
her with paternal pride and pronounced that she was
"heartbreakingly fetching!" while her mother had
pulled on her gloves and reminded her in her crisp
manner, "Pretty is as pretty does!"

She had drawn everyone's eye at the dedication…everyone's but Percy's. Her brother's other
friends had teased her fondly, Ollie remarking at how
grown up she was becoming and how the green satin
set off the color of her irises.

Mary closed her eyes. She remembered the heat
and humidity of that day, how she'd thought she'd
die of thirst, when suddenly out of nowhere, Percy
had appeared and handed her an ice-cream soda from
the drugstore across the street.

Percy…

Her heart began to race as it had then to find him
suddenly standing there, tall, blond, and at nineteen
so handsome that one could hardly bear to look at
him. She had once thought him awfully gallant, the
hero of all her secret dreams, but when she became "a
young lady," she'd felt a change in his affection. It was
as if he saw in her some private cause for amusement

Many times she'd stood before her mirror puzzling over his new attitude, hurt by the mockery she saw in his eyes. She was pretty enough, though there was nothing of the pink-and-white Dresden doll daintiness about her. She was too tall for a girl and too long in the arms and legs. Her olive complexion was a constant bone of contention between her and her mother, who hardly allowed her out of the house without gloves and a bonnet. What was worse, while others lovingly called her "Mary Lamb," Percy had nicknamed her "Gypsy," which she took as an insult to her Toliver coloring.

Still, she knew there was something striking about the combination of her black hair and green eyes and oval-shaped face with its marked Toliver features. Her manners, too, were lovely, as befitting a Toliver, and she made good marks in school. No cause for mockery there.

And so, because she could not pin down a justifiable cause for Percy's recent disdain, a sort of antipathy grew between them, at least on her part. Percy seemed as unaware of her dislike as he had been of her admiration.

On this day, she had looked at the soda with an outward scorn but an inner acute longing. (It was chocolate, her favorite.) All through the long July morning, she had managed to strike a pose impervious to the heat and cloying humidity, keeping her arms a discreet distance from her body to allow a negligible breeze up

her sleeves. And now without warning, Percy's grin
and soda were implying that he saw through her crisp
outer appearance and knew that inside the eyelet dress
she was dissolving into her underwear.

"Here," he said. "Take this. You look about to
melt."

She perceived it as a deliberate affront. Toliver
ladies never looked about to melt. Throwing up her
chin, she rose from the park bench and said in her
best haughty manner, "Too bad you're not gentleman
enough not to notice."

Percy had laughed. "Gentleman be damned. I'm
your friend. Drink up. You don't have to thank me."

"You are quite right about *that,* Percy Warwick,"
she said, sidestepping the proffered soda. "However,
I would thank you to give it to someone whose thirst
requires refreshment."

She stalked off to congratulate her father, who
had finished his speech, but halfway to the courthouse steps she glanced back. Percy was watching
her as she'd left him, grin still in place and the soda
sweating in his hand. A sensation unknown to her
fourteen-year-old body flushed through her, dizzy-
ing in its intensity as their gazes locked in a kind of
recognition across the shimmering distance. A cry
of surprise and protest rose and died in her throat,
but somehow Percy heard it. He grinned wider in
response and raised the glass to her, then drank, and
she could taste the cold chocolate in her mouth.

Mary could taste the cold sweetness now. She could feel the sweat collecting under her arms and between her breasts and the same sensation tightening her stomach and thighs. "Percy...," she murmured.

"Mary?"

She turned at the sound of the familiar voice, as agile as a girl of fourteen, but she was confused. How had Percy gotten behind her? She had just seen him standing beneath the elm on the courthouse common.

"Percy, my love...," she greeted him in surprise, hampered by the cane and handbag from holding out her arms. "Did you have to drink *all* my soda? I wanted it that day, you know, as much as I wanted you, but I didn't know it. I was too young and silly and too much of a Toliver. If only I hadn't been such a fool—"

She felt herself shaken. "Miss Mary...it's Matt."

Chapter Four

Matt?" Mary repeated, blinking into the concerned face of Percy's grandson.

"Yes, ma'am," Matt said.

Oh, Lord, Mary thought as her confusion cleared and she read Matt's expression. She'd let a very old cat out of a very old bag. How could she explain her way out of this? But she was loath to let go of the memories of that day while the feelings still lingered. How great it had been to go back for those few throbbing minutes when the juices still flowed and her blood had thrilled. To see Percy again at nineteen....

Senility did have its rewards.

She smiled at Matt and patted the starched front of his shirt. Like his grandfather, he dressed in coat and tie, even in summer. "Hello, dear. Did you catch me talking to myself?"

"I can't think of a better person to have a conversation with than yourself, Miss Mary," Matt said, his eyes, bright blue like his grandmother's, alight with curiosity and surprise. "It's good to see you. We've all missed you this past month, Granddad especially. Were you headed somewhere special? Let me walk you there."

"Actually, dear, I just got back," Mary said, smiling cryptically, indulging herself. "From the past," she added, seeing his brows raise. She suspected he'd been watching her from a courthouse window and knew she hadn't been anywhere. What difference did it make now, anyhow? Matt was young enough to get over anything and old enough to understand the indiscretions of which he now suspected her and his grandfather guilty. She looked at him fondly. "You haven't lived long enough to have a past, but you will someday."

"I'll soon turn thirty-five, creeping up there," Matt said with a grin. "Now, come on, where are you going?"

"Nowhere, I guess." She suddenly felt tired. She saw that Henry's hunger pangs had driven him out on the sidewalk to look for her. She nodded toward her limousine, and he struck off eagerly toward Amos's office.

"Henry's gone for the car," Mary said. "Walk me back to the corner, will you? It's been a while since we talked." She slipped her hand under Matt's arm, wielding the cane with the other. "When are you going to marry, Matt? You can't be hurting for choices."

"You'd be surprised. Lots of choices, but none

too choice. How is that great-niece of yours, by the way? Any hope she'll be paying us a visit soon? You know, I haven't seen her since Mister Ollie died. She was around sixteen or seventeen, I recall—already a beauty then."

"Seventeen," Mary murmured, her throat suddenly tightening. "She was born in 1956."

It was something else she'd have to account for, her hand in keeping Matt and Rachel apart. Ever since they'd met the first time, when Rachel was fourteen, she'd speculated on the supreme irony of the two of them attracting each other and something coming of it down the line. At their second meeting—Ollie's funeral—three years later, they had already developed into the breed they would become—Rachel the planter and Matt the lumberman—a combination that never would have worked...not for Somerset.

She'd felt the spark between them on that occasion, had seen the interest in Matt's eye, the admiration in Rachel's, and decided right there and then that the two should never be in Howbutker at the same time. It had not been difficult to arrange. Matt had already graduated from college by then, and for most of his young adult life his grandfather had had him out of town learning the business of Warwick Industries' far-flung operations. When he did manage to get home for short visits and holidays, Mary had made sure that Rachel was occupied elsewhere. Any lingering curiosity her great-niece may have had about

Percy's handsome grandson, she'd discouraged by simply never bringing up his name and changing the subject when it invariably was. There was five years' difference in their ages, and she'd counted on Matt being married by the time Rachel had graduated from Texas A&M and was ready to settle down.

Of course, all that conniving had happened a number of years before the full picture of the tragedy she was creating had begun to emerge...before Rachel's falling-out with her mother and the breakup with her air force pilot. How could she have foreseen that Rachel—within sight of thirty and Matt nearly thirty-five, the same age difference between her and Percy—would be unmarried still? Matt had moved home for good. He had taken over as head of Warwick Industries, and, but for the codicil, Rachel would have been coming home, too.... She halted. *What if she had destroyed another what-should-have-been?* The thought was like a knife plunged into her lungs.

"Miss Mary, what is it?" Matt covered her clutching fingers with his hand, his brow furrowed in concern. "Tell me."

Mary turned her disturbed gaze up to him. He had inherited his grandfather's height and build and a rougher-cut version of his handsomeness. She had always preferred his face to Percy's. It comforted rather than devastated and had an appeal entirely his own. She could see nothing of Percy's wife, Matt's grandmother, about him except his light brown hair and bright blue eyes. "How's Lucy?" she asked.

Looking baffled, Matt eased into his grandfather's grin. "Why, the same as always. Full of piss and vinegar. I just got back from a visit with her in Atlanta. Should I mention that you asked about her next time I talk to her?"

Mary threw up a hand. "Oh, good Lord, no! She might have a heart attack."

Matt chuckled. "You two. I don't suppose I'll ever learn what came between you." I imagine you have a pretty good idea already, Mary thought, amused, and wondered if Matt would question Percy about what he'd overheard. Probably not. He'd let the creek lie still, rather than go fishing. No telling what he might drag up that would embarrass his grandfather. It had all happened so long ago, anyway.

"I can see that you're not going to relieve my curiosity," Matt said, "so let's go back to Rachel. When can we expect her next visit?"

"Oh, in about two or three weeks, I'd say," Mary said, her attention on her limousine drawing up to the curb. It was white, ancient, and in impeccable running order, much as she'd once thought of herself. "Here's Henry, so I'll say good-bye, Matt."

She gazed up at him through her sunglasses, a constriction suddenly in her throat. He'd always been such a good boy. She remembered when he and his mother, Claudia, Percy's daughter-in-law, had come to live at Warwick Hall. Matt had been only a few months old. He had reminded her of Matthew, his namesake. Matt had been their rainbow after the storm. Pain swelled in her breast. "Matt—" she started to say, but to her dismay, a sob blocked her words.

Matt said, "Hey, here now…what's this?" and drew her into his arms. "You look too lovely to cry."

She felt in her purse for a handkerchief. "And you're wearing too nice a jacket to cry on," she said, finding a tissue and pressing it to a wet spot on his lapel, appalled at herself. "I'm sorry, Matt. I don't know what came over me."

"Memories do that to you sometimes," he said, his expression gentle and knowing. "How about letting Granddad and me come down for a drink around six? He's missed you this past month—more than I can say."

"If you'll promise not to say a word to him about my…behavior."

"What behavior?"

Henry had come around to assist. "Aunt Sassie's havin' ham and black-eyed peas and collards and fried cornbread for lunch," he said. "That'll fix her up."

"Sounds like just the ticket," Matt said, but Mary caught the look he exchanged with Henry that belied his confidence. Before closing the door, he leaned in and placed a hand on her shoulder. "We'll see you this evening, Miss Mary. Okay?"

She patted his hand. "Okay," she said.

But of course it wasn't okay. She'd think of some excuse and have Sassie call down to Warwick Hall later with her apologies. After their month's separation, Percy would have a fit, but she was in no state to see him. She needed her emotional and physical strength for her encounter with Rachel tomorrow, and she must still attend to that final task in the attic. "Henry," she said, lifting her glasses to wipe away the last of her tears, "I'd like you to do something for me when we get home."

Henry cast her a stricken look through the rearview mirror. "Before lunch, Miss Mary?"

"Before lunch. I want you to go up to the attic and open Mister Ollie's World War One footlocker. Have Sassie get the keys from my top bureau drawer to unlock the lid. Leave the keys up there. Shouldn't take too long, then you can have your ham and black-eyed peas."

In the mirror, Henry's eyes narrowed. "Miss Mary, you feelin' all right?"

"I'm feeling sensible, Henry, if that's what you're asking."

"Yes, ma'am," he said, his tone expressing doubt.

Her eyes were dry by the time they turned into the wide, tree-canopied street of Houston Avenue, passing houses of grand proportions set back on rolling lawns in manicured order. "When we get to the house, let me out in front, Henry," Mary instructed.

Henry shot her another bewildered glance through

the rearview mirror. "In front of the house? You don't want me to drive you round to the side door?"

"No, Henry, in front. Don't bother to get out to help me. I can manage."

"If you say so, Miss Mary. Now about Mister Ollie's army trunk. How'll I recognize it?"

"It's the sickly green one pushed against the far right wall. His name is printed on it: CAPTAIN OLLIE DUMONT, US ARMY. You can't miss it once you get the dust off. The lid hasn't been opened in so long, you'll probably need to use a crowbar."

"Yes'm," Henry said, drawing the limousine to a stop before a wide flight of verandah steps. He watched with anxious eyes as his mistress maneuvered herself out of the backseat and began her ascent to the white-columned porch. She waved him off as she was halfway up, but he waited to pull away until she'd reached the final step. A short while later, Sassie Two, so called because she was the second Sassie in her family to serve as the Tolivers' housekeeper, flung open the front door and came out, demanding, "Miss Mary, what you doin' out here? You know this heat ain't good for you."

"It's not bothering me, Sassie, really." Mary spoke from a deep white plantation chair, one of a number of pairs that graced the wide verandah. "I told Henry to drop me off in front because I wished to climb the steps again, to get the feel of entering my house by the front door. I haven't done that in ages, and it's been even longer since I've sat out here, observing the neighborhood."

"Ain't nothin' to observe about the neighborhood 'cept the grass growin'. Everybody else is inside where it's cool. And you ain't goin' to find a blade of that grass changed since the last time you sat out here, Miss Mary. Why're you doin' it now, of all times? Lunch is about ready."

"*Dinner,* Sassie," Mary corrected firmly. "*Dinner* is about ready. When did we southern folks start calling our noon meal *lunch*?"

"Oh, about the time the rest of the world did, I imagine."

"Well, the rest of the world can be hanged. From now on, we have *dinner* here at noon. Dinner and *supper.* The world can have its *lunch* and *dinner.*"

Hands on her ample hips, Sassie regarded her mistress tolerantly. "That's fine by me. Now about your *dinner.* Will you be ready for it in about ten minutes when Henry comes down from the attic?"

"That'll be fine," Mary said. "Did you give him the key to Mister Ollie's trunk?"

"I did. What in the world do you want it opened for?"

"There's something I need from it. I'll go up after dinner and get it."

"Can't Henry find whatever it is?"

"*No!*" Mary barked, clutching the arms of the chair in panic. Sassie's dark face flooded with alarm, and she added in a mitigating tone, "I'm the only one who knows what I'm looking for. It's . . . something I must do myself."

"Well, all right." The housekeeper looked skeptical. "You want some iced tea?"

"No, I'm fine. Don't worry about me, Sassie. I know I'm acting a little odd today, but it feels good to kick the traces a bit."

"Uh-huh," Sassie murmured. "Well, now, I'm comin' back to get you soon as Henry comes down."

Mary sensed Sassie's concerned backward glance and regretted causing her worry. No doubt she and Henry thought she was finally losing her mind. Something cold would have tasted good. She wished she hadn't refused the offer of iced tea, but it was too much trouble for Sassie to have to come back.

She made herself comfortable and directed her gaze slowly up and down the avenue. The Toliver mansion sat high enough to permit a good view of the neighborhood from the verandah. Her great-great-grandmother had seen to that. How she loved this house, this street. Little about it had changed since she was a girl. The carriage houses were now garages, sprinkler systems had replaced the hand watering once done by the household help, and a few of the old trees had finally toppled, but the antebellum grace of the avenue remained the same, a small part of the South not yet gone with the wind.

Would Rachel ever appreciate what it had cost her

to take this place away from her? Would the child ever fathom what it had been like for her to live the final weeks of her life knowing that she would be the last Toliver to reside in the family home place, the house her forebears had built? Most likely not. That would be asking an awful lot from the girl....

"Miss Mary, you talkin' to yourself again."

"What?" Startled, Mary squinted up at her housekeeper.

Sassie Two was standing in front of her. "You talkin' to yourself again. And where are your pearls? You left here wearin' 'em."

Mary felt at her neck. "Oh, I left those for Rachel—"

"For Rachel? Oh, Lawsey, that does it. Miss Mary, you comin' in outta this heat."

"Sassie!" All at once, Mary's mind cleared. The past dashed to pieces in the clarity of the present. She was herself again, and in charge. Nobody told her what to do, not even Sassie, who was family and had the right. Mary pointed her cane at the housekeeper. "I will come in when I'm good and ready. You and Henry go ahead and eat. Kindly fix me a plate and leave it in the oven."

Showing no offense at Mary's attempt to put her in her place, Sassie said, "Well, what about some iced tea?"

"No iced tea, Sassie. Bring me a glass of Taittinger's from that bottle we keep in the refrigerator. Get Henry to open it. He knows how. On second thought, bring the bottle. Ice it down in a champagne bucket."

Sassie's eyes bulged. "Champagne? You want *champagne* in this heat? Miss Mary, you never drink alcohol nohow."

"I am today. Now go on and do what I say before Henry perishes of hunger. I heard his stomach growling like a caged tiger in the car."

Shaking her wiry gray head, Sassie retreated and returned with a tray bearing the commanded items. She set it down loudly on the table next to Mary. "Will that do?"

"Splendidly," Mary said. "Thank you, Sassie." She looked up at her housekeeper with a swell of profound affection. "Have I ever told you how much you mean to me?"

"Not near enough," her housekeeper said. "Now, I don't care what you say, Miss Mary, I'm comin' out here to check on you ever' so often, so you better be careful what you say to yourself if you don't want no secrets let out."

"I'll be sure to guard my conversation with myself very carefully, Sassie. One other thing. Was Henry able to get the lid to Mister Ollie's trunk open?"

"He did."

"Good." Mary nodded in satisfaction.

When Sassie had gone, she poured the flute full of champagne and brought the rim to her lips. She hadn't imbibed anything stronger than a few sips of champagne on New Year's Eve since she was a girl. She knew better. Alcohol had the power to take her back to times and places she'd striven nearly all her life to forget. Now she wanted to go back. She wanted to remember everything. This would be her last chance to return to the past, and the champagne would take her there. Sipping calmly, she waited for the arrival of her magic carpet. After a while, she felt herself spinning back into yesterday, and her journey had begun.

MARY'S
STORY

Chapter Five

HOWBUTKER, TEXAS, JUNE 1916

In chairs ranged before the desk, Mary Toliver, age sixteen, sat with her mother and brother in the funereal atmosphere of Emmitt Waithe's law office. A smell of leather and tobacco and old books reminded her of her father's study at home, now closed with a black ribbon strapped across the door. Tears sprang to her eyes again, and she clasped her hands tighter, lowering her head until the moment of grief passed. Immediately she felt Miles's consoling hand covering hers. On the other side of her brother, dressed completely in black and speaking through a veil covering her face, Darla Toliver gave a little exclamation of sympathy and said with annoyance, "I declare, if Emmitt doesn't come soon, I'm sending Mary home. There's no reason for her to have to sit through this so soon after burying her father. Emmitt knows how close they were. I can't imagine what's keeping him.

Why can't we simply tell Mary the contents of the will when she's up to it?"

"Perhaps it's mandatory for a legatee to be present on these occasions," Miles said with the formal wordiness he'd taken to using since going away to college. "That's why Emmitt insists she be here."

"Oh, fiddlesticks," Darla said, her tone unusually sharp toward her son. "This is Howbutker, darling, not Princeton. Mary is a minor recipient of your father's will. There is not the least necessity for her to be here today."

Mary listened to their dialogue with half an ear. She'd been so emotionally removed from them since her father died—from everyone—that Miles and her mother often discussed her as if she weren't in their presence.

She still could not believe that she would wake up tomorrow and the day after that and all the tomorrows to come in a world without her father. The cancer had taken him too fast for her to adjust to his imminent death. It had been devastating enough to lose her grandfather five years before, but Granddaddy Thomas had lived to seventy-one. Her father had been only fifty-one, too young to lose all that he had worked for...all that he loved. For most of last night, she'd lain awake in her room and wondered what would happen to them now that her father was gone. What would become of the plantation? Miles wanted no part of it. That was common knowledge.

He desired only to become a college professor and teach history.

Her mother had never cared much for Somerset and knew very little about its operation. Darla's interest lay in being the wife of Vernon Toliver and the mistress of the mansion on Houston Avenue. To Mary's knowledge, she had rarely ventured outside of town where the plantation began and stretched for acres and acres beside the road, almost clear to the next county. Dallas lay beyond and Houston the other direction, cities where her mother loved to take the train to shop and stay overnight.

Many Junes had come and gone, and her mother had never seen the fields starred with thousands of cotton blossoms ranging in colors of creamy white to soft red. Mary never missed a one. Now only she was left to thrill at the sight of the blossoms gradually giving way to hard little bolls until August, when suddenly—here and there upon the sea of green— could be spied a white fleck. Oh, to watch the whiteness spread after that, to ride out on horseback as she often did with her father and Granddaddy Thomas into that white-capped vastness billowing on its green undertow from horizon to horizon and know that it belonged to the Toliver family.

There was no greater joy or glory, and now there was the horrifying possibility that soon it could all be gone. A paralyzing thought had struck her before morning. Suppose her mother *sold* the plantation! As the new mistress of Somerset, she would be free to dispose of it as she wished, and there would be nobody to stop her.

The door to an adjoining office opened. Emmitt Waithe, the Tolivers' longtime attorney, entered full of apologies for having made them wait, but at once Mary sensed something strange in his manner that had little to do with the delay. Whether out of commiseration for their grief or something else, he seemed unable to meet their eyes. He bustled about, unusual for a man of his taciturnity and economy of movements, and appeared unduly concerned about their comforts. Did they need tea or perhaps coffee? He could have his secretary run down to the drugstore and get Mary a soda—

"Emmitt, if you please," Darla interrupted in an attempt to settle him down, "we have need of nothing except your brevity. We're all about at the end of our emotional tethers and would ask that you . . . well, get on with it, if you'll excuse my turn of phrase."

Emmitt cleared his throat, regarded Darla oddly for a few seconds, then got on with it. First he withdrew a letter from an envelope on top of a formal-looking document he'd brought in. "This is, uh, a letter from Vernon that he composed shortly before he died. He wanted me to read it to you first before disclosing the contents of his will."

Behind the veil, Darla's eyes dampened. "Of course," she said, reaching over to clasp her son's hand. Emmitt began:

Dearest wife and children,

I have never thought of myself as a cowardly man, but I find that I do not have the courage to apprise you of my will's contents while I am still alive. Let me assure you, before its reading, that I love each of you with all my heart and wish, as deeply, that circumstances could have afforded a more fair and generous distribution of my property. Darla, my beloved wife, I ask you to understand why I have done what I've done. Miles, my son, I cannot expect you to understand, but someday, perhaps, your heir will be grateful for the legacy I leave you and entrust you to retain for the fruit of your loin.

Mary, I wonder that in remembering you as I have, I have not prolonged the curse that has plagued the Tolivers since the first pine tree was cleared from Somerset. I am leaving you many and great responsibilities, which I hope will not force you into a position unfavorable to your happiness.

Your loving husband and father,
Vernon Toliver

"How very odd," Darla said slowly in the silence of Emmitt refolding the letter and slipping it back into its envelope. "What do you suppose Vernon meant by 'a more fair and generous distribution' of his property?"

"We're about to find out," Miles commented, his thin face hardening.

Mary had grown very still. What did her father mean by "many and great responsibilities"? Did they have anything to do with his last words to her, which she'd taken as the incoherent mumblings of a dying man reliving a terrible nightmare? *Whatever you do, whatever it takes, get the land back, Mary.*

"I was instructed to apprise you of one other matter before I read the will," Emmitt said, picking up another document. He handed it across the desk to Miles and explained, "It's a mortgage contract. Before Vernon learned that he was terminally ill, he borrowed money from the Bank of Boston, offering Somerset as collateral. The borrowed money went to pay off a series of plantation-related debts as well as to purchase additional land to put under cotton."

After skimming the document, Miles raised his head. "Am I reading this correctly? Ten percent interest for ten years? That's nothing less than robbery!"

"Where have you been, Miles?" Emmitt threw up his hands. "Farmers around here have paid twice that amount for the privilege of going into debt to these big eastern mortgage brokers and commercial banks. If he'd borrowed against the crop, he'd have paid a considerably higher rate, but by mortgaging the land, he could get the money more cheaply, if you want to call it that."

Mary sat motionless, appalled. The land mortgaged...no longer in Toliver hands? Now she understood the meaning of her father's dying plea...the desperation of it. But why had he directed it to her?

"What if the crop doesn't make?" Miles asked, his tone brusque. "Sure, cotton is bringing high prices now, but what if we have a bad harvest? Does that mean we lose the plantation?"

Emmitt shrugged. Mary, glancing from the lawyer's grim face to her brother's flushed one, spoke up for the first time. "The crops *will* make!" she declared, close to hysteria. "And we're not going to lose the plantation. Don't even think that, Miles!"

Miles brought his palm down hard on the chair arm. "God almighty! What could Papa have been thinking, buying more land when it would put the land we have in jeopardy? Why in hell did he stick us further in debt by buying machinery he felt we had to have right now? I thought he was such a shrewd businessman."

"If you'd taken a little more interest in his affairs, you'd have known more about what he was doing, Miles," Mary said in defense of their father. "It's not fair to blame Papa now for decisions you never once offered to help him make."

Miles looked taken aback at her outburst. They rarely argued, though their differences were many. Miles was an idealist, already gravitating toward Marxism, which advocated removing property and profit from the master class and distributing it more equally to the masses. He loathed the tenancy system as it flourished in the Cotton Belt, believing it was devised to keep the impoverished tenant farmer in bondage to the planter. His father had vehemently disagreed with his view, arguing that the planter system, fairly managed, freed the tenant farmer to be his own master. Mary stood squarely on the side of her father.

"Miles could hardly have been privy to your father's decisions, Mary Lamb, since he's been away to school for the past four years." Darla's veil fluttered from the mild reproof. "What's done is done. If we need money, we'll simply sell off some of Somerset. If your father had known he was dying, he would never have purchased additional acreage. From his place in heaven, he will surely understand why I have to undo the damage he never intended to inflict. Isn't that so, Emmitt? Now if you will please read the will so that we can get this over with. Mary looks ill. We need to get her home."

With another one of those peculiar glances at Darla, Emmitt picked up the document with a slow hand and read aloud. When he had finished, his listeners sat mute, too dumbfounded to utter a word.

"I...don't believe it," Darla whispered at last. Behind the veil, her eyes were glassy with shock. "You mean that Vernon left the entire plantation to...to Mary, except for that narrow strip along the Sabine? That's all our son is to receive from his father? And Mary's to have the house, too? I am to have nothing but whatever money is in the bank? But...there can't be much, since Vernon was using every last cent to pay off the mortgage."

"That appears to be so," the lawyer concurred, consulting a page in a bank book in his possession. "However, you do understand, Darla, that you are legally entitled to live in the house and to receive twenty percent of the profits from the land until your remarriage or demise. Vernon specified that in the will."

"How...very generous of him," she said, tight-lipped.

Mary still sat stiffly, her hands tightly clasped, willing her expression to give nothing away of the relief—the utter joy—flooding the bleakness of her heart. The plantation was hers! Her father—foreseeing that her mother would sell it—had left it in the hands of the one Toliver who would never let it go. It didn't matter that the will had given Miles power of attorney over Somerset until she could legally assume control at twenty-one. For the sake of their mother's 20 percent, he would take care not to interfere with its prosperous operation and the priority of paying off the mortgage.

Her brother had risen and was pacing about with the hard strides customary to him when he was agitated. "Are you telling me"—he turned to the lawyer in exasperation—"that my mother's livelihood *for the rest of her life* is dependent on the success of the plantation, and that she's even to be deprived of ownership of her own home?"

Emmitt shuffled some papers and avoided meeting his gaze. "Entrusting the house to Mary will ensure that your mother always has a home, Miles. Often it is the case, in situations like this, that houses are imprudently sold and money from the sale soon gone. And let me remind you that twenty percent of the profits is not a pittance. With cotton selling so high now, especially if war comes to the United States, Somerset should enjoy enormous revenues. Your mother will be able to live quite comfortably indeed."

"Less expenses and if the crop does not fail," Darla whispered.

Emmitt flushed and peered at Miles over the rim of his spectacles. "For your sake, it would behoove your son to see that it doesn't." The lawyer pondered a moment, as if debating whether he should speak his next words. Apparently deciding to do so, he dropped his pen on the desk and leaned back in his chair. "Actually, Vernon believed he had no choice but to set up his will the way he did."

Still standing, his contempt plain, Miles asked, "Oh? And why is that?"

Emmitt gazed directly at Darla. "He feared that you might sell the plantation, my dear—as you proposed to do only a few minutes ago. This way, you will still be able to enjoy whatever Somerset produces, which would have been the case anyway had Vernon lived, and the plantation and house stay in the Toliver family."

"Except that, as before when I was supported by my husband, I will now be dependent upon my daughter for my bread and roof." Darla spoke in a voice so drained of power that the veil barely moved.

"Not to mention that he's disrupted *my* plans for the next five years," Miles said, his upper lip quivering with anger.

Darla loosened her tight hold of the chair arms and composed her hands in her lap. "So I'm to understand, then, that the circumstances to which my husband referred in his letter had to do with his fear that I might sell the plantation or, in the event that I did not, would certainly mismanage it. Are these the reasons which precluded—how did he express it?—'a more fair and generous distribution of my property'?"

"I believe you, ah, have understood your husband's reasons perfectly, Darla." Emmitt's countenance softened in an obvious hope to soothe. "Vernon believed that Mary is the best Toliver suited to eventually run the plantation. She seems to have inherited an ability for land management as well as a devotion and loyalty to Somerset and the way of life it affords. He thought it was she who could make the plantation pay, benefiting all of you and preserving it for the next generation, which will include your children, Miles."

Miles grimaced in patent disgust and came to stand behind his mother's chair, laying a sympathetic hand on her shoulder.

"I see..." Darla's voice carried no emotion. Very deliberately, she lifted the veil and calmly tucked it among the black feathers of her oversize mourning hat. She was an extremely pretty woman, with cool, alabaster skin and large, lustrous eyes. Her son had inherited their amber shade, her auburn hair, and the shape of her small, saucy nose. Mary, on the other hand, had been favored with the striking combination of features that had characterized the Tolivers since the days of the first English Lancasters. Everybody said she could be none other than Vernon Toliver's daughter.

Mary watched in trepidation as her mother rose from the chair, a cool, distant figure, almost a stranger in her somber black attire. The lifting of the veil worried her, as did the unfamiliar gleam in her eyes. All vestiges of grief were gone. The whites were starkly clear. She and Emmitt stood as well.

"I must ask you one further question, Emmitt, being so unfamiliar with these matters...."

"Of course, my dear. Anything." Emmitt bowed slightly.

"The will's dispensations...will they be made public?"

Emmitt pursed his lips. "A will is a public document," he explained with evident reluctance. "Once it is probated, it becomes a court record which anyone, especially creditors, can peruse. Also..." The lawyer cleared his throat, looking uncomfortable. "Wills which have been filed for probate are listed in the paper. This is for the benefit of those who may have a claim against the estate."

"Family members excluded," Miles commented, clench-jawed.

"Then anyone curious about the details of the will can learn them?" Darla asked.

Emmitt simply nodded. The strength seemed to drain from Darla's stiff carriage. "Damn Papa!" Miles said, jerking his mother's chair out of the way for their departure.

"Uh...there is one other thing that I promised Vernon I'd do, Darla," Emmitt said. He opened a cabinet behind him and withdrew a bud vase containing a single red rose. "Your husband requested that I give this to you after reading the will. By all means, keep the vase."

Slowly, Darla took the slender-necked vessel in her gloved hand, her children watching. After a long study, she set it on Emmitt's desk and extracted the rose. "Keep the vase," she said with a smile so foreign that all of them drew back slightly. "Come, children."

Sweeping from the room, Darla Toliver dropped the red rose into a trash receptacle by the door.

Chapter Six

On the way home in the Tolivers' Arabian-drawn buggy, the family sat in silence, Mary as far in her corner as possible. They all stared out the isinglass windows in much the same somber way they had ridden to Vernon Toliver's funeral four days before. On that day, Mary had felt a palpable void in the carriage, but today it was filled with a frightening, invisible force that seemed capable of separating her from her mother and brother, and they from the memory of the husband and father they both had loved.

She glanced at her mother. She knew about the legend of the roses and understood the meaning of the red rose her father had arranged to be given to her and the terrible significance of her mother dropping it into the wastebasket by Mr. Waithe's door. Mary, worriedly observing her mother's pale, stark profile, believed with a desolate certainty that her father would never be forgiven for what he had done.

And what had he done? Her father had only

ensured that the plantation and family home would stay in Toliver hands. In a financial pinch or in the event of her remarriage—which may have forced her to live elsewhere—her mother would have sold them. And bequeathing the land to Miles would have guaranteed the loss of their birthright. By leaving it to her, he would preserve it for his children's offspring.

Since this was clearly the case, why was her mother so upset? And Miles, too, for that matter? In time, he could pursue a teaching career. Five years was not long. During that time, she would not waste a minute in learning everything possible related to running the plantation. She had Len Deeter to help her. He was an excellent overseer, honest and hardworking, loyal to the Tolivers, highly thought of by the tenants. What she hadn't learned from her grandfather and father, she would learn from him. Miles probably wouldn't need to hang around until she was twenty-one. Two years should do it, then she'd send him on his way, mailing him papers that needed his signature. By then, she would have established herself in charge of Somerset.

In the late afternoon, Mary took these arguments to her mother to defend her father's action. She found Darla lying on a chaise longue in the room she'd shared with her husband, her rich auburn hair brushed out of its elaborate pompadour and spread around her shoulders. The late afternoon sun cast a sickly glow through the sheer yellow draperies. Mary

wondered disconsolately if there was some significance in the bright lavender housecoat she wore—a
kind of repudiation. The black dress and hat were out
of sight, as were the many flowers of condolence her
mother had ordered sent up from the parlor after her
husband's body was removed for burial. Earlier, meeting Sassie coming downstairs with an armload of the
still fresh arrangements, she had asked with a feeling
of dread, "What is this all about?"

"What does it look like?" Gloom darkened their
housekeeper's voice. "I declare, I got a feelin' nothin'
ain't never gonna be the same round here again."

Mary had the same feeling as she stood anxiously
studying her mother lying on the chaise longue. There
was a terrifying remoteness about her white-set features,
the rigid length of her body. All warmth and spirit
seemed to have been struck out of her. A cold, unap-
proachable stranger lay in the lavender satin housecoat.

"You ask me what else he could have done?" Darla
repeated Mary's question. "I will tell you, my dear
daughter. He could have loved me more than he loved
his land. *That's* what he could have done."

"But, Mama, you would have sold it!"

"Or, that failing," Darla continued with her eyes
closed, as if Mary had not spoken, "he could at least
have divided his holdings equally between our son
and daughter. That strip Miles inherited is all but
worthless. It floods every spring. Nothing planted
there can mature before or after the rains."

"It's still a part of Somerset, Mama, and you know Miles has never cared a whit for the plantation."

"At the very least," Darla went on in the same dead tone, "he could have considered my feelings and known how it will look to all of our friends for him to have left his wife's welfare in the hands of his daughter."

"*Mama...*"

Her eyes still closed, Darla said, "Your father's love was my greatest treasure, Mary. What an honor it was to be his wife, to have been picked from all the women he could have married, some prettier than I...."

"Nobody's prettier than you, Mama," Mary whispered, choking on her grief.

"His love gave me life, gave me stature, made me important. But now I feel that it was all a sham, simply something for me to enjoy while he lived. In death, he took it all away, all the things I thought I was to him, and he to me."

"But, Mama—" The words failed to come. They failed because deep down in her sixteen-year-old heart, Mary knew her mother spoke the truth. In the end, the preservation of the plantation had meant more to her father than his wife's pride, feelings, and welfare. He had left her virtually penniless, dependent on her children, and subject to the humiliation of Howbutker society.

Mary, who already had little tolerance for weakness, could hardly blame her mother for feeling shattered and empty, bereft of even the memories that would have brought her comfort. With tears spilling down her cheeks, she knelt beside the chaise longue. "Papa didn't mean to hurt you, I know he didn't."

She laid her head on her mother's bosom, but even as tears soaked the lavender satin, some part of her far below her grief rejoiced that Somerset had come to her, and she vowed that no matter what pain it cost her to keep it, she would never give up the plantation. Not ever. She would make it up to her mother some-how . . . work hard to make Somerset pay to keep her in the silks and satins of which she was so fond. Somerset would grow so big and powerful, the Toliver name so strong, that no one would dare risk a remark against her mother. And, after a while, everyone would forget Vernon Toliver's betrayal and realize how right he'd been to dispense the estate as he had. They would all see in what esteem Darla Toliver was held by her chil-dren and grandchildren, and the pain would go away.

"Mama?"

"I'm here, Mary."

But she wasn't, a deep wrench of her instinct told her. She'd never again be the mother that she and Miles had known. Mary would have given anything in the world to see her on her feet, normal and famil-iar, beautiful and happy, even in her grief. Anything but Somerset, Mary modified her thought, and was shocked at the amendment, at the line beyond which she could not force her love to go.

Exactly as her father had not been able to do.

A sense of loss pierced her to her soul, as great as the moment her father's hand had slipped from hers forever. *"Mama! Mama! Don't leave us, don't leave us!"* she sobbed, feeling the rise of hysteria as she shook the inert form in the lavender satin.

That evening, sitting in the twilight gloom of the front parlor, Mary became aware of someone watching her from the black-draped doorway. It was Percy Warwick. He was wearing the still, serious expression that she'd come to interpret as disapproval. By now, Miles would have told him and Ollie about the will, and doubtless they shared her brother's opinion of it.

They were a fraternity of three—Miles Toliver and Percy Warwick and Ollie DuMont. They'd been inseparable since they were infants, perpetuating the friendships their grandfathers had begun and their fathers had continued. At the graveside service, her attention had been drawn to the three standing together. How different each was from the other. Ollie, short, pudgy, and jolly, the eternal optimist. Miles, tall, thin, earnest, a crusader desperate for a cause. And Percy, the tallest and most handsome of the three, prudent and reasonable...the Apollo who watched over them all. She'd known a moment's envy. How comforting it would be to enjoy the kind of friendship they shared. Her father and grandfather had been her only friends.

"Mind if I come in?" Percy asked, his voice deep and resonant in the close summer dusk.

"That will depend on what you've come to say."

That brought the familiar, amused flicker to his lips. She and Percy never conversed. They sparred. It had been that way for the last couple of summers and during holidays when the boys were home from Princeton. Like Miles and Ollie, he had graduated in June, and he had then joined his father's lumber company.

He chuckled and moved into the room. "Ever the little firebrand when it comes to me. I'm assuming you don't want a lamp?"

"You assume correctly."

How handsome he is, she thought grudgingly. The dusk seemed to intensify the sheen of his blond hair and the deep bronze of his skin. He'd worked outdoors all summer with the other lumbermen, and the results showed in his lean, hard form. There had been lots of girls back east, so she understood...Dresden blue-bloods. She had heard Miles and Ollie laughing over his conquests.

She returned to her original position, head resting on the back of the chair, eyes closed. "Is Miles back?" Her voice was hoarse with grief and fatigue.

"Yes. He's gone upstairs with Ollie to see your mother."

"I suppose he told you about the will. You disapprove, of course."

"Of course. Your father should have left the house and plantation to your mother."

Mary lifted her head in anger and surprise. Percy

was noted for withholding judgment. He never spoke in terms of *should haves* when it came to other people's business. "Who are you to say what my father should have done?" He had come to stand close to her chair, hands in his pockets, and was regarding her solemnly, his face in shadow.

"Someone who cares for you and your brother and mother very much. That's who I am."

That pricked her outrage like a dart to the throat of a puffed adder. She turned her head away, blinking and swallowing at the lump in her throat, on the brink of tears again. "Well, please care enough for us to withhold your opinion, Percy. My father knew what he was doing, and to say he didn't only makes everything that much worse at this time."

"Are you saying that out of defense of your father or because you feel guilty that you were the one remembered?"

Mary hesitated, wanting—*needing*—to trust him with the truth of her feelings, but she feared he'd think even less of her. "What does my brother believe?" she asked, evading his question.

"He thinks you are overjoyed to have inherited Somerset."

There. My brother's opinion is out in the open, she thought, the knowledge as cutting as a knife. She'd been so careful not to betray her inner exultation, yet she hadn't fooled Miles or her mother, and they would detest her for it. Tears stinging, she shoved out of the chair in one angry motion to stand before a parlor window. A pale moon had risen. She watched as it dissolved in a silver stream before her eyes.

"Gypsy...," she heard him murmur, and before she knew it, he'd come to her and tucked her teary face beneath his chin. Within seconds, she was blubbering against his tie.

"Miles b-blames me for...for Papa writing the will as he did, doesn't he? Mama does, t-too. I've lost them, Percy, as surely as I've lost Papa."

"This was all such a shock to them, Mary," he said, stroking her hair. "Your mother feels betrayed, and Miles is angry on her behalf, not his."

"But... but I'm not to blame for Papa leaving everything to me. I can't help it if I love the plantation, any more than Mama and Miles can help it that they d-don't."

"I know," he said, his voice warm with understanding. "But you can undo what's been done."

"How?" she asked, lifting her head to hear this wisdom he proposed.

"Sell Somerset when you're twenty-one and split the proceeds among you."

Mary could not have been more shocked if she'd looked up to find snakes sprouting from his head. She pushed out of his arms. "Sell Somerset?" She stared at him incredulously. "You are suggesting that I *sell* Somerset in order to pacify Mama's and Miles's disappointment?"

"I'm suggesting you do so in order to salvage your relationship with them."

"I have to *buy* a relationship with them?"

"You're distorting the situation, Mary, either to make it easier on your conscience or because you're so blinded by your obsession for Somerset that you can't see the real root of your mother's and brother's grief."

"I *see* it!" Mary cried. "I know how Mama and Miles feel! What none of you can see is that I am honor bound to carry out my father's wishes."

"He said nothing about your not selling the plantation when you're twenty-one."

"Would he have left it to me if he'd thought I would *sell* it?"

"What happens when you're of marriageable age and your husband doesn't wish to share his wife with a plantation?"

"I would *never* marry a man who didn't understand and support my feelings for Somerset."

Percy fell silent at this declaration. Her hair ribbon had slipped to the floor. He reached down and picked it up, folding it in half. He laid it across her shoulder. "How do you know you couldn't love a man who didn't feel about Somerset the way you do? You know no world but Howbutker. You've never been exposed to any other interest but the plantation. You haven't experienced anything but being a Toliver. You've had a very limited existence, Mary."

"I don't care to know any other existence."

"You can't draw that conclusion unless you have something else with which to compare it."

"Yes, I can. Anyway, I'm not likely to have the opportunity to make such a comparison, am I?"

They could hear Miles and Ollie coming down the stairs. To her surprise, Mary found that she regretted the intrusion, as—she had to admit—she missed the solace of Percy's arms. It was the closest she'd ever stood to him. She had never known that a small freckle was tucked beneath the ridge under his left eye or noticed the intriguing radius of silver around his pupils. "You've always disapproved of me, haven't you?" she asked, the question popping out unexpectedly.

Percy's dark blond brows rose. " 'Disapproved' is not the right word," he said.

"Then not *liked* me." She held her breath, waiting for his confirmation.

"That's not it, either."

"Then what *is* the word?" Her cheeks were burning, but she was determined to learn exactly what he thought of her. Then he could be damned, and she wouldn't think about his opinion anymore. It would no longer be an issue of curiosity.

Before he could answer, Miles, with Ollie huffing behind him, entered the room.

"Here you are!" her brother said, and for a hopeful second Mary thought he'd come in search of her. But it was for Percy he was looking, she realized as he ignored her and addressed his friend. "I didn't know if you'd left or not. Will you be staying for supper? There's plenty of food, but Sassie will want to know."

"I'm not staying," Ollie said, looking at Mary as if he wished he were. He smiled fondly at her, and she responded with a warm softening of her lips.

"I'm afraid I can't, either," Percy said. "We've got guests coming, and Mother is expecting me to play host."

"Who are they?" Miles asked.

"The daughter of Mother's roommate when they attended Bellington Hall in Atlanta and her father. The girl's interested in enrolling there this fall. Her mother is dead, and they're here to discuss the school."

"At least that's the pretext her papa gave for bringing her for a visit," Ollie said with a meaningful wink at Miles.

"Well, the father seems the kind who operates with an ulterior motive up his sleeve, and my mother thinks their visit is a ruse," Percy admitted, "but then don't most mothers believe that every girl has designs on their son?"

Here's one girl Beatrice doesn't have to worry about, Mary thought, feeling an irrational nip of jealousy at another girl claiming his attention for supper. Deliberately, she turned to Ollie and placed a hand on his sleeve. "Ollie, are you sure you won't stay? We could use your cheerful company tonight."

"I'd like to, Mary Lamb, but I'm helping my father with the end-of-summer inventory at the store. Maybe tomorrow night, if the invitation's still open."

"It's always open to you, Ollie."

If Percy noticed his exclusion from her sentiment, he didn't show it. Instead, he flashed her his familiar grin. "We'll finish our conversation another time, Gypsy. Remember where we left off."

"If I don't forget," Mary replied, bridling at the use of the nickname he knew she hated.

"You won't forget."

"This houseguest…what's her name, and what's she like?" Miles asked, following his friends from the room.

"Lucy Gentry, and she's nice enough. I don't much care for her father."

The rest of the conversation was lost to her as Miles saw them out. From a parlor window, she watched "the boys," as the families referred to them, walk down the front walk to their spanking new Pierce-Arrows, graduation gifts from their fathers. In June, Miles had been puzzled and disappointed not to find a similar present waiting for him in the stable, yet to be converted into a garage since the Tolivers did not possess one of the new horseless carriages. Now he understood why his gift had been limited to a handsomely bound set of encyclopedias for use in his future position as a history teacher.

A strange sadness deepened her depression. She

wished she and Percy could have finished their talk. She'd certainly never return to the subject, and he was likely to forget about it by the time he'd backed out of the drive. She'd never learn the precise word he would have chosen to describe what he felt for her, but she could guess. It was pity—pity for being a Toliver, for taking her heritage so seriously. She couldn't understand why Percy took his so lightly. He was the only heir to protect and preserve the legacy of his family. Ollie, as casual and jolly as he was, looked upon his responsibilities as a DuMont far more seriously. What galled her was Percy's scorn for what he called her obsession with Somerset because he could not feel the same devotion toward the Warwick Lumber Company.

Well, that was what became of those who disregarded their original roots, if not out-and-out *discarded* them. The Warwicks and Tolivers had arrived as cotton planters to Texas, but Percy's family had converted to lumbermen immediately, while the Tolivers remained true to their calling. She understood that fully now. Percy looked upon the Warwick Lumber Company as a way to provide a living. She regarded Somerset as a way of life.

Satisfied with this distinction, she made her way into the dining room, where the long mahogany table had been set for her and Miles in their usual places. Her brother was already seated. In the hot, yellow glow of the kerosene lamps, they ate their meal in silence, withdrawn and divided, the absence of their parents filling their chairs at the head of the table like dejected ghosts. Who is this Lucy Gentry? Mary wondered as she forced down her meal. And did she have designs on Percy, as his mother suspected?

Chapter Seven

Mary, may I see you in the study for a moment?"

Startled, Mary looked up from shelling black-eyed peas into the lap of her apron. Miles had come to the doorway of the kitchen. "Of course," she said, apprehensive at his tone. He was so brusque these days, so unlike the gentle, teasing brother she'd always known. Eager to please him, she made a bowl of the apron to transfer the peas to the basket in Sassie's lap. They raised brows to each other. This past month, the housekeeper had often expressed that it was a "cryin' shame" the way Mister Miles treated his little sister.

Dutifully, Mary followed her brother's slender figure to the room next to the library, from which their father had run the plantation. Miles had begun referring to it as "the study" rather than "Papa's office." It was one of the many details in regard to the plantation that concerned her. Miles had been coming and going mysteriously, Somerset's red ledger books tucked under his arm. Mary wanted to demand that he let her examine them, but she did not dare. Now was not the time to declare rights of ownership—to insist he let her in on how he was managing Somerset. She feared that Miles was implementing his theory that had caused many a dispute at the Toliver dinner table between father and son.

Vernon Toliver had believed a landowner should be in strict control of everything from how a tenant dealt with his wife to how he treated his horse. His son disagreed with this approach to dealing with human beings, describing it and the tenancy system itself as evil and despotic. Vernon Toliver maintained there was nothing evil about a landowner renting his acres to a man who could not afford a farm of his own in exchange for a part of the crop. Wickedness resulted only when such men did not receive fair payment in return for their labor and when the owner did not provide the "furnishings" agreed upon in the contract. He was not responsible for the evils of other planters. He could not right the abuses of the tenancy system. Only by example could he show how it was meant to work. Could Miles not see that Somerset's tenants were the best clothed, fed, and sheltered, the most fairly treated, of all those in East Texas?

Miles argued that their tenants were still serfs and they the overlords, feared as much as God. There ought to be a law that gave tenants the right to apply their rents against the land they farmed. Once it was free and clear, they could then pay the landowner a royalty for life.

Mary had seen her father's face blanch at these dinner table proposals.

Now she felt a similar drop of her blood at the thought that Miles might be setting out to prove that a laissez-faire treatment of the tenants would result in greater benefits for all. Harvest was less than a month away, and every cent was needed to make the mortgage payments. She longed to talk to Len, the overseer, but Miles took the buggy and Arabians each day, leaving in the stable only an old mare unreliable for the trek to the plantation. She itched to acquaint herself with her father's bookkeeping methods, but when the ledgers were not in her brother's possession, they were in a locked drawer in the study. Miles had the only key.

She loved her brother, but she was beginning to look upon him as an adversary to all her hopes and dreams, and especially to her father's wishes and memory. Two camps had formed in the Toliver household. Only Sassie was in hers. Everybody else—the rest of the help, her mother, and all their friends except for neutral Ollie—was on Miles's side. God forbid, but she was even wishing that something would happen to Miles, a mild accident that would force him to turn over the plantation to her. At the very least, she hoped he'd become bored with his new duties and realize that he wasn't cut out to be a planter.

"Is this about Mama?" she asked, taking a chair opposite her father's big pine desk, a gift from Robert Warwick to James Toliver in 1865.

"It's about you," Miles said in the pedantic tone he'd assumed since becoming man of the house. He seated himself with a professorial air behind the desk, elbows resting on it, long, aesthetic fingers laced, his French cuffs as starched as his manner. "Mary, I'm sure you can appreciate that this is a very awkward time for all of us."

Mary nodded, wanting to cry at the loss of warmth between them.

"Something has happened to our family that goes beyond our grief for Papa. As a matter of fact, our grief should be uniting us. Instead, the will has left Mama and me with very little feeling for Papa at all. We feel bitter and cheated. Mama feels humiliated. Neither of us has been fair to you. I realize that. You've been made to feel that you're to blame for what's happened, and I regret that, Mary, I really do. However, the truth is, I can hardly look at you without feeling that you were somehow responsible for the terms of the will."

"Miles..."

He held up a hand. "Let me finish, and then you may have your say. Lord knows I didn't want the plantation, but it should have gone to our mother. She should have had the right to sell or keep it. She should have been first in Papa's affections, not Som-

erset, and not you. That's how both of us feel, plain
and simple. We also sense that you are delighted with
Papa's decision."

"Only because I will take care of our birthright,"
Mary interrupted. "I will take care of Mama. She will
never want for anything—"

"Mary, for God's sake, Mama doesn't want your
charity. Don't you understand that? Put yourself in
her position. How do you think you'd feel if your husband favored your daughter over you, if he left *you* at
the mercy of *her* charity?"

"I wouldn't repudiate my daughter for something
my husband had done!" she cried, aching from the
pain of her mother now turning her face to the wall
whenever she entered her room.

Miles raised his hands, palms up, to concede her
point. "I can see that's how you've been made to feel,
and I'm truly sorry."

"I could have used a little maternal and brotherly affection this past month, Miles. I miss Papa
terribly...."

"I know you do," he said, his manner softening
briefly, "but all of this is beside the reason I asked you
in here. Now, I want you to hear me out before you
jump up and tell me to go to the devil. I wouldn't do
that if I were you. Understand?"

Mary understood. Miles's pointed stare reminded
her that he was trustee of Somerset. She and the plantation were at his mercy for five years.

At Mary's nod, Miles tipped back in the timeworn chair and assumed his didactic pose. "I think you need to put some distance between you and Mama. I'm going to send you away to finishing school. There's a fine one in Atlanta that should suit you splendidly. I still have some money Granddaddy Thomas left me, and that will pay for a year."

Mary gazed at him in numb disbelief. He was going to send her away to that place where Beatrice had gone...away from the plantation....

"It's called Bellington Hall," Miles went on with an air unperturbed by the sight of his sister's distress. "Beatrice Warwick finished there. You may recall Percy mentioning that fact in regard to his houseguest, Lucy Gentry. It would have behooved you to agree to meet her while she was here, since she's to be your roommate."

She was too horrified to speak.

"You'll leave in three weeks for the fall term. I'll instruct Sassie to get your clothes ready."

She finally found her voice. Her insides felt on fire, as if a conflagration had been lit in her stomach. "Miles, please don't send me away. I have to stay here and help Len run the plantation. The quicker and the more I learn, the better. I can't function outside Howbutker. Mama and I can work out this situation."

"The only way you and our mother can work out this situation is for you to agree to allow me to sell the plantation." Miles wagged a cautionary finger when he saw Mary clasp the arms of her chair with the clear intent to disobey his previous warning. "Since you're a minor and cannot own or sell land, as the trustee of your property, I can. Of course, I would never do that against your wishes, as Papa well knew."

Mary leaped up, the blood pounding in her ears. "I absolutely refuse to give you my permission!"

"I am profoundly aware of that, little sister. So...you'll be going to Bellington Hall."

"You cannot do this to me."

"I can, and I will."

Mary stared at him as if he'd suddenly hatched horns. This wasn't happening. It wasn't possible for her brother to be so cruel. "Percy planted the idea in your head to sell the plantation, didn't he? Is Bellington Hall also his suggestion?"

Miles's lip twisted. "Credit me with doing my own thinking in regard to my family. Percy suggested nothing of the kind in regard to selling the plantation, and I learned of Bellington Hall through his mother. If it weren't that school, it would be another. Now *sit down*!"

Mary backed away to her seat. "You are making a huge mistake...."

"My mind is made up, Mary. My main concern right now is not you, but Mama. You may take comfort in the knowledge that at twenty-one the land will come to you. Mama has no such solace. So you will go to Bellington Hall and give her a chance to come to terms with this injustice—and, I might add, her feelings concerning you. Absence could endear you to her. Your constant presence here will not."

His words were so cutting, their delivery so sharp, they could have chipped ice. Mary lowered herself onto the chair, her legs weak. Was he saying that if she stayed, her mother would never love her again? But that was absurd. She was her daughter. Mothers might have a *change of feeling* for their children for a little while, but they didn't stop loving them forever—did they? Feeling forsaken, as if she were single-handedly fending off a pack of wolves, she locked her arms across her chest. "What if I refuse to leave?"

Miles cracked a half smile. "Oh, I don't think you want to hear the consequences of that."

"Tell me anyway."

Her brother drew forward and fastened his gaze on her mutinous face. "I will use the money from Granddaddy Thomas to take Mama to Boston, where I will have no problem getting a teaching position. I'm acquainted with a number of eligible older gentlemen there—wealthy businessmen who wouldn't waste a minute coming to call on our beautiful mother. It's likely she'd remarry in no time, putting this"—he waved a hand to indicate the house and all that it represented—"*unpleasant reminder* behind us. I have a right to my own life, and Mama has a right to rebuild hers. If that means I'm out of reach to be of assistance as trustee, so be it. In addition, I will sell that strip along the Sabine to further fatten my purse. I promise you, Mary, that if you do not compromise with me in this very tragic situation, I will do exactly as I've threatened."

Very slowly, Mary's arms came apart as she realized the extent of her brother's power. This was no idle threat. Miles had thought of another option for their mother. Only a very slender thread of allegiance to Somerset, their father, and her kept him from pulling up stakes and taking their mother to Boston. Even without the mortgage to worry about, he knew that to leave her and Len to run the plantation without the presence of a Toliver male and his available signature would surely be detrimental to Somerset. Spiriting their mother away would besmirch the family name. It would confirm to the wagging tongues that Vernon Toliver had indeed done an injustice to his wife by willing his property to his daughter.

Once again Miles reclined in his chair, inserting fingertips into the pockets of his waistcoat. "Well?" he asked with the smug lift of an eyebrow.

Mary was not yet willing to capitulate. "You could sell that strip along the Sabine anyway. What's to keep you from it?"

Miles was silent for a moment. "Papa's wishes that I keep it for my son."

Tears sprang without warning, blurring her vision. "Miles, what's happened to us? We used to be so happy together."

"The plantation's what happened to us," her brother said, rising in dismissal. "The plantation is a curse for anyone obsessed by it, Mary. It always has been, and I'm inclined to think it always will be. Obsession for that land caused a good man like our father to disavow a loving wife and split a family in two. He knew what he was doing. That's why he asked Mama to forgive him."

Mary came around the desk and gazed up at her brother through watery eyes. "Miles, I love you and Mama so much."

"I know, Mary Lamb. I miss all of us, too, the way we used to be. I especially miss my little sister. So does Mama, I'm sure. So do the boys. You were so precious to us."

The tears overflowed. "*Were?* But...not anymore?"

"Well, it's just that...you've become such...a Toliver."

"And that is bad?"

Miles sighed. "You know my answer to that. It will be especially bad if you suffer the curse Papa mentioned in his letter."

"What curse are you talking about? I never heard of any curse."

"It has to do with the procreation of children. None in possession of Somerset have ever been copious child bearers—or keepers," he concluded dryly. He turned to take a leather-bound volume from a shelf behind him. "You can read all about it in here. This is a picture and genealogy album. I found it among Papa's papers. I never knew it existed. Did you?"

"No. Papa never mentioned it." Mary read the title on the ancient cover: *Tolivers: A Family History from 1836.*

"Papa was afraid that in leaving the land to you, he would be condemning you to a childless state or to one in which your children would not live long lives. Until we came along, there was never more than one surviving Toliver to inherit the plantation, but who knows? Our youth is not yet spent." A sardonic gleam lit his eyes. "Granddaddy Thomas was the only heir of his generation to survive, and Papa of his. After you read what's in there, you'll understand Papa's meaning... and concern."

An uneasy feeling slid through her. She had never once considered the oddity of her grandfather and father being the single survivors to perpetuate the legacy of Somerset. They'd each had several siblings, now dead. Where had this album been all these years? Had her father deliberately kept it from her—she, the appointed repository of family lore?

Miles lifted her chin with cool fingertips. "Now," he said gently, "will you go to Bellington?"

She felt her answer squeezed from her lungs. "Yes," she said.

"Good. Then that's settled." He adjusted his French cuffs and sat back at his desk to indicate the interview was over.

"Lucy says you'll like Bellington Hall," Miles commented when she was at the door.

She paused to look back. "What's this Lucy like?"

"Not as pretty as you, if that's what you're asking."

She blushed hotly. "Of course not!"

"Oh, poppycock. Of course it is. She's petite in height and figure and round as a ball in all the right spots. Cute, I'd say. I like her, although I don't think you will. Why didn't you see her while she was here?"

"I'm in mourning, Miles, in case you haven't noticed."

"That, my sweet, is a cut beneath you. You were simply jealous of her for having so much of Percy's time."

"What nonsense," Mary said, her tone dripping scorn. "If I won't like her, why am I sharing a room with her?"

Miles dipped his pen into an inkwell. "It was thought best for both of you," he said, writing.

She knew he was avoiding her eyes. "By whom? You? Percy? His mother?"

"Beatrice and Percy are not involved. It was Lucy who suggested it when I voiced the possibility that I might send you to Bellington, and it was I who decided you should room together. You can look out for each other. You have a lot in common. Neither of you has any money. You won't have to suffer sharing a room with someone who does. You're both the same age. It's a perfect arrangement. I've already spoken to the headmistress about it."

Furious, Mary glared at her brother, his head bent pointedly to his letter. Were all men fools, or was only Miles in that category? *A lot in common, her foot!* She'd heard through Sassie by way of the Warwicks' cook that the girl had gone ga-ga over Percy. *He* was the only thing she and Lucy Gentry had in common. The girl perceived her as her connection to Warwick Hall.

"Was there anything else?" Miles asked, sounding weary of her.

The tender moment of a while ago was now history, ashes in a cold grate. Mary felt nothing but a chilling dislike for her brother. Clutching the book to her chest, she jerked open the door without answering. "Happy reading, little sister, " Miles called as she slammed it. "I hope you won't find the book disturbing."

She stuck her head back in. "I'm sure I won't, because I don't believe in curses. I intend to have many children."

"We'll see," Miles said.

Mary carried the volume to her room and sat in a window seat to examine it. The aged leather binding was held together by a leather cord running through two eyes and tied in a fast knot. She straightened against an odd feeling of dread and opened the book to the first page.

Some of the genealogical facts she knew. Others, she did not. Silas Toliver, Mary's great-grandfather and patriarch of the Texas clan, was born in 1806. He was thirty years old when he came to Texas with his wife and son Joshua. A year later, in 1837, a second son was born, Thomas Toliver, Mary's beloved grandfather. Joshua died from a fall off a horse at twelve. His surviving brother took possession of Somerset in 1865 after the death of Silas. That same year, Thomas became the proud father of a baby boy, Vernon, Mary's father. In the following years, he fathered another son and one daughter. Neither child was living at the time Vernon inherited Somerset. His brother had died of a water moccasin bite at fifteen, and his sister had succumbed at twenty to complications from the delivery of her only child, a stillbirth, leaving Vernon the single Toliver heir.

Faded photographs of all the Toliver offspring accompanied the chronicle. Mary studied them. Each of the children looked high-spirited and healthy. Their deaths had been sudden and unexpected. Here today and gone tomorrow. With a wrench of sympathy for their parents and surviving offspring, she snapped the book closed and shut it away in a drawer of the window seat. Then, to raise her low spirits, she stripped off her pinafore and dress and stood before her full-length mirror. She was pleased with what she saw. She might not be petite and cute and "round in all the right spots," but she knew she was alluring, and her long, supple body was made for childbirth. Her periods were as regular as clockwork. She would have many children—Miles needn't doubt that. Her father—God rest his soul—should not have worried that he had threatened her prolificacy or shortened her children's longevity by entrusting her with Somerset. No matter what he'd believed or the book implied, there was no Toliver curse. The fatalities befalling the heirs were normal to the times in which they lived. Percy and Ollie were the only living heirs to their families' enterprises. Were they under a curse, too? Of course not. She ran her hands over the firm flesh between her full breasts and slender hips. And Percy Warwick, too, could spare himself the trouble of thinking she might fall in love with someone unwilling to share her with a plantation. She wouldn't look at a man who had such a failing. She would marry no one who would separate her from her destiny. The man she married would support her in procreating the Toliver line and in carrying Somerset into the next century. The idea of a curse was absurd.

Chapter Eight

Her packing completed, Mary latched the last of her suitcases, relishing the finality of the sound. It signaled an end to her incarceration at Bellington Hall, thank God. The year was finally over, and she was going home. In three days' time she'd step foot onto hometown soil, never to leave it again if she so desired. And she so desired, she thought savagely, yanking the suitcase off the bed. If she'd gained nothing else from this wasted year at Bellington, it had reaffirmed what she'd arrived knowing—that there was nowhere else she wanted to be but Howbutker, nothing else she wanted to be but a planter of cotton.

Where in the world was Lucy? She'd be damned if she'd let that girl delay her departure. The headmistress had probably sent her off on some errand to prevent her from showing up on time. Well, if Miss Peabody thought she'd miss her train in order to say good-bye to her roommate, she was as mistaken about her now as she'd been the day they met.

She lugged the suitcase outside her door and placed it with the others to be picked up by the porter. She was the last in her dormitory to leave. Miss Peabody had seen to that, too—a final thrust to the armor Mary had built up against Bellington Hall and the headmistress in particular.

Up and down the corridor, the doors to all the dormitory rooms stood open, their occupants gone, the silent echoes of their voices lingering in the quiet. Mary stood in the doorway and listened, already recalling with difficulty the faces of the girls who'd shared her wing. Although they were her age, they had seemed intolerably young, their heads filled with the fluff the teaching staff had tried to stuff into hers. Mary had sensed their pleasure in knowing she'd be the last student permitted to leave the premises.

All except Lucy.

She felt a pang of contrition. She should be ashamed for hoping that Lucy wouldn't make it to her room before she left for the station. It was simply that Lucy would turn their farewell into an awful, sloppy scene, and she'd had enough of those from her roommate.

Besides, she was going back to enough emotional turmoil. Everything had fallen apart at Somerset. As she'd feared, Miles had relaxed the landowner image he'd disputed so long with their father, and with predictable results. In March, sick for news of the plantation because Miles had included precious little about Somerset in his infrequent correspondence, she'd written to Len. The overseer had replied by return mail and, in a laborious script written with a lead pencil she pictured often touched to his tongue, related as respectfully as his chagrin would allow the sorry state of affairs at Somerset.

Horror-stricken, Mary had visualized the situation. To prove that a laissez-faire treatment of the tenants would result in greater benefits for all, Miles had ordered Len to put away his quota book, frown, and imaginary whip and go fishing. The tenants did not need overseeing, he was informed. Each man would work according to his own dictates. They had families to feed, land to look after, cotton to grow. They would do it and more besides. Len would see the results at settlement time. Give a man his dignity and a freer hand to govern himself and his energies would know no bounds.

Consequently, Len reported, the tenants who didn't mind less for themselves and their families had slacked off. They'd bale fewer acres this year, taking in mind what they'd lose to the boll weevil. Mister Miles's handling of matters didn't seem to be working, and maybe Miss Mary needed to come home and have a talk with her brother.

Mary was all but weeping by the time she'd finished Len's letter. "Damn Miles!" she'd cried, pacing about her room. She had known this would happen. Without Len brandishing his "imaginary whip," which was nothing more than the constant supervision of the tenants, production was bound to drop. With money needed for seeds, fertilizer, equipment, maintenance, and repair, there would hardly be enough to meet the mortgage. "Damn him! Damn him! Damn him!" she wailed, of a mind to pack right then to have it out with her brother. He had no right to indulge his socialistic leanings at the expense of the plantation!

She had decided to pack her bags, when a letter arrived from Beatrice Warwick.

In her blunt style, Beatrice wrote that she had learned from Miles that Mary was not fitting in well at Bellington Hall. In that case, if she knew anything about their spirited Mary Lamb, she suspected that Mary would be planning to come home before the term ended. Beatrice was writing to advise her against it. Her mother's situation had not improved. She saw only Miles and Sassie and Toby Turner, their handyman. She had shut out everyone else, including her. The house was dark and shuttered, and no one went calling there anymore. In her opinion, Houston Avenue was no place for Mary at this time. Her presence would add to Miles's burdens and hinder her mother's recovery. Time to adjust to the terms of the will, which were now widely known and discussed, was all that Mary could give Darla for the present.

Mary read the letter in despair and anger. It was unheard of for a member of one of the families to interfere in the personal business of the other two unless asked. Miles must have asked. He had painted a terrible picture of her rebellion at Bellington, and out of concern for her best friend, Beatrice had agreed to write the letter.

Heavy of heart, Mary had folded the letter and decided that she had no choice but to wait out the year at Bellington and pray for the best concerning her mother and Somerset. Cotton prices were soaring right now owing to the demands of the war in Europe. Their profits would offset Miles's idiocy for the time being, and she would be home before the next planting season.

Then several other blows fell. In April, the United States declared war against Germany. Congress passed the Selective Service Act mandating that all able-bodied men from eighteen to forty-five register for compulsory military service. Mary, fearing the worst, held her breath. Sure enough, Len Deeter was among the first in town to receive a draft notice. Who would be left in the county to replace him?

Then, to add horror to horror, she received a letter from Miles on the first of June informing her that he and Percy and Ollie had enlisted in the army and would be reporting to officers' training camp in Georgia in July. Her first thought was the question of how Miles could serve as trustee of Somerset when he was an ocean removed from Howbutker. Her second was to realize that Miles could be killed or maimed and the same might be true for Percy and Ollie. In shock, devastated, and furious, she had wept. How could Abel DuMont and the Warwicks permit such stupidity? As only sons, the boys could have argued for deferments based on their indispensable duties at home, Miles especially since his family was dependent on him. How could he go off and leave their mother? How could he do this to his little sister? She had to get home and talk him out of this insanity.

"You're all packed, I see."

The crisp observation came from Elizabeth Peabody, headmistress of the school. She stood in the open doorway, pince-nez in place, clipboard affixed to her arm.

"Yes, I am," Mary said, surprised. She had not expected to be cleared for departure by Miss Peabody herself. The housemother or her student assistants, of which her roommate, Lucy Gentry, was one, had seen to the discharging of the other girls on the floor, and now that Mary was the last in the dormitory to leave, there was no lack of personnel available for the task. It was typical of Miss Peabody's mean-spiritedness not to send Lucy. *She has come for one last shot at me,* Mary thought, deliberately turning from the woman to pull on the jacket of her traveling suit.

"How many pieces of luggage?"

"Four."

Elizabeth Peabody marked something on the clipboard with quick, precise strokes. After entering the room, she darted a critical eye about the stripped beds and walls, the open, emptied drawers and cupboards.

"Have you checked thoroughly to make sure you've not forgotten anything? The school is not responsible for items left behind once a student has officially departed the campus."

"I've left nothing behind, Miss Peabody."

Miss Peabody's focus swung to Mary, and the agate eyes behind the pince-nez flashed. There was dislike in the gaze, which Mary met with the cool indifference that had set her apart from the other students from the beginning. "You can be sure of that," the headmistress said. "I don't think we've ever graduated a student who contributed and gained so little from the school."

Mary thought over the statement and said with her composed smile, "Well, now, that's not true, Miss Peabody. I learned that the sentence you just spoke contains perfect parallel structure."

"You are impossible." The headmistress's hand tightened perceptibly on the pencil. "An impossible, willful, selfish girl."

"In your eyes, perhaps."

"I've learned to trust my eyes, miss, and they see in you a young woman who will live to regret the decision she has made."

"I doubt it, Miss Peabody."

The headmistress was referring to her refusal to become one-half of the famous pairs Bellington Hall was noted for matching. Early on, Mary had discovered that many parents sent their daughters to the school to seek suitable husbands among the rich brothers, cousins, youngish uncles, and even widower fathers of classmates. The man Mary had refused was Richard Bentwood, a wealthy textile manufacturer from Charleston and the brother of one of the few girls of whom Mary had grown fond. "Since Amanda will have one more year here," she offered, "perhaps you'll have greater success in introducing her brother to someone far more suitable for him than I."

"Mr. Bentwood does not need my services in introducing him to suitable women, Miss Toliver. You can be assured that they abound in *his* social circles, whereas you are not likely to meet another Richard Bentwood in *yours*."

Mary turned away to pin on a floppy-brimmed hat before Miss Peabody could see that her shot had hit home. The headmistress was right in a way, though Percy and Ollie and Emmitt Waithe's son, Charles, could measure up to any man, including Richard Bentwood. The problem was, none of those boys were for her, and she had wondered, when she turned down Richard's marriage proposal, where and when she would ever meet his like again. He had been correct for her in every way but the one that mattered. He would have expected her to turn Somerset over to a land manager when they married, in order to live with him in Charleston. That was unthinkable, of course, but the night they had parted forever, she'd experienced an unfamiliar panic. What if no one came along who could stir her blood like Richard? What if there was no one in her future whom she would want to marry and have father her children?

To her relief, Mary heard the porter pick up her luggage in the hall, but the headmistress was not yet through with her. As Mary pulled on her gloves, she continued. "I understand that the lusty heirs of your ruling families will be going to war. Let us hope that fate will be kind and spare them to perpetuate their lines. However, from what I have read of the trench warfare in Europe, there is reason to doubt its beneficence. Should the young men be lost"—the headmistress touched her cheek in feigned horror—"there will not be much of a pool from which to make a choice, will there?"

Mary felt herself grow pale. The images that had haunted her since hearing of the boys' enlistment flashed through her mind. She saw their bodies lying in pools of blood on some godforsaken battlefield, Miles sprawled like a scarecrow, Percy's blond head forever still, the light eternally snuffed from Ollie's twinkling eyes.

She opened her handbag, a small beaded affair with a tortoiseshell frame, one of her last purchases from the DuMont Department Store. "Here is the key to my room," Mary said without a trace of regret. "That should do it, Miss Peabody. I have a train to catch."

Mary expected to be called back as she sailed from the room. It would be so like the witch to conjure up some reason to detain her—a fee not paid, a trumped-up damage charge, a lost book. Apparently, the headmistress was as happy to be rid of her as she of Bellington Hall, and she fled unassailed down the hall to the stairwell and freedom.

At the bottom of the stairs, she found Samuel, the porter, waiting for her. He greeted her with a gold-toothed grin. "I knowed you be anxious to leave, Miss Mary. A cab, it be on the way. How long it be since you been home?"

"Too long, Samuel." She handed him a nickel tip with a grateful smile. "Have you seen Miss Lucy?"

"She be up the Hill. Went that way 'bout twenty minutes ago."

"The Hill?" Mary cried. "Why would she go now, of all times?" The Hill was the campus post office, so called because it sat on a rise of land a good trek away. Lucy never received mail of her own but insisted on accompanying Mary when she checked her box in case there should be news of Percy.

A horse-drawn cab rattled through the wide wrought-iron gates. "Here be your ride, Miss Mary," Samuel announced, and thoughts of Lucy blew away like the dust beneath the coach's wheels.

"Thank goodness!" Mary exclaimed.

Samuel had loaded her luggage and was about to help her into the two-seater cab when a familiar voice called, "Mary! Mary! Samuel, stop that cab!"

"It's Miss Lucy," Samuel said unnecessarily.

Mary sighed. "I'm afraid so."

She watched the petite figure run toward her, holding up the full skirt of her outmoded dress, and felt the nick of annoyance followed by the flash of guilt often associated with Lucy Gentry—annoyance because the girl had attached herself like a leech since the first day she'd arrived at Bellington Hall, and guilt because she was the only schoolmate besides Amanda who had been friendly toward her. Aggravated, she faced the girl. "Why did you choose to go to the post office when you know I have a train to catch?"

"To get this." Lucy waved an envelope before Mary's face. "Go ahead and get in. I'm coming with you. Samuel, call Mr. Jacobson and have the milk truck swing by the station to pick me up, will you?"

"Miss Peabody goin' to have yo' hide," Samuel warned.

"Who gives a damn," Lucy said, pushing Mary into the coach and gathering her skirts to clamber in behind her.

With ill grace, Mary made space for her voluminous-skirted roommate. "What is that?" she asked, indicating the envelope.

Dramatically, Lucy withdrew a folded letter. "What you have here is my acceptance for employment. You are looking at the new freshman French teacher at Mary Hardin-Baylor in Belton, Texas."

Mary caught her inner lip between her teeth to keep from betraying her chagrin. Secretly, she'd hoped Lucy would not get the position. Belton was only a half day's train ride from Howbutker, and she would become a nuisance. Weekends, while Mary was busy restoring order to Somerset and seeing after her mother, Lucy would expect to be put up at Houston Avenue. Mary would feel differently if her roommate visited out of fondness for her, but they both knew that was not the case. Lucy suffered from a ridiculous, insane crush on Percy, inspired by the one time they had met. Mary was her link to Percy, and Mary Hardin-Baylor was a means to Warwick Hall.

"I don't understand," Mary said. "Why do you want the job now that Percy will be leaving for the army? Hasn't Miss Peabody offered you a better-paying position here?"

"What more convenient place to wait out Percy's return?" Excitement lit Lucy's summer blue eyes. "This way, I'll be close to Houston Avenue. I'll get to see him when the army lets him come home for a few days between the fighting. You *will* have me down, won't you...when he comes home on leave?" She batted her stiff, straight lashes that followed the circular line of her lids like a doll's.

The presumption of the girl! Mary thought, struggling to hide her annoyance. What made her think Percy would want to see her? "Lucy, the boys are going to France. I doubt very seriously if any of them will be sent home, over the ocean, for a few days' leave. They may be gone until the war ends."

Lucy thrust out her lower lip and stuffed the letter back into its envelope. "Well, it doesn't matter. I can still come for visits and walk down the street to his house and blow kisses that will find their way into his room, his bed..."

"Oh, Lucy..."

"Don't take that moaning tone to me, Mary Toliver. Those are the kinds of things that will bring him back. I *know* they will!" Lucy's small, dimpled hands clenched, and the porcelain purity of her complexion became mottled with the heat of her intensity. "I'm going to confession every day and light a candle for his safe return as well. I will say fifty Hail Marys every night and give a tenth of my salary to the church so that the priest will say a special mass for Percy—and for your brother and Ollie DuMont, too, of course."

Mary coughed delicately into her handkerchief. Lucy was a Catholic, another strike against her hopes to win Percy. The Warwicks were staunch Methodists and Jeremy a thirty-third-degree Mason. Mary doubted whether the family's well-known tolerance toward all creeds, races, and religions stretched to their only son marrying a Catholic.

"As soon as I finish up here," Lucy went on, "I'll make a trip to Belton to find a place to live. Then from there..." She arched a brow at Mary. "Perhaps my dear friend will invite me to spend a week or so for the purpose of seeing you-know-who."

Mary shifted uncomfortably in her seat. "I don't

mean to thwart your plans, Lucy, but I have no idea what Mother is like now, and what with Miles leaving, and the harvest to get in . . ."

Lucy's pleased expression became that of a rebellious child. "Harvest isn't until August."

"Which will give me barely enough time as it is to do the thousand and one things that have to be done—and undone, if I know Miles." Inwardly, Mary sighed. Lucy was well aware of her distress over the mismanagement of Somerset. "There simply will be no time to entertain you."

"Then how am I to see Percy before he leaves?" she demanded. "I certainly wouldn't expect Mrs. Warwick to invite me. The family will be busy getting him ready for war duty and spending as much time with him as possible."

Why can't you have the same consideration for my family? Mary felt like shouting. It was an example of Lucy's insensitivity, a basic disregard for the delicacy of a situation, that added to the many reasons Percy would never be interested in her.

"I won't be a bother to you, Mary, honest." Lucy's blue eyes flooded with appeal. "You won't have to go the itsy-bitsiest step out of the way for me."

"Because you'll be busy throwing kisses at Warwick Hall, is that it?" Mary grinned, relenting as always. On reconsideration, maybe more contact with Percy would be a good thing. Percy was nothing if not honest. When he saw Lucy's infatuation (and who could miss it?), he'd snip it at its root. He'd never go off to war leaving her to think he returned her affections.

Feeling better, Mary patted her roommate's hand. "I'll probably be glad of your company. Let us know when you're coming, and I'll have someone meet you at the station." Reading her friend's hopeful expression, she added, "No, Lucy, I cannot promise it will be Percy."

Chapter Nine

Settled on the train at last, Mary waved good-bye to Lucy waiting on the platform for the milk truck, her face fixed forlornly on Mary's window until the train curved and cut her from view. Mary removed her hat and tiredly expelled her breath. Lucy Gentry wore her out.

She had still not recovered from the shocking scene two nights before when Lucy learned of Percy joining the army. That evening when she asked if there had been a letter "from home," a presumption that never failed to grate, Mary had handed over Miles's letter and waited for the roof to fall in. It might as well have. As anticipated, Lucy wept and railed, screamed and cursed at the top of her lungs, sending books flying, clothes scattering, and her little stuffed bear out a window. Mary had never witnessed such grief and rage or heard such language. Every girl on the floor had come running, as had the housemother, who kept repeating, "I declare!" as they all watched Lucy shadowboxing the demons that possessed her, fighting off any who tried to calm her.

Mary had stayed out of her way, and at long last, Lucy had slipped to the floor in a corner of their room and buried her tear-streaked face in her arms. The girls who had gathered began to leave, and Mary quietly assured the housemother that she, too, should go back to bed. Lucy would be fine. She'd received some devastating news, and this was simply her way of handling it.

Mary then went to Lucy huddled in the corner and put her arms around her as if she were a child. Through the flannel of her robe, her sturdy little body felt unnaturally moist and warm. It gave off a faint, offensive odor, as if the bitterness of her rage were seeping out through her pores. Still, Mary held her until she felt the last shuddering sobs leave her body.

"Wh-why didn't he ta-take a deferment?" Lucy hiccuped between snatches of breath. "H-he's entitled to—to a deferment."

"Why didn't any of them?" Mary answered, smoothing Lucy's damp bangs away from her forehead. "It's not their way."

Lucy clutched Mary's hand. "He won't be killed!" she cried, her blue eyes bright and feverish. "I know he'll come home. I *know* it! I'll make a pact with God. I'll promise to be good. I *know* I can be good. I'll give up—"

"Cursing?" Mary suggested with a grin, and was relieved to see a sheepish smile crawl across her roommate's face.

"That, too, by God, if I have to."

The next morning, Mary awakened to find Lucy gone, her bed unmade. She had left a note: "Gone to mass. Lucy."

Still awed by the depth of the emotion she had witnessed, frightened by its sincerity, Mary made the bed and exchanged fresh pillowcases for those sodden with the tears Lucy had continued to shed through the night. She was deeply disturbed for her roommate. How was it possible to have such feelings for a man she barely knew and to cling to hope that he might care for her?

Lucy Gentry hadn't a chance with Percy Warwick. The woman he chose would be beautiful, intelligent, and cultured, a lady through and through. He would never settle for less, and Lucy, as captivating as she was in her unexpected way, struck Mary as definitely very much less. There was a coarseness about her in speech and manner that Percy would find offensive. She made good marks and was considered an adroit student, but what others perceived as intelligence, Mary pegged as sheer craft. It was her observation that Lucy had perfected the impression of being lettered. She was a book skimmer, a headline reader who had an amazing ability to suggest, with a few crumbs of information, that she possessed the whole loaf. Also, Mary suspected that Lucy's high academic rating was a result of cheating. As a staff aide, she had access to examinations and test schedules that Mary believed accounted for her uncanny ability to know what and when to study for exams.

Even her impoverishment was a sham. True, Lucy was a "scholarship girl," a student who had the credentials, but not the means, to attend Bellington Hall. However, she had a small trust fund left by her mother that would have updated the hopelessly outmoded clothes that hung in sparse number in her dormitory closet. The clothes were a banner of some sort. If Lucy could not flaunt the finest, she would the shabbiest. Mary could not quite understand the point of the statement or believe in its sincerity. It was a ridiculous rebellion, more of a pose than a stand, although Lucy's Victorian wardrobe endeared her to the girls and staff alike.

Mary shrugged off these small imperfections as minor blights on an apple. She could eat around them, but not Percy. Percy would pick the finest from the barrel.

One day, in exasperation, Mary had informed Lucy that she was aware of her futile infatuation with Percy and that she was a nitwit to allow it to influence a decision about her future. It was then that Lucy had reacted with her absurd claim: "You want him for yourself!"

Mary had been so taken aback that she could hardly speak. "What?" she'd squeaked.

"You heard me," Lucy said, sulking. "Don't try to deny it. You've had your eye on him all your life."

Mary heard her roommate's voice as if it had come from a deep well. She—set her cap for Percy Warwick? Why, Lucy would have better luck with him. "That's ridiculous," she disputed. "In the first place, I'm not interested in Percy, but even if I were"—she held up a hand to check Lucy's immediate contradiction—"he isn't the least interested in me. He doesn't even *like* me."

"Doesn't like you?" Lucy looked puzzled. "Why not?"

"It has to do with the way we look at our families, who we are, what we're about."

"You mean the Tolivers and the Warwicks?"

"Yes. Percy and I differ on the importance we put on our heritage, our...duties. I think one way and Percy thinks another. It's too complicated to go into, but believe me, we are not high in each other's affections. As far as I'm concerned, you have a clear field with Percy. It's...just that..."

"Just what?" Lucy urged, blue eyes narrowing.

Mary pulled in her lip and held her tongue. She longed to say: *It's just that you're not the kind of woman he could care for. You haven't the beauty, or the brains, or the delicacy of feeling that would appeal to Percy.*

Lucy observed her closely, then threw back her head with a bark of a laugh. "It's just that I'm not good enough for him, is that it?"

Mary considered her words. Since she'd opened the door, now was the opportunity to deliver the blunt truth, but she hadn't the heart to do it. "Being good enough isn't the question, Lucy. You're good enough for any man, for heaven's sake. I happen to know Percy's type, that's all."

"And I'm not it."

"Well...no, you're not."

"What is, then?"

"Dresden. Porcelain. Sweetness. Kindness. Not a drop of vinegar in the blood."

"What an utter bore!" Lucy exclaimed. "What about passion? Sex?"

Mary's jaw dropped. How did the girl *know* of such things? If Miss Peabody were to hear her, she'd have a stroke. She said equably enough, "I would imagine Percy finds feminine sweetness, if it's genuine, sexually stimulating."

"Mary Toliver!" Lucy stamped her small foot. "You mean to tell me you've lived practically side by side to Percy Warwick all your life and never realized what kind of woman he likes? Why, Percy requires spirit and fire in a woman. Dresden and porcelain be damned. He likes a woman he doesn't have to worry about breaking, that he can grab hold of, that can match him thrust for thrust—"

"Lucy!" Mary was on her feet, two spots burning on her cheeks and her heart racing as it had three summers ago when Percy had held her gaze across the courthouse common. "I can't understand how you know so much about Percy's sexual preferences since you've barely met him, but keep the subject to yourself. You may be right, but if you are, you're out of luck."

"Why?" Lucy demanded.

"Because you're too... you're too *short*."

Lucy laughed again. "Well, we'll see. There are ways around that little problem, and I'll bet Percy knows all about them."

That discussion cleared the air between them, and they were seen together so frequently, they were thought of as best friends. They were nothing of the sort, and they both knew it. Mary would never entrust her private thoughts to someone of Lucy's doubtful ability to keep confidences, and Lucy was well aware of Mary's frank disapproval of her pursuit of Percy, an objection she met with her usual unflappable good nature.

"I may not be good enough for him in *your* eyes, Mary Toliver, but I'll be good enough in *his*. My love for him will blind him."

"He has known the love of many, Lucy. None has succeeded in blinding him."

"Ah, but he's never known a love like mine. It will so dazzle him that by the time his eyes clear, I *will* be the woman he deserves. Loving him will make me so."

In the train, grateful for the sound of its wheels chugging her home, Mary laid her head back and closed her eyes. Poor, poor Lucy. She had as much hope of Percy falling in love with her as a ship had of plying dry land.

Chapter Ten

The next morning, Mary was ready for the first call to breakfast at six o'clock. It had been a dreadful night. She'd thrashed about, dreaming that she was doomed to ride the Southern Pacific forever, glimpsing the far-off landmarks of Howbutker only through her Pullman window as the train whistled through the station without stopping. She awoke shaken, her heart thumping in the sultry, close air of the compartment. No sooner would she doze off again than the nightmarish scene was back, this time with Lucy Gentry smiling and waving from the station platform as the train whizzed by.

A large breakfast and three cups of coffee, unusual for her, dispelled the aftertaste of her disturbing night, and Mary returned to her compartment to await the final leg into Howbutker. She would delay pinning on her hat until she saw the whitewashed outskirts of the Hollows, the Warrick-built company town where mill workers lived in trim pine houses with wraparound porches, white picket fences, and bricked streets. Only then would she know that the long journey was soon to be over.

She had not been home since Miles saw her off on the train last August. He had looked uncomfortable when she mentioned returning for Christmas.

"Wait until I send for you, Mary. In case things don't work out for you to come home, try to arrange for an invitation to spend the holidays with a friend."

"But, Miles, Christmas..."

Shamefaced, he'd taken her into a clumsy embrace. "Mary, Mama's in a bad way. You saw that for yourself when she wouldn't see you before you left. You can only help by going away and...staying away until she gets better. I'm sorry, but that's the way it is."

A strange terror had shaken her. She'd fastened her arms around her brother's waist and asked in a small, beseeching voice, "Miles, Mama doesn't hate me, does she?"

She had heard his answer in his silent reply. "Miles, *no....*"

"Shush, don't tear up now. You'll mar your pretty face. Try to make the best of this year. Do us proud."

"I truly have lost her, haven't I?" Her stricken look begged him to contradict her.

"You'll adjust to it, Mary. You'll adjust to all the losses in your life because you care only for the one thing that cannot leave you." One side of his mouth had ridden up mirthlessly. "Betray you? Most certainly. Let you down, suck you dry...absolutely, but it will never leave you. In a way, you're luckier than any of us. You're sure as hell luckier than Mama."

"I could lose Somerset," she reminded him. "If those mortgage payments aren't made, I could lose the plantation, too."

Miles playfully touched the tip of her nose and eased himself from her arms. "See how quickly the pain of one loss is forgotten at the possibility of one more important to you?" he half joked, wounding her with his stranger's smile. Once she was seated by her window, he'd waved briefly but had turned and walked away even before the train pulled out of the station.

She'd gone with Amanda to Charleston for the Christmas holiday, during which her darkly handsome older brother, Richard, had given her the experience of her first kiss upon the lips. It happened under the mistletoe. He'd tilted up her chin to meet his intent, and she'd been too surprised to step away. After a moment, she'd found herself responding to the pressure of his mouth and the clasp of her body to his male form. "Oh," she'd said breathlessly when they parted, amazed and embarrassed at herself, more so because of the spark in Richard's eye and his small, knowing smile. They seemed to say he'd discovered an untapped vein that he intended to mine for himself. Immediately, her defenses had gone up. She'd stepped away from the danger zone of the overhanging greenery. "You shouldn't have done that."

"I don't think I could have refrained from it," he'd said. "You are very beautiful. Surely that's reason to forgive me."

"Only if you promise never to let it happen again."

"I'm afraid I never make promises I am powerless to keep."

She'd accepted his hand to lead her into the dining room, but the experience had shaken her. Instinctively, she'd known she must keep this...new self-discovery sealed from men who could use it against her. I will not let him kiss me again, she had vowed—a promise that she, too, had found herself powerless to keep.

Mary shook herself from the recollections of their mutually enjoyed passion. Through the pine trees, the first white gleam of the Hollows had come into view. Mary scarcely noticed the increased number of houses as the train, slowing and blowing its whistle, skirted its periphery. She saw the flash of a handsome modern structure with its sign, WARWICK LUMBER COMPANY, written in fresh bold letters. She remembered that Miles had written of the expansion of the company's facilities and the building of a new office complex on landscaped grounds. The brief sight of it barely registered. She had her mind on other things.

Miles was to meet the train, but there had been no reply to a note she'd written weeks ago to alert him of the time and date of her arrival. In the days that had followed, she'd worried how she'd get the money for her ticket if Miles did not send her the sum. Finally, unable to bear the suspense any longer, she'd sent a collect telegram to Miles, an extravagance the Toliver budget could ill afford, pleading her urgent need. Within the week, he'd wired her the correct amount with no message attached. Stung, she had thought the absence of a few lines from her brother to welcome her home unforgivably rude, and she'd lived in a state of apprehension about the kind of reception she'd receive.

The train whistle blew again, and Mary, her heart beating uncontrollably, adjusted her hat in the small mirror above the lavatory. It was as out of fashion as her other clothes, though not as much as Lucy's. The fashion silhouette of women's styles seemed to change every season, and she'd had only a few new things in her wardrobe since her father had died.

The Tolivers' fiscal reverses were apparently well known in Howbutker. Shortly after she'd arrived at Bellington, Abel DuMont had written to ask if Mary would consider wearing his clothes as advertisement for the DuMont Department Store. "Your figure and bearing are superb for the new style of women's wear," he'd explained, "and I can't tell you what a service you would render if you would agree to model our line. You would, of course, keep all garments and accessories as a small token of my appreciation."

Mary had run a hand over the exquisite garments mailed along with the letter, then reluctantly boxed and returned the collection. "Thank you so much for your kind proposal," she had written, "but you and I both know that your clothes do not *need* advertisement here in fashion-knowledgeable Bellington Hall. Everyone is aware of your establishment and the beauty and quality of your merchandise. However, be assured that as my fortunes allow, I will never purchase my clothes anywhere but from the DuMont Department Store."

It had caused her pain to deny Abel the opportunity to show her kindness, but she was certain he would understand that she'd look upon the gesture as a breach of the agreement the families had followed since the founding of Howbutker.

Studying her face in the compartment mirror, she wondered if it had changed in the year she'd been away. Richard had brought to her attention the perfect symmetry of her features. With his forefinger the last night they were together, he'd drawn a line straight down from the V of her hairline to the dimple in the center of her chin. "See? Everything over here"—he'd kissed her left cheek—"parallels everything over here...." And he'd kissed the right. Then with both hands cradling her face, he'd drawn her forward to kiss her mouth, but she had stiffened and pulled away.

"No, Richard."

Chagrin had flashed in his fine dark eyes. "Why not?"

"Because it's...pointless, that's why."

He'd frowned. "Why is it pointless?"

"You know why. I've told you many times."

"Somerset?" The name seemed to curl his tongue, like something rancid. "I thought I was wooing you away from that rival."

"You were mistaken. I'm sorry, Richard."

"Not as sorry as I fear you may be someday, my dear."

The train finally drew to a stop. Mary stepped off and inhaled deeply of the hot, sultry air of her hometown, scanning the platform for Miles. It was Saturday, and the station was bustling. She inclined her head at the stationmaster and several farmers and townspeople she knew, including the mother of a former classmate. Had it been only a year ago since she'd greeted the woman, wearing the same hat, as she'd waited to board for her annual trip to California to visit her daughter? She herself had been waiting to collect Miles on his return from Princeton because their father was ill at home and their mother was tending him. Even so, back at the house, all was in readiness for his homecoming, the table set, the champagne chilling, and the house vibrant with arrangements of spring flowers. In less than a month her father was dead, and none of their lives had been the same.

"Good morning, Mrs. Draper," she said. "You're off for your June visit with Sylvie again, I expect." *Where in the world is Miles?*

With a gloved hand, Mrs. Draper touched the

cameo at the high neck of her blouse in a gesture of demure surprise. Mary had always thought her pretenses a way to project an image of good breeding. "Why, as I live and breathe, if it isn't Mary Toliver. You're home from that school they sent you off to, I reckon. I would never have known you, you've changed so. Become *older,* I guess would be the best word."

Mary smiled faintly. "It will do as well as any other," she said. "You, however, do not seem to have changed a bit, and I'm certain Sylvie hasn't, either."

"You're too kind for words." Behind the simpering smile, Mary could easily read the woman's thoughts, overheard one time when she'd expressed them aloud to a shopkeeper. Her Sylvie and the uppity Mary Toliver had never gotten on as well as one would expect, the two of them having grown up together and all, and her Andrew making as good a living as he did from the saddle-and-boot shop. There was nothing wrong in earning a livelihood from a shop. Didn't Abel DuMont do it every day, only on a grander scale? No, Mary's snootiness came from being a landowning Toliver. Everybody knew the Tolivers considered themselves treetops above everyone else in town, except for the Warwicks and DuMonts. Never mind that those they looked down on could pay their bills while the high-and-mighty Tolivers could not.

All this Mary divined while impatiently casting an eye about for Miles, and it was a few seconds before the implication of Mrs. Draper's running commentary sank in:

"...and we were all so shocked when we found out. Poor thing. If there's anything any of us can do...Just imagine. Darla Toliver in those...particular straits."

Mary dragged her attention back to Mrs. Draper. "I beg your pardon? What particular straits? What are you talking about?"

Mrs. Draper's fingers once again fluttered to the cameo. "Oh, dear me," she said, her small eyes bright with delighted horror. "You mean you don't know? You poor girl. I do believe I've said too much." Her expression gladdened further at someone approaching behind Mary.

Miles! Mary thought in desperate relief.

"Why, hello, Percy," Mrs. Draper crooned. "You caught me welcoming our Mary home!"

Chapter Eleven

So I heard," Percy said in a tone as pointed as a stiletto. "Hello, Gypsy," he addressed her in a quality of voice markedly warmer, and drew her into the custody of his arm. "Welcome home."

Somehow the familiarity of the hated nickname fell on her ears like a beloved song. She lifted her face gratefully to accept his kiss upon her cheek. "I'm so very happy to see you," she said, meaning it. "You've come in place of Miles?" He wore a cream-colored suit and thickly knotted tie, and never had he looked more handsome, more glowing with youth and health and masculine vigor.

"He's at home making sure everything is fit for your arrival. Didn't trust anybody but himself to see to it, so I snatched the opportunity to be the first to welcome you home."

It was all a lie said for the benefit of Mrs. Draper's pricked ears, Mary knew, but she was as thankful as if his words had been the truth. Something must have happened back at the house. Her mother was behaving badly, having second thoughts about her daughter coming home, and Miles had been forced to stay behind to deal with the situation. He'd probably called Percy at the lumberyard office—he wouldn't have dressed in such a natty suit simply for her—and he'd dropped everything to rush to the station.

"How nice of you," Mary said, giving Percy a look that revealed she'd grasped the truth and appreciated the deception.

His arm still around her waist, Percy turned to Mrs. Draper. "If you'll excuse us now, I'd better get our girl home. Her mother is eagerly awaiting her arrival."

"Really?" Mrs. Draper purred. "What a nice change. I'm sure Mary will be just what the doctor ordered."

"Without a doubt. Have a good *long* trip, Mrs. Draper."

"Why, thank you, Percy." Her hand at the cameo again, she batted her eyes in the insipid manner that Mary had noticed he inspired in her sex.

"Thanks for the rescue," she said when they were out of earshot of Mrs. Draper. "What an abominable woman."

"The very worst," Percy agreed. He took her hand and placed it in the crook of her arm. "I'm sorry I wasn't here to prevent her from waylaying you."

"Well, actually, I'm the one who approached her. She didn't seem to recognize me."

"I can see why not."

"Meaning what?"

Percy halted and said in feigned surprise, "Why, Mary Toliver, don't tell me you're fishing for compliments—and from me, no less!"

Her hackles rose. She felt herself slipping into her old defensive position until she glanced into his eyes. She saw amusement there, but no mockery. His expression was admiring, even proud. She laughed lightly. "As curious as I might be to see what I'd snag, you won't ever catch me casting a line into *your* pond, Percy Warwick." They walked on. "So tell me what that dreadful woman was implying when she said my mother was in particular straits. Is Mama the reason you came instead of Miles?"

He folded his hand over hers, holding it firmly as if to prevent her stumbling when he answered. "Your mother has a drinking problem, Mary. She's . . . become addicted to alcohol."

"What?" Mary stopped abruptly, immobilized. "You mean . . . Mama is an alcoholic?"

"I'm afraid so."

"But how? Where did she get the liquor?"

"Your father kept quite a cache of it in your cellar against the possibility of Prohibition. She found it, and before Miles or Sassie discovered what she was up to, it was too late."

The horror of it numbed her. Her mother...an alcoholic? She'd heard the word *alkie* used to describe those addicted to the bottle, a vile, disgusting word depicting individuals lacking self-will. "And everybody knows but me," she said. "The whole town, apparently."

Percy's expression changed. A pointed light appeared in his eye. "Is that your major concern, that the Toliver name will be sullied?"

Of course not! she wanted to cry, stung by his implication. She was concerned for her mother. This last public shame would keep her bound to her room forever. She let go of his arm. Nothing had changed in her absence, certainly not between them. All and everything remained the same. "I should have been told."

"Miles didn't want you to know. What good would it have done?"

"I could have come home. What good did my going away do, after all?"

"It was worth a shot, Mary—a small enough sacrifice for you to make, don't you think?"

What was the use of a rebuttal? He'd made up his mind about her. Feeling sick, she opened her beaded bag and said in her Bellington-trained manner, "Here are the claim tickets for my luggage. There are four pieces if you'd be good enough to collect them. They're inside the station house."

Percy gently enclosed the proffered hand. "I'm sorry this is not the homecoming you'd hoped for, Gypsy."

"I'm learning not to hope for what I can't control," she said, lifting her chin, steeling herself against the inclination to cry. He judged no one but her.

He slipped the tickets from her fingers and brought the back of her gloved hand to his lips, his gaze exploring hers. "I certainly hope I'm an exception to that policy."

Her breath caught sharply, and she withdrew her hand. "The only exception to that policy is the hope that I will not be misjudged by the people I care about. Now, how are we getting home?"

Percy shook his head as if there were no reasoning with her. "I have a Pierce-Arrow, a red-and-yellow job. It's parked under the trees in the livery yard. Wait for me there in the shade."

The shining, open-seated, low-slung motorcar stuck out in the parking area like a Thoroughbred among mules. Mary stood disconsolately on the passenger side, barely cognizant of its elegance. The thrill of her homecoming had evaporated, and she dreaded the first glimpse of her mother and the encounter she expected with Miles. What a fool she'd been to look forward to seeing him from her compartment window when the train steamed into the station. She'd imagined riding home with him in the buggy, chatting of local gossip and plantation news. She'd even halfway hoped that her mother would be glad to see her and that they could be a family again before Miles went off to war.

"Has my mother been under a doctor's care?" she asked as Percy stowed her luggage into the back-seat of the two-bodied car. "Has she responded to treatment?"

"Doc Goddard has been seeing her, but his skills are limited in that area. He's recommended total absti-nence, which Miles and Sassie have been enforcing."

"Dear God," Mary said, imagining what an ordeal that must have been. "Is she recovering?"

"Not from the need for alcohol, but at least now she's clean of the stuff. Miles has had to watch her like a hawk to make sure she doesn't get her hands on a bottle. He and Sassie take turns, and my mother spells them when she's asked. Sometimes, in order for them to get rest or for Miles to go out to the planta-tion, they've had to tie her to her bed. I'm sorry, Mary. I'm telling you this only to prepare you. You need to know what you're heading into."

A sickening pressure spread beneath her breast-bone. "Surely all the liquor has been disposed of."

"All that she didn't drink or hide. There are still bottles hidden in and around the house." He opened the door to the passenger seat. "I have road gear if you want to cover your clothes and hat. Some gog-gles, too. I wear only the goggles. The road dust is terrible this time of year."

"It's too warm. Besides, I want to see the countryside."

"I'll try to keep us under thirty miles an hour."

They climbed in, and Percy started the motor. Mary listened fascinated as the engine coughed to life beneath the long, shiny red hood. She had ridden in only one horseless carriage before—Richard Bentwood's Rolls-Royce, which he'd imported from England. "I hope to high heaven Miles did not spend good money on one of these," she remarked with distaste as they took off to the gaping admiration of those waiting on the platform.

Percy chuckled. "No, you know Miles. He thinks motorcars are another example of degeneracy brought on by capitalism." He turned onto the road leading into Howbutker. "By the way, I meant it when I said welcome home."

"That's hardly for you to say, considering that in less than a month, you'll be gone for God only knows how long." She didn't add, *Maybe forever,* as her heart contracted with the familiar fear. "My brother and his causes! He's dragged you and Ollie off with him, hasn't he?"

"Ollie thought that somebody ought to go along to look after him, Gypsy. Otherwise he'll get his bloody self killed."

"And where Miles and Ollie go, you go—to look after them both."

"That's about it."

The sadness, the waste, of it were too much. Her anger at Miles rose like the aftertaste of bad fish. How could he do this to his best friends and their families?

How could he leave their mother in these new throes, abandon his responsibility to the plantation? But it would never do to confide her disgust to Percy. He would hear no word against Miles.

"What's to become of this thing when you leave for Europe?" she asked.

"I'll either sell it or give it to Dad to hold for me until I come back. Mother refuses to ride in it, but Dad's not above taking it for a spin to keep the joints oiled."

Her eyes suddenly burned, and she was compelled to watch the countryside more closely. After a short while, she said, "Give it to your father to hold for you."

She sensed his head turn in surprise. "All right," he said. "I'll give it to Dad to keep for me."

They drove awhile in silence, Mary keeping her attention averted to her side of the road. The dogwood was spent now, but the climbing vines of wisteria were still in splendor, their lavender blooms cascading off fence and trellis and the limbs of trees. Out at Somerset the cotton fields were in bloom, their blossoms the myriad colors of East Texas sunsets in high summer.

Mary concentrated on that image. All her loves were gone, her grandfather and father, her brother and mother. All that remained was Somerset, waiting for her. The land was hers to care for year after year, harvest after harvest, for as long as she lived. As

Miles had said, it would never desert her. The boll weevil could come and drought and floods. In the time it took to run for cover, hail could wipe out a crop worth a fortune, yet the land would still be there when the devastation was cleared away. There was always hope with the land. There wasn't, oftentimes, with people.

Percy said, "I suppose your first order of business will be to ride out to Somerset."

It was uncanny how he could read her thoughts. "Yes," she said shortly. He made it sound as if such a prompt visit were the height of impropriety.

"Well, before you come down too hard on Miles for the way he's run the place, there are a few things you need to know."

"Oh?" She raised a brow at him. There was nothing Percy could say that would mitigate her brother's mismanagement of their livelihood.

"Remember that your brother has the final say over the plantation until you're twenty-one."

"I don't need reminding of that."

"But you do need reminding that if your brother is of a mind, he can change the character of the plantation so that it's no longer the Somerset you want to preserve. Remember that as well."

Mary froze in her seat and fixed him with a shocked stare. "What do you mean?"

"There are other ways that land can bring in revenue than producing cotton, Gypsy."

"Percy, what are you talking about? What has Miles done? What is he proposing to do?" Her words whipped angrily out of her mouth, torn by the wind as the Pierce-Arrow with its open body sped along. They were shouting, she realized. To have a conversation in one of these bloody things, you had to shout.

"Will you listen, you little fool, before you go jumping to conclusions about Miles? I'm telling you what he *didn't* do, and all on account of his little sister."

"Tell me," she said, drawing a deep breath.

"He could have put the acreage under sugarcane. A grower out of New Orleans came to see him right after you left for school and made him a very handsome offer. He turned him down, as he did my own father. Dad wanted to lease the plantation and put it under a ten-year growth of timber."

Mary could not speak. She felt her eyes straining from their sockets. Swallowing hard, she said, "The land could never be reclaimed if he did that."

"Would that be such a tragedy, Mary?" Percy's hand left the steering wheel and sought hers. "Cotton is dead anyway. Synthetic fibers are on the way. Other countries are beginning to compete for the world markets Texas has had to itself for so long. And as if that's not enough, the boll weevil has just about wiped out the Cotton Belt in the South."

"Percy—Percy—" Mary yanked her hand away. "Be quiet, you hear me! Be quiet! You don't know what you're saying. My God, what have I come home to?"

Percy said nothing, his eyes on the road. After a moment, he said quietly without looking at her, "I'm sorry, Mary. Believe me, I sincerely am."

"Well, you should be," she retorted. "The very idea of your father taking advantage of our situation and offering Miles—gullible, vulnerable Miles—the opportunity to grow timber. I promise you one thing, Percy Warwick, it'll be a subzero day on the Fourth of July in Howbutker, Texas, before a single Warwick pine ever sinks a root into Toliver soil!" She was so angry, she was quivering.

They had arrived at a point beside the road that allowed for a U-turn. Into this space Percy spun off, raising dust and bringing the Pierce-Arrow to a squealing halt. Startled, Mary instinctively reached for the door handle to seek escape, but Percy grabbed her free wrist at the same time he tore off his goggles. Mary had never seen him angry, and the sight stunned her mute. She remembered Beatrice describing to her mother the rage of which he was capable: *It's not often his temper flares, but when it does, it's the most frightening thing you'll ever see. His mouth tightens like a steel trap and his eyes lose color. And he's so powerful! My goodness, he could break you like a toothpick. Thank God my boy never gets angry without just cause.*

Just cause. . . .

"Don't you dare misconstrue my father's attempt to come to your family's aid as a way to serve the Warwicks," he said through clenched teeth, his eyes like chips of ice in his flushed face. "If you don't know better than that, you're more pigheaded than I thought."

"*He* should know better than to go behind my back to make such a proposal," Mary countered, struggling to free herself from the pain of Percy's grasp. "He knows what cotton meant to my father. That's why he left Somerset to me and not Miles!"

"Maybe Dad doesn't take your father's obsession as yours. Maybe he thinks that since you're a woman, you'll want something else besides a weevil-ridden plantation, a system of outdated servitude to devote your life to. Maybe he thinks that since you're going to marry me, Somerset will be under timber anyway."

Her jaw dropped. "What?"

"You heard me."

"Wha—Marry you?" She stared at him, dumb-struck. "Put Somerset under timber? You're joking, right?"

"Does this seem like a joke?"

He reached for her. She was so shocked by the pre-posterousness of his assumptions that her mouth was still open when he locked his over it. She struggled and pushed, sputtered and squealed, but to no avail. The woman in her, traitor to the chaste girl who'd withstood Richard's advances, bloomed full grown under Percy's assault. Her body flared, her senses blazed. Caution and decorum flew from their restraints in surrender to her need of him, and she welcomed his possession as much as the restrictions of their clothing permitted. Eventually, time and the present returned and she lay spent and hot in his arms, aware that her traveling suit was rumpled, her hair disheveled, her lips smarting, and somewhere her hat lay in the dust of the road.

"Lord have mercy," she said, too enervated to move her head from the hollow of his shoulder.

"Now after that, try telling yourself we don't belong together."

It was not possible to dispute it. She'd felt as tightly bound as a bale of cotton when she'd seated herself in this contraption, and now the wires were cut and she was spilling everywhere, and they both knew it. But this would never do. *They* would never do. "It doesn't matter," she said. "I can't—I won't marry you. I mean it, Percy."

"Well, we'll see how you feel when I get back from Europe, after you've had the responsibility of overseeing a five-thousand-acre plantation, fighting the boll weevil, caring for a couple of hundred sharecropping families, and keeping your overseer sober. That's not to mention taking care of your mother and living from hand to mouth. I wish it were fair to you to marry you before I leave, but"—he kissed her forehead, leaving the implication between them—"at least you'll have Mother and Dad to look after you until I get back."

"What presumption!" Mary scoffed, finding the will to push out of his arms. "And what if I feel the same way about us when you return?"

"You won't." He smiled, not with the smugness of Richard Bentwood, but with the quiet, unshakable confidence of his knowledge of her.

Somehow she managed to flounce back to her side of the car, straightening her dress. "Put it out of your head, Percy Warwick. It's not going to happen." She looked around for her hat and saw that it had landed in a field, where a cow was happily munching it for its dinner.

"It will happen," he said, starting the motor.

Mary could not look at him as they pulled back onto the road. There was now a new enemy in her midst, far more insidious than the boll weevil, more deadly than hail or flood or drought, more frightening than a cartel of Boston bankers lying in wait to foreclose on Somerset. Now she knew what was behind her strange antagonism toward him these last few years. He had the power to make her love him. He could weaken her will to his. Marriage to him would mean combining their interests, expanding the Warwick timberlands at the expense of Somerset. She would become absorbed into the Warwick identity, lose the special distinction associated with a Toliver.

Their children would be raised as Warwicks, and the Toliver line would perish. Miles was no Toliver. He was his mother's son, a Henley, a weak-willed visionary. *She* was the only true remaining Toliver. From her would come the sons to sustain the line, but only if she married a man who shared her commitment. Percy Warwick was not such a man.

"It would behoove us both," she said, staring straight ahead, "never to put ourselves in this position again."

"I promise nothing, Gypsy," he said.

At her door, she extended her hand formally. "Thank you for meeting my train, Percy. It's not necessary for you to come in."

Percy ignored her hand and slid his arm around her waist. "Now, don't worry about what we discussed," he said. "The subject can wait until I return."

She lifted her face to stare straight into his eyes. "I want with all my heart for you to return, Percy, but not to me."

"It must be to you," he said. "There can be no one else. Now, go easy on Miles. He's been like a hound beset with wolves this year. If there's one thing he's learned, it's that he's no farmer. He's made a mess of things, as I'm sure you'll point out, but the man has done the best he could."

Mary nodded to indicate she understood. "That's my girl," he said, and drew her to him to kiss her lips lightly. She tensed against the rise of passion, a self-betrayal his amused gaze indicated he'd felt. "I'll see you later," he said, leaving her to descend the steps. Behind her, she heard the door open and Sassie's exclamation of welcome, but it was a long few seconds before she could take her gaze from his confident stride to the Pierce-Arrow.

Chapter Twelve

The train was late. For the tenth time in as many minutes, Mary glanced at the lapel watch pinned to her outdated dark green serge suit before once more staring down the empty track.

"The train was probably late in leaving Atlanta," Jeremy Warwick offered, to ease the mounting tension in their little group gathered on the platform. There were four of them—Jeremy and Beatrice Warwick, Abel DuMont, and Mary—waiting among a larger crowd that had come to the station to welcome "the boys" home from the war. The high school band was there, lined up and ready to strike into "Stars and Stripes Forever" the moment a uniformed figure stepped down from the train. A banner reading WELCOME HOME, HOWBUTKER'S OWN was draped over the entrance to the station, and one like it stretched across a section of Courthouse Circle for the parade scheduled later that day.

The war had been over for nearly a year, but not for Miles and Ollie and Percy or for thousands of other members of the American Expeditionary Forces (AEF) delayed in France—either by the scarcity of ships to bring them home or by occupation duty in Germany.

Only Percy would be coming home unscathed. Miles had been severely gassed toward the end of the war, and rather than leave him behind, Captains Warwick and DuMont volunteered to remain after the armistice to help demilitarize a hostile Rhineland. Shortly after Christmas, as a member of the occupying garrisons, Ollie had been injured by a grenade that had all but severed his leg from his hip.

It had been a long twenty-six months for the returning soldiers' families. The war years themselves had been worrying enough, with newspaper accounts of soldiers enduring unspeakable anguish and hardships of combat, and then of influenza raging throughout the AEF, striking as many as ten thousand a week. But then reports at the war's end had caused even more agony with tales of wounded men still in critical condition being moved from base hospitals to forwarding camps, where they were left to convalesce without medical supplies and attention.

At news of this, the families' hopes sank to their

lowest depths of the war. It had been bad enough imagining the boys engaged in trench warfare, shivering in tents on quagmire floors without sufficient fuel or blankets during the coldest winters Europe had ever known, but to think of Miles and Ollie wounded and forgotten, cut off from home, and Percy facing the same possible fate every day was an even worse nightmare.

There had been virtually no mail received on either side of the Atlantic. The few letters that had trickled in from overseas complained of the abysmal mail service, and the families—who shared every letter among them—could hear their sons' plaintive cries of loneliness between the raillery of their lines.

Beatrice Warwick, unable to deny her, had allowed Lucy, too, to pore over her son's letters, reading after reading. By now, Mary's former roommate was installed at Mary Hardin-Baylor and had made frequent weekend visits to Houston Avenue, where she had managed to insinuate herself into the Warwicks' reluctant good graces, which included a guest room. Lucy preferred their forced hospitality to the lack of any at all in the Tolivers' cheerless mansion up the street.

Naturally she would be here today, Mary thought with familiar irritation as she glanced in Lucy's direction. Slimmer and fashionably turned out in a becoming mauve dress whose hugging lines and shorter length showed off her new figure, Lucy had strolled away to check her reflection once again in the station house windows. Lord, how that girl could wriggle in where she was determined to be. Mary had learned through the Warwicks' cook that Beatrice—a formidable woman hard to outmaneuver—was at a loss as to how to deal with the nuisance Lucy had become.

Earlier that day when Percy's parents had called for her in their shiny new Packard—Lucy preening in the backseat—her onetime roommate had looked delighted to see her appear in her old green serge. "You look marvelous!" she'd cried as Mary lifted her outdated long skirt to get in. "I've loved you in that for years!"

"So has Percy," Beatrice drawled from the front seat. "How thoughtful of you to wear something he will remember, Mary Lamb. So much has changed around here since the boys have been away."

Lucy lapsed into silence, and a glance at her pouting lips told Mary she realized she'd been put firmly in her place. Mary felt a warm glow of appreciation toward Beatrice Warwick. She knew she stood high in her respect and affections, higher than in her own mother's. She would brook no one patronizing one of their own, especially an outsider whose designs on her son were as clear as well water.

Mary looked affectionately at her sitting stoutly beside her husband—suited, gloved, and hatted in expensive black. She had donned what everyone called her "widow's weeds" the day the boys left for war and had dressed in black ever since. It wasn't that she had no faith in the boys' deliverance from the jaws of death, she said. It was her way of protesting war in general, the stupidity of nations to engage in barbarity to settle their differences. She wore mourning, she said, for all the sons who would not make it home.

On the platform, Mary turned her glance from Lucy to Abel DuMont. From his expression, she could tell that already Ollie's father, a widower since Ollie was ten, was visualizing the tragedy of his son descending the train on crutches. Surgeons were already scheduled in Dallas to restore the leg as much as possible. Moved by sympathy for him, she slipped her hand under his arm, gloved to hide the giveaway signs of her labor. His deepened crow's-feet crinkled in lieu of a smile, and he patted her hand in understanding. Mary hoped that he'd forgiven her for not wearing the beautiful day dress with a matching cape she'd left hanging in her closet. She had modeled it in a fashion show for the DuMont Department Store. As a reward for participating, all the young women who had paraded down the ramp, town girls like herself, were given the dresses they had modeled. Mary was certain the fashion show had been arranged for her benefit, as yet another way that Abel might introduce a new dress into her wardrobe for the homecoming events. She'd appreciated the gesture, but the Tolivers were not ready for charity yet.

From far away came the sound of the long awaited train whistle. "I hear it!" someone shouted, and the crowd stirred anew, moving into the small, elite group that had stepped closer to the edge of the platform.

Mary felt as if her heart were ready to burst through her chest wall as the whistle blew again and a thin spiral of smoke rose in the distance. How would he be changed...Percy Warwick, the town's golden boy? Surely war must have altered him. Would he return with the same easy manner, the quick laugh, the confidence with which he'd always met life? Would he still want to marry her?

Even now her blood warmed at the memory of their last moments together on this very spot over two years ago. In front of everyone, he had drawn her into his arms...a small enclave of intimacy in the midst of the crowd. She hadn't seen much of him between the time he'd brought her home from the train and the day he left for officers' training camp, or in the week's interim between his return home and his departure for overseas. Even if she hadn't spent every day at the plantation and evenings unraveling Miles's ledgers, she doubted he'd have tried to see her. He was playing a waiting game, she was sure of it— waiting for her to tire of running Somerset, hoping she'd be run to earth with the struggle of it by the time he came home.

"My intention still stands, Mary," he'd said that day. "When I come home, I intend to marry you."

"Never," she'd vowed, her heart pounding so hard, she was sure he could hear it. "Not if it means giving up Somerset."

"You'll have it out of your system by then."

"Never, Percy. You'll have to accept that."

"I accept only that I want us to be married."

"Why?" She'd thrown the question at him, memorizing how the sun struck his hair, the deep tan of his skin, the clarity of his eyes. He'd held his billed hat under his arm. "I've thought it over and decided it's...simple lust between us. That's it, isn't it? I don't think you even like me."

He had laughed. "What has liking got to do with it? And of course there's lust, but I want to marry you because I love you. I've loved you all your life, ever since you smiled at me through your cradle bars. I've never considered marrying anyone else."

She'd heard him in disbelief. Percy...who could have any girl he wanted...in love with her since she was born? How had she missed it?

She'd relived that moment thousands of times in the twenty-six months of his absence...remembered how he'd placed his hat back on, slipped his arm around her waist, and pulled her to him and kissed her...how they'd parted numb with desire, drowning in each other's eyes. She'd been vaguely aware of the ripple of shock around them, of her brother's startled gaze, Beatrice's raised brows, Abel's quickly averted glance, and finally...Ollie's resigned smile when he approached her as Percy left to join his parents.

"Don't worry, Mary," he'd said, his eyes grave, the twinkle extinguished. "I'll see he gets home in one piece."

"Ollie, dear..." There had been a catch in her voice as she'd said his name. She'd only then realized what she'd been too blind, too single-focused, to see. Ollie was in love with her, too. Now he was bowing from the competition, yielding the field to Percy.

"See that you take care of yourself, too, Ollie," she'd said, and hugged him hard, his custom-fitted uniform already too snug from the extra pounds he'd gained while home on leave.

Thinking now of Ollie, she was chilled by a suspicion that had haunted her often since the telegram arrived informing them of his injury. The few subsequent letters had offered sparse details. The families had learned only that Percy and Ollie were together on patrol duty when a grenade landed close by. In the still, dark hours of her many sleepless nights, Mary had asked herself, Could it be—was it possible—that Ollie had sacrificed himself for Percy?

A mauve sleeve pushed in beside her, and Mary turned in exasperation to her friend. "Lucy, do give the Warwicks the first opportunity to embrace their son."

Lucy's blue eyes darkened in offended injury. "Do

you think I wouldn't, Mary Toliver? You, of all people, should understand how I feel about Percy."

"I don't think there's anybody who doesn't understand how you feel about Percy."

"You know perfectly well what I mean." Lucy spoke in an edgy whisper so the Warwicks would not overhear. "Everybody else might think that I believe I have a chance with Percy, but you know that I know I can never win him. But what's to keep me from loving him, praying for him, being glad he's home safe until he falls in love with someone else?"

"Your pride, maybe?" Mary suggested. How could any woman lay herself so unabashedly open for pain, like a puppy happily exposing its underbelly to be kicked?

"Pride?" Lucy chortled. "Horsefeathers! Pride is nothing but a hobble that confines you to a small space with no chance of ever seeing what's over the mountain. You'd better take a long look at pride, sweetie. It could be your undoing."

"Here they come!"

The train was slowing, nearing the station. Every neck craned in the direction of its approach. Abel, tightening his grip on his cane, solemnly drew himself erect. Lucy forgotten, Mary felt her eyes smart. Already tears were running down Jeremy Warwick's cheeks, and Beatrice withdrew a voluminous lace-edged handkerchief from the black sleeve of her dress and held it to her mouth. The band director raised his baton. The stationmaster took his stand importantly beside the place the train would stop.

"I see them!" whooped a man who had moved on down the track. Mary recognized him as a farmer who had lost his oldest son at Belleau Wood. He whipped off his hat and began to wave and shout at the faces peering from the train windows. Mary experienced a sudden, aching desire for her mother to be standing beside her, but she was lying at home, a wasted figure swallowed by her bed. Her long battle with alcoholism was finally over, but the end had been bought at what may have been too dear a price. Only time would tell, and her mother's willingness to live. Maybe Miles's homecoming would help. Maybe he was in time to save her, and they could be a family again.

Lucy squealed in her ear. The train was gradually screeching to a stop, and all on the platform stared at the open windows, looking for familiar faces smiling back, the sight of uniforms. The stationmaster hopped on board.

"What's keeping them?" Lucy demanded.

"They're probably gathered in the corridor, waiting to get off," Beatrice said.

"Maybe Ben is alerting the boys to the mob that's waiting," Jeremy surmised, referring to the stationmaster.

"Or maybe my son needs help," Abel remarked. "The T and P wires such information ahead, you know."

"Ben would have said something to us about that," Beatrice said in her rational tone.

"Well, where the hell *are* they?" Lucy whined as the crowd fidgeted and waited.

The stationmaster reappeared and stepped quickly down from the platform from which the honorees would descend, holding up his hands to the crowd. "All right, everybody, Captains Toliver and Warwick and DuMont will be out in just a moment. I'll ask you all to move back except for the families. Remember that there are other passengers aboard. I'd ask you to allow them to get through to the station house."

"Oh, for heaven's sake, Ben," snapped Beatrice. "Stop talking and get the boys down here!"

The stationmaster bowed and stepped again onto the platform. "Gentlemen!" he called into the car.

The crowd held its collective breath, then let it out in a huge cheer as Percy stepped out. The band struck up, and the Warwicks and Lucy rushed forward, but he appeared to be searching over their heads for someone else. Mary slowly put up her hand, and his gaze lit upon her and held for a long, heart-stopping moment before he descended the steps and was lost to her. She caught only a glimpse of his uniform hat before he was set upon, blocked from sight by Beatrice's towering hat and his father's broad-shouldered figure. Poor Lucy hopped up and down behind them like a bright little fledgling pushed from the nest, unable to break through the barrier of their embraces.

Mary felt her whole body explode with joy. Relief thundered through her. He was alive...he was well... he was whole. He was home.

After another breath-held minute, Ollie appeared, his smile as beaming as ever. Mary's gloved fingers flew to her lips. Beside her, Abel stiffened and uttered a strangled cry. "Oh, my God. They've cut off his leg."

Chapter Thirteen

Miles followed shortly, stepping out onto the platform with the blinking gaze of a man seeing sunlight after a long confinement underground. Both Mary and Abel stared mutely. Ollie waved at the suddenly quiet crowd with one of his crutches, then adroitly maneuvered down the steps with his usual jauntiness. The right leg of his army jodhpurs had been brought up and pinned at the knee, leaving the rest of the pant hanging as flat as an empty bellows.

Shockingly thin, his face ghastly pale, Miles descended behind him laden with luggage, his concentration focused on managing the steps. With grim composure, Abel offered Mary his arm and together they went to meet son and brother.

"Miles?" Mary said uncertainly, wondering if he'd allow her to embrace him.

He stared at her blankly. "Mary? Is that you? My God, but you're beautiful. I guess I am, too, huh?"

He smiled with a touch of his old irony, revealing teeth that had begun to decay. "Where's Mama?"

"At home. She's so eager to see you, Miles. I... have been, too." She felt her chin trembling and tears spurt to her eyes.

Miles set down the bags and held out his arms. "Well then, come here and give your big brother a hug."

She threw her arms around him and held him fiercely, dismayed at his appallingly thin frame. "You're all bones and hollows," she moaned. "Sassie will have a job fattening you up."

"How is Sassie?"

If she'd answered truthfully, she would have said, *Tired, Miles. Worn out from seeing after our mother, trying to run the house without help, to put food on the table from our limited larder.* But his battle had been worse than theirs. "The same," she said. "A bit older. Wearies a little easier."

"And Mama?"

"The same, too, I'm afraid. I'll tell you about her away from here."

She heard a shuffle behind her. "Hello, Mary Lamb."

It was Ollie, so much the same, so much changed. As with the others, his uniform hung on him, but the twinkle in his eyes for her had not altered. His father, who'd held up until now, turned to Miles and embraced him with an audible sob.

"Dear Ollie," she said, her eyes brimming again as she leaned to kiss him lightly upon the lips. "Welcome home."

A smile broke across his face. "That was worth coming home for, I can tell you. You're even more beautiful than I remembered. Don't you think so, Miles?"

"I said the same," her brother agreed, his voice choked from Abel's emotional welcome. "I'd worry about her beauty going to her head if I didn't know Mary."

"Part of her charm," Ollie said. While Miles showed Abel the luggage belonging to his son, he took her hand and squeezed it affectionately. "Thanks for the letters."

"They reached you?"

"Four of them did. Percy was jealous as hell that you sent them to me, but I let him stew. It did him good."

"They were meant for all of you, as I'm sure he knew. Was it unpatriotic of me not to write to each of you individually?"

"Hell, no! He had plenty of mail from other girls."

"Did he really?" Over his head, she saw Percy trying to extricate himself from Lucy's tenacious arms, his tall, much sparer figure bent to accommodate her diminutive height.

"But it was your letters he kept looking for," Ollie confided quietly in her ear.

Hearing the drop of his voice, she studied his face for confirmation of her predawn fears. "Ollie? You didn't do anything absurdly self-sacrificial out of regard for Percy and me, did you?" But another thought, lightning quick, struck her: *God forbid, what if he had not...?*

"How could I ever do anything absurdly self-sacrificial out of regard for Percy and you?" he asked, swiping at the dimple in her chin.

"My turn, Ollie," Percy said behind her, and Mary felt her legs turn as limp as boiled noodles.

"All yours," Ollie said, and hopped back on his crutches with the smiling regret of someone who must return a found treasure.

She'd rehearsed the scene of his homecoming as often as she'd remembered the one in which they'd parted...what she would say, how she would act. Everyone would be looking at them, expecting some sort of romantic drama, but she would give no tongue an excuse to wag or Percy a reason to hope—that is, if he still wished to marry her.

But now that they were face-to-face, her carefully prepared speech and practiced demeanor flew from her mind like puff weed on the wind. Without thinking, she put out her hand, not to be shaken, as she'd rehearsed, but to touch the war-hardened ridge of his cheekbone. "Hello, Percy," she said, all that the hot rush of her gratitude and relief would allow her to vocalize.

"Hello, Gypsy." He stood with his usual ease, his hands in the pockets of his jodhpurs, holding himself from her as if she were a rare wine that must be sipped rather than gulped down. "Why didn't you write?"

"I—I—" She was vaguely conscious of the others leaving them—Ollie hobbling off with his father to waylay Lucy from bearing down upon them and Miles to greet Jeremy and Beatrice. "I was afraid," she said. It was the first question she knew he'd ask, and she'd decided to tell him the truth.

"Afraid?"

"I...was unable to write what you wanted to read. You were at war. I was afraid my letters would disappoint you more than if I'd not written at all."

"You misjudged the risk."

"I'm sure," she agreed, ashamed. Any letter from home in the midst of what they were going through would have been better than no letter at all. Shyly, she reached up and again touched the tightly drawn flesh of his jaw. "You've all lost so much weight."

"Would that were all," he said.

"Yes," she said, understanding. They had lost an essence of themselves—innocence, she supposed. She could see it in their old, young faces, both familiar and strange. In her mirror each morning before setting out for another backbreaking day at the plantation, she could see the loss of it in herself. She removed her hand, seeing that he did not seem moved to take it. "You had my prayers, if not my letters, Percy. I'm happy more than I can say that they were answered." It was impossible to break away from his gaze. He still had not touched her but stood with an awesome containment that unsettled her.

"They were answered, but at the cost of Ollie's leg."

She covered her mouth in dismay. "You mean...?"

"That German grenade was meant for me. He saved my life."

Before she could speak, Miles appeared beside her, frowning. "Mary, when are we leaving? I want to go home to see Mama."

"And the boys could use some sleep," Percy said. "Neither one slept on the train."

"If you noticed, you didn't either," Miles said, punching his shoulder.

Dazed by Percy's revelation, she glanced around in confusion at the crowd milling about for their cue to depart and saw Beatrice swooping toward them like a large black bird. Lucy followed in her bright plumage and Jeremy loaded with flowers presented in honor of the boys' homecoming. "I came with the Warwicks, Miles," Mary managed to explain, aware that Percy still held her in his quiet gaze. "Beatrice will have to tell us how we're to get home."

"It's just as I expected," Beatrice announced irritably. "I told Mayor Harper that the parade ought to be scheduled for later in the week when we've all had the opportunity to catch our breaths, but he wanted to save all these people a second trip into town. Abel wants to take Ollie home. The poor boy is worn out."

"So is Miles," Mary said, "and he's eager to see Mama."

"Well, we can't all fit in the Packard," Lucy pointed out, sidling close to Percy with an oblique look at Mary.

"We are aware of that, Lucy." Beatrice cast her a sour look. "Miles, dear, you and Mary go with Abel, and let's all meet up at the house about four o'clock to drive into town. With hope, that will give the boys time to have some rest."

There were murmurs of agreement as bags were gathered and hoisted. Beatrice took the flowers from her husband's arms and shoved one of the arrangements into Lucy's. "Kindly help me take these to the car, Lucy," she said.

"But, I—" Lucy protested through the spikes of gladiola screening her face.

"Now, if you please," Beatrice ordered, giving her son and Mary a wink over her shoulder as she marched Lucy off.

Left alone, Percy removed his hands from his pockets and took her by the shoulders. "I'll take you and Miles home after the hoopla is over tonight," he said. "Plan to stay up with me so we can talk. Don't deny me this, Mary."

"I won't," she whispered, almost woozy from the blood pounding in her head.

He smiled for the first time. "That's my girl," he said with a swift stroke of her dimple before following his parents and Lucy to the Packard.

Chapter Fourteen

Mary waited in the parlor while Miles went upstairs to their mother's room. Hugging herself—her tendency in times of despair—she stood before one of the French doors that opened to what was once a magnificent rose garden. A few bushes had survived her mother's vicious attack several nights after the will was read. Most had succumbed to the crowbar used to beat them to the ground while the household slept. Toby had found the severed red and white blossoms and slashed stalks early the next morning and gone in search of the weapon, fearing his mistress might take it into her head to give her daughter the same treatment as she lay in her bed.

The rosebushes had not been replanted, and now weeds and grass grew over the desecration, mercifully hidden from the street by a trellis in need of a fresh coat of white paint. Only a few bloomed bravely on spindly stalks here at the end of the season.

There was no liquor in the house, and Mary wished she'd thought to ask Toby to buy a bottle of champagne for her brother's homecoming. They wouldn't have been able to share it with their mother, of course, but the two of them could have celebrated with a quiet toast in the parlor.

Not that there was much to celebrate. Her brother was a sick, fractious man, even more of a stranger now than when he had left. On the drive home, he had sat in a resentful silence broken only by fits of coughing into a handkerchief. Once in the house, he'd set his army duffels by the door, as if he didn't mean to stay but had merely stopped by to see his mother before setting off for another war. He'd embraced Sassie warmly but left her welcome-home meal cooling on the table set with their finest tableware. "I don't feel like eating," he'd said. "I'll have a sandwich later in my room."

And poor, dear Ollie. The jollity he'd assumed for the crowd had evaporated once he was seated in his father's new Cadillac, one of the first of its kind manufactured by Henry Ford. Abel had bought the elegant motorcar as a homecoming present, but Ollie was unable to drive with his right leg gone. Abel was still in shock over his son's amputation. It was an old man who led the group to the Cadillac where it was parked with the Packard among Howbutker's less modern conveyances.

And then there was Percy. He owed Ollie his life. Did Percy know of Ollie's promise to her? Had he taken the blast on their behalf? Those two were closer than brothers. Maybe Ollie had acted instinctively out of love for his best friend, with no thought of his vow to her at all. But if Ollie *had* saved Percy for their sakes, what was her obligation to either of them?

She'd get a better picture of the situation when she and Percy had a chance to talk tonight, but the answer to her most pressing question she already knew. Percy's feelings for her had not changed.

Neither had hers for him. If anything, they had strengthened in the time he'd been away. Every morning she'd awakened thinking of him, and every night she'd gone to bed with his safety the utmost concern on her mind. There had been times when she'd shaken awake from a nightmare in which the worst fear of her life had come to pass—worse even than losing the plantation. She'd dreamed that Percy had been killed.

So that left her in a dilemma. Percy would expect her to be over Somerset by now, but she was more determined than ever to hold on to it. By all that was holy, she deserved that reward for her sacrifices. When Miles left, naming Emmitt Waithe as trustee in his absence, she'd fired Jethro Smart, the overseer she'd hired to replace Len Deeter, and assumed his job, sometimes working eighteen hours a day. With

Emmitt's cooperation and under her uncompromising hand, Somerset began to pay. Its profits allowed her to increase the mortgage payments, making it possible to repair the debt several years in advance of the bank contract.

True, there had been no money left for nonessentials. She was sure to catch grief from Miles when he saw the run-down condition of the house and the lack of help, but the day was drawing nearer when they'd be able to modernize the house and replace their horse and buggy with a motorcar.

Also, if her mother's health did not require further expensive treatment and if the harvest was as abundant as predicted, there would be money to pour back into the land, making it more productive. Already, now that the war was over, industry and science were addressing the needs of the farmer. New methods of cultivation were being tried. More efficient equipment, improved seeds, and a new substance called insecticide for combating destructive pests like the boll weevil were coming on the market. They were all within Somerset's grasp once the mortgage was settled.

How in the world would Percy fit into her plans? Would he be willing to accept her *and* Somerset? Had his war experiences softened or hardened his views against sharing his wife with the risky venture of a cotton plantation? He would soon turn twenty-five.

He would want to settle down, have children, return to the family business. She wanted that, too, more than anything in the world.

But not at the cost of Somerset. She could never, ever give up the plantation. That would mean betraying her father and his father and all the Tolivers before them who had wrested the land from the forests, had sweated and toiled, sacrificed and died, for the thousands of acres they lived to see swelling with the pride of their labor. No way in tarnation would she sacrifice Somerset for the sake of male pride! But...she loved Percy. He was a thorn in her side she couldn't pull out, no matter how hard she tried. She wanted him, she needed him. She had no doubt of that now. He meant to wait no longer, and she was not confident of her strength to resist him.

"She looks bad."

At the window, Mary jumped.

"Sorry. Didn't mean to startle you." Miles slouched into the room with his hands pushed deep into the pockets of his ill-fitting trousers. He had changed into civilian clothes and was looking around the parlor with the air of someone in a waiting room, uncertain of where to sit. "Mama looks terrible, doesn't she? That place you sent her to really wrung her out."

Mary felt a sting of indignation. "Actually, she looked quite well when she left the sanitarium," she said, careful to keep a calm tone. "Emmitt thought she seemed a lot like her old self, but she caught a cold in the train on the way home from Denver that turned into pneumonia. It's taken a toll on her."

"She says you sent her away to that sanitarium in Denver to get her out of your hair while you got in last year's harvest."

"Oh, Miles, that's not true!" Her voice rose in frustration. "She required professional help to cope with her. You can't believe the ruses, the lengths she went to, for a bottle. She was so offensive to the sitters I hired that none of them would stay on, and Sassie was worn out."

"What about you? Where were you?"

"You know very well where I was. I had to get the harvest in. You're aware of the work involved in running a plantation. It's a year-long, day-in-and-day-out, sunup-to-sundown business."

Miles's look was piercing. "It doesn't have to be. If that land had been sold when Papa died, none of this would have happened."

Mary bit off a reply, but not before a tremor passed through her. It was a question she refused to consider—how different things might have been. She lifted a silver pot from a tray. "Would you like a cup of coffee? And there's gingerbread here. Sassie made it especially for you."

"No thanks. Tell me about Mama. Do you think she'll ever get better?"

"She's not yet what is called a recovered alcoholic." Mary sipped the hot coffee to soften her tight throat. "She still craves liquor, and we were warned—"

"We?"

"Emmitt Waithe and myself. He's been helping me to deal with her. I don't know what I would have done without him. He found the sanitarium for Mama. He went with me on the train to Denver and helped me bring her home."

"Out of guilt, no doubt."

"It was out of compassion." Mary forced patience into her defense of their lawyer. "We were told that Mama would have to be watched for years before she could be allowed to come and go as she pleased. Sit down, Miles, and we'll talk. Or would you rather go to your room and rest awhile?"

"We'll talk." He plopped down on the sofa and hung his hands between his bony knees, his head down. After a moment he said, "She asked me for a drink."

"Oh, Miles, no. . . ." Mary had not considered the possibility that her mother would try to wheedle a drink out of Miles—depended on it, come to think of it. Ever since she'd been told of Miles's arrival date, her mother's color had been higher, her eyes brighter, as if she were harboring a secret. Mary thought the new animation was due to her son coming home, but now she realized she'd been anticipating he'd supply her with liquor.

"What did you tell her?" She eyed her brother

warily. Miles had always been putty in their mother's hands.

"I told her no, of course."

"What did she do?"

Miles raked a hand through his dull, thinning hair, releasing dandruff that caught like dust motes in the autumn sunlight filtering through the sheers. "She didn't throw a fit, if that's what you're asking. At least she's past that stage. She looked like a doll with all the stuffing yanked out, that's all."

Mary sat next to him. "I thought you were the reason she was getting better, not the bottle she'd hoped you'd bring."

"Well, I wasn't, was I," Miles said, his tone peevish. He linked his hands and gazed downcast at the floor.

Mary placed a hand on his shoulder. "What is it, Miles? You seem so disappointed in everything. Aren't you happy to be home?"

He stood abruptly and jammed his hands into his pockets, then commenced to pace about the room, shoulders hunched—a familiar indication to Mary that he was working up nerve to tell her something. "I'm not staying," he said at last. "I want to go back to France. There's a nurse there, a woman who brought me back to health, what little there is left of it—" A bout of coughing interrupted him. When he'd recovered, he faced his sister directly. "My lungs are shattered, Mary Lamb, and I don't know how much time I have left."

"Miles, dear..."

He held up a desisting hand. "I'm not being maudlin. You know me better than that. I'm only being frank. What time I have left, I want to spend with Marietta. There's something else. I've...become a Communist."

"Miles!" Mary leaped up. "You can't be!" She was surprised at the depth of her dismay. This was nothing unusual. Her brother tried on every new political affiliation to come along, only to discard it when the next faction appeared waving its flags. But a Toliver...a *Communist*!

"I knew you'd react this way," Miles said, "and I know you think this is just another cause I've leaped onto, but you're wrong. The Bolshevik rebellion is the greatest revolution in the history of mankind. It will do more for the world than—"

"Oh, stop! *Stop!*" Mary covered her ears. "I will not hear another word in this house in defense of a political system more bloodthirsty than the one it replaced. Communist indeed!" She could not tone down her disgust. "What about this Marietta? Does she share the same political delusions?"

"She's a sworn member of the Communist Party."

"Oh, good Lord!" Mary turned away wearily. "So what are you saying—that you want to go back to France to become a Communist?"

"I want to go back to France to marry Marietta. I already am a Communist."

"Bring her over here."

"No. The political climate for a Communist is easier over there."

"Oh, I see...." Mary let the innuendo hang, her lip curling. "What about Mama? I'd counted on you to help out with her, to give Sassie some relief. She and Toby and Beatrice are the only ones she'll allow into her room. She can't abide me."

"In the state she's in, dreaming of nothing but deliverance by the bottle, she doesn't need me, Mary. You don't, either. I'm betting that Somerset hasn't been in as good a shape since Papa died. You've probably got every poor sod out there picking a bale a day. I'd think you'd want to get rid of me so that I won't muck everything up."

She wasn't concerned that he'd interfere with her efficient management. She and Emmitt would make sure he didn't. "It's not the plantation that needs you. Mama and I do. We need to become a family again."

"I'm going, Mary." Her brother faced her, his jaw set. "I've got Marietta to think of and myself, too. I only came home because I wanted to make sure the boys arrived okay and to see you and Mama one last time."

Tears of disappointment filled Mary's eyes. Where did Miles get this fascination for political causes so far removed from his upbringing and heritage? His family and friends would have taken his convictions seriously, if he hadn't forever been changing them, but when he acted upon them this time, he'd be lost to them forever. He wouldn't have the strength for a return ocean crossing. Somehow, she must get him to stay until this new fervor abated and Percy and Ollie could prevail upon him to change his mind.

She drew her fingers down his unshaven face. "At least stay until you are stronger. Give us a little more time with you."

Miles captured her hand and, after bringing up the other, turned them over for his inspection. "What toil these hands have seen at such a young age. Mary... Mary..." His voice softened with a concern she'd not heard in years. "If you're smart, you'll marry Percy. He's the best catch in Texas, and he's insane for you. But I don't think you are smart, not in the way of a woman. A smart woman knows what's important at the end of the day. What benefit is a bountiful harvest if you can't go home to the one you love? No, you'll listen to your planter's heart, which says you can have both Percy and Somerset. You can't, Mary. His pride won't permit it."

She pulled her hands away, raw, red things that she stuffed into the pockets of her skirt. Her face burned. "Why do I have to be the one to sacrifice? Why can't Percy give up what is so dear to him?"

Miles's mouth twisted. "Because he's dumb, too. But I'm not. That's why I'm going home to Marietta." He turned his back to her and walked away, as he'd done after every one of their arguments since the will was read. At the doorway, he tossed over his shoulder, "Tell everybody when you meet them at the Warwicks' that I won't be joining them. I don't want to be a part of all that patriotic folderol the mayor has planned."

Chapter Fifteen

Mary remained in the parlor long after Miles had left. Heaven help her, she was weary to the marrow of her bones, sad to the core of her being. She wondered what her father would say if he could see his family now, divided, each member lost to the others with no hope of reuniting...and all because his wife and son couldn't appreciate the importance of Somerset to the preservation of their heritage.

Miles had volunteered no information concerning Ollie's injury. Mary admitted to herself that she hadn't asked for details because she didn't want to know. She wanted never to know...the reason she'd decided not to see Percy alone tonight. Right now, she longed for nothing more than to dissolve in his arms and have him prove to her that he was home at last. But Miles was right. Percy's pride would never allow him to marry a woman who served two masters. She couldn't be sure of his attitude until they talked. But not tonight. She was too tired, too lonely, too susceptible to her need of him, to risk facing him tonight. She might agree to anything. She'd wait until nearly time to meet at the Warwicks' to send word that Miles was not up to the celebration and they'd all be retiring early. Lucy would be delighted at her absence. Of Percy's reactions, it didn't bear thinking.

Later that evening, lying awake in her bedroom, she could hear the muted sounds of revelry—band music, blaring horns, and fireworks—coming from the town circle. Not long afterward, she padded down to the front parlor in her nightgown to await the sounds of motorcars returning from the festivities. There would be three, if Percy drove the Pierce-Arrow his father had removed from storage. At eleven o'clock, she heard first one and then another make its way up Houston Avenue. A peek through the sheers revealed Abel's Cadillac and a minute later the Packard. When the street was silent again, a third swung into the Toliver driveway and stopped before the verandah. Her heart began to pound.

She stood beside the front windows in the darkened room, listening and watching. The simple sound of the motorcar door shutting carried a sexual implication, quiet but firm, suggesting a man determined but in no hurry. She heard the faint jingle of keys, the soft crunch of footsteps on fallen leaves, and thought she would die from the sheer anticipation of seeing Percy step from the shadows into the light of the October moon. The moment was as devastating as she'd feared. The moonlight illuminated the full glory of him. It fell on his tall blond head and the breadth of his shoulders, smartly tailored in a new dark suit; the shine of gold cuff links and the latest in men's timepieces, a wristwatch; the gloss of handmade shoes...a prince come to call on a pauper.

Almost to the verandah, he stopped, dumbstruck. *"What?"* she heard him cry, and peeked out to see him scale the steps two at a time. She heard the rip of her note down from the door and watched as he moved to read it under the porch lamp she'd left burning. He took a step back and stared aghast at the window where she stood, pressing a fist to her mouth. "Damn you, Mary! How could you do this?" he demanded, speaking to the draped glass in a voice hoarse with outrage and disappointment. "You know how much I want to see you—how I've waited for nothing more than to see you. You said you wouldn't deny me, damn you!" He crushed the note in his hand and marched to the window he'd singled out. "Mary, come out here. I know you're in there, goddammit!" He braced an arm to the window frame and bent forward to listen for a reply.

Mary did not dare move and wondered how he could not hear the pounding of her heart inches separated from his golden head. She closed her eyes at the beloved sight of it, grinding her fist into her mouth to resist the overpowering urge to throw open the door and fling herself into his arms.

"Okay," he said, straightening, and she could see the hard shine of determination in his eyes. "So maybe tonight's not a good time for us, but tomorrow will be. I'll see you then. Expect me."

Mary remained stock-still until she saw the beam of the Pierce-Arrow's headlights swerve up the street, then released her cooped-up breath. Good. Tomorrow would be a better day all around. They'd both be less emotional, less on tenterhooks. She'd have Sassie invite him for coffee in the afternoon, and she'd come in early from the plantation and make herself presentable, do something to her unseemly hands. She'd be ready to see him by then.

She rose early and was in the fields with the other tenants by seven o'clock. They were making a final pass over the rows, extracting the last of the bolls before the autumn rains began. Mary was emptying cotton sacks into the wagon that would transport the day's picking to the weighing station when one of the Negro tenants tapped her on the shoulder. "Miss Mary, they's somebody here to see you."

She made a sun shield of her hand and gazed in the direction of his pointing finger. Her heart nearly flew out of her mouth. "Oh, good Lord, no—" Percy, suit coat flapping open, strode toward her between the rows of picked cotton. She blew out her cheeks. There was no hope for it now: He had caught her looking her worst, which put Somerset at its worst. Resigned, she whipped off her wide-brimmed hat, wiped the sweat from her brow on her sleeve, and went to meet him.

He stopped and waited. Typical of a man, she thought in annoyance, expecting him to put his hands on his hips and frown in disapproval at her appearance. He did neither. He slipped his hands into his pockets, and his face remained as bare of expression as a blackboard before the start of a school day.

But how could he not be thinking what any man would? She was wearing an old flannel shirt of her father's with the sleeves rolled up and baggy, stained pants tucked into weather-beaten workmen's boots. The hat was a recent addition, decided upon when she realized her skin was turning as brown as a walnut and the boys would soon be home. Gloves were a nuisance when picking cotton, and hers, threadbare besides, had been discarded long ago. Her hair was tied back with a rawhide string, and her face and forearms were grimy with dirt. In his eyes, she must look no better than the itinerant women who often came begging at their back doors.

She stopped a few yards short of where he stood in his immaculate business attire, conscious that her tenants had stopped picking and were watching them, their rapt expressions clearly wondering what Mister Percy of the Warwick Lumber Company was doing way out here. Percy spoke first. "Hail, Mary, full of grace."

Her chin went up. "I didn't think mockery was part of your verbal arsenal."

"There's quite a bit about me you don't know." His hooded eyes bristled with anger. "Why didn't you open the door to me last night?"

"I thought my note explained that."

"It said that all of you had gone to bed early, but you were up, behind the parlor window watching me, weren't you?"

Mary thought a moment, then admitted, "Yes."

"Is that any way to treat a soldier returning from war?"

"No, it isn't, but you and I both know what would have happened if I'd opened that door, Percy."

He took a step toward her, his face anguished. "Well, hell's bells, Mary! Would that have been so bad? My God, we're both adults."

Mary looked around, feeling a fluttering beneath her breastbone and a weakness in her knees. The tenants had gone back to work but were casting curious glances over their shoulders. She wondered if their voices had carried in the thin October air. "Let's continue this conversation over there," she said, pointing toward the Pierce-Arrow parked under a tree.

"Let's," Percy said, and gripped her arm as if she might bolt in the opposite direction.

He had brought cups and a vacuum bottle designed to keep beverages hot, a new product on the American market called a Thermos. The Warwicks were always the first with the newest gadgets. He poured out coffee, but Mary refused to drink her steaming cup in the Pierce-Arrow, remembering what had happened the last time she'd sat in it. She helped him spread a car robe in the shadow of the tree, and they sat down, blocked from view by the large trunk and the Pierce-Arrow. Mary saw that he'd noticed her chapped, burr-pricked hands.

"Well," she said, "you see how it is with me. Every pair of hands are needed out here, including mine, and it will be that way until the mortgage is paid."

"It doesn't have to be that way."

"Yes, it does."

"Mary, look at me." He set down his cup and firmly imprisoned her chin between his fingers. "Do you love me?"

The flutter increased to a wild beating. She nodded. "Yes. Yes, I do."

"Are you going to marry me?"

She did not answer at once. "I want to," she said at last, returning the intensity she saw in his eyes. "Now let me ask you a question. Would you take me *and* Somerset?"

His gaze did not falter. "The way I feel now, yes. Mary, I thought of no one else but you all the time I was away. I want you now more than ever. I can't imagine my life without you. I don't *want* a life without you. So, yes, right now I'll agree to anything, if you'll only marry me."

He had given her the answer she'd prayed for, but she heard it with a sadness that almost made her weep. He was five years older than she, better educated, wiser in the ways of the world, more experienced with human nature, and yet for all her naïveté, she was the one who could see the future as it would unfold if they married. In the two years he'd been away, her thoughts, too, had been constantly occupied with him and their life together, and last night before dawn she'd reached a conclusion.

"Percy," she said, removing his hand from her chin and holding it against her heart, "you say the way you feel now. But what about *after* what we feel for each other now is spent? What then?" She silenced his immediate answer with her fingers over his lips. "I'll tell you how it would be. You'd come to resent sharing my love with a plantation. You'd be jealous of Somerset and furious with me for allowing it to take time away from you and the children, from our home, our social obligations, from the life you envisioned with a wife. You'd come to despise Somerset, and you'd come to despise me. Now tell me how that wouldn't be so."

Her voice was firm but gentle, carrying the soulful regret he must surely know she felt. She waited for his reaction, asking herself for the thousandth time how she could bear letting this man go. But in all fairness to them both, how could she not? Percy was studying her in that all-seeing way he had, and she hoped he saw in her grimy face and pricked hands the future as it might be for Somerset, always a bad harvest away from debt, a constant drain on her energy, a never-ending source of worry. She saw Somerset someday prosperous and herself groomed and dressed in the finest that befitted a planter, but two years of dealing with lazy tenants, the boll weevil, the vagaries of nature, and unpredictable cotton markets had put a more realistic frame around that rosy picture. Still, she was and always would be a planter, a *Toliver* planter, and no matter what the future threw at her, these past years had taught her she could handle it.

Finally Percy said, "Now would you like me to describe the picture I have of us married?"

She released his hand. "If you must," she said with the resigned air of someone forced to listen to a pipe dream.

He anchored a strand of hair that had escaped its rawhide bond behind her ear. "Call it male conceit or arrogance or the power of love, but I believe I can make you want to give up Somerset. I believe I can make the woman renounce the farmer, and you won't want to spend your time and energy fighting your tenants and the boll weevil and the weather. When you experience what I have to offer, you'll want to be with me always, making a home for me and our children. You'll want to be there, looking fresh and beautiful, when I come home in the evening. You'll prefer to spend Sunday mornings in bed making love, rather than getting up at dawn to work on the books. Your Toliver blood won't be nearly as important to you when you see it combined with mine in our children. And in time…"

Smoothly, before Mary realized what was happening, he pulled her to him and kissed her in the way she'd never forgotten. "And in time," he repeated, releasing her with a smile, his eyes aglow, "you'll wonder how you ever thought a backbreaking plantation could take the place of a husband and children who adore you."

Mary stared at him, her lips feeling plump and mellow as ripe fruit. He was dreaming! He was spinning a fairy tale! Renounce the farmer for the woman? They were one and the same!

In exasperation, she brushed away the strand that had again slipped free, ignoring her carnal stirrings. "Percy, how is it that you've missed what I am all these years?"

"I haven't missed it," he said, looking ready to kiss her again. "You're simply not aware of what *I've* seen plainly. And I mean to show it to you, Mary." The light in his eyes turned serious. "You owe it to yourself. We owe it to ourselves."

We owe it to ourselves. That made Mary think of Ollie and the crucial question that had haunted her throughout the night… that she'd believed she hadn't the courage to ask. But now she must. "And to Ollie? What do we owe Ollie?"

His forehead knotted. "Ollie? I know what *I* owe him, but *we*?"

Mary examined his face for evidence that he knew what she was talking about, but his expression showed only perplexity. She laid a hand on his sleeve. "Tell me about that day."

He sat back from her and, after a hard swallow of coffee, directed his answer to the fields. "Our garrison was herding columns of defeated soldiers out of France into Germany. Most of the Jerries were glad the war was over and only wanted to get on with their lives, but a few were still fighting for the motherland. They were the ones we had to be on the lookout for. They'd conceal themselves by the side of the road and try to pick us off when they caught us separated from the columns. It was one of those buggers that lobbed the grenade." Percy threw the remains of his coffee onto the grass and grimaced as if it had left a bitter taste. "It landed right behind me, but I didn't see it. Somebody hollered, but by the time I'd have reacted, it would have been too late. Ollie pushed me out of the way and threw himself over it." He turned his gaze to her, his face bleak with memory. "Greater love hath no man, you know."

He doesn't know, she thought, relief mixing with horror. She had listened with an eye and ear alert for the slightest reference to Ollie's promise to her but could detect none. It remained Ollie's secret and hers. As far as Percy knew, Ollie had acted out of love for a friend whose life he had put above his own. Perhaps it was true, and she was under no obligation to marry the man his sacrifice had brought safely home. But a wave of thankfulness for his act washed over her. "I'm so grateful to him," she said.

"Are you?"

"You know I am, Percy."

Their gazes had held for a long, unbroken moment when a new light popped into his eyes. "You know what I'd like to do right now?"

"Dare I guess?"

"I'd like to take you to the cabin, stick you under the shower, and soap you all over. Then . . ."

"Percy, shush—" Dizzy from a rush of desire, Mary pressed a hand over his mouth to prevent his words from carrying across the cotton fields.

He continued to speak through her fingers. " . . . I'd dry you off and carry you to bed and make love to you under the sheets for the rest of the day. How does that sound?"

Breathless, she said, "Impossible," and got quickly to her feet. "I must get back to work."

"Whoa," Percy said, snaring the top of her boot in his grip. "We haven't finished our conversation, Gypsy, the one we started before you asked me about Ollie. You haven't heard what I'd like to propose."

"I thought you just stated it," she said.

"I have a more serious proposal."

"I thought I'd heard that, too."

"Not this one." He scrambled up. "But first, I have a question."

She glanced at the tenants who were still sneaking peeks in their direction. "Well, make it fast before we're a subject for gossip."

He brushed a streak of dried dirt from her face. "The plantation might fail anyway, my love, and then what would you do?"

It was as if the sun had gone behind a cloud. It was not about her financial ruin he was asking, but how she'd feel if she lost him *and* the plantation. It was a question she'd not let herself contemplate. She decided to hedge. "I'd think that my losing Somerset would suit you just fine."

His smile turned cool. "I'd be happy to win you by default, in other words? Well, that wouldn't suit me at all, Gypsy. I'd settle for sharing first base, but not coming in second. I'd want you to come to me not out of necessity, but by choice, realizing you need me as much as Somerset. So, back to the subject of what we owe ourselves..."

"What are you proposing?" she asked, swallowing quickly.

"I propose we give ourselves the opportunity to see who's right—you or me. I propose we give ourselves a chance to see if we can live without each other."

"And we do this... how?"

"Not like you're thinking—unless it happens. We do it by spending time together. Talking, sharing meals, going for walks..."

How will I have time? she thought, dismayed.

He moved closer, his gaze ironic. "You win either way, Gypsy," he said. "I'm the one who could lose."

She felt the blood quicken in her loins, hot and throbbing. Did she dare accept his proposal—risk subjecting herself to his magnetism, her own perfidious needs? Or was this an opportunity to prove to him that they were wrong for each other, settle this madness once and for all? "I'll agree if you understand that I can't always be available when you'd like, and if you promise not to rush me or to take advantage of my...inexperience. I'll be off like a scared rabbit if you do."

"I will be the soul of understanding and patience. You won't even feel my net."

That's what I'm afraid of, she thought, both thrilled and frightened. "And there's one other thing...one other promise I require from you."

"Name it."

"Will you not call me 'Gypsy' anymore?"

He laughed, a rich, deep sound that she'd prayed nightly to hear again. "I promise. Now do we have a deal?"

"We have a deal," she said, her nerve ends dancing. "Now I must get back to work."

She knew his eyes followed her as she started back across the fields. She wouldn't blame him if he was having second thoughts. How could he find her desirable in her baggy pants and flannel shirt, her hair streaming between her shoulder blades like an Indian squaw's? She had not gone far when she thought of something. She swung back around. "By the way, what about Lucy?"

"Lucy?" He frowned as if he had difficulty remembering the name. "Oh, Lucy," he said. "I told her last night that there was someone else."

Mary stood stone still. "Did you tell her who it was?"

"No. I spared her that. She didn't seem to want to know. I told her she was someone I've loved all her life and plan to marry. She left early this morning. We won't be seeing her again."

Chapter Sixteen

Miles was gone within the week. Mary found a note pinned to his pillow when she went to his room to inquire why he had not come down to breakfast. It read simply: "I'm sorry. I have to go. Explain to Mama. Love, Miles." Beside it lay a red rose.

Mary slowly picked up the rose, surprised that he would make use of a symbol so hateful to their mother and inherent in Toliver tradition. Silent tears gathered as she pressed the rose to her lips. Scenes returned from the past when the four of them had been happy and loving. She heard her mother's laughter again and the deep response of her father's voice, her own squeal of delight as Miles swung her high in the air and caught her before she fell. Recalling those family times, she stayed on in her brother's boyhood room a few minutes longer before summoning Toby to run get Mister Percy.

He was there within minutes. She had caught him as he was dressing for work. Sassie led him into the parlor, where she sat staring vacantly into space, the rose still in her hand. When she discovered him standing quietly by her chair, she experienced a sense of déjà vu. Hadn't she lived this scene before when the light caught Percy's blond head and shadowed his face in exactly the same way?

"He's gone," she said. "Miles has gone back to France, to Marietta and the Communist Party."

"I know. He called before he left. Ollie knows, too."

She frowned up at him, accusation glinting in her eyes. "And you didn't warn me?"

He sighed, hitched up his pants, and squatted beside her chair. Again, Mary had the odd sensation of having experienced this moment before. Then she remembered that Percy had come to her and knelt by this very chair the night following the reading of her father's will. His face wore the same still expression now as then. He touched one of the petals. "He left this?"

She indicated yes with a barely perceptible movement of her head.

"Then you must forgive him."

Again a slight nod. She said listlessly, "He'll die in France. He'll never come home again. And now I have to tell Mama." Her eyes felt bright with tears. "You promised to talk him out of this."

"I promised to try, Gyp—Mary, but his mind and heart were made up. He was going back to a woman who makes him happy. Forget the Communist rot. With Miles it won't last until the first snow flies. It won't last with Marietta, either, I'm betting, now that she can devote her energies to Miles."

"He should have stayed here." A surge of anger made her sit up and swipe at her eyes. "We need him. Now more than ever. He's always shirked his responsibilities to the family."

Percy thumped the arm of her chair and stood up. "That's not fair, and you know it. Because your brother's concept of family duty is different from yours doesn't mean he's irresponsible."

Mary's frustration with him was mounting. She should not have asked him to come. In the days since their meeting at the plantation, they'd both had a taste of what they were in for if they were to keep their deal. Twice they'd made evening plans, and twice unforeseen difficulties at Somerset had kept her at the plantation. Percy had arrived at the appointed time to find no Mary. The first time she stood him up, she had rushed into the house wet and muddy from the beginning of the October rains and sent a note of apology, only to have one returned that Percy had gone to the office to catch up on paperwork. Miles had sat watching the situation from his chair by the fire, shaking his head as if she were the greatest fool to inhabit the earth. The second time she didn't appear, Percy and Miles had collected Ollie and the three had gone to the country club to get drunk.

Other nights, Percy wasn't available. At the moment, the Warwick Lumber Company was negotiating new labor contracts in meetings that often lasted long into the night. This morning was the first time they'd been together, and they were on the verge of quarreling. She was not up to it. She was tired. She was always tired. She stood and laid aside the rose.

"All I'm saying," she said, attempting to mitigate her tone, "is that it would have been considerate of Miles to have stayed at least for a few months to help Sassie care for our mother. Mama would have liked that very much."

"Miles believed he hadn't a few months to spare," Percy said.

"All the more reason he should have shared them with Mama."

"I see...," Percy drew out, infuriating her further.

She gritted her teeth. "What do you see, Percy? What do you see that I don't?"

He appeared to be undisturbed by her annoyance. "If your mother allowed you to spell Sassie, would you?"

"That's a moot question. You know she won't have me in her room."

"But...what if she did? Who would receive your time—your mother or Somerset?"

"We're riding that old horse again, are we?"

"I'm merely trying to get you to see that Miles has the same right to his choices as you do to yours."

Exasperated, she turned away to the fireplace, in need of its comforting warmth. Indian summer was over. A cold autumn had arrived, but feeling as she did, she'd have welcomed a fire on a summer day. Percy was saying that Miles was as entitled to his selfishness as she was to hers. They would never work out their differences. She was more convinced of that each day. She said with her back to him, clasping her elbows, "I regret more than you will ever know what's happened to my mother, but none of us could have predicted she'd take the dispensations of my father's will the way she has. If Papa had known she'd feel disgraced, he might have made different arrangements, but he had no idea."

"No idea? Then why did he ask Emmitt to give her one of these?"

She whirled around. He held the rose aloft, a cape before a bull. She snatched it from his fingers. "That's Toliver business! Please leave, Percy. I'm sorry I asked you to come."

"Mary, I—"

"*Get out!*"

"Mary, you're tired and overwrought. Please…let's talk this out.…"

"There's nothing to talk out. Our dissimilarities are too great. I don't want to be loved *in spite* of what I am, but *because* of it—which you seem to find impossible."

"I don't give a damn what it seems." Color flooded

his face. "I love you, and that's that. These disagreements have nothing to do with love."

"They do to me. Our deal is off!" She sailed past him into the hall. "And you're bleeding," she cast back. She'd noticed a small trickle of blood on his hand where he'd been pricked by the rose. "Kindly go tend to your wounds, and I'll tend to mine."

He reached out helplessly. "Mary..."

But she flew up the stairs, her heart aching, and was nearly at her mother's room when she heard the front door close, its sound echoing the finality of her hope for them.

A florist's box containing a long-stemmed red rose arrived from Percy the next day with a note attached: "Forgive me. I'm a dolt for bringing up a touchy subject at such a time. You needed comfort, not criticism. I am sorry that I failed to show the love that I feel for you with all of my heart. Percy."

Mary responded with the last white rose in the garden. It was bedraggled from the recent rain, but it would convey her message. She sent it by Toby up the street to Warwick Hall with a note that read: "No need to ask forgiveness for speaking the truth as you see it. It proves the irreconcilable differences between us. Mary."

She expected him to roar up to the house or out at the plantation to refute her statement, but the Pierce-Arrow did not appear. She heard from Ollie the next evening that Percy had gone out of town on business.

"Really?" she said. The news pierced her to the quick. They were chatting on the verandah after he'd spotted her sitting forlornly in the porch swing after everyone had gone to bed, the loneliest time of the day for her. "He didn't tell me."

"No doubt with good reason. He's heading to Oregon. The company's bought timberlands there, and the loggers are causing problems. They're mighty tough customers, but Percy can handle them. He didn't want to worry you, but I thought you'd like to know."

Dear Ollie...ever the peacemaker between her and Percy. He had learned of their rift and must surely think his sacrifice had been for naught. "Thank you," she said. "I won't look for him for a while, then."

Bereft, she sat on the swing after he'd left. Two losses in one week, and there was no one left in her family to turn to for solace. She recalled when Granddaddy Thomas had died. It was as if a wall of her house had blown away and a cold wind were rushing in. After the funeral, her father had driven her out to the plantation in the late afternoon. It was almost picking time, and the fields were a blinding white. She was eleven years old, and she'd thought she'd burst from her grief. Her father had taken her hand, and together they had walked between the cotton rows, up one and down another, until the sun set. They had talked, as always, of cotton. Never did he mention death or sorrow, but in their clasped hands, their feelings met, flowed one into the other, and her grief was assuaged.

How she would like in this moment to slip her hand into her father's.

The next week, she received a brief note from Lucy.

I'm thinking of reapplying for that position at Bellington Hall at the end of the school year if old Peabody will have me back. As you may have heard (and predicted), Percy sent me packing the day after he came home. He is in love with someone else, somebody he says he's loved all her life. Do you know who she is? No, don't tell me. I don't want to know. I'd be eaten up with jealousy. I imagine she's all those things you told me he admired in a woman. I'm surprised you never mentioned her to me so that I wouldn't have misspent my dreams thinking there was a chance for me. You tried your best to dissuade me, though. I'll let you know my decision. In any event, I'll probably not be seeing you again unless fate joins our paths. Best of luck, Lucy.

Mary folded the note with a sense of guilt threaded with relief. Unless they married, it was unlikely now that her roommate would ever learn that she was the girl Percy had loved all her life. Katie bar the door if or when she did. Lucy would believe that she'd deliberately lied to her and—knowing Lucy—would live the rest of her life convinced she'd been betrayed.

Upon Percy's return three weeks later, he sent a note from his office. Mary read it eagerly, thinking its purpose was to state a time he'd drop by, but the quick scrawl was only to let her know he'd arrived safely and expected to be busy with sundry business obligations in the weeks to come. Disappointed, Mary could not resist an ironic chuckle. Now Percy knew what it was like to keep his nose to the family grindstone.

A few days later, his duties increased when Jeremy suffered a serious head injury. Percy was forced to take charge of the company, overseeing interests now stretching into Oregon, California, and Canada. Even if they'd been seeing each other, Mary realized ruefully, he would have found it difficult to find space in his days and calendar to coordinate with her unpredictable routine. In a roundabout way, they'd been given the opportunity they owed themselves— the chance to see if they could live without each other. Apparently, they could.

By the middle of November, things had wound down at Somerset. The fields were lying fallow under a blanket of snow, and the tenants and Mary enjoyed a respite from their labors. She turned down invitations to the DuMonts' and Warwicks' for Thanksgiving dinner, hoping her mother could be enticed downstairs to eat Sassie's stuffed turkey, prepared with all the trimmings. She refused, so Mary and Sassie and

Toby shared the holiday meal in the kitchen and sent a tray upstairs.

Christmas proved as bleak and unfestive. Percy, who'd kept in touch through occasional notes (the Tolivers did not possess a telephone), invited her to attend the Christmas ball at the country club, but she begged off, writing that she had nothing to wear. "It wouldn't matter if you wore a sack," he wrote back, his script dark and strident. "You'd still be the most beautiful girl there."

In truth, she'd withdrawn entirely from society. She felt the weight of its judgment against her father for disregarding his wife—and against her for not making it right. Descriptions of herself as working in the fields "like a field hand" reached her ears. They angered and isolated her but strengthened her determination to restore the Toliver name to its former glory.

Meanwhile, she missed Percy sorely and wondered if that wasn't his intention. He'd played this waiting game before. Was he trying to impress upon her how lonely she was and how much she needed and wanted him? If that was so, it was working, especially when she considered the paralyzing possibility that he might be seeing other girls.

A visit from Ollie forced her to agree to one small ceremony held Christmas Eve. "I won't take no for an answer," he said. "Percy and I will drop by Christmas Eve with gifts and champagne. So dress up in your best party dress, Mary Lamb, and ask Sassie to make some of her divine cheese crackers. Shall we say eight o'clock?"

Mary gave the order for the cheese crackers and decorated a small Christmas tree in the parlor. To prepare for the evening, she manicured her nails and spent time soaking in a long, fragrant bath. She dressed in the dark green velvet gown she had worn the night Richard Bentwood kissed her under the mistletoe, and with Sassie's help, she coiled her shining, shampooed hair into a party creation atop her head. She borrowed her mother's pearls for her ears and throat, and when she inspected the result in her mirror, she hardly recognized the girl staring back at her.

Neither did Percy or Ollie. "What's the matter?" She laughed at their amazed faces when she answered the door. "Haven't you ever seen a girl in a party dress?"

Mary pretended to be unaware of their close observance of her through the exchange of gifts and champagne toasts—Percy's expression guarded and Ollie's frankly awed. Feeling gauche and a little like a doe run to ground by two rutting bull elk, she avoided their gazes from a lack of knowing how to handle the attention.

"Ollie, how thoughtful!" she exclaimed when she unwrapped his gift of a delicate silver pencil disguised as a handsome brooch. "You remembered that I'm forever misplacing my pens." She pulled the pencil on a retractable chain from its holder. "I'll be sure not to lose sight of this one." She smiled at him and got up from her chair to kiss his round, rubicund cheek.

Percy's gift was a pair of ladies' finely sewn work gloves of buttery leather, dainty but durable. She flushed at their implication. "How thoughtful of you as well, Percy, but they're much too fine for what they're intended." A note was tucked inside one of the cuffs, and she deliberately appeared not to notice it. She'd read it later, away from Percy's disturbing scrutiny.

"Not for your hands," he said, catching her eye in a way that made her heart leap as she bent to deliver the same reward she'd given Ollie.

Her gift to Ollie was a volume of verse by Oscar Wilde, his favorite writer, and for Percy, a pictorial history of North American trees. When the evening was over, she saw them both to the door, Percy seemingly not of a mind to stay behind for a private word.

"Wish you were going with us," Ollie said.

"Next year, perhaps." She smiled, determined that they not sense her loneliness. They were off to Ollie's, where Abel was hosting his usual Christmas Eve party for friends and their families. It seemed so many years ago since her own family—her mother swathed in fur and herself skipping along in a white fox muff and matching hat—had walked hand in hand to the party and returned home singing "Silent Night" under the star-filled sky.

"We'll hold you to it, Mary," Percy said, and she found herself missing his nickname for her.

When they had gone, she leaned against the closed door for a few moments, listening to their male repartee as they went down the steps. Then, despondent, she returned to the parlor, banked the fire, and took the remainder of the champagne to the kitchen, where she poured it down the sink. She gathered her gifts and later in her room ensconced herself on her window seat to read Percy's note by the light of the moon: "For the hands I want to hold for the rest of my life. Love, Percy."

Chapter Seventeen

Your mama wants to see you, Miss Mary."

At her father's desk, Mary looked up with arched brows from the ledger where she was calculating expenses and profits for the coming year. It was the first of January 1920. "Mama wants to see me? What for?"

Sassie lifted her shoulders. "Don't ask me, but your mama is sittin' up in bed, pretty as a picture. She got herself bathed this mornin' all by herself, combed her hair, and tied it with a pretty blue ribbon. She wants me to dress her to come downstairs after her nap."

Mary rose with cautious hope from the desk, glancing at the clock on the mantel. If this was another game of her mother's, she really hadn't time to play it. She must have her figures in order before meeting at noon with Jarvis Ledbetter, a neighboring planter. But if her mother had turned a corner...

Mary marked her place in the ledger. "What's come over her, do you suppose?"

"I don't know, Miss Mary. Somethin's goin' on behind them yellow eyes of hers."

"I don't know what could be going on that we don't know about. She's been nowhere, seen no one in over a year. Did she get a letter from Miles?"

"If she did, I didn't take it up to her."

Mary patted Sassie's shoulder. "I'll go see what she wants. Bring us up some coffee, will you, and didn't I smell cinnamon rolls a while ago? Put a couple of those on a plate, and maybe she'll eat one."

"You smelled 'em all right. I expect Mister Ollie by this afternoon, and you know how that man do love my cinnamon rolls." She chuckled, following Mary out into the hall. "He's a man I sure wouldn't mind cooking for. Mister Percy, neither, though he don't get the pleasure out of food that Mister Ollie does."

Mary studiously avoided a return comment by tying her green hair ribbon more firmly in place before going upstairs. Sassie's hints that it was time she married were about as subtle as pitched bricks. Already, since he rarely came calling anymore, their faithful old housekeeper considered Percy a lost hope.

As she started up the stairs, Mary thought of him with the usual curling of anxiety in her stomach. Had he truly lost interest in her? Was he banking on her loneliness to send her running into his arms? Did his absence mean he agreed that their union was hopeless? Daily she recalled the words he'd written on the note slipped into the cuff of her Christmas present: "For the hands I want to hold for the rest of my life."

Mary hesitated before knocking on her mother's door, dreading the gravelly, woeful "Come in" that marked the beginning of every distasteful visit. Mary never heard it without feeling a prick of annoyance. One had only to look at how Ollie was dealing with his situation to feel scornful of the way Darla Toliver was handling hers. No sulks or self-pity for Ollie! After a short hospitalization in Dallas, he'd returned to work in the executive offices of the DuMont Department Store, wielding his onyx-and-silver-headed crutches like a fashion extension of his smashing wardrobe.

"Come in!" Darla's voice, strong and vibrant, answered her knock. Surprised, Mary opened the door and peeked in cautiously.

"Why, Mother, how...how lovely you look," Mary declared in astonishment. She could not remember when she first began calling her mother "Mother." It had evolved out of the distance that had grown between them, the years of estrangement. "Mama" was an endearment; "Mother," an address.

At once, Mary saw that "lovely" was not the word. She doubted that her mother would ever look lovely again after such prolonged abuse to her health. But today, propped up in bed on clean pillows, scrubbed and combed and dressed in a filmy peignoir like the kind she'd worn when Mary's father was alive, she looked fresh and rested. Mary approached the bed.

"What's the occasion?" she asked, shocked to see that without the dark accumulation of oil and sweat, her mother's hair was streaked with gray.

Darla laughed in her natural, light way, a sound Mary hadn't heard in years, and flung a flaccid arm toward the windows. Sassie had pulled open the draperies to a pale January sun, the first outside light that had been allowed to enter the room since Mary's father's death. "The new year—that's the occasion. I want to celebrate it, get up out of this bed, leave this room. I want to walk out into the fresh air and feel the sun on my face. I want to feel alive again. Do you think it's too late for that, Mary, my lamb?"

My lamb. It had been four years since her mother had called her that. Mary's throat tightened at the echo from their past. "Mama," she murmured sadly. There had been these mood changes and resolutions before that had proved to be ruses to gain freedom of the house and access to a hidden bottle.

"Mary, I know you're skeptical," Darla said, ducking her chin to give her daughter a fond look. "You think I want to get out of here only so that I can run down a drink somewhere, but frankly, I'm out of ideas as to how to go about that. I . . . simply want to feel human again, darling."

At the foot of the bed, Mary squeezed her eyes shut to stanch the sudden rush of tears. *Darling.* She was stunned at how starving her heart was for that word of affection.

"Oh, my darling, I know...." Darla threw back the covers and swung her frail, ghostly pale legs to the floor. "I know...I know," she crooned, tottering unsteadily in the diaphanous gown toward Mary. "Come to Mama, precious child." She held out her arms, and Mary went into them, allowing herself to be stroked and petted as if she'd come in from play with a scraped knee. She submitted with a desperate hunger even while a long-embedded wariness warned this could be another game whose objective only her mother knew.

Nonetheless, she held her hands when they were seated on the chaise longue and asked, "What do you want, Mother? What would you like to do that would make you happy?"

"Well, first, I'd like to take a stroll about the house to regain some strength in my legs. Then I was wondering if I might help Toby do a little tilling of the garden. Sassie tells me he's got some potatoes ready to go into the ground."

Mary had been studying her mother as she spoke. She saw none of her former craftiness, the quick shift of her eyes that betrayed another motive behind her requests. Had she forgotten that the vegetable garden had yielded its last bottle of bourbon years ago, turned over by Toby's hoe?

Darla read her concern and squeezed her hands. "Don't worry, darling. I know there's nothing left to dig up. I just want to feel the earth again, plant some things. I'm sure Toby can use the help."

"You know someone will always have to be with you," Mary reminded her gently.

"Yes, I realize that. Well, Toby can watch me in the garden in the mornings, then I'll take a nap after dinner and be locked in as usual. Sassie can stand guard over me in the parlor in the afternoons. I'd like to sit in there and read. Do we still take the *Woman's Home Companion*?"

Mary winced at the cruel-sounding words, but Darla spoke without rancor, using the matter-of-fact tone with which she once apprised her family of their schedules at the breakfast table.

"I'm sorry, we don't," Mary said, "but we still have the copies from a few years ago. There seemed no point in continuing the subscription...."

Mary drew in her breath, expecting to see Darla's golden eyes smolder with offense at her reasoning, but she said, "That was wise since I was the only one in the house to read the magazine. I know we're poor. No use spending money on things we don't need." She withdrew her hands. "I won't ask how things are going out at Somerset. As well as anyone could hope, I imagine, with you in charge. You are spending most of your days there?"

Mary looked for signs of her old wounded anger, but Darla had put the question mildly, as a matter of curiosity. Perhaps she had finally emerged from the dungeon of her bitter resentment after all. "Yes, ma'am. We're getting the fields ready for the spring."

"Well, no need to feel bad about having to spend time at the plantation. When you and Sassie are tied up, maybe Beatrice can sit with me. I know she's offered countless times. How does she look, by the way?"

"Much better now that Percy's home and she's no longer wearing black."

"I always thought that was a mere affectation, a way to gain sympathy and be noticed. We all had sons in the war. But I'd love to see her. Will you arrange it for tomorrow? I have something I want her to do for me." She cocked her head in the saucy way Mary thought of as singularly her mother's, opening a bank of memories and a well of despair.

"Is it something that I can do for you instead?" Mary asked, suspecting the worst. Everybody in town, including the Warwicks, had stored up liquor before the passage of the National Prohibition Act, which forbade the buying and selling of alcohol for consumption after midnight, January 16.

Darla clearly perceived the reason for her question. She waved a clawlike hand. "Silly girl, I'm not going to ask her to part with a bottle, if that's what's worrying you. No, I want her to help me to plan a party."

"A party?"

"Yes, my lamb. You know what's coming up at the beginning of next month?" Darla giggled at Mary's astonished expression. "Yes, darling, your birthday! Did you think I'd forgotten? We'll have something elegant but simple and invite the Warwicks and Abel and Ollie, and even the Waithes, if you'd prefer. I haven't seen the boys in a long while, have I?"

"No, Mother," Mary said quietly. "Not for a few years." Of course she hadn't forgotten the date of her birthday. She would become twenty, one year removed from the time she would take full control of Somerset. She was simply surprised that her mother had remembered. There was the thump of Sassie's footsteps on the stairs and the rattle of china cups. "Sassie is bringing us coffee and cinnamon rolls," she said. "Shall we have a tea party like the old days and discuss what you have in mind?"

"Oh, let's!" Darla patted her hands together. "But I can't discuss everything I have in mind, Mary Lamb. I want to surprise you so there will be no doubt of the love I bear you."

Later, returning the coffee tray to the kitchen, Mary asked, "Well, what do you think, Sassie?"

"She puttin' on, Miss Mary. I know your mama, and just as sure as my rheumatism tell me when we in for rain, I know she be up to somethin'."

Mary wasn't so sure. The house and garden and grounds, the gazebo, carriage house, and tool shed, had been thoroughly searched for contraband liquor. Of course, her mother might believe they'd missed a bottle or two, but if that was the case, she'd have tried to get out of bed earlier. Escape was out of the question. She had no money, no way of getting any, and no place to go even if she had the strength to get there. She had seemed genuinely, pathetically contrite for her behavior these past years and determined to make up for it.

"Did you notice that all the family pictures are gone on the mantel 'cept the one of Mister Miles in his army uniform?" Sassie asked.

"I noticed. She took them down after Papa died."

"Well, your mama can have a little fire in her fireplace like she done have me lay this mornin', and she can have me open the drapes, and she can get herself all fixed up, but until I see them pictures of you and your papa and the whole family back out, I ain't gonna believe nothin' she say."

Mary nodded thoughtfully. "That would be a sign of her sincerity," she agreed, doubtful that she and Sassie would ever see photographs of her family smiling from their silver frames on her mother's mantel again.

Chapter Eighteen

Driving out to the Ledbetter plantation later that morning in the only horse-and-buggy conveyance still used among Howbutker's elite, Mary ruminated alternately between the latest caprice of her mother's and Jarvis Ledbetter's reason for sending around an invitation asking her to "luncheon." It was common knowledge that a big eastern bank, like other distant investors seeking to buy up ever more of the rich farmlands of the Cotton Belt, had approached the old gentleman with an offer for his plantation. His only children, twin daughters, had married disappointingly, and he had often hinted that he would rather sell his plantation, Fair Acres, and live in grand style off its proceeds than leave it to his daughters for their husbands to do likewise. Mary believed the invitation was for the purpose of offering her the first chance to buy Fair Acres.

Fair Acres was a long, narrow stretch of cotton land situated between Somerset and the strip along the Sabine that Miles had inherited. On it sat a handsome plantation home that would be included in the land sale. Mary had been up since dawn calculating the financial feasibility of purchasing the acres that would unite the Sabine strip to Somerset and provide a convenient home away from home on Toliver acres.

It had always been her father's dream to acquire the two sections that severed Somerset. He envisioned a sea of Toliver cotton stretching from one unbroken boundary to another, but no matter how Mary manipulated the figures, the ledger showed that the dream was not to be. The only extra money constituted no real surplus at all, but funds held in reserve as a hedge against disaster. Even if this coming harvest was wiped out, there would be money to pay those bloodsuckers in Boston who waited each year for her to go under. They'd never get the satisfaction. She had scrimped and saved, sacrificed and endured, to make sure of that. Within two years, the Tolivers would be in sole possession of Somerset once again.

Mary lived for the day the deed would arrive. She would have a party, a huge bash to show Howbutker that her father had been wise in leaving her Somerset. Everyone would see that under her hand it had become a mighty plantation again. Quietly, the household would emerge from its penury. She'd hire help for Sassie, install modern bathrooms to replace the privy in the far corner of the backyard and the honey pots under the beds. She might even buy a motorcar and retire old Shawnee, their faithful Arabian who'd outlived his buggy mate. Her mother would want for nothing. She could hold her head up again, under the finest hat money could buy. Knowing Darla, once she was dressed in the latest fashion and the house was restored to its former grandeur, she would not care whose hand provided her the best. She would take as much pride in the fact that it was her daughter's as she had when it was her husband's.

But if Jarvis Ledbetter wanted his money before the last boll was picked, she'd have to turn him down. She couldn't risk their cash reserve for any reason. Nonetheless, it was worth putting work aside for a while to hear what he had to say.

Two hours later, having heard it, Mary sat staring at the plantation owner, shocked beyond speech in her chair. They were seated in the study of the small plantation home, having after-luncheon coffee. "The First Bank of Boston, you said?" Mary repeated. "The *First Bank of Boston* wants to buy Fair Acres?"

"That's what I said, Mary. Every square inch of it. However..." The master of Fair Acres, still a reputed womanizer at seventy, tapped his fingertips together playfully. "I haven't said yes yet. I'm giving you first chance to buy it and unite your acreage."

Mary resisted the urge to wail aloud. The First Bank of Boston was the lending institution that held the mortgage to Somerset. Like an undertaker waiting close at hand for a dying man's last breath, they

expected her to default on the mortgage. By buying
Fair Acres, if Somerset failed, they would be in possession of a plantation on a major waterway, making
it the most valuable plantation in East Texas, worth
triple their investment. Why else would they be interested in buying that particular stretch when there
were other cotton farms vulnerable for the snatching?
Mary thought she would choke on the insult.

She had come to look upon the financial body as
a personal enemy bent on destroying families such
as hers and the system that went with them. One by
one, all across the Cotton Belt, planters like Jarvis
Ledbetter were selling out to eastern bidders, selling out the tenants who depended upon them for
their livelihoods, selling out the land to be diverted
to other, more profitable crops than the cultivation
of cotton. She couldn't blame them, she supposed. It
was getting harder and harder to maintain the plantation way of life. Inclement weather, maintenance
costs, diminishing markets, pests, and the disinclina-
tion of heirs to carry on in the rural tradition—they
all represented reasons for getting out from under the
constant struggle to survive.

Still, Mary felt a surge of resentment toward the
toadlike man whose pale blue eyes observed her with
rheumy delight over his fingertips. She made up her
mind at once. "If you're willing to wait until after the
harvest, I will certainly buy it," she said.

The silver-haired old planter shook his head. "I'm

sorry, my dear. I can't wait until after the harvest, which may or may not come in, as we are all too painfully aware. I'm selling everything—lock, stock, and barrel—and moving to Europe. Plan to live in Paris for a while. I've always wanted to go there, see a little of the world before I die, and I can't think of a better place to start than the Moulin Rouge. Miles still in Paris?"

"He was the last we heard. Mr. Ledbetter..." Mary's mouth went dry as she heard herself ask, "Exactly what are you asking for Fair Acres?"

When he quoted the sum, she sucked in her breath. It was far less than she had expected. "But that—that's most reasonable," she stammered, her mind working, going over the figures in her ledger back home.

"Far more reasonable than I intend to be with the bunch back in Boston," Jarvis said, his pale eyes glittering.

"Why are you making me such a generous offer?" Mary was suddenly wary. All through the meal, she'd half expected the old man to make an inappropriate advance toward her.

Her host sighed and reached inside his black wool jacket for a cigar. After biting off the tip, he studied the end of it. "To ease my conscience a bit, perhaps. If I sell to them, I'm opening the back door in this part of Texas for the jackals to move in. I know it, and I'm sorry about it, but if I don't, my girls and those worthless husbands of theirs will. I figure that by offering you the chance to buy Fair Acres, I'll have done something to save the old way of life. I figure if anybody can last out here, you will. They don't make offspring—heirs—of your kind anymore, Mary. You're the last of the breed. I can take a little less and still be happy. Besides..." The old planter lit up. "I figure it's all you can afford."

"You're right," Mary said. She was more relaxed with him now. He offered an opportunity she'd be a fool to pass up. Never again would she be able to buy that land as cheaply, and certainly not if the First Bank of Boston purchased it. She said quickly, "Mr. Ledbetter, I do believe I see a way to buy those sections. When do you have to know?"

"I'm hoping to close out the deal by the end of the week. I know that's short notice, Mary, but I want to be out of here by the last of the month. If you buy it, I'll see that the fields get tilled, but my responsibility ends with that. And you'll have to give me cash. Mind, I'm sorry about it, but I'm in no position to carry you on a note. I need my money now, and I don't want to leave anything on the books before I sail. A man's affairs are too hard to handle from across the water."

Rising, Mary extended her hand to her host. "I'll let you know something by the end of the week. As you know, I must consult with Emmitt Waithe, who's the trustee of Somerset."

Jarvis Ledbetter set aside his cigar, got to his feet, and shook her hand. "My dear, if you can get past

Emmitt with this, then you're even more of a cracker-jack than I thought. Good luck."

She needed more than luck, Mary thought as she clucked Shawnee down the dirt road on the way into town. She needed at least twenty good reasons to convince Emmitt to release the last of their security to buy Fair Acres, and the chances of that were very slim. Not once since Miles had named him trustee had he given her a moment's argument concerning expenditures, but he would dig in his heels at this one. As much as he thought of her personally, and admired her ability and leadership, his allegiance was first and foremost to her father. They had been best friends. No other man in the county had respected and liked her father more. Mary would have to get around Emmitt's fiduciary responsibility to the memory of his late friend, and that would be no mean task. In no way would he risk losing Vernon Toliver's Somerset on what he most certainly would consider a whim of his daughter's.

Yet the more she thought about it, the more she was persuaded that buying Fair Acres was a prudent move. First of all, she would own Fair Acres outright. She must convince Emmitt that she'd simply be exchanging one form of asset in the trust for another. She would be exchanging cash for land that would actually have a greater monetary value than its asking price. Should the harvest come in short or fail, she could borrow against Fair Acres and manage both mortgages for the brief time left to repair the debt on Somerset. She would not let herself think of what that would mean for the household, when they were already scraping the marrow from the bone.

As she flew along the road into town, she thought of other important considerations as well. She prayed—*begged*—for the power to make Emmitt see them as clearly as she did.

She found him in, relieving her worry that she'd find the CLOSED FOR DINNER sign in his window.

"Mary, my dear," the lawyer said in quiet astonishment when she explained the reason for her visit, "I can't believe that level head of yours would ever entertain such an idea. That reserve you have in the trust is your only source of security. I can't possibly let you have it to purchase additional property that would compromise the land you have."

"But, Mr. Waithe," Mary implored, standing before his desk, too wrought up to sit, "you don't know these people. Why would they want to buy Fair Acres if not in hope they'll foreclose on Somerset?"

Emmitt parted his hands in a reasonable gesture. "I don't deny they have done exactly that for the reason you cite, but, my dear, why not? It's their prerogative, and actually it makes good business sense."

"All the same, they could make very unpleasant neighbors. There are all kinds of ways they can inflict damage to Somerset from Fair Acres with the intention of making me go under."

Emmitt hiked a skeptical brow. "Like what?"

"Well, they can sabotage irrigation from the Sabine, for one. The Tolivers and Ledbetters have always worked together in keeping the canals open across our properties. Think of all the ways that flow could be diverted or even stopped, and nothing could be done about it. Without irrigation, Somerset is doomed. And the Bank of Boston can refuse to work with us to eradicate pests. Mr. Ledbetter and I have always treated our fields simultaneously. If we didn't, the other's efforts would be futile. I'm sure they have other means to wipe me out that I haven't conceived. Fire, for instance."

Emmitt made an agitated sound in his throat, obviously loath to argue with her. "Mary, that would be cutting off their nose to spite their face. The Bank of Boston wants that land as an investment, not as a means to drive you out. The location of it is an advantage because of the irrigation from the Sabine. They're buying it to sell for a profit."

"They can afford to wait, Mr. Waithe. They can let that land go to seed for a year, then sell it as part of Somerset and still make a fortune."

"Only if the Bank of Boston's motive in buying the land is as nefarious as you suspect, which I wholeheartedly doubt," Emmitt said.

But Mary saw that she had given him cause to reconsider his objections. He frowned, tilting back in his chair. She leaned forward to press her argument.

"By adding Fair Acres to the trust, it becomes more valuable," she contended. "And remember, I'm only in trouble if the harvest fails. But isn't that an improbable *if*? We're looking for a bumper crop this year. If we get it, I'll have more than enough money to put something in reserve for next year. But if the year after that is good...oh, Mr. Waithe..." Mary stood back and clasped her hands, her eyes shining. "Think of it! Somerset united, a sweep of white from one boundary to the other, clear down to the Sabine! It would be a dream come true."

Emmitt shook his head sorrowfully. "No, Mary. Not a dream come true, but pride gratified. This is not about vision. This is about blind desire that falls short of greed only because you love the land. Forgive me for speaking bluntly, but I owe it to your father to do so. It's your pride pushing you to buy Fair Acres. You will then own one of the biggest plantations in Texas and prove that your father was right in writing his will as he did. It's pride at work in you, not the hope of a dream fulfilled, and it's blinding you to the harsh realities of your situation."

Hurt by his words, disbelieving that he could so mistake her motives, Mary cried, "No, Mr. Waithe, it's you who are blind to the harsh realities of my situation. If the Bank of Boston buys those sections, they will destroy Somerset. Are you willing to bet they won't?"

"Are you willing to bet everything you own that

they will?" Emmitt countered. "You're gambling on what you *think* the Bank of Boston will do. You're gambling on the next two years' harvests. If they fail, you're gambling that you can borrow against Fair Acres. What if you can't? Remember that you'll only be twenty. You have to be twenty-one before you can borrow on your own signature. A cosigner will be required, and who will that be?" Emmitt's expression told her to rule him out as a possible candidate. He didn't have the money to cover her losses should disaster fall.

"In that case, I have to hope the Toliver name will be enough." Mary's chin lifted confidently. "Everybody knows that we Tolivers are good for our promises."

Emmitt sighed and scrubbed a hand across his face. "Oh, dear child...Another point I don't think you've considered. How can you run Fair Acres and Somerset without an overseer? You're stretched to the limit as it is. Can you afford to keep Ledbetter's man? Think of all the extra duties you'll be taking on, the exaction in time and effort and money and, I might add"—Emmitt gave her a look of fatherly concern—"your youth."

"Mr. Ledbetter said he'd see to the tilling before he leaves," Mary said, but her tone was subdued. She finally drew up a chair and slumped in it. No, she hadn't thought of the extra work or what to do about the overseer. She never swam a current until she had to, and as far as her youth was concerned...it had been a long while since she'd felt young. She gazed across the desk at Emmitt Waithe, obstinate in his conscientious duty. "I know you're looking out for my best interests, Mr. Waithe, but how are you going to feel if I'm right about my best interests and you're wrong?"

"Terrible." Emmitt sighed. "But not nearly as terrible as I'll feel if I'm right and you're wrong. If you're right, at least I can plead that my better judgment caused me to refuse you the last of your funds. I won't have that refuge if *I'm* right."

"Papa would agree with me," Mary said evenly, her gaze steady on the lawyer. "He always foresaw this danger. Papa would take the gamble. And I must tell you, dear friend, that if the Bank of Boston buys that land and my fears come to pass, I'll have a very hard time forgiving you."

Emmitt pursed his mouth. His mulling expression made her think that she had said the magic words: *Papa would take the gamble.*

After a few seconds, the lawyer gave her a pensive smile. "You are so like him, Mary Toliver. Did you know that? Sometimes, for all the obvious evidence of your gender, I honestly think I'm talking to him sitting in that chair. Yes, your father would have taken the gamble. And, as with you, I'd have tried to talk him out of it."

"Would you have succeeded?"

"No." The lawyer pulled forward in his chair as if

he'd made a decision. "You have until the end of the week to get back to Jarvis, you say? Let's both think on this. I'll let you know my decision by Friday, and then you can contact Mr. Ledbetter." Emmitt peered at her long over his glasses. "And I must tell you, Miss Mary Toliver, that if my answer is yes and *my* fears come to pass, *I* shall have a very difficult time forgiving me."

Chapter Nineteen

Striking off to the study to rework her figures when she'd returned home, Mary came to a halt when she heard her mother call from the parlor, "Mary? Is that you? Come in here."

Incredulously, she approached the open door of the room to find her mother sitting in her favorite rocker before the French windows, fully dressed, and Sassie holding watch from the couch. The look of consternation Sassie gave her reminded Mary that it was four o'clock, long past the time she'd promised to be home to relieve her to do the marketing, a chore she looked forward to as her only means of getting out of the house for a change of scene.

"Sassie has been waiting to fix supper," Darla scolded, her scowl and tone recalling to Mary the many times she'd received such reproofs as a child. In those days, they had bothered her. Now she welcomed her mother's reproach as a sign that she was returning to normal. Darla flicked a critical eye over the blouse and riding skirt that she'd chosen to wear to Fair Acres before heading to the plantation. "I'm assuming those are not your usual work clothes. Where in the world have you been?"

"I...had some business to attend to in town. I'm sorry I'm late. Sassie, I'll make it up to you. You can go to town in the morning. I'll see to the noon meal, and you can take your time. Mama, it's so good to see you downstairs."

"You can go now, Sassie," Darla said with a dismissive wave of her hand. "And see that you don't burn the cornbread."

"Yes'm," the housekeeper said, giving Mary a long-suffering look as she left the room.

Mary pulled a chair close to her mother's rocker. She was wearing her spectacles, and the *Howbutker Gazette* lay in her lap. It had been over four years since she had read a newspaper. In the fading glow of the afternoon, Mary was struck once again by the tragic depletion of her mother's once blooming beauty. She'd been among the first of her contemporaries to use rouge, but now it only accentuated her sunken cheeks. Her hair, formerly thick and lustrous, had lost its shine and fullness. It lay in a dull, brushed-out mass as fine as down on shoulders so fleshless that Mary could see the sharp outline of her bones beneath her shawl.

"I imagine you've found that a lot has changed in town since you last read the *Gazette*," Mary offered gently.

"Why, it's like entering a new world!" Darla turned to a page and showed it to Mary. "Would you look at these fashions Abel is featuring in his advertisements? Skirts up to the calf! And you mean to tell me that Howbutker has a moving picture theater?"

"Well attended, so they say," Mary said, smiling. "I haven't been yet. Would you like to go one evening?"

"Not for a while. I must save my energy." Her mother laid aside the newspaper and removed her glasses. "Did you speak with Beatrice?"

Mary grimaced. "Mama, I'm sorry. I completely forgot. I'll do so tonight."

"Don't bother." Darla drew her shawl closer around her thin shoulders. "I've changed my mind about seeing her. I don't need her help in planning the party. I want it to be as much a surprise to her and everybody else as it will be to you. But I have an objective before that."

Mary felt a prickle of apprehension. "Are you still thinking of helping Toby in the garden?"

"Well, yes, there's that. Toby can indeed use an extra hand. The grounds and garden are a mess. I took a brief tour of them today. I'll have to get out my old garden bonnet and coverall. I don't want to get as brown as you. I'm sure you're still not protecting yourself from the sun. You don't deserve your complexion, the little care you take of it—" She broke off, seeing Mary grin. "What's so amusing?"

"You." Mary's grin widened. "It's good to have you fussing at me again."

"You never listened. I don't know why I bothered."

"Because you loved me, I guess," Mary said.

Her mother appeared to have heard the hopeful inflection in her voice. Her face softened, and she patted Mary's hand. "Yes, because I loved you," she said. "You must never forget that. Now, this is my objective. I want to knit you something for your birthday, and I must get started immediately. I'll need every second to work on it, so you'll have to take me to town to buy the yarn. There *is* sufficient money for me to afford a few skeins of yarn, isn't there?"

"Yes, Mother. You have a separate account at the bank to which I've monthly deposited your twenty percent."

She regretted mentioning the amount set aside from the profits the minute she said it for fear of refueling her mother's resentment against her father and the will, but Darla's expression remained only one of concern. "Oh, I don't want to bother with going to the bank. Can't you lend me the money and next month deduct the cost of my purchase from the amount you'd deposit?"

Relieved, Mary said, "Of course I can, but you

don't need to make me anything, Mama. It's all I could ask that you're up and getting on with things again. That's present enough."

"No, it isn't," Darla disputed with a smile, and caressed her daughter's cheek. "It's been a long time since I made my lamb something with my own hands. What I have in mind is something you'll have to remember me by always."

"I'll have you, Mama," Mary said.

"Not always, darling. Time is not that kind." She drew back her hand. "I'd like to get started as soon as possible. Will you be free to drive me to town tomorrow afternoon for a little shopping? We'll avoid Abel's. I'm sure he has nothing I can afford to buy." Her pale brow contracted when she saw Mary wince. "What's the matter? Will that inconvenience you?"

"No, of course not." Mary forced a smile. She'd already promised the morning to Sassie, and if she drove her mother to town in the afternoon, she'd lose a whole day at the plantation. The drainage ditches were scheduled to be cleaned out tomorrow, but her crews would have to start without her supervision. It was more important that her mother get out of the house. "We'll enjoy a full, lovely day together," she said, "and when we get in from our outing, we'll take the chill off with a good cup of hot chocolate, like we used to when we'd come home from shopping."

"That will be very nice," Darla said, and snapped the paper back to its original folds in a way that suggested to Mary that she did not like her raking up memories of their bygone days but preferred they remain under the leaves of the past. They were too painful. From now on, she'd make references only to the future.

Later in the kitchen, Mary questioned Sassie about her mother's tour of the grounds. "Did she visit the rose garden?"

"Uh-huh," Sassie said.

"Do you think she remembers the last time she visited it?"

"Uh-huh. You can't tell me she don't remember takin' a crowbar to it. Toby say she stop a few minutes in front of the Lancasters, then went on without sayin' nothin'. I tell you, she up to somethin', that one."

"For goodness' sakes, Sassie," Mary remonstrated her sharply. "What would you expect her to say? How terribly sorry and humiliated she feels? Have a little heart for all the woman's been through."

"I'll try for your sake, Miss Mary," Sassie said.

At the appointed time the next afternoon, Darla was dressed for her first appearance in town since walking out of Emmitt Waithe's office. The fashion world had revolved 180 degrees since it favored her large bird's-nest hat and modified bustle. Mary felt shame and embarrassment watching her come downstairs pulling on her long gloves, regally unconscious of her pathetically outdated attire.

As they entered Main Street in the buggy, Darla exclaimed, "Good Lord! Look at all these horseless carriages! Why, they've quite taken over Courthouse Circle."

"We'll have a motorcar one of these days, Mama."

"I wouldn't think in my lifetime, Mary Lamb," Darla said.

At Woolworth's, Darla made her purchases. To Mary's relief, the store was practically deserted of other customers, and Darla had the salesclerk to herself. Together they collected rolls of knitting yarn in a soft cream that they heaped upon the counter. Wary of letting her mother out of her sight, Mary hung anxiously out of earshot of their whispered conversation. At one point, Darla instructed, "Now, Mary, turn your head. I absolutely cannot have you peek at my next purchase."

Mary obeyed, and a hushed consultation between Darla and the clerk followed. She heard the sound of something unrolled from a spool, a snip of scissors, and then the crackle of tissue paper as the item was packaged. "There now," her mother said in satisfaction. "You can turn around."

Her mother's color was rosy and she was smiling to herself as they bounced along in the buggy toward Houston Avenue. A thrill of delight at the pure joy on her face caused Mary to ask, "Happy, Mama?"

Darla turned her bright countenance to her daughter. "I haven't felt this happy in a long time, Mary, my lamb," she said.

Mary flicked the reins over Shawnee's back. She would have to write Miles to tell him the news of their mother's resurrection—that Darla Toliver had finally made it home from the dead.

Chapter Twenty

At the end of the first week in January, Mary purchased Fair Acres. A dour Emmitt Waithe reluctantly opened his office late Saturday afternoon for the transaction, and by five o'clock the deed was signed. Ordinarily, Emmitt would have brought out a bottle of whiskey on hand to toast such momentous legal occasions, but the Wild Turkey stayed in his desk.

The news was out by Monday. Ollie and Charles Waithe dropped by with congratulations, but Percy did not appear. A reporter from the *Gazette* called upon her, asking for an interview. Mary granted it only because he was a school classmate back in town to work for the paper and was desperate for a byline. He wished to write an article on the modern woman's role in society, politics, and business from the perspective of the youngest mistress of one of the largest plantations in Texas, he explained. Mary did not feel particularly modern when she saw the photograph that accompanied the article. Until she saw herself, unsmiling, in a blouse with muttonchop sleeves and high collar, her long hair tied back in a wide bow, she had not realized how seriously out of fashion she'd become.

With the purchase of Fair Acres, Mary's days were filled from before dawn to long after dark. In addition to overseeing the chores reserved for the winter months at Somerset, there was much to do to acquaint herself with her new property. In the buggy, she rode out to visit with each of the Fair Oaks sharecroppers, meeting their children and drinking untold cups of coffee in their mean little shacks, which she hoped someday to replace with the three-room cabins and separate kitchens Vernon Toliver had built for his tenants. She inspected her new fields, fences, equipment, storage sheds, and the plantation house that Jarvis was busy vacating before he set sail for Europe in February.

Apprehension and fatigue were her constant companions. Worry went to bed with her at night and awoke with her in the morning.

Her speculations concerning Percy lay like a shadow over her days. She still had not heard from him. Her last contact was on Christmas Day when he came by to wish her a Merry Christmas and to ask if she would join his family for the holiday meal. She declined, explaining that she must stay with her mother. Sassie balked at preparing another Christmas dinner for appetites as small as theirs, and Mary sent her to be with her granddaughter on Christmas Day and Toby to his brother's. After that, Percy and Ollie took off to Dallas to serve as groomsmen in an army buddy's wedding, Ollie's crutches notwithstanding. They were back by New Year's Eve, and Mary learned Percy had squired Isabelle Withers, a banker's daughter, to the dance at the country club.

Even with her mind in turmoil over plantation concerns, she had burned with jealousy for days. Isabelle was the porcelain-skinned, blond, blue-eyed Dresden type she'd described to Lucy as the kind of woman Percy preferred. She remembered how Lucy had scoffed. *Dresden and porcelain be damned. He likes a woman he doesn't have to worry about breaking, that he can grab hold of, that can match him thrust for thrust....*

Ruthlessly, she closed off that mental picture, forcing her mind to other daily tortures. Percy had every right to see other women. He was a man with a man's needs, and what did she expect, if she wasn't willing to satisfy them? But why did it have to be Isabelle, that silly, simpering simpleton? She was sure he had taken great umbrage at her purchase of Fair Acres. He would know what that would exact in tolls of time and commitment and look upon this latest folly as the final scuttling of the deal they'd made.

She would know more how things stood between them when he came to her party.

It was an event she both welcomed and dreaded. She had no time for such foolishness, but it would be a "coming out" party for her mother, and she was grateful the occasion had given Darla impetus to concern herself with her appearance. "I must eat more to get some flesh on my bones," she'd say to explain her second serving at meals. "I must exercise to get color into these cheeks," she'd say when Mary came upon her wielding her spade in the garden. And while the results were slow in showing—Sassie reported that often she'd seen evidence that her mother had thrown up her meals—her former imperious mien and manner reasserted themselves.

"I believe I preferred your mother outta my way and off my nerves," Sassie commented after one particularly trying day.

Mary returned a sympathetic smile, thrilled but a little alarmed at her mother's high-handed demands of the household now that she was back in charge. "Bite your tongue, Sassie, but I well understand what you mean." Still, she reveled in the tender affection that Darla, unlike in former days, went out of her way to show her and the relief she felt to know that Darla now had a reason to get out of bed in the mornings. Ever since their trip into town, she'd rise at dawn, dress, and come downstairs to commence knitting the cream yarn into something whose purpose stumped all who saw the growing pile in the basket beside her rocker.

"What all that yarn goin' to be, Miss Darla?" Sassie inquired.

"Never you mind, Sassie girl. This is to be a surprise for Mary on her twentieth birthday. All will be revealed then."

"I know you don't want to hear it, Miss Mary, but I don't like this one little bit," Sassie confided. "She gives me the willies sittin' there in the parlor rockin' and smilin' to herself, them needles flashin' away, like she got a secret. She up to somethin', mark my words."

"She's simply lost in the past, Sassie, reliving some amusing moment when she was young and beautiful. Leave her to the comfort of her memories. And have you noticed that the family pictures are back on the mantel?"

So she and Sassie and Toby prepared for the party. Invitations were written and delivered, the menu planned, the food purchased, the house cleaned and aired. The Warwicks, Ollie and Abel, several other neighbors, and Emmitt Waithe and his family were invited. Mary shook out an outdated red taffeta evening gown from the back of her wardrobe for herself—risking Abel's ceiling-cast eyes when he saw her in it—but ordered an amber velvet creation from his store for her mother.

"Lawsey, Lawsey! What we goin' to have to do without to pay for *that*?" Sassie moaned when the dress was delivered.

"Meat for the next month," Mary answered, taking the gilded box upstairs to surprise her mother. "Be sure and cancel our delivery, Sassie."

The night of the party, she dressed joylessly in her antiquated red taffeta. It required she wear a corset, though corsets were passé now, replaced by brassieres, which Mary didn't own. She looked tired, strained, dated, and plainly not in the mood for a party. At least her hands were in fair shape. She had started wearing work gloves, but not the ones Percy had presented her at Christmas. Those she had put away with the note because they were too lovely for fieldwork. Nonetheless... looking at herself in the mirror, she knew she didn't stand a chance against Dresden.

"Now get that frown off your face and them worry lights out of your eyes, chile," Sassie commanded, coming into the room and catching her forlorn inspection. "This is your night to howl, and I want to hear some *howlin'*."

Mary had adjusted the festive twist of plaits she'd pinned on top of her head while Sassie was downstairs tending to last minute refreshments. The arrangement did little to elevate her appearance. "I'm afraid I don't feel much like howling. Have you checked on Mother?"

"I tried to, Miss Mary, but she say go 'way. Wouldn't let me in. Say she can get herself dressed, and she don't want nobody to see her 'fore she make an appearance."

"I wonder what she's going to do with all those strips she knitted."

"I wish I knew. They all be part of your present,

but what that goin' to be, I guess we all have to wait
to find out."

"I'll come show you and Toby once I've opened it.
Now I'd better go make sure she's all right."

Going down the hall, Mary reflected on the long,
dogged hours her mother had plied her knitting
needles in the parlor in what was plainly a sincere
effort to ask her forgiveness. A simple red rose would
have served as well, and she in turn would have done
something creative with the Snow Whites pictured in
the seed catalogs to assure her that all was forgiven.
Only twice had her mother ever made her a garment.
Once, a scarf, and long ago for Christmas, a pair of
mittens. Other mothers, when she was growing up,
embroidered smocks and bonnets, crocheted dresses
and shawls, and knitted sweaters and hats for their
daughters, but Darla preferred to needlepoint sam-
plers. Mary told herself that whatever the present, or
her distaste for the party, she would show just appreciation for her mother's gift and be grateful the dark
days were over.

She knocked on her door. "Mama, are you all right?
Don't you need help dressing?"

"Absolutely not!" Darla's answer came with a flut-
ing laugh. "The dress is smashing, darling. You're
going to love me in it. Now run downstairs and let
me prepare my grand entrance."

Mary turned away, disappointed, wanting to be the
first to see her in her new finery, as she'd been allowed

to admire her all those many social seasons ago. Once a little girl, always a little girl, when it came to seeing her mother in a party dress, she thought.

Starting down the stairs, she caught sight of Percy's hatless blond head through the fanlight above the front door. He was coming up the walk, early and alone. The panic that had been lying at low ebb all these past weeks surged through her like a tidal wave, and she descended at a breathless run, yanking open the door before he reached for the bell pull.

She knew at once what he'd come to say. His eyes were colorless as glass and his jaw hard as rock. "I know I'm early, Mary, but I have a few things I want to say before the others get here. Mother and Dad are coming in their car later. I walked to get some air into my lungs."

Her smile flickered. "You must have a lot to say."

"I'm afraid so."

"On my birthday?"

"It can't be helped."

"Well, then, do come in. Mother's not down yet."

"Mother?" He frowned at the unfamiliar reference.

"I . . . suppose I've taken to calling Mama that sometimes. . . ." She flushed under his measured squint. "Here, let me take your coat."

"That won't be necessary. I'm not staying."

His words struck like a blow. "Percy, you can't mean that. It's my birthday."

"You don't care a fig that it's your birthday, other than it brings you one year closer to taking possession of Somerset."

"This is about my buying Fair Acres, isn't it." Pressure was mounting in her solar plexus, threatening to close off her breath. "You view it as sealing my commitment to Somerset."

"Doesn't it?"

"Percy..." Mary searched her mind wildly for a convincing explanation. "Buying Fair Acres wasn't a choice between you and Somerset. It was an opportunity I couldn't afford to pass up. My decision had nothing to do with you. I...I had so little time to consider. I didn't even think of you at the time, how buying it might affect us...how *you'd* think it would affect us."

"If you had, would it have made a difference? Would you have gone ahead and bought it anyway?"

She felt trapped. How could she make him understand that she'd had no choice? She stared at him wordlessly, anguish burning in her chest.

"Answer me!" he thundered.

"Yes," she blurted.

"That's what I thought." His nostrils flared. "I wonder what that cost you—besides me. God, Mary—" He raked his gaze down the length of her, and she cringed inwardly, imagining how overblown she must look in her outmoded taffeta with its nipped-in waist and her breasts pushing for attention above the lace trim of her bodice. Loose waistlines and flat-tened chests were the fashion of the day, the likes of which he must be accustomed to admiring on Isabelle Withers.

"You're halfway through your youth, and you haven't known a day of it," Percy said, his mouth twisting contemptuously. "You ought to be going to parties and dances, wearing pretty clothes and flirting with the boys, but look at you. You're drawn, worn out, putting in eighteen hours a day working like a field hand, and for what? To live in poverty, with con-tinuous worry about where you'll get the next loaf of bread? To wear clothes that went out with high-button shoes? To relieve yourself in a bucket and read by the light of a kerosene lamp? You've lost a brother and a mother, and now you're about to lose a man who loves you, who could give you everything, and all for the sake of a backbreaking, heart-shattering plantation that will never, *ever* make your sacrifices worth it."

"It won't always be this way." Mary held out her hands to him. "In a few years—"

"Of *course* it will always be this way! Who are you kidding? You made sure of that when you bought Fair Acres. I don't have a few years!"

"Wha-what are you telling me?"

He turned away, his handsome face crumpling. She had never seen him cry before. She stepped toward him, but he held up a hand to stop her, while the other snapped out a handkerchief from inside his coat. "I'm telling you what you've tried to tell me all along. I thought I could lure you away from Somerset, but I see now that I can't. Your buying Fair Acres proved that. I kept away from you to give you time to realize how much you need and want me, but you simply filled it up with more land, more work…like you'll always do to handle days when we're divided. They'll tear the guts out of me, but, hell, you'll simply plant another row of cotton."

He wiped his eyes and faced her. "Well, that's not for me. You were right about me, Mary. I need a woman who will love me and our children above all and everyone else. I cannot share her with any endeavor that will wear her to the bone and leave nothing for me and our family at the end of the day. I know that now, and I won't settle for anything less. If you can't give me that…"

He looked at her with desperate hope, his face full of appeal, and Mary knew this was a now-or-never moment. If she let him go, he was gone forever.

"I thought you loved me.…"

"I do. That's what's so damn tragic. Well, what's it to be—me or Somerset?"

She wrung her hands. "Percy, don't make me choose.…"

"You have to. What's it to be?"

She stared at him in a long, resigned silence.

"I see…," he said.

The slam of motorcar doors and voices drifted

up the walk. Sassie swung out of the kitchen at the end of the hall, a stiffly starched white apron over a black dress she wore to funerals. "They all comin'," she announced. "Mister Percy—why you still in your overcoat?"

"I was just leaving," he said. "Give my best to your mother, Mary, and . . . happy birthday."

With a puzzled frown, Sassie watched him spin on his heels and stride to the door, closing it behind him without a backward glance. "Mister Percy is leavin'? He ain't comin' back?"

"No," Mary answered in a voice as empty as a rain barrel in drought. "Mister Percy is not coming back."

Chapter Twenty-one

Mary was still standing numbly in the hall when the guests streamed into the house. They all arrived at once, everyone looking elegant, prosperous, and delighted at the prospect of seeing Darla again, the house opened up, and the Tolivers back on course. Abel's expression showed the barest trace of horror when he saw Mary in the red taffeta—it had, after all, come from his store—but Charles Waithe, who had recently joined his father's law firm, beamed in admiration. He bent over her hand with great gallantry and said, "What a stunning dress, Mary. The color becomes you. Happy birthday."

Mary greeted them with a smile stiffened by the overwhelming awareness of her loss. No one but Ollie seemed to notice. He hung behind when Sassie ushered the others into the parlor, where refreshments were laid out.

"What's wrong with Percy? Why isn't he staying?"

"We've had . . . a falling-out."

"*Another* one? What happened?"

"Fair Acres."

"Ah," he said as if no further explanation were necessary. "I feared as much. Percy was very, very angry when he heard you'd taken on another plantation, Mary Lamb. Unappeasable. He read it as your making a choice between him and Somerset."

"It was a decision, not a choice."

"Then we must get him to understand that."

Mary looked into his kind face, moved, as always, by his love for them. She laid a hand on his shoulder. "Ollie, you've sacrificed enough for Percy and me. Don't spend another minute on two people so bent on mishandling it."

Ollie took her hand and fondled it against the velvet lapel of his dinner jacket. "I've no idea what you mean, but no sacrifice is too great for two people who mean the world to me."

A movement came from the top of the stairs. Mary and Ollie glanced up at her mother, her hand on the balustrade, striking an imperious pose like the Darla of old. In the parlor, Beatrice caught sight of their arrested, uplifted faces and beckoned to the others. "Darla is coming down," she announced excitedly, and within seconds they had gathered to watch Darla descend the grand staircase.

The dress had been an excellent choice. Its amber color and straight, curveless silhouette softened her wasted figure. The textured velvet added weight to her frame, and the long chiffon sleeves disguised arms grown flabby from years of lying in bed. Her lip and cheek rouge and the extra attention to her pompadour did little to boost her gaunt face, but her smile and poise, the tilt of her head, were the same as in years past when Mary had stood rooted in this same spot to watch her mother glide down the stairs to her guests.

"Hello, everyone," she greeted them in her lilting voice. "How good of you to come."

Eyes misted as applause filled the hall and everyone expressed their delight at seeing her again. "You chose the perfect gown," Abel whispered in Mary's ear.

"Well done," Ollie said.

Darla made her laughing way around the circle of old friends, stroking Mary's cheek to remind everyone of the reason for the party before it was forgotten in the celebration of having her among them again. Mary was relieved. The attention on her mother diverted it from her and her obviously distracted air. Ollie took charge of the conversation when they were settled in the parlor, and she was able to fade further into the background. There were plenty of national happenings for spirited discussion—Prohibition, the presidential campaign, the Nineteenth Amendment.

"I hope never to see the day," declared Jeremy Warwick, "when women will get the right to vote."

His wife gave his arm a smack. "Not only will you live to see that day, my dear, but you will live to see your wife cancel out your ballot. I'm voting for Warren G. in the November election, if the amendment passes."

"Which proves my point that women have no place in the ballot box," her husband rejoined to the general laughter of all.

A hush fell when time came for Mary to open Darla's gift. It was packaged in the same gilded box in which her dress had been delivered and sat on a table among the flowers the guests had sent to circumvent the invitation's request that no gifts be brought. Everyone watched attentively as Mary removed the lid, and a chorus of oohs and ahs greeted the cream-colored, beribboned confection that Mary drew out of the box.

"Why, it's…the most beautiful thing I've ever seen!" Beatrice declared.

"Darla, my dear!" Abel gawped at the huge afghan Mary held up. "I would be most happy to buy as many of these as you can make. I assure you they'll sell as fast as ice cream in July."

A wan smile, as if the very thought of his offer tired her, parted Darla's lips. "Thank you, Abel, but I knitted this specially for my daughter as a memento of her twentieth birthday. I'll not knit another."

She remained silent while everyone fingered and complimented the meticulous detail, workmanship, and pattern of the voluminous bedcovering. The lengths of knitted cream strips had been joined with pink satin ribbons tied in perky bows that formed a pattern of exquisite design.

"Mama, I...am without words," Mary said in awe and pleasure, reverently tracing the intricate handi-work. "You did this for me?" She still could not quite believe the generosity of her mother's labor; it seemed so beyond the bounds of her demonstrations of affec-tion in the past.

"Only for you, darling," her mother said, her eyes glowing tenderly. "It is the only gift I could contrive that would express what you mean to me now."

Remembering her promise, Mary left the guests to their cake and coffee and hurried to the kitchen to show her gift to Sassie and Toby. The housekeeper was not impressed. "Now, why you suppose she go and choose pink ribbons when your room done in blue and green? It won't go with nothin' in there. I tell you, they is no understandin' that woman."

"You know she's always tried to push pastels on me, Sassie. Her choice is a subtle way to let me know she's back at it, and that's another healthy sign. When the harvest comes in, I'll have my room redecorated in pink and cream."

"Pink'n cream! Them ain't your colors. They too weak and puny. They your mama's colors!"

When she returned to the parlor with the afghan, her mother said, "Here, let me have that. I'll refold it and take it up with me when I go."

The guests traded amused looks. Beatrice remarked,

"Your mother's worked so long and hard on your gift, Mary, who can blame her for not wanting to let it go?"

Strain marked the rest of the evening. The life had drained from Darla. She sat in her rocker tired and distant, her pallor more pronounced. Mary, too, could no longer hold the smile she'd forced all evening. Despair was overtaking her. The certainty that Percy was lost to her for good was worse than her worst imaginings during the war.

Without preamble, Darla rose from the rocker, clutching the gilded box to her bosom. "I'm afraid I must call it a day, dear friends and daughter," she said. "But please don't leave because of me. Stay and enjoy the party as long as you can. I do insist." Immediately, everyone gathered around, offering endearments, hugs, pecks on her cheek. Mary stood aside until the flurry was over, then carefully embraced her mother's fragile frame.

"Thank you, Mama," she said, gratitude overwhelming her voice.

Her mother pressed her cheek to hers. "It pleases me that I've provided my dear girl a birthday she'll always remember."

"I could never forget, Mama. Your gift will guarantee it."

"That was my purpose." Darla disengaged herself. "Stay down and help Sassie clean up when everyone's gone. She's getting old, and I don't want her up half the night tidying the kitchen." Clasping the box, she turned with a smile to the group and twiddled her fingers in farewell. "Good-bye, everyone."

It was Ollie who ended the evening. "I'm sorry, folks," he said, "but I feel like a bottle of champagne with its cork popped and the fizz gone. Dad and I ought to be pushing home." In the hall, as everyone donned overcoats and hats and gloves, he asked in an undertone of concern, "Want me to stay?"

Mary was tempted to say yes. He knew she had not enjoyed her party and understood why. She'd have appreciated his company while she cleaned up, but Abel would have had to return for him in the Packard, and it was already late. "Thank you, Ollie, but I'll be fine. Please don't concern yourself with Percy and me. We were...never meant to be."

He brought her hand to his lips. "You were made for each other, Mary Lamb. You're like oil and vinegar—you're a perfect blend when shaken. Perhaps that's what you both need—a good shaking."

She had always been amused by his way with words and smiled despite her sadness. "Seems to me we're constantly being shaken, but we resist blending."

After everyone had left, Mary sent Sassie and Toby off to bed and carried the party dishes to the kitchen herself. She welcomed the task of cleaning up to avoid lying awake thinking of her future without Percy. Though she'd told herself a hundred times they hadn't a chance together, in her heart of hearts she hadn't

believed it—and she'd counted on Percy not believing
it. Somehow, some way, things would work out. Percy
loved her. He could never let her go. Time would take
care of everything—if he were willing to wait.

Apparently, he wasn't.

She thought fleetingly of checking on her mother
as she stacked the dishes, but the stairs seemed insur-
mountable to her leaden feet, and she had no wish
to explain her red-rimmed eyes. Besides, her mother's
bedroom door creaked loudly and she might awaken
her if she was already asleep. She'd wait until morning to peep in on her.

It was long past midnight when she finally climbed
into bed. The gilded box was on her dresser. She
would wait until tomorrow to take out its treasure and
spread it on her bed. Though exhausted, she expected
to lie wide awake in her misery, rolling from shoulder to shoulder; but sleep came immediately. She was
dreaming of snow falling on cotton when she was
awakened roughly the next morning by Sassie shaking her shoulder. "Wha-what is it?"

"Oh, Miss Mary!" Sassie wailed, the wild roll of
her eyes stark in the early morning sunlight. "It's your
mama—"

"What?" Mary tossed off the bedcovers, blurrily
aware that Sassie had gone to the water bowl to retch.
She stumbled down the hall to her mother's room and
lurched to a dead stop at the open door. A scream tore
from her throat. *"Mama!"*

Still in the amber velvet dress, her mother hung from the ceiling by a noose of knitted cream-colored wool around her neck. On the floor beneath her suspended feet lay a mound of pink satin ribbons. Slowly, understanding at last, Mary knelt before the pile and gathered the ribbons in her hands. *"Oh, Mama...,"* she sobbed, the ribbons falling through her fingers like the stripped petals of pink roses.

Chapter Twenty-two

She was still sobbing uncontrollably and clutching the ribbons to the bodice of her nightgown when Percy appeared beside her and scooped her up in his arms. "Sassie, close the door behind me and go call Doc Tanner," he ordered. "Keep Toby out of this room, and don't say a word to him about what happened here."

"No, sir, Mister Percy."

"And bring up some hot milk. We've got to get Miss Mary warm before she goes into shock."

"Mama...Mama..."

"Shush," Percy said gently, laying her in her bed and pulling the covers tight under her chin.

"She...hated me, Percy. She...hated me...."

He stroked her forehead. "She was a sick woman, Mary."

"The...pink ribbons...You know what they mean...."

"Yes," he said. "That was very cruel of her."

"Oh, God, Percy...Oh, God...."

He stoked the dying fire and found other blankets and piled them high. When Sassie arrived with the milk, he helped Mary lift her head from the pillow and put the warm cup to her lips. "Try to get this down. Come on now, Mary."

"Doc Tanner'll be here in a few minutes, Mister Percy. What you want me to do when he get here?"

"Send him up, Sassie. I'll meet him in the hall."

Mary grabbed his hand, staring at him out of eyes wide with horror. "What are you going to do? What will happen now?"

He wiped away the milk trickling down her chin. "Don't worry. I'll see to everything. This will stay between us and Sassie and Doc Tanner. No one else—not even Toby—has to know. I'll send a cable to Miles."

"What...will you tell him?"

"Your mother died of natural causes. That's what Doc Tanner will state on the death certificate. She went to sleep and did not wake up."

Mary fell back against the pillows and turned her head away. His distaste for dissembling was plain to see. He would lie to Miles and call in an IOU from Doc Tanner that the Warwicks never expected or wished to be repaid for their many generous contributions to his medical causes through the years. "Thank you, Percy," she said to the wall, her teeth chattering.

Buried beneath the blankets, she listened to the

hushed voices and footsteps of Percy and Doc Tanner and Sassie going in and out of her mother's room. When the housekeeper reappeared, she reported that her mother's body had been cut down and sewn in a sheet. "The undertaker goin' to come pick her up like that," she said, adjusting Mary's blankets. "Mister Percy, he goin' to go with her to the funeral parlor and make sure the coffin be nailed shut. He goin' to tell everybody that Miss Darla's long years of bad health left her *ravaged*—that Mister Percy's word—and her daughter want her to be remembered as she was."

Percy stayed at her side during the strain of making funeral arrangements and receiving visitors. He voiced no judgment, made no accusations, but the significance of the pink ribbons writhed between them like a poisonous snake they'd tacitly agreed to ignore but of which each was keenly aware. His grim silence expressed to Mary what she herself believed: She was responsible for her mother's suicide. It was another consequence of her pigheaded obsession with Somerset.

"What you want me to do with them strips and ribbons, Miss Mary?" Sassie asked when she was out of bed and moving about blankly like a shell-shocked war victim. "Mister Percy say to burn 'em."

"No!" Her cry felt scraped from her throat. "They are from my mother's hands.... Bring them to me." In possession of them again, she compressed the pink ribbons into a ball and wrapped them in a casing of

the cream-colored strips, then packaged the bundle
in tissue paper and hid it far back in her wardrobe.

At the funeral, she felt the same silent condemnation from the townspeople that she sensed from
Percy. Even though none were aware of the cause of
her mother's death, her demise was enough. Darla
had died of a broken heart by her husband's hand,
unrectified by his daughter. Mary even saw Emmitt
Waithe shake his head as though he, too, believed this
tragedy the result of Vernon Toliver's will.

A few days after the funeral, she said to Sassie, "I'm
moving into the Ledbetter house temporarily. It will
be easier for me to manage things from there. Why
don't you take this opportunity to visit your daughter? Toby can look after things here, and the house
has a telephone. Here's the number."

"Miss Mary, how you goin' to look after yourself
alone out there?"

"I'll manage."

"Mister Percy and Mister Ollie ain't goin' to like
this one little bit."

"I know, Sassie, but I'll enjoy the respite from their
well-meaning concern." *And Percy's silent judgment,*
she thought.

By April, the fields were planted. Mary shielded
her eyes from the spring sun and gazed at the infinite
stretch of neatly mounded rows awaiting germina-
tion of their seeds. Behind her stood Hoagy Carter,
the white overseer she'd inherited with her purchase

of Fair Acres, and Sam Johnson, one of Somerset's tenants whose father had once tilled the same soil as a slave. At ginning time, Sam and the others would receive one-third of the profits from the crop they surveyed today. Both men waited with hats in hand for Mary's pronouncement.

"They look good, Sam. The best ever," she said. "If it all makes, we'll have a bumper crop."

"Oh, Miss Mary..." Sam sighed and shut his eyes in pleasure. "I can hardly stand thinkin' about it. If the good Lord'll just keep the good weather comin' through the pickin', we goin' have us some money in the bank."

"We've been blessed all right," Mary agreed. "Rain at the right intervals and no late frosts. But I'm like you. I won't rest easy until the last row is picked."

"Then we can start worrying 'bout next year." Hoagy chuckled, but his eye on Mary turned sharp and anxious. "That is, if a good wind don't come along and blow you away first."

Mary made no comment as the men replaced their hats and got in step beside her to walk to Sam's cabin. "Mister Hoagy's right, Miss Mary," Sam said with the same expression of concern. "You got to start eatin' 'fore you waste away. How's 'bout stayin' and havin' dinner with us? Bella's got a big pot a spring peas and backbone on the stove."

They had reached the porch, where Sam's wife was waiting for them. She had overheard her husband's invitation and now added her own: "And I just gone and taken a blackberry pie out of the oven, Miss Mary."

Hoagy watched her with hope-filled eyes. Mary knew he wanted her to say yes. It would be another two hours before he sat down to his own table, and then to eat a meal gone cold on the back of the stove. She could see the pie cooling on the sill of the open kitchen window, smelling of bubbling blackberries and buttery crust.

"Thanks just the same," Mary said, "but we've got a few more houses to call on. Hoagy, you ready?" The sight of the pie and its fruity smell turned her stomach. Since her mother's suicide, she could hardly abide the thought of food.

Sam and Bella followed Mary and the disappointed Hoagy into the breezeway that divided the house, where they were met by Daisy, the Johnsons' fourteen-year-old daughter. "Mama, they's a fancy automobile headed this way. I just seen it turn off the road."

"One of them horseless carriages?" Bella said. "Who be comin' out here to see us in one of them?"

Through the screen door, Mary saw the object of discussion draw to a stop beneath one of the pecan trees in the front yard.

"Why, it's that Percy Warwick feller," Hoagy said, his eye narrowing. "What you expect he's doin' out here?"

"I believe he's come to see me," Mary said. "You all remain here, and I'll go see what he wants."

He had finally run her to earth, Mary thought, already weary from the encounter to come. He'd apparently trailed her on her rounds, going from house to house to find her here. He lounged with crossed legs and arms by a new Pierce-Arrow that had replaced the one his father had held for him during the war.

"Hello, Percy," she said, her greeting unenthusiastic. "I know why you're here."

"Ollie was right." His gaze ran over her critically. "You do look more skeleton than flesh."

"You're making that up. Ollie would never say such a thing about me."

"I'm paraphrasing, maybe. I believe he said 'more bone than flesh' after he saw you at your house the other night, but both are apt."

She knew he was referring to Ollie's waylaying her when she returned home to replace a harness for Shawnee. With relentless vigilance, he'd waited on her verandah each night hoping to catch her when she returned. "Ollie shouldn't waste his evenings waiting for me, not after working all day at the store. He needs his rest."

Percy unwound his legs and straightened up. "Well, you can appreciate his concern. He doesn't understand why you've put yourself beyond the comfort of those who love you."

But you understand, don't you? Mary thought. He understood why she had cut herself off from everyone and lived like a hermit away from the house. He'd been privy to a scene that had changed her forever, and seeing him only reminded her of it and added to the crushing guilt she felt every waking minute. She was surprised to see him dressed in layabout clothes. It was a weekday, and typically he'd be wearing a business suit. Still, as always, he shone like a Greek god under the noonday sun, and ordinarily her pulse would be racing. But not now—not anymore.

"Ollie says you've moved into the Ledbetter house," he said. "No wonder we never found you at home. Toby wouldn't tell us a thing." He grimaced as if he could picture the emptied, dirty house she returned to every night, the cast-off mattress and left-behind cans of soup she heated when she felt like eating. But at least she could enjoy the comforts of an indoor toilet.

"It was for convenience sake," she said. "I sent Sassie to her daughter's, and Toby has been looking after things at the house."

Percy let out an exasperated sigh. "Mary, this has got to stop. I can't stand what you're doing to yourself."

"You'll have to." She cast a nervous glance at Hoagy, impatient to get on with their rounds so he could have his dinner. "I know you and Ollie and your families are worried about me, but there's nothing you can do about it. I am where I want to be, doing what I want to do. I don't mean to sound like an ingrate after all you've done, but now I want to be left alone."

"I can't leave you alone."

Conscious of Hoagy's tuned ears, Mary hissed, "Percy, *listen* to me. There's absolutely *nothing* you can do."

"Yes, there is. That's why I'm here. I have a proposal."

"I've already heard it."

"Not this one." Percy moved closer, and a dogged flicker in his eye warned her not to step away. "Don't you think you owe it to me to hear what I've got to say?"

Ah, there it was. Something to hold over her head for the rest of her life. But he was right. She did owe him. Always.

"If you'll keep your voice down," she said, her teeth gritted. "I don't want this conversation discussed on every front porch in the county."

"Then go tell Hoagy you have business in town and get in the car. I have a meal waiting for us. He can take your horse and buggy to his place, and we'll pick it up later."

She stared at him as if he'd lost his mind. "I will not! I've got two more rounds, and then Hoagy and I have to discuss weeding schedules."

He stepped closer. "You are coming with me or I will pick you up and throw you into the car. How would that be as a topic for front porch gossip?"

Mary knew he meant it. The glint in his eye indicated she had maybe a few seconds to decide. "All *right!*" she snapped, and whirled around to march back to the cabin, where three pairs of goggling eyes hastily withdrew behind the screen door. On the porch, Hoagy regarded her with curiosity. She saw that he'd heard enough of the conversation to deduce something was going on between her and the almighty Percy Warwick. "Hoagy, I'll be driving back to town with Mr. Warwick," she said, attempting an offhand tone. "You go on and finish up our rounds and then get yourself some dinner. I'll pick up my rig at your place."

Hoagy squinted at her. "Must be important for you to be leaving in the middle of the day."

"That's as may be," she said, annoyed, "but I'll be back this afternoon." His face soured, and she read that to mean he'd have taken the rest of the day off if she weren't returning. *I'm firing his hide first chance I get,* she thought as she strode back to the Pierce-Arrow and Percy.

"This visit of yours will be on the tongues of every tenant on the place by suppertime," she said, plopping onto the passenger seat and slamming the door.

Percy grinned. "Well, hell, Mary, don't you think we'll be more interesting than boll weevils?"

Chapter Twenty-three

Once the dust of the road was billowing at their backs, Mary turned to Percy. "And just where are we going?"

"To the cabin. We're going to have a picnic, drink something cool, talk."

"The cabin..." A nerve jumped in the pit of her stomach. She remembered Percy mentioning the cabin as the place he'd like to stick her under the shower and soap her all over. It had been the day he'd caught her in the fields at Somerset looking a fright—a lifetime ago.

"I still use it for fishing and hunting."

"And as a place to take your women, I suppose."

He glanced at her. "If you like."

"Well, I don't like, Percy Warwick. I do not intend to become one of your women."

"I don't want you to become one of my women. I want you to become my wife."

Now every nerve in her body was jumping. "That's impossible."

"I once thought so, but now I'm ready to compromise."

She let out a little yelp of surprise. "Compromise? Is that what this proposal is about?"

"Uh-huh. I'll tell you more after I've fed you."

Mary willed her heart to a steady beat. They had been in this snare before. She recalled Percy's words from that long-ago day at Somerset: *Call it male conceit or arrogance, or the power of love, but I believe I can make you want to give up Somerset.* Surely by now he knew he couldn't. He ought to know that if her mother's suicide had not deterred her commitment to Somerset, nothing he could say or do would. She'd lost too much, sacrificed too much. In a perverse way that Percy would never understand, she owed it to her mother to make the plantation a success. She would never agree to a compromise that would interfere with that goal.

His *wife,* he'd said, not his mistress. Why would he even want to marry her now? She would never expunge from her mind the sight of her mother's body suspended by the cream strips she'd knitted for a hangman's noose. Despite her grotesquely swollen face, her protruding tongue, there had been an unmistakable look of triumph on her lips. Percy could not have missed it when he'd cut her down.

A sound of regret escaped her throat. Percy heard it and asked quietly, "A shadow pass over your grave?"

"Something like that," she said.

Mary had never been to the log cabin that Miles and Ollie and Percy had started building on the bank of Caddo Lake as boys of ten. The project had taken the whole of their summer that year and a number of subsequent summers and holiday vacations to complete and refine. She could still remember table discussions regarding its construction and furnishings, and her mother's words of caution: *Now, Miles, remember that it must be a place where you wouldn't behave any differently than you would in your own room at home.*

Even at her ages of five and six, Mary had thought that an inane admonition, judging that the reason the boys built the place was to behave precisely the way they wouldn't at home. She'd grown up thinking of it as a highly secret, exclusive, male hideaway—a place where the boys took girls and drank spirits.

"So this is the cabin," she said when Percy drew up before the rough pine door. "I've never been here before. Not in all these years."

"Ever been curious about it?"

"No."

"Right," he said.

They entered a twenty-by-forty-foot room partitioned into a kitchen, sitting area, and curtained bedroom consisting of one double bed and two bunks. Percy left her to study her surroundings while he went to retrieve the "something cool" from the well. She recognized a cast-off couch from her father's study, a couple of chairs that had once graced the Warwicks' back parlor, and a washstand and mirror of French design, undoubtedly a contribution of the DuMonts. The cabin was clean and cool. She had expected it to be a hot, dark, airless cave infested with flies and mosquitoes and Lord knew what creepy crawlies from the riverbank. Instead, despite the shade of the trees, light flowed in from the tightly screened windows, and ceiling fans moved the crosscurrents of air that drifted in from the lake.

The small table in the kitchen area had been set for two, complete with napkins and a bowl of spring flowers. The carefully placed items, arranged by Percy's muscled, lumberman hands, moved her in a curiously tender way.

"Why have you brought me here, Percy?" she asked when he returned with a bottle of wine he had chilled by lowering it in a bucket into well water. "Alcohol is not going to help your case, whatever it is. And you better hope Sheriff Pitt doesn't come poking around out here and find a bottle of that cooling in your well."

Percy was busy uncorking the wine. "The sheriff knows better than to look where he shouldn't."

"You're saying the Warwicks are exempt from the law?"

She regretted the remark as soon as she'd said it. Percy had the grace to say nothing, allowing his silence to remind her that the Tolivers, too, did not feel obliged to abide by every letter of the law, as events had recently proved. "Only those laws it's nobody's business if we break," he said, filling two glasses of Sauvignon Blanc. "Sit down, Mary. A glass of wine isn't going to hurt you. You're wound tighter than a watch spring. Drink up while I set out our picnic. Then we'll talk."

"I'd rather talk now," Mary said, taking the glass with no intention of drinking it. "Why do you want to marry me, Percy? Especially...after all you've seen?"

He guided her to a chair, where he took her glass, set it aside, and gently pushed her down onto the seat. Then he pulled up another chair so that their knees almost touched. "Listen to me carefully, Mary," he said, taking her hands. "I know what you believe I've been thinking. You're wrong. You didn't cause your mother to take her life. It may be true that she would still be alive if your father had written his will differently, but he didn't. That's not your fault, either."

Stunned, Mary sputtered, "How—how can you deny that you've always blamed me for Papa leaving Somerset to me? It's been the cause of all our arguments. And don't tell me you don't hold me responsible for Mama taking to her bed and—and dying. You *know* you have."

"My argument with you has been about your *obsession* with Somerset to the exclusion of everything and everyone else, but your mother did not have to *die* because of it. She did not have to languish in her bed. She could have chosen to live, to love you and support you no matter who your father favored in his will."

Mary gawked at him. "But you believe Somerset should have gone to her!"

"Of course I do. But I also believe her death should not have been a consequence of your father's action, and it was despicable of her to leave you thinking it was."

Hot, incredulous tears shot to her eyes. "You...you really mean that, Percy?"

"Oh, honey, with all my heart," he said, standing and pulling her into his arms, cradling her like a child rescued from a bad dream. "I'm an idiot for not realizing what you must have been thinking. That's one reason I brought you out here, to clear up that misperception. We have our differences, but your mother's death isn't one of them."

"Oh, Percy..." She sighed, letting her resistance fall. His arms were a dangerous place to be, but what utter heaven to have them around her, offering refuge and strength and...forgiveness.

He kissed her between the eyes and set her back from him. "I'm feeling nothing but bones here," he said, kneading her shoulders. "Let's get some food into you, then we'll finish this discussion. Drink your wine. It will whet your appetite."

Mary sat down again, feeling light and unburdened, even a stirring of hunger. She watched Percy set to work in the kitchen alcove, humming quietly.

He was so comfortable with himself, she thought, sipping her wine. He seemed to live life effortlessly, rolling with its waves like a seaworthy ship. Was it possible for them to be happy if they married? He was a man of steel, like her father. Vernon Toliver had needed no alloy to complete him, the reason he could afford to marry a woman like her mother. But she was made of sterner stuff. It was inevitable that she and Percy would clash... steel against steel.

The alcohol was beginning to take effect. She must watch herself. This was the reason her mother had started drinking. To feel better, to stimulate her appetite, to dull her pain. "Need any help?" she called. He was at the counter, chipping at a block of ice melting in the sink.

"No. Sit there and relax."

Yes, she would do that, Mary thought. She would enjoy these rare moments of peace. Settling more comfortably, she let her gaze wander about the objets d'art the boys had deemed worthy to drag from home. On one wall was an Indian chief's headdress that had once hung in Miles's bedroom. Mary thought of her brother with a sorrow that was like a dull, persistent ache. There had been no reply to the long letter she had written describing their mother's last days. She had tried to make them sound happy, relating how Darla had sat in the parlor day after day and seemed content to knit the afghan with which she'd surprised her on her birthday.

"Chow's on," Percy announced, and Mary laughed when he bowed with mock formality and took her by the hand to lead her to the table. She made an effort not to make a face when she saw the heaped plates. Her stomach felt the size of a thimble.

"It looks...enticing," she said, forking up a bite of the concoction on her plate, new to her palate. It was a salad of diced chicken, green grapes, and toasted almonds combined with a clear, sweet dressing that burst tart and refreshing in her mouth. After she'd chewed and swallowed, she closed her eyes in bliss. "Hmmm. Percy, this is delicious."

He held out the breadbasket. "Try one of these."

She helped herself to one of the light, buttery rolls in the shape of a crescent and bit into it. "Oh, my," she said.

"They're called *croissants,* one of the few pleasures I enjoyed in France. The DuMonts' cook has taught our cook how to make them."

She ate every bite of the salad and two of the croissants. At the meal's end, she pushed away her plate and put her hands over her stomach. "I don't know where I would put the peaches and cream, Percy. There's absolutely no room in here."

"That's all right," he said. "The cream's on ice. We'll have it with the peaches later."

The mention of "later" brought Mary back to the reason he'd brought her out here. All through the meal Percy had steered the talk to news of local happenings, family, and friends while their knives and forks clinked companionably on the Willow Wood plates. The main topic of discussion had sat far off in the distance, like a potential rain cloud.

Now she folded her napkin and laid it on the table. "Percy, I think it's time for you to present your proposal."

Percy picked up their plates. "I'll wash these up first. Privy's outside if you care to use it. Select any tree and be careful of the chiggers. Well water's drawn and towels beside it. We'll finish up the wine on the porch."

She was feeling too logy to argue, like a contented, well-fed cat. She strolled outside into the green stillness of the waning afternoon and found herself a private spot, washed and dried her hands at the well, then returned to the porch, where Percy was pouring out the last of the wine. Shaded by cypress trees, the porch had been built to catch the lake breezes and screened to protect against mosquitoes.

"I don't need any more of that," she objected, drawing out the chain of her lapel watch. "It's after three o'clock. I really do need to get back."

"What for?" Percy asked. "Can't Hoagy handle things?"

"Hoagy has to be supervised. He's too fond of visiting and taking coffee breaks."

"The joys of running a plantation, huh?"

"Let's not ruin a perfect picnic by bringing that up, Percy."

"Oh, but I have to. The plantation's the main point of my proposal."

Mary tensed. Here it comes, she thought. Another ruin to another perfect day together. "And what is that?" she asked.

"Well, I've been doing some reconsidering of what's important—what I can live with and what I can't live without. And I've decided"—he swirled the wine in his glass with utmost attention—"that I can live with a weevil-infested plantation, but I can't live without you."

Mary strained to make sense of his words, sure she'd heard him incorrectly. "What...are you saying, Percy?"

"I want us to get married—just as we are...I, a lumberman, and you, a planter."

She felt her eyes grow as large as the Willow Wood plates. "You mean you'd take us both—me and Somerset?" It wasn't possible, she thought. Her ears were tricking her.

Percy turned his face to her. "That's what I'm proposing. Will you marry me if I'll promise to back off with my objections to Somerset and accept things as they are?"

Still, she could not trust her ears. "I don't believe it," she said, her voice hardly above a whisper.

He set down his glass and held out his hand to her. "Believe it, Mary. I love you."

Cautiously, she laid her hand on the large surface of his palm. "What's caused this change?"

"Seeing what's happening to you. And to me." His fingers closed around her hand. "How many more burdens do you think you can bear alone? How many more years can I go on alone, without you? Our days are filled from dawn to dusk, honey, but our lives are empty."

"What about…all the things you said you needed in a wife? Someone who'll put you and the children first?"

"Well, maybe that will happen, but I promise I won't go into our marriage counting on it. If I can't come home to you, then you can come home to me. Simply living together, married, under one roof will be enough for me, I promise."

Disbelief still constrained her joy. "But you're doing all the compromising. What do I have to give up? What do I have to promise?"

His hand tightened. "You have to promise that if Somerset fails, you'll let it go. That will be the end of the matter. No coming to me for money to save it. It will be hard to say no to you, but I will, and you must promise that my refusal will not affect our marriage. You know how I feel about growing cotton. I consider plantations such as yours a losing proposition whose time has come and gone."

She reached forward with her free hand and pressed

her fingertips to his mouth. "You don't have to say any more, Percy. I know how you feel and, no, I wouldn't expect you to come to my rescue. It would be a violation of the rule we've always lived by."

"Then you promise?" he asked, looking as if he held his own joy in abeyance until she gave her word.

"Of course I promise," she cried, scooting out of her chair like a child ready for a romp. "Percy...do you really mean it?"

"I really mean it," he said, laughing. "You haven't said yes, by the way."

Mary knelt before him and flung her arms around his neck. "Yes, yes, *yes!*" she shouted between hard, quick kisses on his mouth. God was smiling upon her at last. "Oh, Percy," she said, "I've wondered for such a long time what it would be like to be married to you."

"Well," he said, "let me get out of this chair, and I'll show you."

Chapter Twenty-four

He carried her into the curtained bedroom. She noticed the crisp sheets as he laid her upon the bed. He'd planned for her seduction, she thought, not minding at all, only relieved that she was soon to be with the only man who could quiet the beast prowling inside her. "Percy...," she said in a small voice, "I am..."

"Afraid?" he said, unbuttoning her blouse. "Don't be."

"But I don't know what to do...."

"It doesn't matter. We'll find our way together."

And they did. Hours later, when the room had darkened and the moon risen, she lay in his arms along the comforting length of his body and said, "You know what it felt like?"

"No, my love," he said, smoothing her hair. "Tell me."

"Home. It felt like coming home."

"You are home," he said.

Toward dawn, he took her hand and led her outside to the shower rigged in a screen of pine trees and
together they stood naked beneath its flow, Mary
squealing and splashing to Percy's deep laughter.
This is Eden, she thought, and we are Adam and
Eve. Were there ever a man and woman so made for
each other? After a while, she ran her hands up the
bronzed breadth of his chest and whispered, "Percy,"
with urgency, and he led her back to the cabin.

When morning came, he made them breakfast—
bacon, eggs, and the peaches and cream they'd for-
gone the day before. Mary ate ravenously, her appetite
soaring. Afterward, as they dressed, Percy said, "At
least I've got a change of clothes to make this look
good when I drive you to Hoagy's, but what about
you?"

Mary touched the collar of her blouse and looked
down at her brown riding skirt. "This is my everyday
costume when I'm not filling in for somebody in the
fields. Hoagy won't notice that I've not changed."

Loath to leave, she gazed at the lake from the
screened porch, and Percy came to stand behind her,
pushing his face into her hair. "Are you all right?" he
asked.

"I'll be fine," she said. "You were very considerate."

"There will be some tenderness. I'll bring by a salve
this afternoon."

"You won't be able to find me. I don't know yet
what sections I'll be inspecting."

His arms tensed slightly. "Tonight, then. Will you be home?"

"Yes, I'll make a point of it. I'll have supper for us, and...you can stay. Toby won't be around. Thursday he spends the night at his brother's. They go fishing."

His hold tightened, and her blood pounded. "I'll leave the car and walk down," he said, his voice husky. He turned her around and lifted her chin, his thumb caressing its cleft. "Are you happy, Mary?"

"More than I ever thought possible," she said. She touched his face in wonder. It was somewhat bristly now, the blond hair hardly visible. Her breath caught in her throat. This was love, she thought, not lust. How could she ever have been so afraid of loving him? They would work out their differences. They needed each other. She would be good to him. He would never be sorry that he had married her. Desire rose in her, mindless of the throbbing rawness left by their lovemaking. If she didn't leave now, she never would, and she had to get back to Hoagy. She stepped away. "We must go, Percy. If I'm much later, Hoagy will suspect something, and I'm sure he hasn't fed Shawnee."

Percy watched her tie back her hair. "Do you think we could discuss a wedding date tonight, honey? I want us to get married as soon as possible."

Her hands fell. She turned toward him with a desolate face. It had not occurred to her that he would want to marry before the cotton was brought in. A wedding wasn't possible, not with all the preparations it would entail. From now on, she must spend every day, every working hour, at Somerset. "I...thought we'd wait until after the harvest," she said, her expression pleading with him not to be wounded that she must put him off. "So much is riding on this one, as you know. It has to make. There can be no delays, no interference. I'll have to be at the plantation constantly. I...thought you agreed to understand."

He swallowed, and she saw the hard knot of disappointment slide down the strong column of his neck. "Well, then, when do you foresee would be a good time?"

"The end of October?"

"The *end* of October! That's a long time away, Mary."

"I know." She slipped her arms up around his neck. "But it will come. In the meantime, if we're discreet, we can be together. And I'll make the delay up to you, I promise. I love you."

Surrendering, Percy closed his arms around her. "All right," he said, "but I wish it were tomorrow. I have a feeling that it's a mistake to wait."

"It would be a mistake *not* to wait," Mary said. "That way, there will be time to plan a beautiful wedding and prenuptial activities and have a proper honeymoon. We can *relax.* You'll see."

April ended, then May, both dry and hot. Mary worried. But at the beginning of June, shortly before the bolls released their white treasure, a soft rain fell, soaking the cotton plants with the right amount of moisture to succor their thirst. Providence continued to shine, but Mary rose every morning with a tightness in her chest. If only the rain held off now, and all other forms of disaster, then the final chapter of the Tolivers' long adversity would end.

Cautious about her happiness, she could not resist imagining the harvest in, the mortgage almost paid, money in the bank. She could begin her marriage to Percy on a clean page, and as long as he abided by his promise, she would make sure he never suffered because of Somerset. She would juggle her time and energies, beginning with the hiring of a manager to relieve her of some of her duties. She'd scour the state, if need be, to find a replacement for the lazy and unreliable Hoagy Carter.

Already, they were planning their life together. They would live in the Toliver mansion. That would please the senior Warwicks immensely, having their son and daughter-in-law and eventually all the little Warwicks a few houses away. Percy had immediate plans after the marriage to install electricity *and a telephone, by God*! Bathrooms were to be added, the kitchen modernized, and the carriage house converted into a garage. The overhaul included the rose garden and grounds and new paint for the exterior. They would keep Sassie and Toby on, of course, but they would hire extra staff, and Percy was adamant they employ a bookkeeper to free Mary from her ledgers when she was home.

Their main concern became keeping the comings and goings of their meetings—and couplings—secret. Mary made no bones to Percy about the importance of safeguarding her reputation from sexual scandal. People might frown at her because she didn't atone for her father's favoritism, but never did they look down their noses. She was a Toliver! But her name would not save her if it was discovered that she was sleeping with a man out of wedlock, and certainly Percy did not want it suspected that he'd bedded his wife before he married her.

Therefore they schemed their liaisons and hideaways carefully. Most often, they met in Percy's isolated cabin by the lake. Not a soul suspected the activities going on behind the rough plank door. With the harvest at hand, the returned Sassie assumed that Mary was spending every night she was absent from home at the Ledbetter house. Hoagy believed his mistress was turning Shawnee toward Houston Avenue at the end of a long, hot day, oddly happier now, more filled out, some flesh on her bones at last.

Thursday evenings they spent at the Toliver mansion when both Sassie and Toby were out for the night, hardly allowing themselves enough time to eat the simple supper Mary had prepared before they dashed up the stairs to her bedroom, shedding clothes as they went. Mary, once living only for her days at Somerset, now lived for her nights with Percy.

Only Sunday afternoons could they bear to share, and these were with Ollie and Charles Waithe, who made a fourth for bridge. Though Mary could hardly endure them, the Sunday occasions were necessary as subterfuge. She was sure that simply by glancing at her and Percy, the others would know where the two of them would rather be. It was agony to sit at the table with him, sometimes as partner, sometimes as opponent, sensually aware of his every movement while unable to risk a smile or even a look in his direction. The afternoons stretched interminably, and it was always with huge relief that she heard the grandfather clock strike the hour for her guests to leave.

Despite his objections, Percy came to see the prudence of keeping their intention to marry secret for a while. Secrecy protected them from speculation about the extent of their intimacy, which Mary lived in fear of being exposed. They both agreed that there would be no end to Beatrice's flurry once she learned of a wedding at hand, and, of course, there was Ollie to consider.

They had discussed Ollie at length. "He has to be told soon, Mary," Percy said.

"Why?"

"Because he's in love with you, you beautiful simpleton. He's loved you as long as I have."

"I suspected so once, but I thought his feelings had mellowed to friendship."

"Believe me, they haven't. If I'd thought there was the slightest chance you'd return his love, I'd never have pursued you. If it weren't for Ollie, I'd be lying in a French grave by now."

"I know," Mary said, gripped by the usual chill at the thought. "Do you think he still holds on to his hope?"

"Not consciously, but until a ring is on your finger, a part of him will believe he has a chance."

"Give me until the middle of August, then buy me a ring," Mary said.

Chapter Twenty-five

It was the end of the second week in August. The time had come to make the first pass at the fields. "Monday morning at daybreak," Mary informed her tenants the Saturday before picking began. "Get plenty of rest tomorrow. On Monday we'll start on the south and work east. Tuesday, from west to north. Be ready to leave in your wagons by four-thirty."

That Sunday afternoon, Mary was too restless to play bridge and overbid her hand twice. "I hope that's not an omen," Ollie commented.

Mary interpreted the remark as full of insinuation. "What do you mean?" she demanded, her sharp tone like the crack of a whip in the quiet, tense room, and all three men turned their heads to her in surprise.

"I was referring to the outcome of the game," Ollie said with a quiet smile of apology. "You must have thought I was referring to the harvest. It was a stupid thing to say tonight of all nights. I'm sure you have everything in hand out at Somerset. I predict that by this time next Sunday, you'll be the happiest woman in the county."

"Let's drink to that," Charles said, quickly filling their glasses with champagne smuggled down the block from the DuMont wine cellar. Prohibition was for those who had voted for it, was their mutual opinion. As usual, Mary declined, but she lifted her water glass. "To our queen of cotton," Charles said. "May it always be king!"

"Hear! Hear!" they chorused, and clinked glasses. But Ollie's remark had put an end to any pretense of enjoying the evening. It had thrown into relief the burning question always at the forefront of her mind these days: Had she overbid her hand?

She pleaded an early rise the next morning and sent her guests home before the normal time, including Percy, who usually returned after everyone had gone. "I'm as nervous as a cat in a roomful of rockers," she explained to him out of earshot of the others, and he squeezed her arm in understanding.

It was the stillness that woke her a few hours after midnight. Bolting upright in bed, she listened, sniffing the air. She threw back the covers and unlatched the French doors to the verandah off her room. *"Oh, no!"* she cried in mouth-drying horror. Far off to the east where Somerset lay, jagged lances of lightning split the night sky. There was the smell of rain, the distant crack of thunder. And something else. Mary sniffed. Dust hung in the still air. *Oh, God, no! Don't do this to me. Please, God. Don't do this to me. Papa, Thomas—help me!*

Her heart was threatening to leap from her body as she tore back inside, taking time only to lace on her boots and grab a robe before running downstairs.

She bridled Shawnee and leaped onto his back in her nightclothes, spurring the gelding with her boot heels out of the stable and down the sleeping boulevard to the back road that led toward the plantation. "Go, boy!" Mary urged the aging horse, bending low over his flowing mane to aid his speed. Her mind cleared as they raced through the night. The tenants knew what to do. Only this week she'd given each family their instructions in case of rain. *Yes'm, Miss Mary, we all goin' to get out in them fields with our sacks and start pickin' fast as we can. When them raindrops start fallin', we goin' run get our sacks under the tarps in the wagons.*

Hoagy was up and had marshaled his family. Thank God both his grown sons were home, one on furlough from the army and the other looking for a job, cotton sacks already slung over their shoulders. "Mornin', Miss Mary," they said, pretending not to notice that she was still in her nightgown and robe.

"How bad, Hoagy?"

Hoagy shrugged. "Your guess is as good as mine, Miss Mary."

"Give me a sack."

The night was still pitch black when the Carter

family, seven in all, and Mary, each taking a row, began picking cotton. Not a drop of rain had fallen, but lightning still lit up the sky and dust clung in the air. She prayed for wind. It was the stillness that terrified her. Far across and down the long, stretching fields, she saw the wink of kerosene lamps and kerchiefed heads bobbing low and steady over the sea of white bolls, hands plucking swiftly and expertly while the night sky urged, *Hurry, hurry, hurry.*

The hail came thirty minutes later, followed by the rain. Mary and the seven Carters were way down their rows, too far to make it to the wagons. "Get under your sacks!" somebody called out. "The hail's as hard as river rocks." But even as the hail pelted, Mary kept picking until finally she knew it was useless. She drew her half-filled sack under her, covering it with her body and using her arms to protect her head. After a while she felt nothing of the pounding, only the sound of her heart slamming against the sack.

The rain was falling in sheets when she was finally pried away. "Miss Mary," Hoagy said, "there's nothing more we can do. Let's get our sacks back to the house."

Her nightclothes plastered to her, hems dragging in the mud, and the mire sucking at her soaked boots, Mary grasped her own sack and struggled toward her overseer's cabin.

"You'll catch your death, Miss Mary," Hoagy's wife said.

I wish, Mary thought.

Under the porch roof where they'd all gathered with their sacks, Mary peered through her streaming locks at the circle of faces around her. They seemed to be waiting for her to say something... do something. Their lives were in her hands, and she must find a way to repair the devastation of this night, make it go away. Hoagy, especially, was regarding her with an expectant eye. Unable to pay him outright for his overseer's services, she had promised him a greater percentage of the profits from the ginned crop. She squinted up into the bleak, sodden night, as if she might hear the voices of her father and grandfather advising her what to do, but all she heard was the mockery of the subsiding rain and the shattering of her dreams.

"Damn!" the overseer swore, wiping his face with a towel. "Another year gone for nothing."

"Wha' we goin' do, Pa?" one of the little girls asked tearfully, her face smeared with mud.

"Right now we're going to shake out this cotton to dry and see what we have," Mary said. "Mattie"—she turned to Hoagy's wife—"get the fire going in the front room to dry the sacks as best as they can be. In the morning we'll stuff the cotton back in them."

Through the black hour before dawn they worked, sorting the salvaged cotton into heaps in the three-room cabin to determine its value. "Bad. It looks bad, Miss Mary," Hoagy pronounced.

The rain had stopped and the night was clearing when Mary finally accepted a cup of coffee and stepped out onto the back porch to view her acreage. Dawn was spreading over the fields, slowly revealing the pummeled rows that yesterday had been stalwart stands of top-heavy cotton. Their stalks stood stripped, broken, beaten to mush, the decapitated cotton bolls mingling with hailstones as far as she could see. Not a plant had been spared.

"It looks like a mess of cooked greens and turnips," one of the Carter boys said in awe.

"Hush, son," admonished his mother, cutting a glance at Mary.

Mary heard the front screen door open and close. The Carters were suddenly quiet, and the silence fell like the kind in a classroom when the principal unexpectedly walks in. Before her numbed mind could register the cause, a jacket was draped around her shoulders and a familiar voice spoke in her ear. "I've come to take you home, Mary," Percy said. "There's nothing else you can do here now."

Mary glanced at the Carters. They were all staring tongue-tied at the all-important Percy Warwick with his arm around Miss Mary. If there had been any doubt about the nature of their relationship before, there was none now. Ignoring Percy, she said, "Hoagy, when you finish up here, do your best to make the rounds of Fair Acres and have everybody take their cotton to the Ledbetter weighing station.

Sam and I will assess the situation at Somerset and we'll weigh ours there. Meet me at the house at ten in the morning."

"Yes, Miss Mary."

"Good morning to you all," Mary said, wriggling her shoulders imperceptibly as a hint to Percy to remove his arm. "I appreciate your hard efforts tonight. Mattie, thanks for the coffee, and I'm sorry about the mess."

Percy dropped his arm and, nodding to the family, followed Mary out through the rooms full of soggy cotton to the Pierce-Arrow. She stopped short of scolding him for his needless and embarrassing appearance when she saw the hail-dented fenders and mud-caked wheels. After drawing a deep breath, she asked, "Why did you come, Percy?"

He adjusted the coat around her shoulders. "I came to make sure you were all right and to take you home."

"What makes you think I should go home? I'm needed here. Besides, I came on Shawnee."

The animal was still standing patiently where Mary had left him tied to the hitching post, rain still streaming off his flanks. He turned his head at the sound of his name and cast her a mournful glance.

"I'll get one of the Carters to ride him home," Percy said.

"No, you don't understand. All the Carter boys are needed here, and I need Shawnee to ride over to

Somerset. When I finish there, I have to go into town to see Emmitt Waithe."

"Mary, for God's sake, I'll take you to Emmitt's."

"No!" Her tone brooked no argument. "I must go alone."

The Carters had gathered at the screen door, staring openly.

"Like that?" Percy asked, casting a wry glance over her wet, mud-soaked clothes. "At least let me take you home to get into some dry clothes before you catch cold."

Mary thought quickly. Percy was right. Appearing in a nightgown and robe to her tenants would not inspire confidence right now, and she was feeling chilled. The last thing she needed was to become sick. "All right," she agreed grudgingly.

They tied the gelding to the bumper, and she and Percy sat without speaking as he concentrated on keeping the Pierce-Arrow and Shawnee from bogging down in the mud. Motorcar and horse were forced to take the recently paved road into Howbutker rather than the muddy track that would have offered a less visible entry into Houston Avenue. The town was just opening up, and driver and bedraggled passenger were both thankful that only a few shopkeepers were about to gape at the odd procession making its slow way around Courthouse Circle.

"Okay, how bad is it?" Percy asked when he stopped in front of the verandah. "Are you wiped out?"

Mary sat stiffly, her profile to him. "I still have a few cards to play."

He put his hand on her shoulder and said quietly, "I'm sorry, sweetheart, but a deal's a deal."

"Did I say it wasn't?" She shrugged off the jacket and threw open the door. "Just don't...look so happy about it."

"I'm not happy about it. Mary, for God's sake..." Percy slid out of the car as she hurried around to untie Shawnee. "How could you think that? Honey, I know how you must feel—"

"The blazes you do! How could you possibly know how I feel? Seeing Somerset wasted is like seeing your child dead. There is no describing the...the desolation I feel."

"But, honey, you knew the risk going in...."

Mary could feel her face flame. "Do *not* lecture me, Percy! The last thing I desire from you right now is a dose of Warwick logic. Go to work or something, and let me handle *my* business."

With that, boots squishing and her garments weighted with mud, Mary pulled at Shawnee's bridle and stalked off to the stable to dry and feed him, leaving Percy to watch the woman he loved abandon him in her hour of need.

Chapter Twenty-six

In late morning, bright with sunshine and birdsong as if the night's devastation had never been, Mary and Shawnee arrived at Emmitt Waithe's office.

The lawyer moaned when she entered and waved her to a chair, falling wearily into his. He appeared more stooped than usual, as if his part in the disaster were a weight carted on his shoulders.

"Somerset is not done yet, Mr. Waithe," Mary began, ready to present a rehearsed line of arguments. "We talked about this contingency, and I still have one ace to play. Fair Acres. I want to borrow against Fair Acres." She realized she was talking too fast, but she must erase that look of "if only I hadn't listened to you" regret from the face of her father's trusting friend. "In order to protect the assets of the trust, I'm sure you'll see it as your fiduciary responsibility to help me obtain a loan. It is the only way—"

Emmitt slammed his hand upon the desk, cutting her short. "*Don't* tell me my fiduciary responsibility now, young lady! Not when you were so eager to set it aside earlier! If I had stuck by my *fiduciary* responsibility, you wouldn't be sitting here this morning and I wouldn't have been up all night cursing myself. Vernon Toliver must be squirming in his grave."

"No, he isn't," Mary argued, determined to keep her tone reasonable. "Papa would have understood the risk. He would have understood your allowing me to take it. So, all right, I took it and I lost. Now I have to salvage what I can. The only way is to mortgage Fair Acres. I should be able to get a large enough loan to meet my monetary obligations. Then next year, with a good harvest—" At the look Emmitt fired over his spectacles she stopped and shrugged. "What other choice do I have?"

"Dare I mention the obvious?"

"No, sir. I will not sell Somerset."

Emmitt removed his glasses and rubbed his eyes. "So what do you want me to do?"

"I want you to set up an appointment at the bank today and help me negotiate a loan."

"Why so soon? Go home, get some rest. I'm sure you were up half the night. When you're rested, you'll have a better idea of what you need. What's the hurry to get to the bank today?"

"After last night, I won't be the only one heading for the bank, hat in hand. Howbutker State has a limit it will lend to farmers. I want to be among the first in line. I hope your appointment book is clear."

"Would it make any difference if it weren't?" With a heavy sigh, Emmitt replaced his glasses and pulled the telephone toward him. Within a few moments, he had explained the purpose of his call to the president of the Howbutker State Bank, who agreed to meet with him and Mary later that afternoon.

Mary had come from the plantation dressed in a well-worn riding skirt and blouse, both bearing traces of the mud caked on her boots. Entering the bank, much to her chagrin, she came face-to-face with the fashionably turned out Isabelle Withers, her displaced rival for Percy's affections. Isabelle's father was president of the Howbutker State Bank. "Well, my goodness, if it isn't Mary Toliver," the young woman purred, her amused gaze traveling the length of Mary's shabby work attire.

"It is indeed," Mary returned, her manner equally haughty.

"So sorry about the hail, and coming right at harvest, too. I'm sure Somerset was badly damaged."

"A bit, but we'll be fine."

"Really?" Isabelle twirled the long rope of pearls that set off the dropped waist of her voile dress. "Then this must be merely a social call on Father. He'll be so delighted. I'm sure to hear all about it this evening. How nice to see you again, Mr. Waithe. Here to pay a social call as well, I imagine." She smiled lushly, her bright red lips painted in the Hollywood fashion of

Theda Bara, and stepped around them, leaving a light floral scent in her wake.

Emmitt, blinking rapidly in clear confusion at the tense exchange, muttered, "Dear me."

In Raymond Withers's office, the lawyer let Mary do the talking, sitting in neutral silence as she laid out her case from a sheet of figures she'd hurriedly compiled on the kitchen table in the Ledbetter house. "I have the deed to Fair Acres, and I'm willing to turn it over as collateral right now if we can come to terms," she said, finishing her spiel.

Raymond Withers had listened attentively, drumming the plump pads of his soft, businessman hands only occasionally upon his desk. From a bookshelf behind him, his pride and joy—in sundry poses at various ages—grinned insipidly at Mary from ornate frames. For a few mellow ticks of a fine ormolu clock on his mantel, he remained silent, and Mary could read nothing of his thoughts behind his smooth face, a pose she was sure he assumed to keep his supplicants in suspense. When finally he spoke, a frown appeared. "We can help you to some extent," he said, "but I'm sure it will not meet your full financial requirements."

"What do you mean?" Mary asked, her heart lurching. Emmitt grunted shortly and sat a few inches straighter.

"The bank can loan you only forty percent of the

value of your collateral, which, since the war and cotton prices having dropped so drastically, is considerably less than what it was. Let's see..." The banker consulted the deed. "We're talking two sections. Their value today, what with the house, buildings, and equipment, would be..." As if he could not bear to say the sum aloud, he wrote a figure on a sheet of paper and passed it across the desk.

Mary snatched it up. "But Fair Acres is worth twice that!" she cried, mentally calculating that a loan based on the bank's appraisal would not begin to cover the cost of her expenses. She handed the slip to Emmitt.

"It is to you, but not to the board of directors, I'm afraid," the banker said.

Emmitt cleared his throat. "Oh, come on, Raymond. Surely there's something you can do. You control the board of directors. If Mary defaults—even if you lend her fifty percent of the true value of Fair Acres—you can sell it and still make a profit."

Raymond Withers considered a moment. "Well, there is one condition that might sway the board if Miss Toliver agrees to it."

Mary's hopes rose. "And what is that?"

"That you do not replant your acreage in cotton. It's too risky a cash crop. Peanuts, sorghum, sugarcane, corn, rice—there are any number of crops, even cattle, that land would support. We might see our way to lending you what you ask if you'd agree to put all of your plantation under another, more favorable form of production, but not cotton. That way, the bank would have a better assurance of having its money returned."

"I can't possibly agree to that," Mary said, appalled that the man would even suggest such a thing to a Toliver. "Somerset is a cotton plantation—"

"*Was* a cotton plantation," the banker corrected, his patience clearly growing thin. "You would be wise to accept that point of view, Miss Toliver. The day of cotton is past in East Texas. Its sun is setting. Other countries are producing as much as and a better quality of cotton than the whole Cotton Belt put together and selling it cheaper. Are you aware of a new fabric, a synthetic to replace silk, that is being produced in France?" he asked. "It's only a matter of time that it will replace cotton in garments and be manufactured over here. Synthetic material is lighter in weight, inexpensive to manufacture, and more durable than cotton. That's a mighty lot of competition for a crop that can hardly withstand the devastation of the boll weevil, let alone—as you've now witnessed—the destruction of nature."

The banker leaned back in his chair and laced his fingers over his suit vest. "Now, if you're willing to replant with any revenue source but cotton, I believe I can persuade the board to increase the loan by ten percent of its original value. Otherwise, forty at the appraisal price."

Mary was too numb to speak. Again Emmitt

cleared his throat. "What would it take to get what she's asking, Raymond?"

"Well…" The banker unlaced his hands and addressed Emmitt as if Mary were not there. "If she were able to get someone of whom the bank approves to cosign the note, we might be able to lend her the money. That person would have to understand that he's on the hook to the bank if Miss Toliver defaults. Because she's under twenty-one, she cannot legally be forced to pay him back since, as you know, the law does not hold minors responsible for loans." He returned his attention to Mary. "Do you know of anyone who would be willing to cosign your note under those conditions, Miss Toliver?"

The trace of innuendo in the question sent a shock through her. He knows about Percy and me, she thought in alarm. He thinks I dashed his and Isabelle's hopes that she would become Mrs. Percy Warwick. Did the whole town know about her and Percy, and if so, how much? "Do you have someone in mind?" she asked, keeping her gaze level.

The banker's smile slid into a smirk. "Why, the bank would highly approve of Percy Warwick's signature, which should not be too difficult for you to obtain, Miss Toliver, your… families being so close and all."

Mary gathered up the papers she had brought. "Thank you for your time, Mr. Withers. Mr. Waithe and I will give this some thought and get back to you as soon as possible."

"Don't wait too long, Miss Toliver," the banker said, rising. "We have only so much cash to lend to farmers, and already there are others submitting applications."

Following Mary out of the bank, Emmitt appeared shaken. "Mary, my dear, what are you going to do? What do you have in mind?"

Mary drew in a deep breath. "Something I expect to spend the rest of my life regretting."

Chapter Twenty-seven

On the way back to Houston Avenue, Mary wrestled with the risk she was about to undertake, but what other choice did she have? She would not put Somerset under another cash crop. That was out of the question. She knew what she was jeopardizing by going to Percy for his signature. *A deal is a deal,* he'd reminded her, and he would expect her to honor it. Indeed, she was no Toliver at all if she did not. It was she who had brought up the no-lend policy, but it was not a loan she was seeking, merely a signature. No money need exchange hands. Yes, he would be on the hook for the loan if the harvest failed next year, but he wouldn't lose a penny. Fair Acres was hers outright. If disaster struck, she would sell it and pay Percy back with the proceeds. It knotted every muscle in her body to think it, but she would be forced to sell part of Somerset as well to pay off her remaining debt to the bankers in Boston. The risk, however, was worth it.

All she had to do was convince Percy that her request was not going back on her promise—that it was not breaking the rule the families had lived by for nearly a century. To the clip-clop of Shawnee's hooves, Mary reflected on that rule, examined it for the first time since accepting it without question as part of the strong fabric of the families' history. She asked herself why they had adopted such a principle in the first place. After consideration, it seemed a cold, even heartless approach to friendship. Who better to ask for aid than a friend? Who better to offer it than a friend? They were all as close as family. Why had they agreed to such a practice?

And then, contrary to all she'd prefer to believe, the answer presented itself as clear as the bright afternoon. The head of each family had known that to borrow from the other was to lose power. Worse, to borrow meant to be beholden, and that would diminish, if not destroy, the friendship. To be in the debt of a friend was to lose equality with him. Even if the debt was repaid, the borrower would always owe the lender. It was a reality of human nature.

Well, that's as may be, Mary told herself, but a signature backed by collateral was not a loan. She was not breaking their deal.

On Houston Avenue, Mary stopped at a neighbor's house to put in a call to Percy at his office. Given the probability of the operator listening in, not to mention the party line, on the rare occasions she'd telephone him, they addressed each other as mere neighbors and always veiled their conversations.

"Why, Mary Toliver, this is a surprise," he said, sounding greatly relieved to hear from her. "I'm so sorry about this morning. Is the damage too great for recovery?"

"Not at all, Percy. The fields are wrecked, but the house was barely touched. That's why I'm calling. I'm afraid it will need some repair. Could you send a man out to assess what needs to be done?"

"It will be my pleasure. What time would you like him to meet with you?"

"Shall we say five o'clock?"

"He'll be there."

Mary hung up thinking that as careful as they had been, it was no wonder their relationship had been discovered. It took only the Warwicks' cook telling somebody else's cook about the meals for two she often prepared for Mister Percy to take to Lawsey knew where and on whose account. Since he was not seen with any other belle in town, a good guess was that he was exchanging salt and pepper shakers with Mary Toliver, the girl he'd kissed in front of God and everybody the morning he left for war.

What did it matter, anyway, Mary reflected, if she and Percy were soon to be married? She inhaled sharply, catching herself. What did she mean—*if*?

He was already at the cabin by the time she arrived.

He had not taken time to change out of his suit but had removed his jacket, loosened his tie, and rolled up his sleeves. The second she drove up he opened the door and went out to the buggy to help her down.

"Lord, it's good to have you in my arms again," he said with a sigh after kissing her long and hard.

She pressed her face into his neck. "It's wonderful to be in them, too," she said.

They went inside, and Percy poured two glasses of iced tea. A breeze was blowing from the lake, stirring the ceiling fans, providing some relief from the humidity following the rain. Handing her the tea, he said, "I'm happy as a puppy at his mama's teat that you wanted to see me, but you must be bone-tired and dead for sleep. Are you sure you shouldn't be home getting some rest?"

Mary sat in one of the parlor chairs. "I had to see you, Percy."

"Judging by your tone, this doesn't sound like the usual reason."

"It isn't. I'm in trouble."

Percy sipped his tea casually, but his brows arched over the rim like two warning flags. He took a seat on the couch, away from her. Mary interpreted that as a bad sign. He had guessed why she'd come. "Well, let's hear it," he said.

She swallowed at the gush of raw fear making its way to her throat. She took a cooling draft of the tea and tried to curb the wild thrashing of her heart.

"I went today with Emmitt to negotiate a loan at the Howbutker State bank. We spoke with Raymond Withers...." There was no reaction to the name of his former lover's father, and she hurried to tell him of the niggardly value he attached to the land, deliberately omitting the banker's condition that she grow another cash crop in order to secure the loan she needed. "The amount he's willing to lend won't cover the cost of seeds," she said, exaggerating, "much less see me through another year."

"So, what's your next step?" he asked, his gaze steady.

There was nothing to do but come right out with it. Against the warning shouts in her head, she said, "He's willing to loan me the amount I need if you will cosign the note."

In the ensuing silence, the innocent tinkle of ice in Percy's glass sounded like a gunshot. "And what did you tell him?"

"I... told him I'd let him know."

"I would have thought you'd have given him his answer right then. Why didn't you? We made a deal."

Mary sat forward. "Yes, I know we did," she said, "but this is not going back on our deal. All I want is your signature, for heaven's sake. It's not the same as asking for money. As a matter of fact, you wouldn't be out a penny, even if I default."

"How's that?"

"If we have another bad year, I'll sell Fair Acres and even part of Somerset if I have to. You'd get your money back in full. I give you my word, Percy."

Percy unfolded his powerful legs and stood up. She had the frightening impression of a bull pawing the ground with nostrils flaring. "Your word," he repeated. "You gave your word right here in this room that you'd never ask me to bail Somerset out if it got into trouble. You promised to let it go and be content to be my wife."

"Percy, this is not the same thing. You're not bailing Somerset out. All I want is your signature. It's not the same thing."

"The hell it isn't. You're splitting hairs and you know it. I'm sorry for what's happened, and that's the truth, Mary, but I'm holding you to our deal."

She stood up slowly. Shock whitened her face. "You're... you're not going to help me?"

"No, I'm not cosigning your note."

He had begun rolling down his sleeves. Mary watched in horror. He was *leaving*! She crossed to him and slipped her hands up his chest, beseeching his understanding with all the power of her great beauty. "Percy, I know this looks as if I'm reneging on our agreement, but try to see it another way. My promise was not to ask you for *money* to save Somerset. How am I breaking that promise by asking for your signature? You won't be out a cent."

She felt his chest contract and knew she'd aroused

him, but he continued buttoning his cuffs. "Suppose you get your loan and you have another bad year. What then? With Fair Acres gone, you'll have nothing else to use as collateral."

"I've told you. I'll sell part of the plantation. I promise, Percy. You have to believe me."

"I wish I could." He removed her hands and tightened the knot of his tie. "This will happen again. You know it will. You'll expect to have a cash reserve to see you through, just like you did before you bought Fair Acres. But how long do you think that money will stay in the bank when the temptations of new products, machines, irrigation systems, and *land* come on the market? Mary Toliver Warwick will be the first in line to buy, if I know her, and you'll be right back in the same pickle you are now when disaster strikes again."

"We're not talking about then. We're talking about *now.*"

"And I'm saying that things will be no different then than now." He took a step nearer her, his eyes bleak with dissolving hope. "This isn't about the money, Mary. You know that. This is about the agreement we made. I promised to support your...obsession for Somerset—God knows that's what it is—but if it failed, you promised to let it go without it affecting our marriage. Prove to me you meant what you said."

She turned her back to him, clasping her hands

tightly. Tears darted to her eyes. "This is so unfair. You're trying to force my hand when all I want is your name on a piece of paper."

He came to stand behind her, and she could feel his desperate need that she tell him what he wanted to hear—what he *must* hear. "What would happen to us if you had to fall back on me again after we're married and I denied you—forced you to sell Somerset to meet your debts?"

Once again, she stood on the brink of a now-or-never crisis with him...the final one, an inner voice cautioned her. One step either way would decide her future.

He spun her around. "Tell me, *dammit!*"

She crossed her arms, hugging herself against the coming cold. "I...would hate you," she whispered, dropping her head.

An eternity passed before Percy spoke. "That's what I thought. So you never intended to abide by your promise."

She lifted her head. The same pain was breaking across his face that she'd felt when dawn washed over her devastated fields. "I *am* Somerset, Percy," she said. "I can't help it. That's who I am. That's the woman you love. To separate me from the plantation is to have half of me. I would not be the same. I'm convinced of that now. Share me, and you will have me whole."

A flush of disbelief stole beneath the perennial tan

of his face. "Are you telling me that I can't have one without the other? That if I don't cosign the loan, I'll lose you?"

Mary ran her tongue quickly over her dry lips. "Without Somerset, I'm lost to you anyway, Percy."

"Mary—" Percy clasped her by the shoulders. "Somerset is only *soil and seed.* I am flesh and blood."

"Percy," she pleaded, "I love you. Why can't you fit Somerset into our lives?"

He dropped his hands. "Maybe I could if I knew you loved me as much. You talk of sharing, but Somerset would get the biggest piece of you. You've proved it." He stepped back, his face contorted with pain. "Don't you realize what you're doing? You're about to lose me *and* the plantation. Where is your gain?" Suddenly an idea seemed to occur to him, too incredulous to entertain. He did not move, and his pupils contracted to the gleam of knife points. "But you don't plan to lose Somerset, do you."

When once again she bowed her head, he said slowly, "No...don't tell me you're going to Ollie...."

Her silence along with her bowed head and folded arms seemed answer enough.

He let out a bellow of rage and disgust. "My God, you'll stoop to any level to save that wasteland, won't you?" He grabbed his suit coat, roughly inserting into his pocket a small box that had lain beneath it. Yanking on his coat, he said, "Before you leave today, pack your things. You won't be coming here anymore."

Mary knew that appeal was useless. Without moving from her position, once again, forever, she watched him leave her. She heard the door of the Pierce-Arrow slam, then the crunch of tires on the bed of pine needles as he spun away. It was the middle of August. She realized that what he'd slipped into his pocket was the box containing her engagement ring.

Chapter Twenty-eight

Early the next morning, Mary called Ollie and asked for a ten o'clock appointment at the store. She'd spent a miserable night in the parlor in order to be near the door should Percy pull the bell rope. Countless times, she'd gone out on the verandah to peer up the street toward Warwick Hall, and once she'd wandered up the sidewalk in her robe, hoping to see the light still on in his bedroom as proof that he was unable to sleep from thinking of her.

No light shone.

With firm resolution she dressed in her outmoded traveling suit, drew her hair back into a sleek chignon, and hitched up Shawnee for a trip to the DuMont Department Store. Ollie had apparently been on the lookout for her and was waiting at the top of the stairs when she reached the upper level. "I am so sorry for your loss, Mary," he said, taking her hands in his, the crutches balanced deftly beneath his arms. "Was it as bad as we all feared?"

For a heartrending instant, Mary thought he was referring to Percy, but then she realized his concern was for the damage inflicted by the storm. Ollie was apparently unaware of their breakup. His face would have shown it. "Worse," she said briefly. "And that's why I'm here, Ollie."

Seated before his desk, Mary explained her purpose in coming, this time omitting nothing of the terms put forth by the banker. "I realize that in asking you to cosign the note, I'm going against the code our families have honored since our existence in Howbutker," she said.

"Oh, pshaw." Ollie waved an immaculate hand. "An archaic convention. Of course you can't put Somerset under anything but cotton. The very idea. Raymond Withers should know that there will always be a market for natural fibers, despite the ingress of synthetics. It will be my pleasure and honor to cosign your note, my dear."

Deeply moved as always by his unstinting generosity, Mary said, "There is one other thing I must tell you, Ollie. I asked Percy first."

"Ah," he said. "And he turned you down?"

"Yes."

He turned up his hands in a typical Gallic gesture. "Perhaps it's for the best. You wouldn't want to start off marriage with . . . complications."

Mary's eyes widened. "You . . . know about us?"

Ollie chuckled. "The way you feel about each

other is about as easy to miss as an elephant at a tea party. Of course I know. So does Charles. When's the wedding?"

Mary dropped her eyes to straighten a pleat of her skirt.

"Oh, no!" Ollie clapped his hands to his cheeks in dismay. "So that's why Percy took off this morning for the back of hell and begone. He called me around six, told me that he was catching the train, heading off to one of the Warwicks' logging camps in Canada, and didn't know when he'd be back. You all must have had *some* rift!"

Mary stiffened. Percy gone? To Canada? How typical of him! A clammy fear raised her flesh. It was one thing to be apart in the same neighborhood, divided by a few houses, but to be separated by a country... "He knew I was going to ask you to cosign the note," she said.

"And he did not approve?"

"He thinks I'm taking advantage of your affection for me."

Ollie sighed and shook his head, dislodging a strand of fine, light brown hair, skillfully trimmed to minimize its sparseness. "What troubles befall proud men," he said with mock pontification, and ducked his head to peer at Mary. "Not to mention proud women. It distresses me to know that I'm the cause of this huff."

"You're not," Mary quickly assured him. "Percy and I are to blame for our huff. We have... fundamental differences that we seem unable to work out. If you'd rather not pursue this further..."

"Oh, nonsense." Ollie motioned that she stay in her seat. "He'll get over it by the time he crosses the state line and will take the next train back. You two have never gone too long without making up. It's perfectly natural that you should come to me when he refused you. Why shouldn't you? I'll speak to him when he gets back, make him realize what an ass he's being." He beamed at her. "Now, sit right there while I call Raymond."

But as he reached for the telephone, Mary laid a hand over his wrist. "I'm in no position to lay conditions, Ollie, but I must extract a promise from you before we go through with this."

"Anything," he said quietly. "It's safe to say that I would promise anything you asked."

"Then it is this. If you are ever in financial straits and I'm in a position to help, you must allow me to assist. You must promise me that, Ollie."

Ollie patted her hand, his smile indulgent. "All right, *mon amie,* if you insist, I promise," he said, his manner suggesting doubt that his promise would ever be tested.

She took a handkerchief from her purse and dried her eyes. She was so emotional these days. "Ollie, you are the most wonderful friend, a treasure to us all. I'm asking only for your signature, mind. Your name will be off the loan next year after the harvest."

He lifted the telephone receiver from its hook. "Then let us hope for good weather and fair skies."

Their business with the bank concluded, Ollie escorted her to the stairs. "Are you sure Percy didn't say when he would be back?" she ventured.

His shoulders lifted in the way of his French ancestors. "No, Mary Lamb, but when he realizes how much he misses you, he'll hightail it home."

But Percy did not hightail it home. Throughout the next week as she supervised the cleanup of her fields, she kept an eye out for his red motorcar throwing up drying mud on one of Somerset's roads and each evening looked for his message on the hall table. Every time she turned Shawnee into the drive, she glanced down the street for a glimpse of the Pierce-Arrow and one evening even directed the faithful animal to the cabin by the lake. She found the windows dark, the door locked, a deserted air about the place, as if their times together there had never been. Depression like a flu virus set in, robbing her of energy and spirit.

August gave way to September, and her deepening sense of loss did not abate. Even Ollie was not around to comfort her. He was attending the fashion shows in New York and would be away until October. After that, he would be leaving for Europe on another buying trip that included Paris, where he planned to visit Miles and reunite with the French comrades with whom he'd served during the war. He would be gone for the better part of a year.

Her misery eventually manifested itself in bouts of nausea, suffered mostly in the mornings shortly after waking. Sassie termed the sickness "water fever," a strange summer illness afflicting those who drank from creek beds and lakes. Mary did not dispute her diagnosis, thinking perhaps the germ was a carryover from her swims in the lake with Percy. But one morning, as she bent over the basin in yet another fit of dry heaves, she debated whether or not her condition warranted an appointment with Doc Tanner. It was such a busy time, but she'd missed a period—

Her head popped up. In horror, she stared at herself in the mirror over the water stand. Fearfully, she felt her breasts. They were sore and swollen. *Oh, God!*

Down the stairs she flew to the library, where she yanked a heavy tome from a shelf. It addressed family illnesses, symptoms, and treatments and had been published in 1850, but certain ailments and their diagnoses had remained the same since the world began. Her head spinning, Mary read the symptoms of her feared infirmity. All applied to her—missed menstrual cycle, swollen breasts, darkened nipples, nausea, frequent urination, fatigue, loss of appetite...

Sweet Jesus, have mercy—she was pregnant!

She realized it was out of the question to go to Doc Tanner to have her suspicions confirmed. She'd have to consult a doctor out of the county, and that would require making an appointment by telephone. Her call would raise all kinds of talk on the party

line, even if the operator did not spread the word that
Mary Toliver was snubbing Doc Tanner to seek professional services elsewhere.

She sped immediately to Beatrice, finding her
snapping green beans with her cook. "Why, Mary!"
she exclaimed when she was ushered into the kitchen.
"What a wonderful surprise. What brings you down
the street?"

"Beatrice, I'm looking for Percy," Mary said in a
rush of words. She discovered she was wringing her
hands and jammed them into the pockets of her skirt.
"It's extremely important that I speak with him."

"Well, I wish I could speak with him, too, dear,"
Beatrice said, handing her bowl to the cook. She took
Mary's arm and directed her out of the kitchen into
her morning room. "He's somewhere in the Canadian Rockies working with one of the company's logging crews. He left two weeks ago, and neither his
dad nor I can get hold of him. Now, tell me, what's
the matter?"

"I...I need to speak with him, that's all," Mary
said, struggling to steady her breathing. Beatrice's
abilities of perception were as sharp as a honed saw,
and it would take little for her to discern the cause of
her anxiety. "We've had a falling-out," she explained.
"I came down to apologize and to tell him that I...I
can't seem to get through my days without him."

Beatrice smiled. "I'm happy to hear that, and he
will be, too. I rather suspected you all had had a row

when he took off to Canada to work on a logging site. When he calls, I'll give him your message, and that'll get him home soon enough." She cocked her head fondly. "Don't you think it's about time you children tied the knot? Any longer and I'll be too old to be a grandmother."

Mary's smile burst full and glowing, despite the worry twisting her nerves into knots. "We'll see that doesn't happen. But please tell Percy to hurry home as fast as he can. I... need him."

"I most certainly will, child." Beatrice held out her arms. "You've made me very happy."

Weeks passed. October arrived. Still no word from Percy. Each morning, Mary examined her abdomen for outward signs of the life forming inside her and was relieved to find none. But something else was growing within her as well. Like a worm, it had waited until all her losses were complete before inching from its burrow. She'd become aware of it shortly after the hail. One morning, tired from worry and lack of sleep, she had looked out over the ruined acres of Somerset and felt the land jeering at her, reveling in the failure of all her hard work and sacrifices. The feeling continued throughout the arduous weeks of cleanup, sorting the salvage, and struggling with the tenants' low morale. It was her condition, she told herself. She had read that pregnancy affects a woman's mental and emotional outlook. It could not be true that the land and nature had conspired against her, turned gloating traitor to all her hopes and dreams. Still, the notion persisted, and often as she rode Shawnee down the pummeled rows, one arm cradling her womb, it seemed that she could hear Percy's voice in the sway of the bordering pines: *Somerset is only soil and seed. I am flesh and blood.*

By the middle of October, she had come to accept with certainty that she could live without Somerset, but never, ever without Percy.

Now at night when she couldn't sleep, she sat in her window seat facing northward, where Canada lay. Hugging her knees to her chest, she prayed, "Please, God, have Percy come home. I'll give up Somerset. I'll be content to be his wife and the mother of our child the rest of my life. I know what's important now. I know that I can never be happy without him. Please, God, send Percy home."

Then one morning, Sassie huffed upstairs to tell Mary, hardly able to drag herself out of bed, that Miss Beatrice was downstairs and wished to speak with her. She ran down in her bare feet, but her surge of relief froze to incredulity when Beatrice explained that Percy had not returned to Seattle with the logging crew. He'd sent word by way of one of the men to let his parents know that he'd gone on a surveying trip deep into the Canadian Rockies and wouldn't be returning for another month. Mary barely heard Beatrice's rant of chagrin. "What could Percy be thinking to go off and leave his father to manage everything alone? Jeremy is not yet entirely well, and our son is needed at the plant. You all must have had one humdinger of a row, Mary Lamb."

Slowly, Mary felt for the safety of the chair behind her, feeling that the earth had opened beneath her feet. She cupped her hands over the imperceptible swelling of her belly. What am I going to do? she asked herself.

And then she knew.

Chapter Twenty-nine

That evening, at Mary's request, Ollie came to call. He had returned a few days before from his trip to New York and brought her an adorable teddy bear from Macy's department store. "I would have preferred something from Tiffany's," he said, "but you would have refused it." The humid heat of summer was over. It was a perfect time to sit in the gazebo and enjoy the first nip of fall in the air. Seated in the swing, his crutches propped on the trellised wall, Ollie sipped a cup of chocolate and waited for Mary to state the reason for the invitation. Night closed in, the stars drew close. An owl hooted from the fence.

"I know there's something else on your mind besides a desire to hear about my trip, Mary. What is it?"

She said in a voice dulled by pain, "I'm pregnant, Ollie. The baby is Percy's."

Complete silence fell, disturbed by the indifferent sounds of night creatures in shrubs and trees.

After a moment, Ollie coughed. "Well, Mary, that's wonderful."

Her face in profile, she said, "It would be if Percy were here."

"Does he know?"

"He'd left before I found out."

"What is the problem, *mon amie?*" His baby-smooth brow creased. As usual, the empty trouser leg had been pulled behind at the point of his knee and pinned discreetly. "You and Percy have been in love with each other since puberty. Once you tell him, he'll come home and marry you like a shot. From the way you've moped around since he's been gone, I do believe you'd both be better miserable together than apart. Who else but you could have sent him off to the wilds of Canada?"

"The problem is that I have no way to reach him. The last word to his parents was that he'd be gone for a month or longer. That was yesterday."

"You mean...Oh, Mary Lamb..." Ollie reached for her hand. "How...far along are you?"

"I'm not really sure. I would guess I'm into my third month. I'm beginning to show a bit."

"Oh, my dear girl, we'll have to think of something. You wouldn't...you're not thinking of destroying the baby, are you?"

"No, of course not. I wouldn't even consider it."

"Well, we'll have to set about finding him, that's all." Ollie wriggled in the swing as if he meant to strap on his crutches and lead the search. "I can hire trackers."

"No, Ollie." Mary put a restraining hand on his arm. "There isn't time for that. Finding Percy could take weeks or longer. By the time he got home and we were married, we could never pass off the baby's birth as premature."

Ollie looked at her helplessly, his eyes deeply troubled. "Well, then, what are you going to do?"

She drew a deep breath and quickly—before she lost her nerve—turned to face him and asked point-blank, "Ollie, would you... would you consider marrying me and raising the child as your own? Percy need never know. He mustn't ever know. I'd... be a good wife to you, Ollie. I promise. You'd never be sorry you married me."

Ollie's soft mouth rounded in mute astonishment. When he'd caught his breath, he said, "Marry you? *You,* Mary? Never...."

She heard his refusal like a thunderclap in her ears. She could not believe it. Hope plummeted like a dropped anvil, replaced immediately with shame. "Ollie, dear, forgive me. I'm so sorry I put you in this position. How awfully insensitive and ungrateful of me, after all you've done—"

"No, no, Mary! You don't understand!" He waved his hand frantically. In his distress, he'd moved peril-ously close to slipping off the swing. "Never in my wildest dreams did I ever think I'd have the chance to marry you. As God is my witness, I've loved you since the day you were born, but..." His face puckered as if he were on the verge of crying. "But you see, I...can't marry you. I can't marry anybody."

She placed a gentle hand on his shoulder. "Is it because of your leg? Ollie, your loss doesn't make you any less a man. In fact, the way you've coped with it...the courage you've shown, makes you an even better man than before, if that's possible."

"It's not only the loss of the leg, Mary Lamb..." Even in the darkness, Mary could see his face reddening. "There were...other losses as well. You see, the grenade injured...my...manhood. I cannot give you children. I cannot be a husband to you. I could only love you."

Paralyzed with disbelief, she listened to his halting description of his injury as her father's parting words to her in his letter blazed in her memory: "I wonder that in remembering you as I have, I have not prolonged the curse that has plagued the Tolivers since the first pine tree was cleared from Somerset." She saw Ollie's lips move, but she heard only the prophetic voices of Miles and Miss Peabody jeering in her head. She pressed her hands to her cheeks. *Oh, please, God, no. Not this.*

"So you see that I can't marry you, Mary, though I'd like to with every fiber of my being," Ollie said, looking on the verge of complete collapse on the swing.

She dropped her hands and with all her might forced a demeanor that showed none of the emotions rocking her soul. "Does Percy know of the extent of your injury?" she asked.

"No. He is never to know. It would add to the guilt he already feels."

Mary strained for a smile. "Then I can't imagine a woman needing more from a man than to be wanted with every fiber of his being," she said.

His sandy brows rose almost to his hairline. "Does that mean that you—that you still would marry me?"

"Yes," she said, "if you will have me."

"*Have* you?" His cherubic face exploded with joy. "Of *course* I will have you! Mary, my dear...I never dared hope—" He stopped in midsentence, struck dumb. "But...what about Percy? What will this do to him? *Mon dieu*, Mary, he'll be crushed. He'll think I *betrayed* him!"

She put her hand on his sound knee. "No, he won't. He'll think *I* betrayed him, that I enticed you to marry me so that I could be assured of the plantation always having your financial support. He'll believe that because he understands clearly that I would do anything to save Somerset. It was the cause of our row."

"But, Mary, how can you allow him to believe that of you, when it's not true?"

"I can allow it in order to spare him the truth of why we married. Believing I married his best friend on behalf of Somerset will hurt him far less. You must surely see that, Ollie."

Ollie wagged his head as if it were buzzing with bees. "Oh, Mary Lamb, I want to marry you. I want the baby. I want it more than anything in the world, but to hurt Percy..."

Without hesitation, Mary knelt before the swing. She gripped both his hands. "Listen to me, Ollie. Percy will never blame you for marrying me. He knows how you feel about me. We must let him believe I married you because of Somerset. It is the only way to spare this baby from scandal. Imagine what the stigma of being born out of wedlock would do to the child—what it would do to the Warwick name, to mine, to the child's. You're leaving for Europe soon. I'll go with you. By the time we return, the baby will still be young enough to convince everyone it was born a couple of months later. If I wait, I won't have that advantage."

"But Percy loves us so...how can we do this to him?"

Mary took his face in a firm grip and stared deep into his eyes. "We will make it up to him, Ollie. We will love him as we always have, with the deepest love of friendship."

"But...now that you've...known each other, how will you bear to be apart, Mary? I couldn't share you, not even with Percy. How can we go on together, the three of us, as only friends?"

"We will have to, my dear," Mary said, drawing up to kiss his forehead. "For the sake of all those we love—your father, Beatrice and Jeremy, Percy, the baby, and . . . ourselves—we have to. Percy will marry, have his own children, and the time we were together will become a distant memory for us both." The lie flowed glibly off her tongue, but she spoke with her deepest sincerity when she said, "I will always be faithful to you, Ollie. I promise you that."

Ollie fished a handkerchief from the inner pocket of his suit and pressed it to his eyes. "I can't believe this," he said. "To think that you . . . would marry me . . . that my most impossible dream has come true. The only blunt to my happiness is Percy. . . . He will be devastated, but . . . I don't know anything else to do."

"Exactly," Mary said, and rose to sit beside him on the swing. There would be a place in her heart for this man, she thought, holding back her tears. He would never lack for her affection, commitment, and respect, but in that moment, she felt a movement within her, as if the part of her that belonged to the only man she would ever love had stolen off to curl up in some remote, hidden corner of her being, like an animal whose time has come to die.

Chapter Thirty

They were married in the DuMonts' elegantly appointed parlor a week later and left the same evening on the first leg of their journey to New York, where they would board an ocean liner to Europe. Mary wore a short, loose-fitting chemise of white satin, the first wedding dress ever worn in Howbutker that deviated from the traditional long gown and train. Only Abel, Jeremy and Beatrice Warwick, the Emmitt Waithes, and their son, Charles, were in attendance. Emmitt gave her away. The ceremony was conducted by a justice of the peace, with a small reception following that consisted of tea cakes and punch spiked with an excellent bootlegged rum.

Announcements of the couple's union were sent after Mary and Ollie were well on their way out of the country. Howbutker understood that the wedding had to be hurried in order for the honeymoon to coincide with the junior DuMont's buying trip to Europe. What spiked its collective brow was Mary's sudden and unexpected marriage to Ollie DuMont when everyone was anticipating an exchange of nuptials with the handsome Percy Warwick. They puzzled, as well, over Mary's unprecedented leavetaking of Somerset, entrusting its supervision to her rather shiftless manager. It was finally determined over tea, porch, and supper tables that the only reason Mary married Ollie so soon after the hail disaster was to ensure the salvation of Somerset. It was an opinion Mary sadly hoped the Warwicks shared to relieve their disappointment that she had not married their son.

But she couldn't be sure. She'd expected a no-bones-about-it reaction of disapproval from Beatrice but instead received resigned acceptance. "Are you sure you don't want to wait until Percy comes home to get married?" she asked. "He'll be so disappointed."

"No, Beatrice," Mary said. "It will be too late then."

Beatrice had given her a long, despairing look, and Mary was left to wonder if she'd guessed the real reason the wedding could not be delayed. Only Jeremy remained a bit stiff when Mary stood on tiptoes to kiss him after the reception.

The couple were no sooner landed in Paris and checked in at the Hotel Ritz than Ollie whisked Mary off to a family practitioner for her first medical examination. It was too early to estimate her baby's due date, the French physician told her. Privately, Mary was projecting the end of April. When she mentioned this to him at her next appointment, he shook his head. "From what I can tell, your baby will arrive later than that. My diagnosis puts the date at least two, most likely three, weeks later."

"What?" Mary felt the room sway. "You mean I'm . . . not as fully pregnant as I thought?"

The doctor smiled. "A most American way of putting it, but yes. Conception must have come at a later date than you figured, perhaps shortly before your first missed period."

Bile rose to the back of her throat. She remembered the "later date" quite well. The memory came rushing to her with such painful poignancy, she had to lean against the dressing room wall for support. It happened the week before the first picking, when her blood had thrilled at the prospects of having money in the bank, of paying off the mortgage, of exonerating her father. It was the first truly "good feeling" day she'd known since her mother's suicide. Percy was waiting for her in the cabin when she pushed open the door, an apron around his waist and spoon in his hand. His foolish grin softened to an understanding smile when he saw the yearning on her face. Calmly he set aside the spoon, moved the pot from the burner, untied the apron, and went to her.

Mary's knees buckled as she relived their passion of that afternoon, how their bodies had melded, become one, inseparable, inviolate, holy, and eternal . . . the day their child was conceived. She slid down the wall and hugged her knees to her chest. *Oh, my darling Percy, what have I done to us? What have I done?*

She was white-faced and trembling when Ollie collected her. He took her back to the hotel, where she stayed in bed for two days, eating crusty French bread and broth, the only food her stomach could tolerate. (She refused croissants.) Within two months of their departure from Howbutker, Abel DuMont passed around cigars at a small dinner party to which the Warwicks were invited. He was soon to be a grandfather, he announced. The child was expected in July 1921. Ollie wanted the baby to be born in their mother country, so the couple would return to Paris for the birth and sail home from France. Actually, Matthew Toliver DuMont was born in May of that year. Money exchanged hands with the delivering physician—a great deal of it—with the result that the birth certificate read that the only child ever to be born to the Ollie DuMonts had entered the world two months after his birth date.

It was with as much relief as pride that Ollie first inspected the child brought to suckle at his mother's breast. Rather than the blond hair they both had tacitly feared, the infant's curls were as black as Mary's own, his teal blue eyes suggesting the green they would become. The faintest depression could be detected in the middle of the tiny chin, and all who saw him remarked at the way his hair grew to a decided peak on his forehead—"so like his mother's."

"Well, my dear, you've got yourself a Toliver," Ollie pronounced, his face wreathed in happiness.

He became an instant slave to the child and could hardly bear having him out of his sight. One evening as Mary watched him rock the small bundle, cooing and patting, forever brushing his lips to the soft little head, she wondered if the supreme irony of his situation had yet occurred to him. He had lost his leg and the ability to sire children to save his friend's life for the woman whom he himself had wound up possessing, along with her child.

Somerset was rarely out of her mind. She mailed letters of instructions weekly to Hoagy Carter. Before she left, they had struck a deal. If, upon her return, Mary found that he had run the plantation with care and efficiency, monitored by Emmitt Waithe, she would allow him to keep all the profits from his cotton crop for three years. If she returned and found fault with his management, she would turn him and his family off the land with nothing.

One evening as they watched Matthew sleep, Ollie said, "Mary, I can't help but still wonder if we are wrong to keep the child all to ourselves."

Feeling a moment's panic, Mary drew him away from the bassinet. "It is not wrong to protect this baby from a mistake that Percy and I made. You are his father now, and you needn't feel guilty because you believe you've taken Matthew from him. Percy will have many sons. You and I will have only Matthew.

Think of what it would do to Percy, knowing the child was his."

She had struck the right chord. His hand closed over hers. "We will not bring the subject up again. It was only a passing thought."

On this, their second stay in Paris, eight weeks after Matthew had supposedly been born, they tracked down Miles and arranged a meeting. Ollie left Mary to finish dressing for their luncheon date while he went downstairs to answer a summons by the concierge. He returned with two letters, one unfolded in his hand. His expression was grave. "These are from my father," he said. "They've followed us around Europe. This one is four months old."

"What's wrong?" Mary asked.

"It's Percy. He's . . . married."

She was still at her dressing table. The necklace she was fastening fell from her hands and clattered onto the dresser top. "Who?" she whispered, staring stunned into the mirror.

"Lucy."

The blood drained from her face so fast, she thought she would faint. "Lucy? Did you say *Lucy*?"

"Yes. Lucy Gentry."

"Oh, my God! *Lucy?*" Mary gripped the table and let out a short, hysterical laugh of disbelief. "Percy married Lucy? How could he? How *could* he?"

"I wouldn't doubt but what Percy had the same thing to say about you," Ollie remarked with a rare frown of disapproval. He opened the second letter, postmarked two months later. After a quick perusal, he met her eyes in the mirror. "Perhaps you'd better prepare yourself for another shock. Lucy is pregnant. She and Percy are expecting the baby in April next year."

When they met Miles later, Mary found it difficult to concentrate on their conversation and barely touched her food. Ollie did most of the talking. Marietta was not with Miles. She was "incapacitated," he explained briefly, his eyes constantly shifting away from Mary's. He looked worse than when he had left Howbutker. His complexion was sallow, his teeth the color of tobacco. Flakes of dandruff from his thin, dry hair spotted the shoulders of his shabby suit.

When Ollie excused himself to go to the men's room, Miles looked at his sister directly for the first time. "I always thought it would be you and Percy, Mary."

"Well, it's not, is it?"

Her brother shook his head. "You and Ollie. Percy and Lucy. It doesn't make sense. What happened?" Receiving no reply, he bared his bad teeth. "Let me guess. After the hail wiped you out, you saw Ollie as a way to save Somerset. Knowing how Percy feels about the plantation, he wouldn't have given you a cent, but he would have married you. Fool that you are, you chose Somerset."

"Let's change the subject, shall we?" Mary said, her jaw tight.

"To what? To Mama? I know in my gut she didn't die in her sleep from heart failure."

"If you'd been there, you could have seen for yourself."

Miles combed a bony hand through his hair in the familiar gesture that Mary remembered. "I'm not accusing you of anything, Mary. It just sounds so unlike her, getting out of the bed she wallowed in for years to give you a birthday party."

"I thought so, too, but she did. The effort was obviously too much. And I certainly hope you're not accusing me of anything, Miles. A brother who ran out on a mother and sister who needed him is hardly in a position to point a finger at anyone else's dereliction of family duties."

They tried as best they could, but the family bond was broken. Miles was a stranger to her, and Mary wished they'd never tried to locate him. He looked the perfect down-and-out picture of the failure he was. It was not an image she wished to carry home, most likely the final one of her brother. Courtesy, and the last shred of sisterly attachment, dictated that she invite Miles back to their hotel to see his nephew, but she hoped he would decline.

Ollie was returning. Seeing his brother-in-law deftly wending his way toward them with the use of his crutches, Miles said, "See that you're good to Ollie, little sister. That one comes from the gods. You won't find any better. I hope you appreciate that."

"I do," Mary assured him.

Miles did not accept the invitation to be introduced to his nephew, and the DuMonts left Europe without seeing him again. They sailed for home within the week, in time for the last pass of the fields at Somerset. It was the end of September. Their son was almost five months old, but none who cooed over the small infant on the return ocean voyage doubted the parents' assertion that he had lived eight weeks short of that time upon the planet Earth.

ON THE VERANDAH, MARY TOLIVER DuMont opened her eyes. The sun had edged beyond the roof, and the glare had lessened. The skirt of her green linen suit was damp and wrinkled across her lap. For a confusing moment, she had no idea where she was or in what year. On the table next to her was a champagne bucket and nearly empty bottle of Taittinger's sweating in melted ice. The lipstick-imprinted flute told her she'd been drinking—and by herself.

Nineteen eighty-five, she recalled. It was August 1985. She was sitting on the front verandah of her house and had been reminiscing about the past.

It had been a long journey back. Only the remembrance of her son's birth had brought her spinning back to the present—that and a strange sensation along her spine. The magic carpet ride was definitely over. She wanted off. She felt a painful twinge beneath her sternum, but there always was when she thought of Matthew. Stupid little chit she'd been not to have known when he was conceived. Girls knew so little about their bodies in those days, especially girls without mothers, and she'd been virtually motherless for a long time by then.

If only she had known, how different her journey into the past would have been. How different their lives. Percy had arrived on the inbound train the day after she and Ollie had pulled out. If only he had called to let his parents know he was on the way, she would have canceled the wedding, and she and Percy would have had time to make things right. If only she hadn't stopped by the cabin that particular afternoon, hot for his flesh against hers, his mouth, his hands. If only he'd agreed to lend her his signature. As it turned out, he wouldn't have lost a dime. The next year produced a bumper crop that enabled her to get Fair Acres out of hock. The following year she paid off the mortgage, and Somerset was hers free and clear.

But, of course, it hadn't been about the money. They'd both understood that.

It proved a successful cover, everybody believing that she'd married Ollie to bail out Somerset. The town had expected him to be her puppet, but he surprised them. Ollie was nobody's puppet, for all his amiable ways, his willingness to please. They'd had a good marriage, based on respect, humor, boundless understanding, and support. She remained faithful to him, even when he was gone and she and Percy could have been together, but by then, of course, it was too late.

Mary shook her head sadly. So many *if onlys*, and their consequences had affected them all. Percy and Lucy. Matthew and Percy's son, Wyatt. Miles and Mama. William and Alice. And Mary Toliver DuMont. All impoverished because of Somerset.

Well, there was one life that she would save from the Toliver curse—one that she would spare the regrets she was taking to the grave. It had taken her long enough to see what must be done, but she had in the end, and before it was too late. Tomorrow, she'd fly to Lubbock and relate the real history of the Tolivers to Rachel, tell her the stories Amos never read, reveal the truths the lies had hidden all these years. She would make Rachel understand. She'd get her to see that she was making the same mistakes, taking the same wrong turns, offering up the same sacrifices to the Toliver altar as her dear old great-aunt, and for what? She had once read: "It's not the land that's important, but the lessons learned from the land." She had scoffed at the notion, but now she believed it. Somerset had been a good teacher, but she hadn't listened. She'd get Rachel to listen, and maybe she'd learn.

But first she must attend to one final task, and then she could leave this earth in peace. She must get up to the attic, to Ollie's army trunk. She'd come down afterward and have a bite of Sassie's good dinner. Not that she was hungry. She felt nauseated, in fact. The pain persisted under her sternum and was radiating to her jaws. Thank goodness Sassie was coming.

She rose unsteadily to her feet. *"Miss Mary! Miss Mary!"* she heard from far off as another pain, wickedly sharp, cut deep into her jaws. She grabbed for the porch rail.

"No!" she gasped, realizing fully what was happening. "I must get to the attic, Sassie. I must—"

Her legs gave way, and for a few seconds, as she strained to keep the light, she thought she saw the outline of a familiar face taking shape in the gray mist rolling toward her. Ollie! she thought, but it was Rachel's features that emerged—beautiful, outraged, and unforgiving. *"Rachel!"* she cried, but the vision disappeared in the darkening fog, and she felt the return of the arrows she had slung.

PART II

Chapter Thirty-one

With briefcase in hand, Amos was adjusting the thermostat in his office prior to leaving for the day when the phone rang. Let the answering machine get it, he thought. He was in no mood to take a call, and besides, he was slightly drunk.

"Amos, if you're there, pick up," he heard Percy say.

Immediately, he plucked up the receiver. "Percy? I'm here. What can I do for you?" There was a pause, the kind that made his heart lurch. "What is it? What's the matter?"

"It's Mary. She...she's suffered a heart attack."

He edged around his desk, groping for his chair. "How bad is it?"

"She died, Amos. Right out on her verandah a little while ago. Sassie sent Henry to get us. Matt's here, but I thought I ought to be the one to tell you—" His voice cut off with a strangled sob.

Amos pressed his palm to his throbbing forehead.

Holy hell! Mary dead? It wasn't possible! My God, where did that leave Rachel? Now she'd never hear Mary's reasons for the codicil.

"Amos?"

"I'll be right there, Percy. Are you at Warwick Hall?"

"Yes. The EMS has just taken the body to the coroner's. There won't be an autopsy. Cause of death was obvious. You'll have to let Rachel know."

Amos's despair sank deeper. "I'll call her from your house."

SWINGING HER DARK GREEN BMW into her reserved space in the parking lot of Toliver Farms West, Rachel was surprised to find her foreman and indispensable right-hand man of eight years sitting in the shade of the awning, apparently waiting for her. He had been scheduled to take delivery of a new compressor out at the south sector while she was at her noon business meeting. Another odd feeling of unease rippled through her. The New York representative of the textile mills with whom Toliver Farms had dealt for years had arrived at their meeting with no contract. Out of courtesy to their long association, he had shown up merely to offer apologies but no explanation.

"What's wrong, Ron?" she called as she got out of the car and knew immediately that something was amiss from the reluctant way he got out of the chair, pushed back his straw hat, and stuck his fingertips into his jeans pockets.

"It may be nothing," he said in his West Texas drawl, "but when I came for the invoice, I took a call from Amos Hines. He sounded agitated. You're to call him soon as you can. I thought I better hang around...well, in case it's bad news. I've contacted Buster to take care of the delivery."

She gave his arm a squeeze as she rushed past him. "Is Amos at his office?"

"No, at the house of somebody named Percy Warwick. The number's on your desk."

Rachel threw down her handbag and grabbed the phone, steeling herself for the likelihood that something had happened to Percy. If so, she'd fly immediately to be with her great-aunt. Aunt Mary would have a terrible time adjusting to life without Percy.

Amos answered the phone before the ring was completed. "Rachel?"

"I'm here, Amos. What's happened?" She locked eyes with Ron's and held her breath to await the impact of Amos's answer.

"Rachel, I'm...afraid I've got bad news. It's about Mary. She died a couple of hours ago from a sudden heart attack."

It was as if she'd taken a gunshot to the chest. She felt the numbing shock, then the spread of pain like the slow seepage of blood from a wound. Ron caught her arm to help her back into her desk chair. "Oh, Amos...."

"Dear girl, I can't begin to tell you how deeply sorry I am."

She heard the break in his voice and the struggle with his own pain and tried to get a grip on hers. "Where was she? Where did it happen?"

"On her verandah around one o'clock. She'd come in from town and had been sitting in one of the porch chairs. Sassie found her in her...death throes. She lived maybe a minute longer."

Rachel closed her eyes and pictured the scene. Just in from town, probably dressed to the teeth, her lovely old great-aunt had died on her verandah with her last view on earth the street where she'd lived all her life. She'd have preferred no other place to breathe her last. "Did...she say anything?"

"According to Sassie, she...said something about needing to get to the attic. Earlier she'd had Henry go up there and unlock a trunk. It must have contained something she wanted. She...also cried your name, Rachel...there at the end."

Tears began to course from beneath her tightly squeezed lids. Quietly, Ron retrieved a box of tissues from the coffee table and laid it within reach.

"My dear child," Amos said. "Is there anyone who can be with you?"

She pressed a tissue to her streaming eyes, knowing that he asked because he knew of the strained relations between her and her family and that they were not likely to be a source of comfort. "Yes, my foreman

is here and my secretary, Danielle. I'll be all right.
I'm so glad you and Matt are there for Percy. How is
he?"

"Taking it pretty hard, as you can imagine. Matt
has sent him upstairs to have a rest. He sends his love,
though, and Matt asked me to tell you he's at your
disposal when you get to Howbutker."

Matt... His name sent a shock of remembrance
through her—a comforting one. She hadn't seen
him since she was a teenager, when she'd cried on
his shoulder. "Tell him I'll gratefully take him up on
that," she said. "And you, Amos? How are you?"

There was a moment's silence while he seemed to
be groping for the right word. "I am... devastated,
child... especially for you."

Kind, loving Amos, she thought, swallowing down
a fresh surge of tears. "I'll be all right," she said. "It
will just take time. Aunt Mary used to say that the
only thing time was good for was to get past bad
times."

"Yes, well, let us hope it will not fail its one at-
tribute," he said, and cleared his voice loudly, as if a
huge obstruction were in his throat. "Now, do you
have any idea of the time of your arrival? I ask because
I can make preliminary arrangements for you—set
up appointments with the funeral director and florist, that sort of thing. The plane is gassed and ready
to go. Mary had planned to fly out to see you tomorrow, you know."

Her surprise momentarily stanched her tears. "No, I didn't know."

"Then I'm afraid she died before she could inform you, but I know she planned to see you. She told me so in my office this morning when she came for...a visit."

"You saw her today? How wonderful for you to have seen her one last time, Amos. I wish she could have made it here. Did she say why she was coming? It's not...it wasn't like her to surprise me."

"It had to do with some...recent changes, I believe. All she told me for sure was that she loved you."

Rachel closed her eyes again. That, too, was unlike her great-aunt. Had she known she was seriously ill? "Did she tell you she had heart trouble?" she asked.

"No, she never told me she had heart trouble. That came as a surprise to all of us. Now back to the question of your arrival...."

"I'll try to be there by ten in the morning," she said, "and I would appreciate your making those appointments. I don't know if I'll have any luck persuading my mother and brother to come with me and Daddy, but would you also alert Sassie to the possibility that she may have to make up an extra guest room?"

There was another pause, as if Amos were carefully considering his next statement. "I would suggest that you convince at least Jimmy to come with your father. I'm sure Mary would have wanted them both at the reading of the will to hear her...last regards to them."

"I'll see what I can do," she said, hoping that Amos's phrasing might convince her mother to come, too. Aunt Mary's will had been the source of all the trouble between them. Rachel could hear her mother now: *I'll never forgive you, Rachel Toliver, if your great-aunt leaves the whole ball of wax to you and nothing to your father and brother!*

"Well, then, I'll see you tomorrow, Rachel," Amos said. "Let me know for certain the time, and I'll be at the airport to pick you up."

Rachel slowly replaced the receiver, niggled by a sense that some other disturbance besides Aunt Mary's death was troubling Amos...like a distinct hum beneath a louder sound. It was the second time that day she'd had the feeling that something else was wrong other than the trouble at hand.

"I take it your great-aunt is gone from us?" Ron asked quietly, slipping a handkerchief from his back pocket to pat his eyes. He'd removed his hat and taken a seat on the other side of the room.

"Yes, she's gone, Ron. A heart attack around one o'clock. You'll have to take charge around here."

"Be happy to, though I'm sorry it has to be this way. We'll miss her, as we sure as hell're gonna miss you."

Her eyes flooded again. "Tell Danielle, will you? I'll be out in a few minutes. I need to notify my parents."

When the door had clicked closed, Rachel sat without moving for a few minutes, listening to the peculiar quiet that had fallen. Silence makes a buzzing sound when someone you love has died, she thought, like a fly in an empty room. She got up and moved to the window, desiring to see the sun before she picked up the phone. At one time, the number she was about to call had represented the truest place on earth to her, an umbilical chord to acceptance, understanding, and love. But that was before Aunt Mary. That was before Somerset.

Chapter Thirty-two

Granddad?" Matt rapped a knuckle softly on his grandfather's sitting room door and spoke quietly to avoid disturbing him if he'd managed to fall asleep in his chair.

"Come on in, son. I'm up."

Matt entered to find his grandfather ramped forward in his recliner, looking none the better for his nap. His face appeared composed, but his red-rimmed eyes and the puffy pockets beneath them spoke to a loss far greater than that of an old friend and neighbor. Matt's heart grabbed as it always did when he realized that his grandfather was nearing the end of his days. He drew up a chair. "Rachel's just returned Amos's call. I told Savannah to give him lunch. He hadn't eaten."

"Johnnie Walker Red, from the smell of him," Percy said. "That's not like Amos."

"Well, maybe he took a belt or two after you called.

Like me, he'd visited with Mary only a few hours before she died. You can tell he's grieving."

"She'll be a severe loss to him. They were great friends. Amos was even a little in love with her when he first came to Howbutker. He was a young man then. If Mary ever noticed, she didn't let on. Goodness, what man wasn't a little in love with Mary?"

Matt couldn't resist asking, "Including you?"

Percy raised his eyebrows at him, dark expressive ledges over gray eyes that on good days were still remarkably clear and alert. "What makes you ask that?"

Matt tugged at his ear, a giveaway to his grandfather that he wished he hadn't spoken, but if it comforted him, what difference did it make now if he told him of the old horse Mary had let out of the barn? "Like I told you, I ran into Mary standing by that old elm near the statue of St. Francis. What I didn't tell you was that I caught her looking confused and talking to herself."

"Is that so?" A light flickered on behind the blood-shot eyes. "What was she saying?"

"Well…" He squirmed a bit under his grandfather's tightened gaze. "She thought I was you. She seemed to have gone back in time and was reliving some memory. When I called her name, she turned around and said…"

Matt could sense his grandfather's sudden tension. "Go on, son. She said…?"

"She said, 'Percy, my love, did you have to drink *all*

my soda? I wanted it that day, you know, as much as I wanted you.' That's it verbatim, Granddad. I hope I'm not dragging up old memories better left buried."

"You're not. Anything else?"

"Well, yes." Matt found himself wriggling again. "She said, 'I was too young and silly and too much of a Toliver. If only I hadn't been such a fool.' And that's when I shook her a little and identified myself." He paused to gauge Percy's reaction. "That's why I asked if you weren't once in love with her yourself."

Percy let out a raspy chuckle. "In love with her *once?*" He swung his gaze to the mantel lined with a series of family pictures. They were mostly of Matt in sports gear and one of him as an infant in his mother's arms, but occupying front and center was the official photograph of his father in his U.S. Marines uniform, the left side of his jacket covered in medals and campaign ribbons. Matt couldn't tell whether Percy's eye fell on the portraits or the murky watercolor—a present from his father—that filled the space above it. In a voice scratchy with memory, he mused, "It was July 1914, at the dedication ceremony of the courthouse. That's where Mary had gone in memory when you found her. She was fourteen, and I was nineteen. She wore a white dress tied with a green ribbon. I was already in love with her and planned to marry her, but she didn't know it."

"Well, I'll be damned." Matt felt a thrill of wonder. "Did she *ever* know it?"

Percy said, "Yes, she knew it."

"Well, then, what happened? Why didn't you marry?" His assertion was plain: His grandfather would have been a hell of a lot happier married to Mary Toliver than he ever was to Lucy Gentry.

"Somerset happened," Percy said, kneading the knuckles of his right hand, a habit when he was deep into himself, Matt had noticed.

"You want to talk about it?" he asked. "That Johnnie Walker Red doesn't seem like a bad idea."

Percy shook his head. "Won't help, I'm afraid. And, no, I don't want to talk about it. It's over and done with...all that might have been."

"Granddad..." Commiseration for his grandfather stabbed through him, bound all these years to a woman he did not love. "You're breaking my heart. Did Gabby ever know about you and Mary?"

"Oh, yes, she knew, but Mary and I happened before I married your grandmother, and there was never any 'about you and Mary' after that."

"Did...you still love her after you married Gabby?"

Percy worked his hands. "I loved her all of her life, from the moment she was born."

Dear God, Matt thought. Eighty-five years....A bereaved silence fell, Percy still massaging his hands. "Did Ollie know?" he asked.

"Always."

Amazed, Matt blew out his breath, sad to the soles of his feet. "Was Mary the reason Gabby left you?"

"She was a factor, but your grandmother had other grievances." Percy adjusted his hips as if he were uncomfortable. "All so much water under the bridge now," he said.

And not waters he cared to go fishing in, Matt gathered, but he wasn't going to let him off the hook now that the line was in. "Well, I'd like to hear about it someday, Granddad. I'd like you to fill in the empty spaces of our family...while there's still time."

Percy cast him a surprised glance. "Is that how you think of...certain periods in our family's history—as empty spaces? Well, I suppose I can understand how you might be curious about them, but they're in the past and don't pertain to you at all."

"Why haven't you and Gabby divorced?"

"That, too, is a part of the past that does not pertain to you." He bestowed his smile famous for disarming opposition. "Maybe you should go down and check on Amos. He'll be even more upset now that he's had to break the news of Mary's death to Rachel. At least he'll be consoled by the thought that she's finally coming to live in Howbutker. He adores that girl."

Matt acquiesced to his brush-off. He supposed he'd never learn why his grandfather had stayed in an absent marriage when it had always been obvious to him that he was born for home and family, for a wife's devoted care. Still, he felt a strange envy. What it must be like to love a woman as he had...for as long...and never to want another. In that regard, he had been a very lucky man.

"I'm looking forward to Rachel living here myself," he said, getting to his feet. "It's time we got to know each other better."

Percy gave him a penetrating look. "I wouldn't be getting any ideas about her, Matt. She's like a young Mary in more ways than her looks, and they're not Warwick-friendly."

Matt gazed down at his grandfather. "That sounds like one of those empty spaces I mentioned, and if Rachel's as lovely as I remember, it would be hard for a man not to get ideas about her."

Percy's face grew serious. "Let's just say that in Rachel's case, the apple fell directly under the tree, and I wouldn't want you to repeat my history."

Matt punched his shoulder. "Well, until you tell me what I'm to look out for, I'll just have to take my chances, won't I?"

PERCY LISTENED TO MATT'S FOOTSTEPS recede down the hall. Confident young pup. He had no idea what he was letting himself in for, if history was indeed so unkind as to give a repeat performance. Percy wouldn't be worried about him if he weren't so much like himself—unable to resist the allure of a challenge, the thrill of the chase, and then when the trap was sprung...

Slowly he rose and let himself out onto the shaded porch of his sitting room. The afternoon felt as hot as it had in 1914, and he remembered that cold chocolate soda and Mary's haughty rejection of it. He remembered everything about Mary, her taste and feel and smell...even now.

He drew a chaise longue farther under the shade of the roof and stretched out. The only way to prepare Matt for Rachel was to fill in those spaces he mentioned, and that he would never do. But if he ever were of a mind to relate the tale of how he'd aborted his happiness, where to begin? He supposed it would have to be the day of his greatest pain, the morning he returned from Canada and learned that Mary had married Ollie....

PERCY'S
STORY

Chapter Thirty-three

The train was late chugging into the station. Percy had slept sporadically during the weeklong trip from Ontario, rising before dawn to smoke on the platform, staying up past midnight in the lounge car, drinking an ocean of coffee, and cursing himself for being a fool. He should have let his parents know to expect him, but his mother would alert Mary, and he wasn't sure what her reaction would be, considering how they'd parted. He planned to take her by surprise, sweep her into his arms, and kiss her senseless, tell her he loved her and that he didn't give a damn about her obsession with Somerset, if only she'd marry him and live with him forever.

Last night, however, he had slept soundly through the last call to breakfast and almost missed the first sight of the Piney Woods this side of Texarkana. He had awakened startled and hurriedly pulled on pants and a shirt to make his way through the berth cars to the rear platform. He had gripped the railing, the wind ballooning out his half-buttoned shirt, and sucked in the pungent air of East Texas on the verge of autumn. He stood there now, recalling when he and the boys returned from France. He'd never in all his life forget the vision of Mary standing on the platform, aloof even in the crowd, her clothes outdated, her expression too tense, but, Jesus, she'd been beautiful...his Mary. *Almost there...almost there...almost there...,* the wheels sang, and he believed the promise of their cadence.

Yes, by God, almost there, almost home, almost back in Mary's arms, which he never should have left. He'd gone away hurt and angry and determined to get over her. He'd never played second fiddle to anything or anybody, and he certainly wouldn't to his wife's affections. He would be first or not at all.

The cold of the Canadian Rockies had burned the arrogance out of him. The isolation had cleansed him of his pride. Lying in camp at night, listening to the men regale one another with tales of women, hearing beneath the braggadocio the wistfulness, the bitterness, the loneliness, he had felt the reach of an icy wind deep into the part of him that only Mary could warm. In the day, as he sawed and loaded and climbed trees whose heights touched the clouds, a need for her grew within him, more gnawing than any hunger, more essential than air or water or food.

At the end of two months, he could stand no more. He was almost twenty-six. He yearned for a wife and home and children...for Mary. He wanted her no more than a heartbeat away in his bed, a hand across his table, a chair's distance from him in the evening. He could learn to play second fiddle. The idea was to be in the band.

He reentered the corridor. The train would be pulling into Howbutker within the next fifteen minutes or so. Once again, he was glad he'd not told his parents of his arrival. He'd be free to see Mary first. Today was his mother's day to play bridge at the country club, and his father would be at his office. He'd take a cab and pick up his car without their being the wiser. If he didn't find Mary at home, he'd drive directly to the plantation, and later when he saw his parents, he'd tell them he'd proposed to her.

In the corridor, he encountered the young Negro porter who hailed from Howbutker and knew his name. "Why, Mister Percy, you missed your breakfast this morning. Want me to see 'bout rustlin' you up a bite?"

"No thanks, Titus. We'll be arriving in a few minutes, and I know where I can get the best breakfast this side of the Sabine."

"And where might that be, sir?"

"At Sassie's table in Howbutker."

Titus nodded. "That be Miss Mary Toliver's residence, I reckon. Or should I say 'Mrs. Ollie DuMont' now." He smiled happily in bestowing this information, the glow of the corridor lamp glinting off the wide exposure of his teeth.

The sudden drop of his blood pressure caused Percy to reach for the railing behind him. "I'm sorry, Titus. What did you say?"

"Oh, that's right. You just now be comin' home, and they be already gone, but I'da thought you knew 'bout the weddin'. Not that it was a big one. Miss Mary and Mister Ollie married rather sudden like 'cause he was goin' over to Paris awhile. The trip had somethin' to do with his papa's store. They goin' to combine business with pleasure."

Percy experienced the total lack of sound he'd encountered in the trenches when the blast of a mortar shell landed close by. For a few paralyzing moments, as the earth blackened before him, he saw Titus's lips move but heard only silence.

"Mister Percy, you all right?" Titus asked, waving his hand before Percy's frozen stare.

Percy's lips moved woodenly. "How do you know all this?"

"Why, 'cause it was all in the paper. There was even a picture of the newly marrieds. Miss Mary, she was all decked out in a white dress, and Mister Ollie, he was turned out in one of his smart suits. Mister Percy, if you don't mind my sayin' so, you don't look so good. Sure I can't get you some breakfast?"

"No, no, Titus. How did they look? In the picture?"

"Well, Mister Ollie, he had that bridegroom look. He got only one leg, you know, but that don't stop him from lookin' at Miss Mary the only way a man can...." He stopped, embarrassed, his color a shade lighter. "I mean...that is, to say—"

"I know what you mean. Go on. What about Miss Mary?"

"Well, now, Miss Mary, she don't look so chipper. Most womenfolks don't, I guess, when they get married...." Again the porter looked uncomfortable. "By that, I mean all the plannin' Miss Mary had to do for the weddin' and packin' for the long trip to Europe. That's enough to take the sap outta anybody...." Titus paused. "Mister Percy, you look like you could use a cup of coffee. Be right back."

Percy let his full weight fall against the paneled corridor wall. It wasn't possible. He was dreaming. Mary couldn't—*wouldn't* have married anyone but him. They belonged together. They were one. Titus was mistaken. He felt along the railing until he reached the sanctuary of his Pullman. He plunked down in stunned disbelief until he heard the porter at the door. He heaved himself to the lavatory and buttoned his shirt. "Come in," he called in a steady voice. He didn't recognize himself. His mouth was thin and bloodless. In five minutes, he'd aged ten years. "Leave the coffee there, Titus. Tip's on the nightstand."

"I'll just help myself to a dime, Mister Percy. Welcome home."

There has to be a mistake, he told himself again. But his mind forced him to realize what his heart would not accept. There was no mistake. Mary had married Ollie to rescue Somerset after he'd rejected her and compounded his stupidity by running off to the Canadian Rockies without a word. But how could she do this to him—to them—marry his best friend, a man she did not love and never would as she'd loved him...as Ollie deserved to be loved?

He slammed his fist into the wall beside the mirror and then sank to the bed to nurse the pain. The enormity of his rage at both himself and Mary overwhelmed him. He finished out the ride into Howbutker with his back against the frame of the Pullman bed, holding his head in his hands, the untouched coffee growing cold on the nightstand.

Before it came to a full stop, he hopped off the train and called to Isaac, one of Howbutker's two cabbies. "The Toliver place on Houston Avenue," he said, throwing his gear into the hansom cab, and he climbed up to sit beside the driver, needing the sobering October wind on his face. As soon as Isaac drew his horse to a stop before the steps of the Tolivers' verandah, he jumped down. "Wait here for me," he ordered, and dashed up to the front door.

Sassie answered the savage ringing of the bellpull. "You better come in," she said, reading his face, her drooped mouth confirming Titus's report.

"It's true, then?" Percy stated.

"They married yesterday and left on the five o'clock train. It was all done so sudden like 'cause Mister Ollie, he had to go to Paris for some clothes show, or so Miss Mary say."

"What do you mean, 'or so Miss Mary say'?"

Sassie shrugged and folded her hands over her flowered apron. "That's just what she say, is all. Mister Ollie, he loves her. You can be consoled by that, Mister Percy."

His voice gave way to his grief. "Why did she do it, Sassie?" he sobbed.

Sassie put her arms around him and pulled his head down to her shoulder and stroked it. "She pine for you, Mister Percy. She grow sick from so much pinin'. She thought you be gone for good. Mister Ollie, he help her out of the jam she be in with Somerset, and I reckon she figure she owe him. If she wasn't goin' marry you, who else good enough?"

Percy sobbed into her shoulder. "What have I done, Sassie?"

"You be young, that's what you and Miss Mary both done. Love ain't got no business happenin' to the young. Only the old be wise enough to treat it right. I'd offer you a bottle of somethin', but they ain't a drop of nothin' in the house."

Percy straightened, extracted a handkerchief, and wiped his face. "That's all right," he said. "I won't have any trouble finding a bottle."

When he returned to the cab, he said, "How much

do you want for that bottle of gin you got stashed under your seat, Isaac?"

"Two bucks. It's only half-full."

"There'll be five more for you if you can pick up another bottle on the way to my destination."

Isaac flipped the reins over the gray mare's rump. "I imagine that could be arranged, Mister Percy."

A half hour later, Percy stepped down before the cabin in the woods. He peeled off a ten and a five and handed the bills to the cabbie. "Isaac, give me twenty-four hours without telling anybody I'm home or where I am. Then I want you to call my parents and tell them to come get me."

"Anything you say, Mister Percy."

Beatrice, alone, came to collect him. Her husband was at his office when Isaac telephoned. Percy heard the story later of how his mother, never having driven a Warwick motorcar, sent word to the stables to ready the surrey and then selected a few items from the pantry. Afterward, she went upstairs to his room to pack a few clothes into a valise. She donned hat and gloves, and without telling her housekeeper where she was going, she drove the matched pair of high-stepping bays to the cabin in the woods.

She found her son lying awake on the sofa in the single room, his face deathly gray and his glassy eyes fixed on the ceiling. The sunlight from the open door illuminated a day's growth of blond beard as well as two empty bottles of bathtub gin on the floor. The cabin reeked of cheap alcohol and vomit, some fresh on the front of her son's shirt.

Beatrice left the door open, raised windows, and got a fire going in the Franklin stove. She stripped Percy of his soiled clothes, then marched him naked to the shower by the lake, pumping while he soaped himself down and shivered beneath the cold spray. He dried off using the towels and wrapped himself in an eiderdown quilt she left him, then returned to the cabin to sit down to a bowl of hot, home-canned soup and a cup of freshly brewed coffee. Then they talked.

"I love her, Mother, and she loves me."

"Apparently not as much as she loves Somerset and you your pride."

"My pride can go to hell. It's not worth what it's cost to keep it."

"Still, it would be mighty hard for a man to live with a wife who put her family name and interests above his. He might be able to at the beginning, but as time went on...when the passion died..."

"I could have lived with her obsession, and our passion would never have died."

Beatrice sighed and did not argue. One look at her face told Percy she agreed with his conviction. "I guess the whole town knows why Mary married Ollie?" The wistfulness in his question held the hope that he was wrong.

She removed his bowl from the table. "Yes, son,

the whole town no doubt believes that Mary married Ollie to save Somerset."

"What do *you* think?"

"You were unwise to leave her, son. She needed you. Who else but Ollie could she turn to when she thought you had left her for good? She was alone. Ollie was here—"

Percy clasped his head with his hands. "Oh, God, Mother. How am I to handle this?"

Beatrice laid her hand on his golden head, like a priest bestowing a benediction. "You must love them as deeply as ever, Percy, but now as one. That will be your gift to them. They will come back wanting your forgiveness, and you must give it graciously and sincerely, like a white rose. And you must forgive yourself, too."

"How can I?" Percy asked, lifting his streaming eyes to his mother's face.

Beatrice bent and gently wiped her son's tears. "By remembering that what you cannot undo, you must accept. And in accepting—especially if they are happy together—you will find the grace to forgive yourself."

Soothed by his mother's words, Percy drank another cup of coffee, cleaned up the cabin, put on the fresh clothes she had brought, and accompanied her home. That afternoon, impeccably dressed and clean-shaven, he surprised his father in his office at the Warwick Lumber Company.

Jeremy displayed unabashed joy at seeing him. His pride in him was evident in his handshake and glowing eyes. His son had come through his baptism of fire and not been found wanting, his manner announced when they made the rounds of the staff to welcome him home. Toughened by war, tested in the field, seasoned by loss, he was a man to be reckoned with now, and his father knew it for sure when he laid a sheath of reports on his desk.

"When you read those," he said in the tone of a man who has nothing else on his mind but business, "you'll agree it's time to expand the Canadian operations."

Chapter Thirty-four

In November, he learned that Mary was pregnant. Abel DuMont, usually dignified and composed, had bounded up the steps of Warwick Hall at suppertime, glued a finger to the bell and, to the startled maid who answered the door, shouted the news that he was soon to be a grandfather. Imagine that! A *grandfather*!

Abel had hosted an impromptu celebration the next evening in his home and passed around cigars and glasses of champagne. Percy had tolerated the event, grateful to his mother for fabricating an excuse that allowed him to leave the party early.

Within days, he turned twenty-six. He declined a party and spent his birthday surveying new timber sites. The glorious autumn usually enjoyed by East Texans melted in rains that lasted through December and intensified his sense of irredeemable loss.

"You ought to get out more, have more social life," Beatrice advised him. "You spend too much time working."

"And with whom am I to have this social life, Mother? Howbutker does not exactly abound in single young women."

He offered the observation to allay her concern that he had no desire for any other woman but Mary and that she had destroyed his trust in her gender for good. She was not far off the mark. Ever since puberty, when the young and likable widow of the choir director had introduced him to the joys of carnal pleasure, the sexual act had been an expression of liking. Not until Mary had he known intercourse for what it was supposed to be, the ultimate possessing and giving of two bodies consumed with love for each other. After Mary, how could he look at another woman?

And she *had* shaken his faith in women. He was willing to bear much of the blame for his predicament, but in hindsight he apportioned an equal share to Mary. How could she have married another if she'd cared as deeply for him as he'd believed? Somerset had mattered more after all. And if he could not trust the love Mary had professed, how would he ever trust the promises of anyone else of her sex?

During the Christmas holiday, to appease his mother, he accepted invitations to parties in Houston and Dallas and Fort Worth from the debutante daughters of oil and cattle barons, but he returned to Howbutker less inclined toward female company than before. At home, he was the only one of his social crowd unmarried, and when he attended alone the dinners and picnics and parties hosted by his married friends, he went away feeling disassociated, depressed, and not a little envious. He longed for a catharsis, a purging spirit to cleanse him of regret and bitterness and self-loathing so that he might feel the sun in his soul again.

And then, in April, when Mary and Ollie had been gone nearly seven months and would not return until September, Lucy Gentry arrived for the Easter holiday.

"I had no choice but to invite her," Beatrice said, announcing her visit at breakfast prior to her arrival. The agitated drum of her fingertips on the starched table linen echoed her chagrin. "How could I say no? The girl practically begged us in her letter to put her up while the school closes for Easter break. She claims that her father can't afford to pay for her transportation to Atlanta, and she'll be the only member of the staff staying in the dormitory."

Her husband and son peered around their newspapers at her fuming at the head of the table.

"Sounds pretty bleak," Percy said.

"Dreadful," agreed Jeremy.

"It's a ruse," Beatrice snapped. "As plain to see as an apple in a pig's mouth."

"See what?" Jeremy asked.

His wife speared him with a look at his end of the table. "You know what, Jeremy Warwick. That girl—with the goading of that awful father of hers—still has her eye on Percy."

"Well, let her look." Unperturbed, he glanced at Percy. "Right, son?"

Percy smiled. "I'd say I'm pretty safe from Lucy Gentry. Don't worry, Mother. I can handle myself."

Beatrice's tight lips expressed doubt as she buttered her toast. "Well, Lord help us if you're wrong," she said.

On the day of Lucy's arrival, Percy overslept and almost missed meeting her train. He'd been in Houston the day before, negotiating a hauling contract with executives of the Southern Pacific Railroad, and had not returned to Howbutker until the early hours of the morning. His mother was in the kitchen when he hurried downstairs. She stood with her back to him, chatting with the cook as they prepared Easter dinner, and for a moment, without announcing his presence, he halted in the doorway and observed her. When had that gray sprung up in her hair, he wondered in surprise, that slight hump appeared at the base of her neck? With dismay, he realized that his parents were growing older and that their suns had begun their declines. Wordlessly, unable to speak, he crossed to her and fastened his arms around her stout figure from behind.

"Why, son!" Beatrice turned in his embrace, startled, until she saw something in his expression that caused her to lay a hand gently on his face. "Lucy's due any minute, you know," she said, her look soft with understanding.

He kissed her forehead. "I'm on my way. Dad call?"

"Only to say not to disturb you. You can make up for today on Friday. A shipload of timber has come in that you'll have to inspect, since your father wants to give his foreman an extra day off to be with his family. That should give you an excuse to get out of the house. Dad and I will see after Lucy. We'll take her to the Kendricks' lawn party Saturday afternoon, and she leaves Sunday after dinner."

The train had already been relieved of its passengers when he parked his car. Lucy, standing with her luggage on the platform, spied him at once as he swung around the corner of the station house. Her whole countenance lit up with a joy so pure and unabashed that Percy laughed out loud.

"There you are, Percy Warwick," she sang out. "I thought maybe I'd been forgotten."

"Impossible," he said, and smiled into her ingenuous blue eyes. "You've done something different with your hair."

"And shortened my hemlines." Primly, she turned full circle in front of him, holding out the skirt of her coat so that he might see the knee-length chemise beneath. "What do you think?"

"I think I like."

"It's the new style."

"So Abel DuMont assures us."

He remembered her now. Short in stature, buxom,

face round like a doll's, and dotty over him. It had been only a little over a year since he'd seen her, but she'd disappeared from his memory as thoroughly as fog before the sun. He reached for her two pieces of luggage, but she snatched up a valise and slipped her hand into his free one with the familiarity of long acquaintance. She came only to his shoulder, and it amused him to look down upon the soft brown crown of her head and see the flurry of her Lilliputian feet working overtime to match his long stride to the Pierce-Arrow.

That evening, laughter lightened the usual mood in the Warwick household. Lucy regaled them with hilarious tales of her students and teaching experiences, rolling her eyes and waving her small, dimpled hands in elaboration so that even Beatrice seemed captivated. At Percy's invitation, she accompanied him to the lumberyard on Friday, and by calling off numbers on the delivery form, she cut in half the time it would have taken to tally the new shipment of timber. Saturday, it was he who escorted Lucy to the Kendricks' lawn party, leaving before his parents' departure, to take her to a supper hosted by one of his friends.

"I thought you'd be married by now," she said that evening. "What happened to the girl you've loved all her life?"

"She married another man."

"She married another man over *you*!"

"He offered more than I."

"I don't believe it!"

"Believe it."

"Where is she now?"

"The groom took her far away."

"Were you sad that she married someone else?"

"Of course, but it's water under the bridge now."

He discovered when he put her on the train Sunday afternoon that he was sorry to see her go. He'd found in their few days together that the traits Mary had disliked in Lucy, he thought refreshing. She called a toad by its name and tolerated little for the sake of good manners that was pretentious, pompous, or pedantic, a ship that wouldn't have sailed with Mary. By nature a listener, he liked that Lucy was a talker with a view about everything, a compulsion that had sent her roommate's head under the pillows at Bellington Hall.

And though her face may not have "launched a canoe in an Indian raid," as Beatrice remarked uncharitably in contradicting the glowing description Lucy's father had sent prior to her first visit, Percy admired the unexpectedness of it—the way her eyes lit up, the impish wriggling of her small nose, the cute rounding of her lips in perpetual O's of surprise and pleasure.

He was charmed by her stature and size, the absurd roundness of her creamy limbs, the dainty joining of wrist to hand, arm to elbow, dimpled knee to leg. Her ears intrigued him. Though pink and delicately formed, they stuck out from her head like little pot handles, the lobes no bigger than the pad of an elf's finger. She would never be svelte, but her waist was small, and he took great pleasure in encircling it with his hands to lift and assist her when her height proved a hindrance.

On the afternoon that he bade her good-bye, he kissed her for the first time. He meant merely to give her a brotherly peck upon a round little cheek, chuck her chin, and wish her well, but when she lifted her china blue eyes and he saw in them nothing but the most profound admiration, he slipped an arm about her waist and drew her toward him. Her mouth was warm and soft and yielding, and it was with great reluctance that he released it.

To his surprise, he heard himself say, "How would you feel about my coming to visit you in Belton next weekend?"

She stared goggled-eyed at him. "Percy! You mean it?"

"I mean it," he said with a laugh.

And so it began.

His mother hovered worriedly in the background. "Do not concern yourself, Mother," he assured her. "The visits are simply a distraction."

"Lucy will not think of your visits as a distraction."

"I've promised nothing."

"It doesn't matter. That girl can hear a note of song and take it as a symphony."

Lucy did not fill his thoughts, his every waking moment, as Mary had done. Indeed, he could go days without once thinking of her, but she was someone available to share his weekends, someone who made him laugh, pampered his ego, and cared for him unreservedly without hope of her feelings being returned.

She was a woman of constant surprises. He expected her to be impressed by his wealth but discovered that, apart from its necessity to provide the essentials, Lucy had little interest in money, especially his. The pleasures she enjoyed were simple and carried no price tags. She preferred a buggy ride through woods draped in springtime splendor to being squired to a party in Houston in his new Cadillac, a blackberry hunt to dancing the night away at the country club, a picnic on the banks of the Caddo to a fine dinner at a grand hotel.

It was during one of these simple excursions that his life turned on an irrevocable course.

They had spread a picnic on a knoll overlooking one of the many lakes in the Belton area. He had come for the weekend, staying as usual at a boardinghouse whose proprietor now greeted him as a regular visitor. It was June and already hot in East Texas. Percy loosened his tie, thinking how much he disliked eating outdoors in heat and humidity. Mercifully, the day was overcast, but as Lucy began to unpack their basket, the clouds parted and the sun's rays bore down.

"Damn!" he swore. "The sun's come out."

"Never you mind," Lucy said in her unflappable manner. "It's merely peeped out to see what we're having for lunch. It'll go back in a minute."

Sure enough, after a quick inspection, the sun disappeared behind clouds and remained hidden all day. Amused, Percy lay back and watched Lucy set out the picnic items, impressed once again by her original way of looking at things. School was almost adjourned, and she was thinking of accepting a position at Bellington Hall in Atlanta for the coming year.

He watched her busily piling his plate with sandwiches, cutting him a large slice of chocolate cake she'd baked especially for him, sugaring his iced tea the way he liked it. "Lucy?" he said. "Will you marry me?"

Chapter Thirty-five

They married the first of July and honeymooned in the Caribbean for two weeks before returning for Jeremy and Beatrice's annual trip to Maine while Percy ran the company. By the time his parents were back in Howbutker from their two months' respite from the heat, Percy's marriage had begun to founder in the unexpected mire of his sexual apathy.

"I simply cannot believe it!" Lucy screamed at him. "The great Percy Warwick with no lightning to his rod! Who would have thought it? Ollie with one leg shot away has probably got more heft to his barrel than you've ever had."

"Lucy, please be quiet. My folks will hear you," Percy implored, astonished anew at her familiar command of such language. Once more, he regretted accepting his parents' offer of a wing at Warwick Hall as a temporary residence until they could build a house of their own.

And once more, he caught himself benumbed by

the fact that he had married Lucy. "You were vulnerable," his mother explained, her look mirroring the despair of Percy's. "I saw it, but I had no way to protect you. Something has to have caused this sudden change in Lucy's feelings for you, Percy. She's always been so slavishly adoring. Has she found out about you and Mary?"

It was as good an explanation as any. Percy turned away to keep his mother from reading the lie in his eyes. "Yes," he said.

The truth was that he had lost all desire for Lucy. As was his wont, he had never engaged in the sex act with a woman he did not like or respect, and he had come to feel neither for Lucy in or out of the marriage bed.

The turn in his affections had not come about inauspiciously. There had been no reason to believe when they left the church for the cruise ship that the sun would not shine brightly on their future together, especially the physical pleasures of marriage both were eagerly anticipating. Lucy's adoring look on that day would have melted the doubt of any man wondering if he'd made a mistake in marrying a woman to whom he had not yet felt inclined to say, "I love you."

But his ardor had begun to cool almost from the point of sailing. Lucy, giddy on champagne and her first taste of sex earlier in their stateroom, had stopped conversation cold at the captain's table when she pronounced to a matron draped in pearls and married to a knight of the English realm, "No need to poke about in that shrimp, Lady Carr. They scare the do-do out of them when they catch them."

By the last night of the cruise, she had reason to ask when he abruptly extricated himself from her tenacious legs, "What happened? What went wrong?"

What could he say? That within two weeks he'd come to feel a heart-sinking disrelish for the woman he had married? Her desire to rut at a change of clothes, her insensibility to his sensibilities, her disinterest in matters cultural or intellectual, offended him. He was now embarrassed by what had attracted him to her—her salty speech, breezy disregard for convention, and carefree opinions that flew out of her mouth like random bullets regardless of whom they might strike. He knew himself well. Despite his own lusty appetites, he was a man of propriety, and it was inevitable that he would carry his distaste to bed.

He muttered an answer: "Nothing, Lucy. It's just me. I'm tired."

"From what, for God's sake? Playing Ping-Pong?" Her aggrieved tone made it clear that once again she'd expected chocolate cake and been given boiled custard.

His mother had tried to warn him. "That ripe little melon has too many seeds, Percy."

"True, Mother," he'd countered, "but the more the seeds, the sweeter the fruit."

How could he have been so blind...so wrong to have thought he'd be happy with Lucy? He could only believe that his despair in knowing there would never be another Mary had led him to marry her opposite.

Yet in no way would he allow her to believe the fault of his failure lay with her. The truth would be more devastating than the lie, and he owed her the lie. She had married him in good faith, believing he accepted her the way she was, while he had married her for the sole reason that he'd not wanted to be alone when Mary and Ollie came home.

"It's not you, Lucy; it's me," he'd say.

In the first month, tears had marked the aftermath of this admission. After that, stony silence followed, and then one night, he heard softly in the darkness, "Why don't you want me, Percy? Don't you *like* sex?"

Not with you, he thought. He knew he had only to give her the satisfaction she craved to make her bearable to live with, but husbandly duty or not, he wouldn't be used as a stud to slake her thirst when all the other pleasures he'd expected from marriage went begging. With that uncanny ability to read his mind, she said, "You—you *eunuch*! You were supposed to be the best stallion that ever covered a mare. By merely looking at a girl, you could get her to lift her tail—"

"Oh, Lord, Lucy, your language—"

"My *language*?" With the ball of her foot, she shoved at Percy sitting on the edge of the bed and sent him toppling, his head narrowly missing a sharp corner of the hope chest at its foot. "Is that your concern in this pathetic situation? My *language*?" Her voice had risen to a shriek. She threw off the covers and stormed around the bed to where Percy, still stunned, sat naked on the floor, legs sprawled apart, manhood exposed. "What about my pride, my feelings, my needs, my *due*, huh? What about *them*, Percy?" She clutched at him savagely, short fingers curved into pincers.

Percy inched back rapidly, slapping her hand away from its target until he'd regained his feet. It was with great restraint that he did not strike her, reminding himself that none of this was her fault. He'd married her knowing it was the idol she loved and not the man. She knew hardly anything about the man, and in the few months of their marriage, she had expended little energy in learning. It was the idol she struck at now, the idol who had deceived her and crumbled to dust at her feet.

He had thought all of this out at length and determined that what he must do was turn her attention to the man. But after such episodes, he came to wonder if he had the heart for that, either.

He'd married Lucy believing that eventually he'd grow to love her, but now he hardly remembered the girl with whom he'd been so taken or why. Her lilting laughter had died, the mischievous twinkle had vanished from her eyes. Her sweet little rosebud lips were perpetually distorted into the bitterest shapes imaginable. Sadly, blaming himself entirely, he watched the girl he could have loved disappear before he'd barely glimpsed her.

Reassurance that it was not her fault had given her neither solace nor compassion. "Well, isn't that mighty white of you," she jeered. "You're damn right it's not my fault. It's yours, Percy Warwick. Your reputation has been a lie all these years. I'll bet Mary sensed it all along. That's why she never set her cap for you."

He preserved a careful inscrutability when she mentioned Mary. Percy wondered how he could have ever thought Lucy fond of her based on their history together at Bellington Hall. His wife had never cared for Mary at all. Lucy had used her, as she'd manipulated his parents, to be near him. To his surprise, Lucy had not asked the name of the girl he'd loved and lost to another man—perhaps because she could not have endured her jealousy—but he saw her sharp eye wander over the faces of women in their social circle, wondering which one had managed to win his heart. God forbid she should ever discover the woman was Mary. "Hell hath no fury like a woman scorned" would be a minor description of Lucy.

By the middle of October, confronted as he was each day by her sulks and her physical and emotional battering at night, he decided to propose an annulment. He was fed up with her obsession with sex, her language, her rages, her resentment toward his mother, whom she blamed as responsible for his "condition," as she called it. He'd set her free and pay her expenses the rest of her life, if she'd only get out of his.

But before he could open his mouth to broach the subject, his wife said, "Get ready for a laugh. I'm pregnant."

Chapter Thirty-six

Beatrice laid Ollie's cable in her lap and removed her spectacles. She looked across the drawing room at her son pouring the round of aperitifs the family enjoyed before the nightly meal. Lucy rarely joined in this ritual. Sometimes she did not even appear for supper. "How nice of Ollie to let us know when they'll be home. You will serve as the child's godfather?"

"Of course," Percy said. "I'm honored to be asked."

"I know they'll be glad to be home," Jeremy said. "Abel can hardly wait to hold that grandson. We'll have to have something for them, Beatrice, a little celebration of some kind?"

They all knew the problem. It was Lucy. In her erratic and unpredictable state these days, how could they rely on her to behave herself at a homecoming party for the DuMonts? "Leave Lucy to me," Beatrice said, responding to the concern in her husband's request. "She'll cooperate."

Percy sipped his Scotch. If anyone could handle

Lucy, it was his mother, but lately she had begun kicking even those traces. The early discomforts of pregnancy, coupled with her disgust of him, were driving her to act in ways that even she had not thought possible. She'd insulted several tradesmen, boxed the ears of the milk delivery boy, and called Doc Tanner a quack to his face. Several longtime servants had quit, and entertaining had been curbed owing to the uncertainty of Lucy being able to suffer gladly those fools the Warwicks had tolerated socially for years. Only the restraints of her Bellington Hall training, awe of her mother-in-law, and a faltering hope for their marriage kept her from popping all her stays, Percy believed. With Mary and Ollie's return, all hell might break loose.

But it was still the senior Warwicks' house and she its mistress, Beatrice maintained. With or without Lucy's cooperation, they would throw a party to welcome the DuMonts home.

On the evening of the event, an emergency at the lumberyard called Percy away, and he missed the arrival of the guests of honor. Invited to come early, they were already seated in the parlor with his parents and Abel, Mary beside the bassinet they'd brought along, when he appeared in the doorway. Lucy had not come down, he noted with relief. He focused first on Ollie rather than the lissome figure in ivory who rose with her husband as Percy entered.

"Percy! You old son of a gun!" Ollie exclaimed, grinning from ear to ear as he pushed toward him on his crutches. They embraced heartily, Percy brought almost to tears by the joy of having him home again.

"Welcome back, old friend," he said. "You've been sorely missed around here, I can tell you." He turned to Mary. "You, too, Mary Lamb."

There was a new look of maturity about her that had settled mainly in her eyes. He would never have believed a woman could look so beautiful. The soft color of her dress gave her skin the hue of honey and deepened the blackness of her hair, bobbed now and set off with a headband of ivory sequins.

They did not embrace. Percy had wondered if she would avoid eye contact, but she looked straight into his gaze with an intensity that broke his heart. Giving him her hand, she said softly, "We've missed you, too, Percy. It's wonderful to be home." He lowered his head to kiss her cheek, the one away from the group looking on, and closed his eyes in a small moment of private grief. Her fingers tightened in his clasp. He pressed them gently and let them go. Turning from her with a smile, he said, "Now, let's have a look at the little fellow, shall we?"

He peered into the bassinet, and the others joined him. "Isn't he beautiful?" Abel said. "I may sound prejudiced, but I don't think I've ever seen a more perfectly formed baby."

"Go ahead and sound prejudiced," Beatrice said. "I intend to when ours is born."

"He's something all right," Percy murmured, gazing

at the sleeping infant. Not so much as a cowlick of Ollie had found its way into the physical makeup of the child. He was a Toliver from the narrow, elegant feet to the cap of rich black hair on the well-shaped head. Stirred by an almost choking tenderness, Percy stroked the tiny palm. Immediately, the child woke and seized Percy's finger in a minute grip, fixing his eyes upon him with a glint of curiosity. Percy drew back and laughed, enjoying the exquisite feel of the small fingers. "How old is this little tiger?"

"Three months," the parents chorused together, and Ollie added, adjusting the armrests of his crutches, "and he's going to have to rely on his godfather to teach him to play ball."

"It will be my pleasure," Percy said, still held captive by the tiny hand. "What is my little godson's name?"

"Matthew," Mary said from the other side of the bassinet. "Matthew Toliver DuMont."

He glanced across at her. "Of course," he said, immediately dropping his eyes back to the child, unable to bear the assault—and memory—of her beauty. He watched, delighted, as the tiny mouth opened in a pink, round yawn, suckled air briefly, then closed in sleep. With great unwillingness, he slipped his finger from the soft clutch and left the side of the bassinet to greet the arrival of the other guests and his wife coming down the stairs.

In a flowing dress Abel had recommended to match the color of her eyes, she was charm itself as she circulated among Howbutker's social elite. She addressed Percy as "darling," slipped her arm through his, and threw him smiles from across the room. He was not deceived. He understood perfectly his wife's motivation for presenting herself as an exemplary hostess. This was her first big party as the wife of Percy Warwick, and plainly and simply, she'd have no one wonder why he had married her instead of the stunning Mary Toliver. She may not be beautiful, but she was warmer in personality, easier to make laugh, to engage in conversation. No one felt intimidated by her. She may have been rumored to indulge in quick flashes of temper and salty language, but weren't they normal aberrations of pregnancy?

After a brief peer into Matthew's bassinet, Lucy ignored the child. "Well," she declared, "I guess you have to claim it, Mary, what with all that black hair and widow's peak and all. And look at the chin dimple! Ollie, is there any part of you in this baby?"

Mary answered for him. "His heart, I hope."

"Yes, let us do hope," Lucy said.

The gazes of the two women locked. The former roommates had greeted each other with reserve. No exchange of hugs and kisses marked their reunion. Now their masks of friendship dropped entirely. A war of sorts was declared in their silent stares.

"Mary dear, perhaps it would be best to take the bassinet into the library and leave the little man to his peace," Ollie suggested calmly.

"What a splendid idea," Lucy said.

That night, when Percy went into his wife's room to say good night, she remarked from her seat at the dressing table, "Well, Ollie certainly cleaned up his mud hen nicely, though she's so tall and stalky, it must be like climbing a tree to fuck her."

Percy's jaw clenched. "Mary is five feet seven, which must make you feel like a dwarf in her presence," he said in a tone that belied his urge to slap her.

Lucy skewed a glance at him, her expression unsure of whether he'd meant the comment as an insult. "I could tell you were mightily taken with her kid," she said.

"His name is Matthew, Lucy. And, yes, he's a handsome lad. If we have a son, I'm hoping he and our child will enjoy the friendship that Ollie and I have known."

"Well, we'll see about that. I wish you'd demonstrate half as much interest in our unborn child as you showed tonight in Ollie and Mary's."

"The atmosphere around here has not been exactly conducive to that," Percy reminded her dryly.

"And you think it'll be any better once the baby gets here? Well, you might as well know now that you are not going to have much say in raising this baby. This baby is mine. You owe him to me."

"The baby is ours, Lucy. You can't use him as a hammer to keep beating me over the head." Percy was unmoved by her threat. His wife understood there was a line she'd better not cross. His guilt would serve only so far in taking her abuse. But he could not fault her for thinking that he had shown little excitement in the coming birth of the baby. Despite their marital situation, he thought his apathy odd and wondered how Ollie had felt before the arrival of Matthew. He must ask him.

The Percy Warwicks now occupied two bedrooms, giving as the reason to the household that Lucy's pregnancy required that she sleep in a separate bed. Percy had no idea what excuse they'd give afterward. He was at the door to leave when Lucy said, "You just watch me, Percy. Why would I want *you* to have anything to do with raising my child?"

"Why wouldn't you?" he asked curiously, coming back into the room. "I'm his father." Like Lucy, he thought of the baby as "him."

"Because..." He saw a bolt of alarm light her blue eyes at his calm, deliberate approach, and she got hastily to her feet.

"Because why, Lucy?"

"Because you're a—you're a—"

"I'm a...?" Percy prompted.

"You're a—a *homosexual*!"

For a few seconds, Percy stared at his wife in frozen astonishment, then he let out a guffaw of astounded laughter. "Oh, Lucy, is that what you believe?"

She set her hands on her hips. "Well, aren't you?"

"No."

"Have you ever done it before?"

"Yes," he answered, still in the throes of amusement.

"How many times?"

He did not wish to cause her pain, but he'd be damned if he'd allow her to believe a misconception that she'd use as a weapon to keep his child from him. "Often enough to assure you that you need have no worry that I may be an undue influence on our son."

"I don't believe you. It's the only explanation that makes sense." Slowly, arching her neck to observe him from beneath her lashes, she parted her robe, revealing her naked body. A slight protuberance of her abdomen disclosed the child to come. She cupped her swollen breasts in her hands. "How can you refuse these? Every man who's ever looked at me has wanted to get his hands around them." She moved toward him, holding out her bountiful endowments. "Aren't these lovely, Percy? Aren't they the most delicious-looking things? Why don't you want me?"

"Lucy, stop it," Percy ordered softy, drawing the robe closed. He did want her. He found her pregnant state erotically alluring, and he'd have liked nothing better than to pick her up and take her to his bed, there to ease into her and give them both the relief they craved. But nothing had changed to suggest their lovemaking would be more satisfying, and it would complicate their situation even more.

She sensed his withdrawal, and her small round face tightened in fury and frustration. She clutched the robe to her tightly. "You bastard! I'll never let you near my son. He'll be all mine, Percy. I'll see to that. No homo is going to have a hand in raising *my* boy! *Homo, homo, homo,*" she jeered as he left the room, closing the door quietly behind him, shutting out the sound of her pain.

Chapter Thirty-seven

The old year ended, and 1922 brought about improvements and acquisitions for the various enterprises of Howbutker's triumvirate. In Mary's absence, Hoagy Carter had managed Somerset with surprising success and brought in a crop that enabled her not only to pay off her loan at the Howbutker State Bank, but to fund an improved irrigation system for the plantation. The Warwicks acquired several lumber-related subsidiaries that resulted in renaming the company Warwick Industries, and Ollie DuMont opened a second department store in Houston.

As the year edged toward spring, Lucy's figure broadened to cumbersome proportions. She waddled when she walked, and her baby-soft skin gleamed with a constant sheen of perspiration owing to the unprecedented heat. Housebound because of her bulk and discomfort, she seemed to draw closer to Beatrice as she entered the final weeks of her pregnancy. Several times, Percy had come across the two women sitting together sewing baby clothes and talking quietly like old friends.

"It's so sad to see her when you come into the room," Beatrice said to her son. "She's like a snarling puppy wagging its tail."

"I know, Mother."

After the party celebrating the DuMonts' return, Percy fell into the habit of visiting them at the end of his workday at least twice a week. There had never been any question but that the couple would reside in the Toliver mansion, leaving Abel to ramble around in the château-style family home at the end of the avenue. At first, Percy had expected a certain awkwardness when he called upon the couple the Monday after the party, but he was lonely for their company and drawn to the baby, whose image hardly left his mind. He might have known Ollie would put him at ease.

"Percy, my boy!" his friend had cried when Percy telephoned him at the store. "My hand was on the crank to give you a ring when the secretary said you were on the line. I wanted to ask you to come by the house and crack open a bottle of something with me when you leave the office today. Mary may not be able to join us. You know how she is during planting season."

"Indeed I do," Percy said quietly.

But Mary was home, sipping lemonade and saying little as she rocked the baby and listened to the men who, within minutes, were carrying on like old times. Percy perceived that Mary's reticence was due to her uncertainty of where she and Ollie now stood with him. He told himself that it would take time for her to be assured that he came only out of friendship. He must not allow her marriage to rob him of the two people essential to his only happiness. And now there was Matthew, too.

Lucy was never present at these gatherings. She was not invited, and as far as Percy could determine, she had no knowledge of his visits. The two women had not attempted to see each other after the party, and he decided not to interfere with the status quo. His wife's absence permitted him greater freedom to enjoy himself, relax, and make a fuss over the child, who now recognized him and pumped his little arms and legs in gurgling welcome when he came into sight.

Before long, Mary appeared more relaxed and returned near enough to her old self for them to laugh together and pretend for the sake of all they had to preserve that their love had never been. By mutual, unspoken consent, they avoided physical and eye contact, Ollie and Matthew becoming the screens through which each saw the other dimly.

Sometimes Percy would arrive to find Mary still out at the plantation, her absence predictable but nettling. She should be home with her husband and son that late in the day, he opined privately, but he and Ollie had his godson to themselves then. Ollie would already have carried the little fellow to the screened back porch to catch the breeze, and he and Percy would talk and drink while one or the other's foot rocked the crib.

"Been down to the DuMonts again, have you?" Lucy asked one evening. She was in their sitting room, hem stitching the latest blue garment for the baby.

He made a wry face that he should be surprised at her knowledge of his visits, since by now he knew that little escaped his wife. "You could have come, too, you know."

Lucy chewed viciously at a length of thread with her small, sharp teeth. Percy took pity on her and handed her a pair of scissors lying beyond her reach. She took them without thanking him, snipped the thread, and said, "To watch you making ga-ga eyes at Matthew?"

Percy sighed. "Isn't it enough that you're jealous of Mary? Must you be jealous of her son, too?"

Lucy's hands came to rest on her mammoth abdomen. She glanced up at him with a softer look. He'd been standing all along. He never stayed long enough in his wife's presence to take a seat. "So all right, I'm jealous. I'm jealous of anything she possesses that should be mine."

He felt as if a sudden breeze had fluttered down his spine. He drew his brows together. "What do you mean by that?" he demanded, more sharply than he intended.

"You know full well what I mean. She...has your friendship, and now her son does, too."

Releasing his held breath, Percy reached to take her hand. "I want to be friends with you, Lucy, but you refuse to let me."

She gazed, mesmerized, at the unexpected contact of his hand. "Well, I'll...try to be friends—for the sake of the baby and since I can't have anything else from you." She lifted her blue eyes, naked with need, to his face. "And I didn't mean it when I said I'd keep the baby from you. I...want him to know his father."

"I know you didn't mean it," he said, releasing her hand. "I know you don't mean a lot of what you say to me."

Several weeks before the baby was due, Ollie asked Percy if he would drive him to Dallas to be fitted for an artificial leg, the first of its kind that he was willing to try. "I'd go by train," he said, "but the damn things are so uncomfortable and unreliable. I hate to ask Mary now that she's smack dab in the middle of ginning. She'd drop everything in a minute, of course, but there's no need for that, and besides"—Ollie indicated his pinned pants leg—"under the circumstances, Percy, I believe I'd prefer your company."

Resentment against Mary curdled within him as sour as bad milk. He agreed that in Ollie's situation, his assistance would probably be more suitable than Mary's, but it galled him that Ollie felt he could not impose upon his wife's duties to the plantation. Mary and her goddamn cotton. "How about Matthew?" he asked. "Will he be all right while we're gone?"

"Oh, of course. Sassie loves that boy like her own."

Percy broached Ollie's request with Lucy. Since the evening of their last parley, they'd been getting along somewhat. He knew she was frightened by the ordeal of childbirth, and he was frightened for her. Since she did not like to read, he'd withdrawn books on childbirth from the library and read them aloud to her in the evenings in their sitting room. She'd listen intently and discuss their contents with him afterward without animosity.

It was a tenuous truce at best, and it was with a feeling of guilt that Percy asked if she minded his leaving her at such a time. But, as usual, she surprised him.

"I think you should take him, Percy. You know the reason Ollie doesn't want to go by train, don't you?"

He confessed that he did not.

"Well, because... How long were you fellows on the train from New Jersey?"

"About six days."

"Can you imagine how Ollie must have felt, what he must have thought, during those days and nights coming home to Howbutker without a leg? No wonder he doesn't like trains. Yes, you should drive him. I'll be fine. Your mother and father will take care of me, but we'll wait for you in any case." She smiled at him, reminding him of the old Lucy. Much of her behavior lately reminded him of the girl she was before their marriage. The change was not—as his mother would say—"put on," but seemed due to a genuine desire to become his friend.

"Thank you, Lucy," he said, returning her smile. "I'll be back as soon as I can."

Percy drove them in Abel's roomy new six-cylinder Packard sedan, but the trip was long and hot to the Veterans Administration Hospital in Dallas. Ollie was flush-faced from heat and exhaustion by the time they reached its entrance. Perspiration stood on his forehead and dampened his shirt collar, and Percy ached for his discomfort as his friend labored to heave himself out of the sedan. An orderly appeared with a wheelchair, but Ollie waved it away and settled his crutches under his powerfully developed arms. "Let's go get 'em, Percy, my boy," he said, and swung after the orderly pushing the empty wheelchair.

After an interminable delay in filling out admittance forms, an attendant arrived with Ollie's medical records under his arm to escort him to an examining room. It was at the end of a long hall, and Ollie looked visibly dismayed at the distance. "Steady, old man," Percy said, following close beside him. "Only a few yards more."

But short of their destination, Ollie gasped, "Percy, I can feel my leg again, and the pain. I think I will take that wheelchair."

But it was too late. His one leg buckled, and he

toppled forward, his face contorted in pain. Crutches and the steel medical file clattered to the floor as the attendant and Percy tried to break his fall. The attendant ran for a stretcher while Percy loosened Ollie's tie and the top buttons of his shirt, his hands trembling, seeing again the body of his friend lying helpless and soaked with blood alongside a shell-shattered road. "Now, get that look off your face," Ollie ordered with a determined smile. "Sometimes this happens, and I'm all quivering flesh and raw nerve ends, but it passes. Just make sure you have a stiff Scotch ready for me when I get out of here."

"If I have to distill it myself," Percy said.

The stretcher arrived, and the two attendants lifted Ollie onto it. "If you'll pick up his file, sir, and bring it along, we'd be grateful," one of them said as he hoisted the framework of poles. Percy picked up the crutches and medical file, his hands still shaking. He took a minute to catch his breath and steady his own nerves before following the white-coats down the hall, but by the time he'd reached the anteroom of the examining area, they'd whisked the stretcher behind the No ADMITTANCE doors.

He decided that while he waited for somebody to return for the file, he'd take a look to learn the extent of Ollie's condition. Until today, he had not known that he could still feel pain in his missing leg. He never complained to him, but Percy was well aware of the reason. Like the wise man he was, the incomparable friend, Ollie knew that nothing drives a thorn deeper or quicker into the side of friendship than guilt.

The initial army report came first, the entries written in the hurried scrawl of a frontline doctor, the kind he'd read dozens of times on the clipboards hanging from the cots of men he'd visited in tent hospitals. In medical jargon, it described Ollie's injury and amputation, and then, at the conclusion of the report, a line—added like an afterthought—stilled the flow of his blood. He read it once, batted his eyes to make sure of his vision, then read it again: "As a result of Captain DuMont's injuries, the urethra is susceptible to infection resulting from retention of wastes normally excreted in the urine, and the irreparable damage to the penis renders the organ incapable of functioning for the purpose of intercourse and procreation."

The metal-covered file fell to the floor with a loud bang. Percy did not hear it. He flung himself out of his chair and staggered to an open widow, struggling for breath. His stomach heaved, his head reeled. He pressed his forehead to the cool white enamel of the window frame to stop the spinning of the room. *Oh, my God... oh, my God...*

"You all right, sir?"

It was the orderly, come to retrieve the file. From his position at the window, Percy mumbled, "I'm fine. Go tend to Captain DuMont."

He fell into a chair next to the open window and pressed his palms to the sides of his head. *Matthew...*

that sweet little boy... his—his! The obvious sequence of events unrolled in his bursting brain like the erratic reel of a silent film. *Mary discovered she was pregnant after he ran off to Canada. She waited, but he did not come home. Finally, she went to the only man who could rescue her and her child.* "Ollie was here," his mother had said. *And so Ollie had married her and agreed to raise her son as his own... shattered Ollie, who could give her no more children... who could not...*

He dropped his head into his hands and moaned—deep, bellowing tolls of grief dredged from the bowels of deepest despair. The orderly returned thirty minutes later to find him sprawled in the chair beneath the open window, staring blank-eyed like a dead man, his face ashen and glossed with tears. "Uh, pardon me, sir," he said, fidgeting with obvious embarrassment, "but I've come out to tell you that Captain DuMont will be hospitalized for observation and treatment until he can be fitted with a prosthetic limb. That'll take about a week. He's been given a sedative and is fast asleep. You can see him in Ward B during visiting hours from six to eight o'clock this evening."

Percy was spared the awkwardness of the visit when he telephoned home from the hospital and Beatrice asked that he return immediately. He was now the father of a strapping ten-pound son.

Chapter Thirty-eight

HOWBUTKER, 1933

Excuse me, Mr. Warwick, but there's a Miss Thompson here to see you."

Percy did not glance up from the report he was reading. It was late October, four years after the financial crash on Wall Street, which had sent the nation spinning into the Great Depression. Every day brought job seekers into his secretary's office pleading for work at Warwick Industries, one of the few stable ships in the county still sailing calmly in the worsening economic waters. "Did you tell her it's a waste of time to see me, Sally? The payroll is splitting at the seams as it is."

"Oh, she isn't here seeking employment, Mr. Warwick. Miss Thompson is a teacher. She's here about your son."

Percy turned up a blank stare, his mind working with the phrase *your son*.

"Wyatt, sir," Sally said.

"Oh, yes, of course. Send her in, Sally."

He rose to greet her, as was his custom when visitors were shown into his office. It did not matter who they were or the purpose of their call. Percy Warwick was noted for the dignity he accorded everyone, even those who, as was often the case these days, came begging, hat in hand, for a job, a loan, more time to pay off debts.

Miss Thompson had not come begging, that was plain to see, but despite her composure, Percy saw that she was clearly nervous and uncomfortable when she took the seat he offered. What the devil had Wyatt done?

"Is there a problem with Wyatt, Miss Thompson? I was not aware that you were his teacher." He made the point not to give the impression that he was one of those fathers who was on top of everyone who affected his son, but out of surprise that he had never met her. For the last few years, he had served as president of the school board. One of his functions was to greet personally the teachers new to the Howbutker Independent School District at the annual welcome reception.

"I was engaged to finish out the term for Miss Wallace, who married earlier in the year," Miss Thompson explained. "She and her husband moved to Oklahoma City. Miss Wallace, as you may recall, was Wyatt's original teacher."

Percy leaned back in his chair, templing his fingers, enjoying her clear, pleasing voice. "I am sure the change has not been to his detriment," he said with a gracious inclination of his head.

"I hope you will continue to think so when you hear what I've come to say."

"I'm listening."

She took a deep breath, lowering her gaze momentarily in an apparent effort to renew her courage. Good Lord, Percy thought. What kind of grief *had* Wyatt given her? He'd make sure he regretted it, if it was as bad as Miss Thompson seemed to imply. Still, it was easy to see how an eleven-year-old boy on the verge of puberty might be guilty of inappropriate behavior in order to gain her attention. She was a very pretty young woman, with clear hazel eyes and neatly bobbed hair evocative of the innocent shade of new wheat.

"Your son," she began, "is deliberately and systematically inflicting injuries upon Matthew DuMont. I am afraid if somebody doesn't stop Wyatt, he'll do serious harm to that little boy."

Percy's chair protested as he snapped forward, his pleasure in her beauty forgotten. "Explain what you mean, Miss Thompson."

"I mean, Mr. Warwick, that every day during school hours, Wyatt manages to hurt Matthew DuMont in some way. It can be anything from tripping him in the hall to deliberately throwing a ball in his face. I can't tell you the number of nosebleeds the child has endured because Wyatt has hit him. I've seen him...I've seen him..." Her cheeks reddened, as much from anger, Percy thought, as embarrassment.

"Go on," he urged tensely.

"I've seen him knee Matthew in the groin many times."

Percy felt his face grow hot. "Why in God's name did you wait until now to tell me? Why didn't you go to the school authorities?"

"I did, Mr. Warwick. I went to the principal, but he refused to listen. I tried to enlist the aid of the other teachers, but they refused to help me, also. They're all afraid of you...of your power. They fear for their jobs. The children, too. Their fathers work for you."

"Good God," Percy said.

"Today was the last straw," Sara Thompson continued, visibly gaining confidence now that she perceived she was making headway.

"What happened today?"

"Wyatt slashed Matthew's prized baseball glove, then threw it into the cesspool at the rear of the school. When Matthew waded out to get it, Wyatt threw a rock and hit him on the temple. It knocked the child nearly senseless and left a deep cut that bled freely. He lost his footing—"

Sara bit her lip, as if the description of the smaller Matthew falling into the muck of the waste pit, blood flowing from a temple wound, were too much to describe, but Percy clearly perceived the picture. He stood abruptly, fingers working angrily to button his suit coat. He knew the glove in question. It had been a present from him last Christmas.

"And does Matthew ask for these beatings?"

"Absolutely not!" Sara's defense was emphatic. "I know Matthew DuMont only as a member of my debate class and from playground duty, but I have observed him to be the nicest student I know. He tries to defend himself, but, though he's a class older, his size is no match for your son's. The other boys...they want to help, but they're afraid of Wyatt...of you."

"I see.... How did you get here, Miss Thompson?"

"Why, I..." Sara grappled with the relevancy of the question. "I walked here from the school."

"That's over two miles."

"The importance of my mission made the distance no consequence."

"So it would seem." Percy threw open the door of his office. "Sally, have Booker bring the car around. I want him to drive Miss Thompson home."

Sara stood up, looking uncertain now and a trifle flustered. "That's very kind of you, Mr. Warwick. I can't thank you enough for hearing me out."

"Why didn't you go to the DuMonts with this?" Percy asked.

"Because of Matthew. From what I know of him, I am certain he would rather die than tattle on Wyatt to his parents or ask for their interference or help.

I could not have appealed to them... before I tried you. It would have been a kind of betrayal. I would have gone to Mr. and Mrs. DuMont next, however."

"You admire Matthew, don't you."

"He has a great deal of character."

"And Wyatt?"

Sara hesitated, then met his gaze directly. "He has a mean streak in him, Mr. Warwick, but only toward Matthew, I've noticed. If it weren't for his... obvious jealousy of the boy, I suspect they'd be buddies. Your son's lonely, Mr. Warwick. He has few friends."

"His fault, I fear."

His chauffeur appeared in the doorway. He'd been on call today at the office rather than at the Warwick residence. Visitors from California had arrived to tour the mills. "You're to drive Miss Thompson to her residence, Booker. Then come back and pick up our guests. My car is here. I'll drive myself to the house." He held out his hand to Sara. "Thank you for coming to me. Booker will see that you get home."

Sara accepted his hand, her look slightly fearful of the mood that had come over him. His secretary and chauffeur seemed to sense it, too. "Mr. Warwick," she said uneasily, "if you'll forgive my asking, what do you plan to do?"

"If what you say is true, I plan to make certain that Wyatt never lays another finger on Matthew DuMont. And you do not have to ask my forgiveness for anything. It is I who should ask it of you."

Percy left his office through a door that provided access to a private garage. Murder foamed in his heart, but reason ruled his brain. He forced himself to remain calm as he drove toward Houston Avenue. He didn't know anything about Miss Thompson. She could be exaggerating accounts of typical schoolboy pranks as a ploy to bring herself to his attention. Such stunts had been tried on him before. These were desperate times, when women as well as men tried all kinds of ruses to ensure job protection and favors.

But he couldn't believe Miss Thompson the kind to play that game. If she was, he'd lost his considerable ability to spot rot in an otherwise sound piece of wood. He judged Miss Thompson to be one of those rarest of human beings—incorruptible. It had taken guts to come into his office bearing those tales. She'd put her job on the line. In not going to Ollie and Mary first, she'd shown sensitivity and an understanding of Matthew, who'd have been humiliated by his parents stepping in to fight his battles for him. Miss Thompson could not have known the other reason Matthew would never have tattled on Wyatt. Wyatt was the son of his godfather, whom he worshipped. He would never say anything about Wyatt that would hurt Uncle Percy. It was the kind of integrity that made Percy's heart break with love and pride, a feeling he'd never had for Wyatt.

He supposed—given the way his life had gone—that it had been too much to hope the boys would become friends. Matthew was willing, but Wyatt had disliked him from the start. There was nine months' difference in their ages. On Wyatt's part, there had been squabbles in the playpen, unfriendly horse-play in the sandbox, and, later, cold indifference at picnic tables as the two families met for outings to which other families were invited to ease the tension between Lucy and Mary.

As Miss Thompson had stated, the cause of Wyatt's hostility was obvious and simply explained. He was jealous of Matthew. Matthew was smarter, better looking, and more likable. Percy took pains to betray no favoritism when the boys were together, but it showed. Lucy often lamented that she wished he'd treat Wyatt with the same warmth he did "the DuMont boy."

But even Lucy liked Matthew, seeing in him all the endearing traits she appreciated in Ollie, and she wasn't above cuffing Wyatt's ear when he played too roughly with the smaller boy. In a strange reversal of her initial threats, she wanted Percy and Wyatt to be close and encouraged them to spend time together. It was a worry to her that from the outset, father and son had not appeared drawn to each other.

Try as he might, his heart went cold at Wyatt's clumsy attempts to win his affections. The boy had no Warwick in him. He was pure Trenton Gentry, Lucy's deceased father, in manner, looks, and attitude…a sullen, bull-necked, barrel-chested browbeater who mistook a kindly nature in the male for weakness. Not a drop of Lucy's humor and gaiety and animation was in him.

Hands tight on the wheel, Percy felt the slow building of the cold, controlled rage that few had witnessed or borne. God help Wyatt if he'd hurt Matthew. God help *him* if Miss Thompson was telling the truth. He parked at the rear of the Toliver mansion and entered the grounds by the wrought-iron gate. Sassie heard its squeak and was waiting for him at the back kitchen door.

"Why, Mister Percy, what you doin' here this time of day? Mister Ollie, he still be at the store, and Miss Mary, she out at Somerset."

Isn't she always? Percy thought with banked resentment. "It's not them I've come to see. My godson home?"

"He sure is. He up in his room. Got into a li'l trouble at school today, or rather, trouble come to him. Somebody threw a rock at him and cut him bad. And you shoulda seen his clothes!"

"Has he had this kind of trouble before, Sassie? Ever come home with a black eye or bleeding nose?"

Sassie's troubled face bunched further. "Yessir, Mister Percy, he has, and *this* time, I'm goin' to say somethin' about it to Mister Ollie. I just don't believe that child is that clumsy. Says he falls down a lot. I never seen him fall down round here."

"How bad was the cut?"

"Any deeper and I'd had to call Doc Tanner."

"Call him anyway, Sassie, and tell him to get here as fast as he can. I'm going up to check on him."

"He'll be glad to see you, Mister Percy. Take up this tray of hot chocolate I fixed him, and I'm addin' another cup for you. That boy like chocolate more'n his papa."

When Percy knocked, Matthew called, "Come in," in a boyish tenor that never failed to pull at his heartstrings. He opened the door to find him looking freshly scrubbed and sitting on his bed, oiling his baseball glove with some kind of putrid-smelling ointment. Apparently he was expecting Sassie. His eyes grew round when Percy entered carrying the tray of chocolate. "Uncle Percy!" he cried in surprise and alarm, quickly stashing the glove behind him. "What are you doing here?"

"I heard what happened at school today," he said, making room for the tray on a nearby table. He sat beside him on the bed and gently turned the boy's chin to study the bandage. "Wyatt do that?"

"It was an accident."

"And this?" Percy slipped the slashed glove from around him and held it up.

Matthew refused to answer or look at him.

"A friend told me what happened. Said Wyatt tossed your glove into the cesspool, then threw a rock responsible for that cut. Is that true?"

"Yessir, but it's okay now," Matthew said.

Percy examined the glove. It was ruined. Last Christmas, he'd given both boys the same kind of baseball mitt, and going to no small trouble, he'd had the gloves autographed by Babe Ruth. Percy had seen a rare smile on Wyatt's face when he opened the box containing the glove on Christmas morning. "Thank you, Dad. It's terrific," he'd said, flushing with joy at the unexpected surprise. Percy had not foreseen that Wyatt's pride and pleasure in his glove would be diminished when he learned that Matthew had been given the same gift. He should have anticipated his younger son's jealousy, but that did not excuse Wyatt's unconscionable meanness.

"I know where you can get another one just like it," Percy said. "A little larger, but your hand will grow into it."

"Oh, no, sir," Matthew protested. "I couldn't take Wyatt's. I wouldn't want Wyatt's glove. It's his. You gave it to him." He fell silent, a small vertical frown between his brows.

"What is it, son?" Percy asked, absorbing the details of his finely chiseled features that were so like his mother's. It was rare for him to have the opportunity to study his older son this closely, unobserved, and he never called him "son" in Ollie's presence. He'd noticed that Ollie didn't in his. It was always "my boy" or "my lad."

"I…don't know why Wyatt hates me," he said. "I've tried to be his friend. I *want* to be his friend, but

I think...I think he believes that you *like* me better than you do him, and...he gets hurt by that, Uncle Percy."

An almost unbearable rush of love for this child he could not claim forced him to stand. From what genetic well did this capacity for understanding, tolerance, and forgiveness spring? Not from him, and not from Mary. He poured a cup of chocolate and handed it to Matthew. "Is that why you've never said anything to anybody about the bruises you've brought home, the scrapes Wyatt has instigated? You know how he feels?"

"Yes, sir," Matthew said, his eyes on the cup he cradled in his slender, developing hands.

"Well," he said, rumpling the boy's black hair, yearning to kiss the top of his head, "perhaps Wyatt and I can come to an understanding of that. Doc Tanner is on the way to see after that cut, and I apologize for your—for my son's cruelty. It won't happen again." He picked up the glove. "I'll see this gets repaired."

In the hall, he telephoned Ollie at the department store and told him what had happened and that he was on his way to deal with the situation. "I believe you need to come home," he said. "Matthew could use your company. Mary needs to be here, too."

"I'll leave immediately. I don't know if I can reach Mary."

The carefully controlled fires of Percy's resentment

leaped. "Why the hell isn't she here this time of day? School's been out a couple of hours."

There was a pause. Though never expressed, Percy's view on Mary's absence from home was no secret between them. Ollie tacitly understood that his chagrin was only out of concern for him and Matthew. "Because she's Mary," he said quietly.

Leaving through the kitchen, Percy told Sassie she needn't worry. There would be no more unexplained cuts and bruises on Matthew. Then he was on his way to Warwick Hall, fury burning within him like glacial fire.

Chapter Thirty-nine

Lucy was in the dining room with the housekeeper, examining a magnificently laid table, when Percy strode through the front door and down the massive hall to the staircase. He never used the front entrance, and she saw his car parked under the portico outside. Breaking off from her inspection, she hurried to the door of the dining room. "Where are you going? Why are you home this early?"

Without breaking stride, Percy called back, "To see Wyatt. Is he in his room?"

"He's doing his homework. What do you want with him?"

Percy made no answer as he hit the wide staircase in a manner that sent Lucy scurrying after him. "Our guests will be here in a little over an hour, Percy. Do you want to change?"

In the two years since his mother's death—which had followed his father's in less than three years—Lucy had become a model hostess, enjoying her life as the wife of one of the most important men in Texas. Having always been cowed by her mother-in-law, she took over as mistress of Warwick Hall with a vengeance, ordering new furniture and carpets, repapering walls, and installing the latest in kitchen appliances. Her maids and housekeeper now wore frilly white aprons over crisp gray uniforms to replace the pinafores and black dresses of Beatrice's day. Her public duties as Percy's wife and her private life as Wyatt's mother seemed fulfilling enough. There were even times when Percy suspected that in spite of everything, Lucy was grateful for the life he had provided her. At least she'd been spared the worry of where the next dime would come from, since he had foreseen the stock market crash and taken precautions against it. They had not shared the same bedroom since her pregnancy, nor—to her often expressed regret—did they share their son.

It was for that reason that Lucy followed her tall, powerfully built husband up the stairs to her son's door. "Percy, what in the world is the matter?"

"Nothing to concern yourself with, my dear. This is between us men."

"Since when have you thought of your son in the same category as yourself?" she demanded, her blue eyes sparked with anxiety.

Percy threw open his son's door without answer and locked it behind him. True to his mother's word, Wyatt was lying on the bed, studying. School was a struggle for him, but apparently he persevered. He looked up at his father's abrupt entrance, his eyes growing wide.

"Get up," he ordered. "You and I are going for a ride."

"All right," Wyatt said, swinging off the bed. For a kid built like a bull, he had the grace of a cat. Percy watched as Wyatt swept his books off the bed into a school satchel, then smoothed the bedspread. A tidy little bugger in the bargain. "Okay, I'm ready," he said.

Lucy was hammering on the door. "Percy, what are you doing to Wyatt? Open this door!"

"Be quiet, Maw," Wyatt called. "I'm all right. Dad and I are just going for a ride."

But when Percy opened the door and Lucy saw his face, she perceived why he had come and what he planned to do. "Percy, for God's sake," she pleaded. "He's only eleven years old."

Percy pushed by her. "Then he ought to know better."

"Percy!...Percy!" Lucy called after him, snatching futilely at his arm as he marched down the stairs, a straight-backed Wyatt in front of him. "I'll never forgive you if you hurt him. Not ever! Percy, did you hear me—no matter what you do, I'll never forgive you!"

"Well, you never liked white roses anyway," he said, and followed Wyatt out the door.

They drove to the cabin in the woods without a

word passing between them. The sun was setting as they arrived, striking ablaze the cypresses at the lake's edge. Percy led the way, opening the door with a key rusting in the dirt of a flower pot that Mary had once planted with geraniums.

Removing his jacket, he spoke for the first time. "Miss Thompson came to see me today. She said you slashed Matthew's glove and threw it into the cesspool. When he retrieved it, you threw a rock at him and cut his head. He lost his balance and fell into all that filth. Why did you do that, Wyatt?"

Wyatt stood his ground in the center of the strange cabin he'd never known existed, his thickset body tense, waiting. His expression was impassive, stolid. When he made no effort to speak, his father thundered, "*Answer me!*"

"Because I hate him."

"Why do you hate him?"

"That's my business."

Percy's brows rose at the defiant tone. Eleven years old and already as hard as a Paris street fighter. He had Trenton Gentry's eyes. They were his mother's blue, but smaller and closer set, like those of the man Percy had despised. They did not waver when Percy began to roll up a shirtsleeve. One thing he had to give him, he thought grudgingly, he was no coward. A bully, but no coward.

"I'll tell you why you hate him," Percy said. "You hate him because he's nice and considerate and gentle.

He doesn't seem quite the boy you think he should be, but I want to tell you something, Wyatt. He's every bit the man you seem to think you are."

"I know that."

The response was not what Percy had expected. "Then why do you hate him?"

A shrug. A quick blink of the defiant eyes.

"And this type of thing has been going on a long time, I understand," Percy said, rolling up the other sleeve. "He's come home with bruises and bumps and cuts, all delivered by you. Is that right?"

"Yes, sir."

"And it's never bothered you that you're bigger than he is?"

"No, sir."

Percy stared at his son, unable to assess the baffling combination of his dispassion and honesty. At eleven, he was already pushing six feet and acquiring the breadth of his father's shoulders. "You're jealous of Matthew, aren't you."

"So what if I am? What's it to you?"

"You watch your mouth, young man, and don't you ever talk to your mother like you did back at the house. You are never again to tell her to be quiet, understand?"

"Why? You do worse to her."

Rage exploded in his head, blinding him. All he could see was the slashed baseball glove and the bandage over Matthew's temple. He saw love in the green eyes and hate in the blue. He drew back his right hand, balling it into a fist, and with his left reached for the jacket front of his other son, the one he did not know, did not love, did not wish to claim. "I'm going to let you feel what it's like to be beaten up by somebody bigger than you," he said through clenched teeth, and brought his fist forward.

The blow landed Wyatt on the floor hard against the front of the couch, a thin stream of blood trickling from his nose and a cut lip. Percy went outside and drew water, brought the bucket inside, and doused a towel in it. "Here," he said, thrusting the wet cloth at his son without pity or remorse. "Wipe your face. And Wyatt—" He reached down and yanked the boy into a sitting position on the couch. "If you so much as look cross-eyed at your—" The blue eyes shot a look into his. For the second time that day, Percy had caught himself from saying *your brother*. "Your neighbor and classmate," he amended, "I will make sure you never bully anybody else again. You understand what I'm saying?" He glared into his son's bloody face. "Do you?"

A nod, then through red-stained teeth, "Yes, sir."

When they returned home, the visitors from California were happily, volubly getting drunk in the drawing room. Dinner had been waiting an hour. "Where have you been?" Lucy hissed, meeting her husband in the back hallway. Percy had already sent Wyatt to his room.

"Getting my son acquainted with me," Percy replied.

It was the last formal event ever hosted by the Warwicks. When Lucy, fearing the worst, attempted to bolt up the back stairs, Percy grabbed her arm and directed her back to the drawing room with a grip that said she'd leave their guests on pain of injury, divorce, or worse. All through the long meal and port afterward, she sat uncommunicative and anxious-eyed while her husband, freshly attired, steered the conversation and poured the wine. When finally the guests had departed, she fled up the stairs to see Wyatt.

He heard her wail of dismay and awaited her fury in his room, where he was calmly removing his cuff links when she burst in. "How could you have done what you've done?" she screeched. "You've nearly beaten our son to death."

"You exaggerate, Lucy. What I did was nothing compared to what he's been dishing out to Matthew DuMont for years. I simply gave him a dose of his own medicine." He related what had happened that day at school and the report of Wyatt's systematic bullying of Matthew.

"What he did wasn't right, I know that, Percy," Lucy cried, "but what you did was worse. He's going to hate you for it."

"He already does hate me."

"Only because of the attention you pay Matthew.

That's why he treats Matthew the way he does. He's jealous of your affection for him."

"Matthew deserves my affection. Wyatt doesn't."

"*Matthew! Matthew! Matthew!*" Lucy struck her palm with the wedge of her hand with each cry of the boy's name. "That's all I hear from you! Holy Mother of God, you'd think Matthew was your son!"

The words held in the room like smoke following an explosion. Lucy stood as if shot, her figure rigid in the satin folds of her evening gown. She stared at Percy, realization dawning across her countenance like the slow breaking of light over the sea. Percy was not quick enough to avert his face before it confirmed the blinding truth of her charge. "*No...,*" she gasped, horror filling her face. "Matthew is your son! It's true, isn't it? He's yours and...and Mary's...." Her voice fell to a whisper. "Mother of God..."

He turned away, knowing that no amount of denying could undo what his expression had betrayed.

Lucy moved to stand in front of him, her scrutiny of his face so intense that he could almost feel her eyes boring into his skin. He refused to look at her. He riveted his gaze over her head to the vista of immaculate, moonlit grounds beyond his bedroom windows, removing himself mentally from the room. It was a trick he'd learned in the trenches when to be aware of the wreckage around him was to go mad.

A hard slap across his face shocked him from his escape. "You have your gall!" Lucy shrieked. "How dare you shut me out at a time like this! Tell me the truth, you prick!"

His cheek stinging, Percy answered wearily, glad to be relieved of the charade. "Yes, it's true. Matthew is Mary's and my son."

Temporarily without words, Lucy gaped at him for several agitated heaves of her enormous bosom. "I should have realized from the way you look at Matthew and never at Wyatt that he is yours, but I believed Mary when she said that you two weren't interested in each other and that I had a clear field. I believed her because I knew she'd never spread her legs for a man who didn't give a fiddler's fart for Somerset...." Her mouth opened wide as another apparently horrifying realization stunned her. She moved back from him as if to give herself room to strike. "So you were able to do it with *her*! At least long enough to get her pregnant."

"Lucy, there's no point in discussing that."

"No point in discussing it?" Lucy circled Percy slowly, dimpled fingers spread, tapered nails like claws itching to get to his eyes. "Tell me, you bastard. *Tell me!* Were you able to get it up and keep it up with *her*?"

Percy looked at the twisted face of his wife and decided that he could no longer live with the lie between them—or with her. The lie had accomplished nothing but to unbridle the inherent meanness within her—as his dissatisfaction with their son had unleashed his.

"Tell me, you goddamn bastard," Lucy screamed at him, "or can't you bring yourself to admit that not even the beautiful Mary Toliver was enough to rouse your manhood? What a shock *that* must have been to her, the lying bitch." She began to laugh, bending down with her hands on her satin knees, the hem of her evening gown pooling on the floor. Hysterical tears streamed from her eyes. "Can you imagine how she must have felt when she discovered that she'd gotten pregnant with so little for her pains? Got her hair blown, did she, and without so much as a ride around the block. What a joke on Mary."

Percy could endure no more. What feeling he'd ever had for Lucy all at once, irretrievably, flowed out of him as if he had a hole in his heart. He reached forward and, shocking her out of her laughter, gripped the bodice of her satin gown and pulled her to within inches of his stalactite gaze. He could not have this little witch feeling sorry for Mary—not his Mary, whose losses were as great as her own.

Boring into the startled blue eyes, he said, "Permit me to answer your question, my dear. Not only did I keep it up, I lifted her with it. Sometimes, I even carried her by it to the bed, where we finished what we'd started somewhere else."

Lucy struggled to free herself, drawing back her hand to slap him, but Percy caught her wrist and gripped it with such force, she cried aloud. "You're abominable when you make love, Lucy. You're like an alley cat in heat. That's why I can't keep it up with you. There's no mystery with you, no tenderness, no sensitivity. Your sweat feels like pus, and your body odor rises up like heat from stones. I'd rather stick my pecker into a pig's snout than slide it into your cunt. Now, does that explain why I don't come to your bed?"

Ruthlessly, Percy pushed her from him. Lucy nearly fell, but she kept her footing, her look on Percy stricken, disbelieving. "You're lying! You're lying!"

"The only lie I'm guilty of is letting you believe the fault was mine."

"I don't believe you."

"What don't you believe, Lucy? That I kept it up with Mary or that you're a terrible lay?"

She spun away from him, hiding her face with her hands. Percy waited. Now was as good a time as any to get everything out in the open, get the tears, the hurt, and the charges over with all at once. He said presently, "Lucy, I want a divorce. You and Wyatt can go anywhere you please. I'll see to it that neither of you ever wants for anything. We can't go on like this. I'm a poor husband and a poorer father. Somehow we have to cut our losses and get on with our lives."

Lucy dropped her hands and swung to face him. Her bodice was torn, her wrist showed the pressure of Percy's grip. Mascara streaked her face. "Just like that. You'd get rid of Wyatt just like that."

"He'll be better off. We all will."

"What is it that you have in mind, after you've gotten rid of us? Try to get Mary and your son back?"

"You know me better than that."

"After what you did to Wyatt, I don't know you at all."

"What I do when you leave here is my business and should not decide your course."

Lucy had begun to tremble noticeably, and her face was shockingly white. Clasping her hands together, she asked in a voice struggling for composure, "Why did you let me believe it was you all these years? Why didn't you tell me that...that I was to blame, if I am?"

"Because I owed you, Lucy. You married me because you...loved me, and I married you for the wrong reason."

"The wrong reason," Lucy repeated softly. Her chin trembled. "Well, I've always known you never loved me. So why did you marry me?"

"I was lonely, and you made me less lonely—then."

Lucy attempted a laugh to cover the patent sadness that scored the soft, round features of her face. "Well, what a couple of sad sacks we make! Feature it, folks—the great Percy Warwick, with all his looks, popularity, and money—*lonely*! An unimaginable picture. Why didn't you marry Mary? Don't tell me she was stupid enough to choose Somerset over you?"

Percy said truthfully, "Somerset has always been first in Mary's heart."

A corner of Lucy's mouth pulled to one side. "And you couldn't be second, of course. Do you still...want her?"

"I still love her."

Lucy fixed him with a glance that dared him to lie to her. "Are you two still going at it?"

"Of course not!" His tone was sharp. "I haven't been with Mary since before I left for Canada."

Inaudibly his breath caught, and he regretted his words the minute they popped out of his mouth. When he saw the quickening of Lucy's eyes, a cold hand gripped his heart. "Canada...," she mused. "That's where you'd gone when Ollie and Mary married, the reason you weren't in the wedding.... Does Ollie know that Matthew isn't his?"

Her tone made him think of the smooth glide of a snake toward its prey. "He knows."

Lucy sauntered to one of the windows and asked with her back to him, "Matthew doesn't know that you're his father, does he?"

Percy could feel the crawl of icy fear down his spine. Why in hell had he mentioned Canada? The truth in the hands of Lucy would destroy them all...all the ones he loved. "No, he doesn't."

She turned around slowly. Her expression was calm now, her hands toying with the ripped neck of her gown. "Of course he doesn't. I do recall asking your mother why you weren't in Ollie and Mary's wedding, and Beatrice explained that you returned the day after the ceremony. The way I figure it, Mary discovered she was pregnant during the time you were in Canada. So she went to Ollie, always her devoted slave, and he was only too willing to take her as she was. Soiled goods are better than none, especially to a man with one leg. And, of course, Ollie knew whose hands had used her—"

"Shut up, Lucy."

"Not before I make several points clear, Percy, my love." She sashayed near him and thrust her face close to his. Percy recoiled, feeling his nostrils flare, and Lucy stepped back, her face blazing. "God, I hate you, you persnickety bastard. All right, here it is, Percy Warwick. I will never give you a divorce. And don't try to get one, because if you do, I promise I will go to Matthew and tell him the truth about his father. I will tell Howbutker. I will tell the world. Everyone, just like me, will put two and two together. They'll remember that Mary was in Europe with Ollie when Matthew was born. They'll remember the hasty wedding, the hurried departure overseas, and how unlike Mary it was to run off and leave the plantation for so long. They'll remember that you were in Canada at the time, unable to make an honest woman of her. No one will find it difficult to believe the truth."

Casually, she removed a pair of pinching diamond-and-ruby earrings as if she hadn't a care in the world. "Are Mary and Ollie aware that *you* know you're Matthew's father?" When Percy remained silent, she said, "Ah, I didn't think so. Their manner makes me think they believe they've kept the secret from you. I couldn't begin to guess how you found out, but I can guess what it will do to them—to all of you—if the scandal of Matthew's paternity comes out."

Percy felt cold to the bottom of his feet. He was convinced she meant every word of her threat. She had nothing to lose, and he had everything. "Why do you want to stay married to me, Lucy? You're miserable here."

"No, I'm not. I like being the wife of a rich and powerful man. I'm going to start enjoying it more. And if I am...abominable in bed, then I wouldn't have much chance of marrying a man of quality again, now, would I? And there's another reason I intend to stay married to you. I never want you free to marry Mary Toliver DuMont."

"I wouldn't be free to marry her in any case, not if I divorced you tomorrow."

"Well, I'll just make sure of it. No, Percy, you're married to me for good—or until Mary DuMont's death."

Her satisfied expression slipped abruptly when Percy approached her, eyes the color of arctic waters. She backed away as near to the fireplace as the lit fire and her flammable gown allowed. "Then you understand this, Lucy. If Matthew ever discovers that I'm his father, you're out of this house on your ear without a cent. You'll wish you'd hightailed it while the getting was good. You said earlier that you didn't know me at all. I'd remember that if I were you."

Lucy inched by him. "I can forgive you for not loving me, Percy," she said, reaching the door and escape, "but I'll never forgive you for not loving Wyatt. He's also your son."

"I am fully aware of that, and it should make you feel better to know that I'll never forgive myself for not loving him either."

Chapter Forty

Here's a letter for you, Mr. Warwick. It was hand-delivered by the Winston boy."

As he took the letter from his secretary, Percy recognized the writer of his name on the envelope. He coughed to regain the sudden loss of his breath. "Did he say who sent him here with it?"

"No, sir. I asked, but he wouldn't tell me."

"Thank you, Sally."

Percy waited until the door had closed before slitting open the sealed flap. He withdrew a single sheet with the message "Meet me at the cabin today at 3:00. ML"

ML. Mary Lamb.

Percy sat back and pondered. What the hell was this all about? It had to be important, and secret, for Mary to ask him to meet her at the cabin, the place so sacred to their memories. They hadn't been there together since the afternoon of their last fateful row fifteen years ago.

She'd not indicated that anything was amiss last evening at the little welcome party she and Ollie had given for William, Miles's son, who'd been sent to live with them after his father's death in Paris. She and Ollie had both seemed edgy, but Percy believed it had to do with the hard times they'd fallen on, like almost everybody else in the county. He wasn't sure how hard. The families never discussed one another's financial straits, but falling cotton prices and bleak retail sales had to have affected them adversely. While he was uneasy about the DuMonts' future, he was more anxious about Matthew's. What affected them affected his son.

Did this note have to do with Wyatt?

There was no accounting for the capricious cards life could deal, the unexpected faces that turned up. After the session with Wyatt in the woods, he'd feared that his son would hate Matthew even more. The reverse had occurred. To his and Lucy's and Miss Thompson's astonishment, within days the boys began to pal around together, and by the end of the school year they were inseparable—as close as brothers, everybody said.

At first, Percy had thought the friendship an attempt of Wyatt's to get on his good side. It soon became apparent that Wyatt hadn't the slightest interest in getting on any side of his, good or otherwise. His son courted no notice or attention from his father, and Percy's opinion of him did not appear to matter in the least. The boy ceased to acknowledge that he existed.

"Do you see what you have done?" Lucy railed. "Have you any idea? You have driven away the only son you can ever call yours. Oh, you may not love him, but there was a chance he would have loved you. And we can all do with more of that, Percy, no matter who it comes from. Look around you. You may not have noticed, but the wells from which you once drank so freely have dried up or disappeared."

She was right, of course, as he'd discovered she often was. With his mother and father dead, Mary removed, and his wife and son estranged from him, only Ollie was left and Matthew, whose affection, while warm and real, was nonetheless that of a nephew for a favorite uncle. It was a good deal less than what he'd hoped to be enjoying at the age of forty after fourteen years of marriage.

Had Mary somehow gotten wind of his ongoing affair with Sara Thompson?

After sending Wyatt back to school with a split lip and swollen nose, he had stopped by her classroom weekly to discuss his son's conduct. One thing had led to another over time, and now they met regularly in out-of-the-way places. He had gone to great lengths to keep their relationship secret, not so much for his sake as Sara's. By now, everyone knew the state of the

Warwicks' marriage, and none would have blamed him for taking a mistress, as long as it was somewhere beyond Howbutker and the eye of his wife and son. Still, he lived in fear that some little something would trip them up and their liaisons would eventually be discovered. They'd had a few close calls already, and now, with a tight chest, Percy wondered if this meeting was to alert him that a scandal was about to break.

He arrived at the cabin early, but she was already there. A shiny roadster was parked under the tree where Shawnee and the buggy were once tied. Percy remained in his Cadillac for a few minutes to quiet the old ache under his rib cage. It was always with him, but buried so deeply that he was hardly conscious of it, like a chronic pain felt only in certain weather.

She was standing in the center of the room, her sleek head cocked to one side, and he wondered if she was caught up by echoes from the past. She turned as he entered, a vision in a red floral dress that brought out the sensuous highlights of her blue black hair. She was thirty-five, in the prime of her womanhood.

"There have been changes here," she said. "I don't recognize the couch."

"It's one I used to have in my office," Percy said. "Matthew conscripted it at Wyatt's suggestion."

She chuckled. "One more generation of boys to enjoy its allure. I'll need to remind Matthew that they should keep the place clean."

"And how will you do that without giving away that you've been here?"

She gestured with an embarrassed movement of a beautifully manicured hand. Every inch of her reflected the attention and excellent taste of a husband who took great pleasure in adorning her in the finest. "Good point," she said. "I know this is awkward for both of us, Percy, but the cabin is the only place where I thought we'd be completely private. If we were seen with our heads together, Ollie is likely to figure out why we met...what I asked you here to discuss."

So this wasn't about Wyatt or Sara. Percy breathed a little easier, but his heart missed a beat nonetheless. "Is something wrong with Ollie?"

"May we sit down? It's early, but I brought us something to drink. Scotch for you. Tea for me." She gave him her usual smile, a small parting of the lips. He rarely saw her smile at full throttle anymore.

"I'll wait," he said.

"Very well." Mary swatted the seat cushion of one of the chairs. Dust flew up, but she took the seat anyway, crossing her legs. "Have a seat, Percy. I could never talk to you while you were looming over me."

A muscle tightened along his jawline at the flurry of memories. He sat forward on the couch in his "no-nonsense mode," Lucy called it, hands locked, forearms on his knees, gaze cool. He and Mary had not been alone together since the last time they were in the cabin. "What's wrong with Ollie?"

An eyelid quivered at his tone, but her air remained calm. "He's in deep financial trouble. He's on the verge of losing the stores. A man named Levi Holstein holds the mortgages, and he refuses to give him an extension. He wants to include them in his chain of dry-goods stores. I'm sure you can imagine what it will do to Ollie and his father if the main store should fall into the hands of a man like him. It will absolutely kill Abel."

Percy knew Levi Holstein by reputation. He bought the mortgages of foundering retail properties from banks desperate to get out from under the loans and foreclosed promptly without mercy when the retailer could not meet his payments. His scheme was to pick up stores like the DuMont Department Store cheaply, keep the name, but strip them of their trademark trappings and stock them with inferior merchandise. "*Both* stores?" Percy asked, dumbfounded. "Including the one here in Howbutker? But I thought it was mortgage-free."

"Ollie wasn't as...wise as you, Percy, in believing that the market was overspeculated. He...put his money in stocks and borrowed to build the second one and buy inventory, using the flagship store as collateral. Even if he were able to sell the Houston store, the money he's been offered isn't enough to keep the one in Howbutker afloat."

Percy's mind reeled. It was worse than he'd feared. Ollie, his friend and brother, no longer the owner of the incomparable DuMont Department Store in Howbutker? Nearly a hundred years of excellence down the drain? It was unthinkable. And Mary was right to believe Abel would not survive it. He was already in ill health, and as much as he enjoyed his grandson, he had been lost since the deaths of Percy's parents. And what about Matthew, who he was secretly hoping would step into Ollie's shoes rather than Mary's?

"How soon?" he asked.

"By the end of the month, if Ollie can't meet the full terms of his note," Mary said. A bleak light broke in her eyes. "I'd sell Somerset, every acre of it, I swear, if Ollie would permit it and if I could get a fraction of what it's worth, never mind find a buyer. Nobody wants a cotton plantation when they can pick up cheaper land elsewhere that's already under a more productive cash crop." She stood suddenly, massaging her throat. "Excuse me," she said, crossing to the sink. "My mouth has gone dry. Before I go on, I must have something to drink."

Percy almost got up to go to her, but a force of will held him to his seat. The strain he saw in those shoulders tore at his heart, but it wouldn't do to put his arms around the beautiful woman he still loved, still wanted, the wife of his best friend, a man he'd give his life for. Talking over the clink of ice cubes, he said, "You called me out here because you obviously think I can help. Now tell me what you want me to do."

"Commit fraud," she said.

"What?"

After a long swallow of iced tea, Mary reached for her handbag on the counter. She withdrew an envelope and a folded document and handed them to him. "These are from Miles," she said. "One is a letter written to me and the other is a land deed. I received them shortly before his death."

Percy inspected the land deed first. He noticed that Mary's name was written on its face. "This is the deed to that section along the Sabine that your father left Miles," he said.

Mary nodded. "Miles transferred the deed to my name with the intention that I hold it for William until his twenty-first birthday. As you know, minors cannot possess land in Texas. His instructions are spelled out in that letter."

Percy read the letter, slowly understanding why she'd asked him out here, the word *fraud* ringing in his ear. He looked up, appalled, when he'd finished reading. "Mary, Miles specifically states that you're to hold his land in trust for William. You're not proposing I buy it, are you?"

"You've said you're interested in buying land along a waterway to dispose of wastes from a pulp mill you're hoping to build—"

"God, Mary!" Fury pulsed in his head. "I'll give you any amount of money you need, but I will *not* buy what Miles intended William to have."

"I believe you will, when you hear me out," she said. "All I ask is that you hear me out."

Percy drew a breath. How could he refuse her? He'd done that once, to his everlasting regret. "All right," he said, suppressing his anger. He pushed back into a more comfortable position and extended an arm along the frame of the couch, as he had those many years and misbegotten dreams ago. "You have my attention."

He could see that she was too wrought up to sit down. The filmy dress floated about her legs as she strode back and forth to present her arguments, sounding as if she'd rehearsed them a hundred times in her head. Percy needed property accessible to water, she said. Without Miles's section, he would have to go outside the county to acquire it, removing potential jobs from Howbutker, which she was sure he did not want to do. The money from the purchase would pay off Ollie's loans and save at least the Howbutker store. Percy needn't worry that she was cheating William out of his birthright. Upon her death, he would inherit half of Somerset, whose worth would far exceed the value of the strip along the Sabine. In some form, he'd inherit a portion of the store as well, an asset that would not be available if it was allowed to be lost.

"But with William receiving nothing at twenty-one and never knowing his father had left him that section," Percy pointed out.

"Yes, there's that," Mary agreed, stopping her pacing to look at him with regret, "but how can he be hurt by what he'll never know? Once he's old enough, I'll be only too happy to turn over the reins of Somerset's management to him, and he'll share in its revenue along with Matthew. Rather than Miles's heir, he'll be mine. How could my brother want anything more for his son, and how could I be more pleased than to have another Toliver on the land?"

Percy remained closemouthed but felt a faint palpitation in his upper lip at Matthew's name mentioned in the same breath as her hopes for William.

"Percy, you know that Ollie will accept no money from you outright," she said, sitting down at last and imploring him from the edge of her chair. "You could empty your bank vault into his lap, and he wouldn't accept it. However . . . if you can convince him of your crucial need for that land and of the job opportunities a pulp mill would provide the community, then Ollie might go along with accepting money from the sale. As a matter of fact"—her tone lifted—"he made an agreement with me long ago when he gave me his signature to save Somerset after the harvest failed. . . ." Her eyes begged forgiveness for bringing up a painful memory. "I made him promise that he would allow me to help him if he was ever in my situation. I'm going to hold him to that promise, if you will help me."

Percy removed his arm from the back of the couch

and hunched forward. Her arguments made good, if criminal, sense. They'd all benefit if he bought that Sabine strip. Even if Mary was unable to keep Somerset afloat—and that was a decided possibility—the store would provide a living and a possible inheritance for Matthew as well. No one stood to lose—except William. "One thing you've forgotten, Mary," he said. "Ollie will never permit you to sell William's land. He'll expect you to abide by the terms Miles spelled out."

There was a small silence filled by the katydids striking up a chorus from the lake's edge. Percy's scalp hair tingled. He recognized the nature of that silence. "What are you not telling me?" he asked.

"Ollie hasn't seen the letter," she said. "I...didn't show it to him when it arrived. I told him only that I'd received a letter asking that we take William in, but I pretended I misplaced it. I showed him only the deed with my name on it and told him that Miles had transferred it to me when he learned he was dying."

Percy forced down a surge of revulsion. He visualized Miles, dying of agonizing lung cancer, writing the letter in trust that his sister would do the right thing by his son. "Then why the hell did you show *me* the letter, Mary? I would have bought the land without ever knowing Miles asked you to hold it for William."

She looked at him helplessly, shamefaced. "I...guess I couldn't bring myself to deceive you, too, Percy.

I... didn't want you to agree to my proposal without knowing the truth." A flush heightened the perfection of her cheekbones. "I wanted you to know everything, so that you... could refuse without... guilt."

"Oh, for Christ's sake. As if you thought I *would*!" He pounced up. "Where's that Scotch?" He struck off to the kitchen alcove and rattled around in a paper sack, Mary watching fearfully as he found the bottle and poured a stiff drink. After a moment of letting the Scotch do its work, he said, "Maybe there's another way."

"What is that?"

"I could go to Holstein, offer to buy the mortgages. Ollie need never know I'm the buyer. I could extend him as much time as he needs to meet his loan."

Hope flamed in her face. "I hadn't thought of that. Do you think it's possible?"

"Let me give it a try. If Holstein refuses, I'll agree to your proposal, but you must swear one thing to me, Mary." His tone warned against any thought of deception.

"Anything," she said.

"You must swear that you're asking this of me on behalf of Ollie and not Somerset."

"I swear... on my son's soul."

"Then you better make damn sure you're not putting it in jeopardy." He set down his glass. "I'll need a few days to meet with Holstein, then I'll contact you by letter. I'll send one of my boys around with it. We can't chance the phone."

A week later, Percy sat at his office desk and composed a letter to Mary. He had failed in his negotiations with Levi Holstein. Not only had the retailer hooted away his generous offer, saying that he'd waited half a lifetime to acquire department stores of the DuMont quality, but he'd sneered that Ollie had only himself to thank for his financial pickle. "He lacks good business sense," he'd declared in his mean little office in Houston, tapping his forehead with a jaundiced-nailed finger. "What store owner in his right mind accepts IOUs for goods in times like these? What landlord refuses to evict tenants who do not pay their rents when the oilfield workers flooding East Texas would pay double for a place to live?"

"A good man, maybe?" Percy had suggested.

"A *foolish* man, Mr. Warwick—of the kind that you and I are not."

"Are you sure about that, Mr. Holstein?" Percy had asked, and watched the man's face pale from the implication.

He sealed the envelope and summoned one of the mail boys up from the basement. "Take this letter to Mrs. DuMont and put it directly into her hands. No one else's. Understood?"

"Understood, Mr. Warwick."

From his top-floor window, Percy, with an acrid

taste in his mouth, watched the boy pedal off on his bike. The pathway to hell was paved with good intentions, but what about the wrongs committed for the right reasons? Were they included as well? Life had taught him that anything that starts wrong, ends wrong. In this case, he supposed that only time and its unpredictable mercies would tell.

Chapter Forty-one

Percy sat in the Warwick pew waiting for the church service to begin, lulled into inertia by the hum of conversation around him and the drowsy whirr of overhead fans. He was the only member of his family present. Lucy had once contemplated converting from Catholicism when they married but never had, and Wyatt had spent the night—as he did every Saturday night—at the DuMonts'. Unless Ollie had cracked the whip this morning, odds were the boys would not make it to church but were probably still in the rack or devouring stacks of Sassie's pancakes drowning in butter and ribbon cane syrup. Of the two families, only he and Ollie attended church regularly. Mary was an inconsistent churchgoer, usually spending her Sunday mornings going over accounts at the Ledbetter place, and Lucy, a nonpracticing Catholic, spent hers sleeping in.

Ollie must have cracked the whip, Percy observed in amusement. A side door of the church opened, and his old friend stepped through, followed by Matthew, Wyatt, and Miles's son, William. Percy smiled to himself. He could imagine the scene this morning with Ollie and Sassie getting that trio scrubbed and brushed and harnessed into suits and neckties. No doubt Mary had left for the Ledbetter place before daybreak, since it was now harvesttime.

All four saw him. Ollie's face broke into its usual broad smile, eyes turning ceilingward in mock long sufferance of the morning's ordeal, and Matthew and William each grinned and waved. Only Wyatt's countenance remained impassive, his eyes sliding away from his father without acknowledgment.

Percy watched the boys follow Ollie down the far aisle to the DuMont pew, Wyatt maneuvering to get a seat next to Matthew. He could not help but feel a stab of envy as he stared at his friend seating himself, both of his sons on one side of him, and now Miles's son belonging to him, too. Ollie would not sit in his pew wondering, with a tug of loneliness, what he would do with himself for the rest of the day, as Percy was now doing. Ollie would go home at the end of the church service, the boys in tow, and Mary would be there waiting, the house smelling of baking ham or frying chicken or roasting beef. He and Mary would sit on the screened back porch, she drinking her iced tea and Ollie his French wine, while the boys did their best not to rend asunder their Sunday suits until dinner was over and they were free to change. Afterward he'd grab a nap while Mary did her bookkeeping and the boys were out on the lawn playing the same games that Percy and Ollie and Miles had played every Sunday of their lives when they were growing up. In late afternoon, there'd be a rousing game of cards followed by a light supper—maybe even fudge—and Ollie would finish the day with his family gathered around the radio. A wonderful Sunday, that. None better. Percy remembered those kinds of Sundays in his own home when his parents had been alive, and before Lucy. Odds were he'd never experience their like again.

The church service began. Percy went through the motions of participation, his attention on his two sons sitting side by side a few pews down the other side of the aisle. How unalike they were. And how odd that both should so thoroughly resemble their mothers. They took only their height from him, Matthew at sixteen and Wyatt nine months younger, already standing a head taller than their peers.

Wyatt possessed the male version of Lucy's solid, compact form, while Matthew had inherited Mary's long, willowy frame. Posture would always be a problem for Wyatt, whereas it never would for Matthew. Percy wished there were a device to stretch Wyatt's stumpy neck and correct the oafish slump of his shoulders. In comparison, his older brother sat in the pew with his head high, back straight, and shoulders squared, all held with Mary's effortless grace.

This is my beloved son, in whom I am well pleased....

Rising to sing with the congregation, Percy remonstrated with himself over the unfairness in being pleased with only one son. He should be pleased with Wyatt, too. The boy tried harder at what came naturally to Matthew and therefore more easily. Only aggression was natural to Wyatt, a sort of controlled belligerence that stood him in good stead in playing football, a sport at which both boys excelled. It surprised Percy that Wyatt took so readily to the bridle of rules and discipline and team play required to play football. But he did, and with a total commitment that Percy could not help but admire.

The boys had been playing the game since each was in the seventh grade and were now co-captains of the junior varsity team. Their group was being predicted to lead Howbutker to its first state championship, a future thrill that both Percy and Ollie looked forward to eagerly.

The two men often attended practice sessions together but saw the game with their wives separately, occupying seats on the fifty-yard line at each end of their row. Matthew played quarterback; Wyatt was an offensive lineman who led his teammates in protecting their leader and opening holes for him to streak through. Lucy's eyes never left Wyatt's bull-like figure on the field. Percy's rarely strayed from Matthew's thoroughbred form. He could not believe the boy's agility in outmaneuvering his opponents, his intelligence in calling plays, the sheer magic of his skill in firing the ball to a receiver in the end zone. It was breathtaking, it was wonderful. Inside himself, as the roar of the hometown crowd filled his ears, he'd shout: *That's my son! That's my son!*

But there was reason to be proud of Wyatt, too. Though slow to comprehend, he retained everything he learned. He was conscientious in his studies, staying up as a matter of routine until all hours of the night to wrestle with the dragons of his homework. Percy kept an eye on his academic progress through Sara, and from her he learned of his son's near failures and close victories, marks that never reflected his effort and perseverance.

Whenever he returned late from meetings or a visit to Sara's and saw a light still on in his son's bedroom, he did not step inside to ask how it was going, the way he once had. Wyatt had not appeared to welcome these intrusions and had merely grunted an answer without lifting his head from his books.

He labored hard when put to work at the mills also. Managers extolled his efforts, as amazed as Percy that he did not take advantage of being the boss's son to shirk his duties any more than he used his father's position as president of the school board to wangle favors from his teachers. Wyatt accepted Percy's praise in these matters with the same dispassion with which Percy suspected his son would take his criticism. His indifference eased Percy's shame that Wyatt's dogged victories, his heroic efforts, never reached his heart like Matthew's easier, more natural ones.

A cough broke the listening silence of the congregation as the scripture was read. A number of heads, including Percy's, turned toward the DuMonts' pew. The perpetrator had been Matthew. Percy saw Ollie discreetly slip him his handkerchief. Matthew coughed into it, a deep, jacket-tightening hack that drew Wyatt's worried gaze.

Percy felt a jab of concern. The boy's coming down with a cold, he thought, glad that Ollie would be there to look after him. He wouldn't have to worry about Ollie running off to the store and leaving Matthew at home ill.

"...give, and it will be given to you; good measure, pressed down, shaken together, running over, will be put into your lap," the minister read. "For the measure you give will be the measure you get back."

Percy listened to the Text and his eyes went again to Ollie. There, sitting beside his friend and waiting at home, was proof of the scripture's promise. Ollie had always given full measure without counting the cost. Of all the men he'd ever known, or would know, Ollie was the most giving. If he'd had to lose the woman he loved to another man, he was glad it was Ollie. If he'd had to give up the son he could not claim to another to raise, he was glad it was Ollie. If his other son turned from him to another father to honor and love, he was glad it was Ollie. Ollie's cup did indeed run over, and deservedly so. Percy was happy for him. He questioned only how it was that he had ended up with a measure so much less.

The service was ending. As the congregation rose for the benediction, Matthew flashed him a grin over his shoulder and jiggled his eyebrows. Percy chuckled, but his concern deepened. The boy looked pale and a little thinner than when he'd last seen him. Once the prayer was finished, he waited by his pew for Ollie and his charges to draw abreast.

"How about coming to the house for Sunday dinner, Percy?" Ollie invited. "Sassie's having chicken and dumplings. Matthew here"—he gave the boy's shoulder a mock punch—"has been off his feed lately, and Sassie thought that might be just the ticket to get him eating again. Me, I don't need an excuse to eat Sassie's chicken and dumplings. I hope nobody heard my stomach growling."

"We did, Dad," Matthew said, rolling his mother's eyes, "but we thought it was thunder sounding on the plain."

"That'll be good for a couple of boxed ears," Ollie said benignly. "How about it, Percy, my boy? We're stealing Wyatt as it is."

Percy wanted to accept. Lucy would be playing bridge with the lowbred cronies with whom she cavorted every Sunday, knowing that Wyatt would be well fed at the DuMonts'. But Wyatt glanced down and shuffled his feet, and Percy took that as a sign that his son preferred he decline. So he said, "Thanks anyway, but I had planned to do a little work at the office." In reality, he'd be going to Sara's house later and eating a grilled cheese sandwich, probably scorched. Her talents did not include cooking. Matthew definitely looked peaked, he decided, and he worried that the DuMont household might not be taking the boy's condition as seriously as it should. "Wyatt, don't overstay your welcome, you hear?" he said. "Let Matthew get some rest this afternoon. Kick him home, Ollie, when you need to."

Ollie looked at Wyatt affectionately and clapped a hand on his shoulder. "Will do, but Wyatt never overstays his welcome."

"Well, then behave yourself," Percy said, and added as an afterthought for Wyatt's benefit, "He always does. Why do I feel I have to say that?"

"Because you're his father," Ollie said, a wise twinkle in his eye.

So it was with some surprise, but no shock, that Percy found Wyatt waiting for him when he returned from Sara's earlier than planned that afternoon.

Chapter Forty-two

He'd driven home with a heavy heart. Sara was leaving him. She'd accepted a job far out in West Texas, where school districts on oil-rich lands could double the salary she was making in Howbutker. There was no future for her here, anyway, she'd said, her look tender but her meaning clear. Sadly, Percy had concurred.

He entered his drive wishing he had somewhere else to go. He'd rather be anywhere but here. He could have gone to his office, but he had no mental energy today for paperwork. He was hungry for food and comfort, neither of which his home provided. His house and grounds had the look and feel of a neglected mausoleum. All the help had gone except for the cleaning women who occasionally came in when Lucy, occupied with her card parties, thought to arrange for them. Since they no longer entertained— once their old cook retired—Lucy saw no need to hire a replacement. She did not like to bother with supervising the kitchen or planning menus or checking accounts, preferring to put together simple meals for her and Wyatt to eat at the kitchen table hours before Percy came home. Sometimes she left a plate warming for him, sometimes she didn't.

As he drove past the house to the garages in back, Percy noticed the overgrown flower beds and newly fallen leaves in need of raking. Nobody lives here anymore, he thought gloomily, spying a crack in one of the mullioned windows of the sunroom. Inside the house, he had knelt to examine it when he heard a throat cleared from behind him. "Dad?"

He threw a startled glance over his shoulder. "Wyatt? What are you doing here? I thought you'd be at the DuMonts'."

Wyatt swatted a cobweb hanging from the door and shuffled into the room. Doesn't he ever pick up his feet? Percy asked himself with a flash of annoyance, then realized that of course he did. He'd seen him lift those size thirteen D's often enough on a football field. It was only around him that he dragged his dogs.

"Something wrong with the window?"

"It's cracked. Probably hit by a bird or a BB. I'll have to get it replaced." He brushed the dust off his hands as he got up. The windowpanes were dirty, like most of the house. "Things are cracking up around here," he said with a grin at his pun. "You look like something's on your mind. What is it?"

Percy thought he could guess. He's come to ask if

he can work out at the plantation on Saturdays with Matthew through the harvest, he conjectured. He should have seen it coming. Each boy understood that he was to work at his family's business on Saturdays throughout the school year and every day but weekends during summer. Percy often wondered if Matthew had ever had a choice as to whether he wanted to learn farming or retailing. From the time he could walk, Mary had dragged him out to Somerset. He didn't believe the kid had ever so much as stood behind a counter in the DuMont Department Store. Matthew didn't appear overenthusiastic about his future as a farmer, but he didn't balk at it, either, minding his chores with the same cheerfulness with which he attended everything else.

Percy was as uncertain of Wyatt's feelings for the vocation for which he was being groomed. The boy labored uncomplainingly and willingly, but silently. He'd never expressed one sentiment about the business he would someday share with his father—and, in time, inherit.

"Well?" he prompted.

Wyat's gaze roved, refusing to meet Percy's—another affliction he suffered in his presence. "It's Matthew," he said with his usual lack of inflection.

"What about Matthew?"

"I think he's really sick, Dad, and he won't let me tell Mister Ollie or Miss Mary or Coach. I didn't promise nothin' about telling you."

It seemed to Percy that all time stopped. "What makes you think he's sick, son?" The address slipped out naturally. Neither indicated he took note of it. "You can tell me. I heard him coughing in church and thought it was a cold. What makes you think it's more than that?"

"He's got a fever. I made him let me take his temperature. It was a hundred and four degrees. He don't look right, neither. I'm awful worried about him."

For once, Percy took no notice of the poor grammar that ordinarily set his teeth on edge. Percy heard only urgency in Wyatt's tone and saw it in the blue eyes that were at last riveted to his. "Where is Matthew now?"

"Upstairs in my room. His folks think we're at the practice field throwing a few balls around. Matthew barely made it through dinner."

Appalled, Percy said, "You mean they let him go? They didn't notice that he was sick?"

"You know Matthew, Dad. The way he can carry on, nobody'd know nothin' was the matter. He's afraid if his folks or Coach find out, they won't let him play Friday night."

"Then I was the wrong one to come to, Wyatt. If he's sick, I'm calling his parents, game or no game Friday night."

Wyatt nodded. "That's why I came to you. I knew that's what you'd do. Matthew is more important than any dumb old football game."

Percy took the stairs two at a time to Wyatt's room, his son on his heels. "Ah, Wyatt, you *told*!" Matthew accused when Percy burst into the room and he saw the look on his godfather's face.

"I never promised I wouldn't tell my dad," Wyatt said. "You're sick, man. You need to see a doctor."

Percy placed a hand on the boy's forehead. It was burning up. His teeth were chattering in spite of the cocoon of blankets Wyatt had wrapped around him. "He's right, Matthew," Percy said. He could taste the metallic bite of fear in his mouth. The boy's color was bad. There was a blue tinge about his eyes and under his nails. Percy had seen that cast in 1918 among his army buddies disembarking for home and carrying with them the deadly virus that would sweep the nation and kill four hundred thousand people in a flu epidemic. Oh, God, please don't let it be what I think it is, he prayed, feeling his legs turn to putty.

It was worse. Staphylococcal pneumonia, Doc Tanner's new replacement diagnosed. The recently discovered antibiotics were powerless against it. How, where, and when Matthew had contracted the particular virulent strain—called the Bowery-bum variety—nobody knew. Those who sat numb with grief by his bedside knew only that it had come with devastating speed and was resisting every attempt at treatment. One week Matthew had been a healthy, active teenager bent on leading his team to victory Friday night, and the next he was lying in bed fighting for breath, coughing up spume, death already behind the sunken green eyes peering out at the faces peering in, desperation meeting desperation.

"Doctor, *do* something!" Mary wailed, clutching the new doctor's sleeve, her face a bloodless mask.

But he and the specialists consulted sadly agreed that there was nothing more to be done except pray that Matthew could ride it out. He was young and healthy and strong, and there were reported cases of victims his age who had survived the disease.

A room was prepared in the Toliver house for Percy and Wyatt to share so that they would be near Matthew's bedside. "It would mean so much to all of us for you and Wyatt to stay here until the boy's better, Percy," Ollie said when it became apparent that Matthew might not recover. "You've been a second father to him. No man could have been more caring, and Wyatt could not have loved him more if they'd been brothers."

Percy looked at his friend—the man who knew that it was his son and Wyatt's brother who lay dying—and could not speak for the love and anguish choking him. He was grateful, too, for Wyatt's presence beside him in the sickroom and in the guest quarters, where they lay sleepless in twin beds, staring at the ceiling, bound together in mutual grief, until finally, toward morning, Percy was relieved to hear the sound of his son's youthful snoring.

It was Wyatt whom Matthew asked to see in the

last hour of his life. Percy found him in the hall roaming like a blind bull, thick shoulders hunched, shaggy head drooped, hands shoved into pockets, dumb with grief. "Matthew is asking for you, son," he said gently, and without speaking, their eyes never meeting, Wyatt followed his father to the sickroom, where he edged shyly around the door.

"Hey, Wyatt," Matthew said.

"Hey, yourself."

"How's practice going?"

"Not so good without you."

"Yeah, well, I'll get back if I can."

Suddenly galvanized, as if an electric current had been switched on inside him, Wyatt lunged across the room and hauled a chair close to his bedside. "No *if* about it," he said, speaking with hard insistence into the pneumonic face. "You have to come back, Matthew. We need you, man. *I* need you."

Matthew was silent. Then he whispered with the wheezy substance left of his breath, "I'll get back, man. You may not see me, but I'll be there. You keep on blasting holes in that line."

"No...," Wyatt groaned. He reached for his friend's hand and crushed it in his great grip against his chest, as if he could keep death from snatching him away. "No, Matthew...you can't leave me, man."

Mary turned away, her eyes wide with terror, and Percy and Ollie bowed their heads. It was the first time they knew that Matthew realized he was dying.

At the end, the ones who loved him best were all with him. Sassie and Toby hovered wet-eyed in the doorway, Abel looked on bleakly from a corner chair, Wyatt and Mary and Ollie hung over his bedside. Only Percy stood apart, gazing out the window at the sun rays slanting through the moss-draped cypress trees that Silas William Toliver had transplanted from Caddo Lake a century before. Toliver history had it that the trees were not expected to survive, but whatever the Tolivers planted on their land survived, year after year—no matter what disaster. Only the Toliver children died.

"Dad…"

Percy's shoulders tensed, but he did not turn around. It was Ollie who answered. "I am here, my boy," he said, and Percy heard his chair creak as he bent closer to his son. Beyond the window, the September afternoon blurred in a sea of blue and gold. The cypresses wept.

"It's okay, Dad," Matthew said clearly, the breathlessness gone. "I'm not afraid to die. I figure heaven's like here and God's like you."

Percy turned from the window in time to catch the last flicker in the green eyes fixed upon Ollie before the lids fluttered closed and the light was gone.

Chapter Forty-three

It seemed to Percy in the days following that Mary never left her stance before her parlor window overlooking the reclaimed rose garden. Morning, noon, and night he'd find her standing there, her back to the room, hands clasping her elbows, an aloof figure, drawn into herself. He was powerless to comfort her. He could not look into the grieving eyes of the mother of his son without betraying the grief of the father in his.

He and Ollie and Sassie received the callers to the house, accepted the telegrams, the gifts of food and flowers, while Mary stood her vigil at the window, often acknowledging the condolences murmured to her frozen profile with only a nod of her dark chignoned head.

"Chérie…," Ollie consoled, embracing her stiff shoulders, smoothing the sleek sides of her hair, brushing his lips against the high, stoic curve of her cheek. *"Ma chérie…"*

Finally, Percy could keep himself from her no longer. She was wasting away, turning to stone before the window. "Mary?" he said softly, laying a hand on her shoulder. To his surprise, as if she'd been waiting for him, she reached up and clutched it to her collarbone. They were alone in the house. Ollie was at the store and Sassie at the market. He'd come in at Sara's behest only to drop off in the hall a basket of condolence letters written by Matthew's classmates.

"I thought it was overexertion, Percy. You know how hard the boys practice and how drained they get the first weeks of football practice, playing in those uniforms in humidity and heat. I begged him to get more rest, to eat more, to drink plenty of water...."

His ears thrummed. What was her point?

"And in spite of what you no doubt think, I didn't haul him out to Somerset to force-feed his heritage to him. I did it because it was the only way I could have him to myself. I lived for summers and Saturday mornings. I knew the time was coming when I'd have to give him up to...his own dreams. He talked of becoming a coach."

Why was she telling him this? But he believed he knew. Yes, she'd perceived correctly that in the first crazed days of his grief, he'd asked himself if Matthew would have survived if she'd been home to notice his illness. But that had been unjust. She could have been around twenty-four hours a day and it wouldn't have mattered. Matthew would have concealed his condition from her. It had taken him years to see it—to admit it to himself—but Matthew had belonged to Ollie. He'd loved Mary, but he preferred the man he thought was his father. Ollie had been his confidant, his friend, his pal. Mary had been almost like an interloper, no matter how hard she tried to create a bond between them. Matthew had shut her out, and—as always when alone—she had turned to the land. He only now realized how hurt she'd been, how lonely.

"Look at me, Mary." He had misjudged her once in thinking she'd married Ollie to rescue Somerset. He wouldn't make that mistake again.

She released his hand and turned around. His heart turned over. Grief had sharpened her features, dulled her eyes, brought out the first threads of gray in the hair drawn back from her temples. Gently, he clasped her shoulders. "Matthew didn't die because of anything you did or didn't do. Forget that nonsense. None of us saw it coming."

"You don't blame me?" Her eyes were wells of despair. "I thought you might think it was the Toliver curse."

At first, he'd considered that, too. How could it be a coincidence that Mary would marry a man who could give her no more children and lose her only child at sixteen, leaving William the single Toliver heir? He remembered that her father and brother had believed in the curse, and Miles had even predicted its evil would befall Mary. But he'd dismissed the brief thought as irrational. A curse was not responsible for the tragedy they'd made of their lives. They were their own curses. "Rot," he said. "Utter rot. Matthew died of viral pneumonia, not some idiotic curse."

"I've even thought"—she wrung her hands—"that we—*I'm*—being punished for selling you Miles's land...that God is getting William's own back by...by taking Matthew from us."

We. Us. She meant her and Ollie, of course. "That's utter nonsense," he said sharply, annoyed now, frightened by the guilt-plagued look in her eyes. If these questions were the demons she was wrestling before the window, she was lost. She would never recover. "We did what we had to do for the welfare of all concerned."

"Did we?" she asked.

Percy had the urge to shake her. What was she getting at? How could she question their motives *now*? "Don't be absurd! We acted on behalf of Ollie. He would have lost his store otherwise, and you would have had to sell the plantation in order to eat."

"It wasn't Matthew you were thinking of?"

"Well, of *course* I was! I had to make sure he'd be left with something salvaged from his parents' monumental stupidity."

After a stunned instant, a new light flowed into her eyes. He let go of her shoulders and stepped back, his angry words *something salvaged from his parents' monumental stupidity* resounding in his ears. Oh, God.

He felt the secret he'd housed so long fall to pieces inside him like slowly breaking glass.

She said calmly, her gaze now serene, "You know, don't you. I was sure of it."

He could not have denied it. He could not have denied Matthew. "Yes," he said, feeling the admission sawed from his heart.

"How long have you known?"

"Since I drove Ollie to Dallas to be fitted for a prosthesis. When I read his medical file and learned the extent of his injuries, I knew that Matthew could only be mine."

Her mouth grew taut. "Then you know... everything."

"Yes, Mary, I know everything."

She closed her eyes and wavered slightly. "Oh, Percy, what a mess I've made of everything."

He took her by the shoulders again. "What a mess *we* made of everything."

"You'd gone to Canada when I found out," she said. "I waited for you, pleaded with God to send you home. But when I didn't know how pregnant I was and nobody knew where to reach you, I was forced to turn to Ollie...."

"I figured all that out in Dallas," he said, folding her in his arms. "I want you to know, Mary, that I was coming home to tell you I couldn't live without you. I didn't care if Somerset came first, last, and always with you, as long as you married me."

She relaxed with a sigh against him. "And I want you to know that I'd discovered I could live without Somerset, but not you. I promised to give the plantation up if only you'd come home and marry me and be the father of our child. It would have been enough, Percy. It would still have been enough."

"I believe you," he said, feeling the warmth of her tears through his shirt. "I know that, now."

They held each other for a while longer, their heartbeats merging, and then their moment was over. It must never happen again. Mary withdrew a ready handkerchief from her sleeve, and Percy asked, "When did you suspect that I knew?"

"It came to me gradually," she said, gesturing that they sit. "When I saw the way you looked at Matthew...in a way that you never looked at Wyatt. The love for a firstborn, I guess...."

"Is Ollie aware that I know?" He followed her motion, and they took chairs before the fireplace, a table apart.

"I'm sure he doesn't. He's always credited your devotion to Matthew as a result of how much like me he...looked."

"That was part of it."

"And Lucy?"

He sighed. "She knows. She discovered the truth about four years ago."

She paused in wiping her eyes. "Good Lord, Percy, how?"

"It doesn't matter. She knows, that's all. That's why she's been rotten to you these past years...and why she hasn't come down to pay her respects." Actually, Lucy had been overcome when she learned that Matthew was dying, but she feared that any attempt to express her sorrow to Mary might betray the secret it was essential for her to keep. "She went to mass every morning on behalf of Matthew and lit God knows how many candles," Percy said. "And to give her credit, she's been exceptionally understanding of Wyatt and me throughout all this, as only Lucy can be."

"Why didn't she divorce you?"

Percy laughed roughly. "I offered, believe me, but Lucy is not about to divorce me. She hates me too much. If I try to divorce her, she's threatened to tell the world about you and me—about Matthew. His death does not change that. There are still you and Ollie to think of, what the scandal would do to you and the memory of Matthew."

"And Wyatt," she said, pale from the shock of this new information.

"Yes, of course...Wyatt."

"Why did you marry her, Percy? You could have had any girl."

He gave her a twisted grin. "The stream was pretty well fished by then. I was lonely. She was there."

"What in the world happened? She worshipped you."

"She discovered her idol had clay feet," he said, his face closing on the subject. "Should we tell Ollie?"

"No," she said immediately. "He deserves to be spared further pain. He's already suffered from the fact that Matthew never knew you were his father. It would be too much for him to learn that you were aware of the truth all along." She dabbed at her tears again. "Our stupidity has hurt so many people. We've kept them from the lives—and maybe the loves—they would have known if we'd married. Matthew was denied his real father and your parents their grandson. Wyatt has grown up the product of a marriage that never should have been. He might have turned out a different boy altogether if he'd been born of a loving union. And Lucy...poor Lucy." Her look held fear that she was treading on dangerous ground. "Let me simply say this, Percy. Her hate is a cover. It's the only way she can bear the love she still feels for you."

He stood suddenly to end the discussion and poured a glass of water from a table still laid for those paying respects. "Regardless, Lucy would have been better off married to anyone but me," he said. "I suppose all we can do now is to somehow deal with the cards we've been given."

"How do we do that?"

He took a long quaff of the water. He wished to God he knew. All his days had a singed quality to them now, like the burnt corners of letters retrieved from the fire. He'd never know an unblemished twenty-four hours again. But if they could make the most of what they had left, they might enjoy a modicum of happiness along the way. He turned back to her with a tentative smile. "Maybe we should begin by forgiving ourselves for the pain we've caused," he said.

She glanced down, toying with her wedding band as if considering that suggestion, the curl of her lashes reminding him achingly, unbearably, of Matthew. After a moment, she looked up. "Maybe we should start by forgiving each other."

The next day, Percy made a visit to the family florist and ordered a single white rose to be delivered to Mary Toliver DuMont, enclosing a note that read: "To healings. My heart always, Percy."

When he arrived at his office, a florist box awaited him on his desk. He opened it and drew out a lone white rose with a note attached that brought a small smile to his lips. Mary had written in her typically brief style, "From my heart to yours. Forever, Mary."

Chapter Forty-four

Percy passed through the next two years like an automaton working of itself without conscious direction. He ran the company, made decisions, built his pulp mill on the bank of the Sabine, acquired more timberlands, and purchased additional subsidiaries without thought of why. The Depression ended. The economy surged forward owing to the newly declared war in Europe. America was on the move, building, building, building, and business boomed for Warwick Industries. The company could barely keep up with the orders flooding its salesrooms.

The distance lengthened between him and his family. For a while after Matthew's death, Lucy's attitude softened toward him, but when she saw how ineffectual his efforts were in comforting Wyatt in his grief, she turned from him once again. "You've lost him, Percy," she said sadly. "You've lost him so completely you'll never find him again. That boy is wandering lost and lonely, all by himself, and even if you should call, he wouldn't answer. He'd never answer the voice of a stranger."

The truth was, Percy did call. He needed Wyatt as much as Wyatt needed him, but there was no reclaiming the man if you'd lost the boy. For his son was a man now, as towering and powerfully built at seventeen as his father, responsible, quiet but cognizant, a presence to be considered in the company meetings Percy invited him to attend. Somehow, as he had emerged from boyhood, his shoulders had lost their loutish slump, his feet their sluggish gait. He walked tall and straight and if not proud, at least resolute, as if determined to reach a goal known only to himself.

Percy did his best to mend fences with his son. He arranged fishing and hunting trips for them, neither of which activity he himself particularly enjoyed. Since the war, he had no stomach for killing, not even a freshly caught trout for a campfire supper. The outings were designed for father and son to be alone together, and if they arrived back at Warwick Hall no more in touch than when they'd left, at least Percy was beginning to make certain discoveries about his second child.

Wyatt, he learned, had the natural instincts of a hunter and fisherman both. For all his bulky size and cumbersome feet, he had an uncanny ability to steal noiselessly and adroitly through tall grass, move surely upon his prey. Percy observed with awe the patience with which his son could wait, hour upon hour, in fishing boat or on riverbank, for his quarry to strike his line. He killed quickly and efficiently, taking in stride the moment of incurred death, an act that Percy always found embarrassing.

He took over the supervision of Wyatt's homework, a duty that Lucy formerly was only too happy to share with Wyatt's more nimble-minded half brother, Matthew. With equal relief, she now surrendered her chair at the kitchen table in the evenings to Percy. These sessions failed in their objective to reclaim the son he'd alienated, but they did provide insight into the makeup of his intellect. By no means did Percy find Wyatt as dull-witted as he'd formerly believed—a point Sara had tried to drill into him often. He was a plodder toward comprehension, certainly, and so deliberate in digesting information that Percy could understand how he'd thought him a dim thinker. But once he'd chewed and swallowed, his recall was complete, a mental ability, Percy explained to his son, that few people possessed. Lucy preened from this unexpected praise for Wyatt, but, as was his way, he merely shrugged, his stolid expression unchanged.

Wyatt continued to play football, serving as captain of his team the last two years of high school. Matthew's gridiron number was retired. No one from Howbutker High was ever to wear number 10 again. His jersey was given to Wyatt at the DuMonts' request, and Percy knew he stowed it away with the baseball glove that he never wore again after he'd destroyed Matthew's, and a copy of *The Adventures of Huckleberry Finn* that Matthew had given him on his thirteenth birthday. The inscription inside had made Wyatt laugh, but he hadn't offered to share its ribaldry with either of his parents. There were times following Matthew's death that Percy had to refrain from stealing into Wyatt's room to rummage for the mementos left of his first son, there to hold the jersey a moment, to read the only lines in Matthew's hand he knew existed.

He never did. He contented himself with going to football games and watching "Bull" Warwick open holes in the defense, wondering if Wyatt ever felt his brother's presence behind him, ever looked up from the ground and visualized Matthew sprinting across the goal line—if it was for him he blocked, making it possible for Howbutker High in his senior year to win its first state championship.

The town went wild. Victory celebrations were held all over Howbutker, but Warwick Industries hosted the biggest party in the company clubroom. Everyone who had been part of the championship dream attended—everyone but Wyatt. By now his mother had grown accustomed to these sudden, unexplained absences of her son. He was known as a loner, preferring his own company to that of his gregarious teammates and the dewy-eyed girls who draped themselves over his hard-muscled shoulders. He was well liked, but no one pursued his friendship, and since Matthew, he'd had no other buddy.

"Go find him, Percy," Lucy said on the night of the celebration. "I want him here. He should be here, enjoying all this hoopla. He was the one who made it happen."

"Keep everybody here until we get back. I think I know where I can find him," Percy said.

It was another inexplicable conundrum concerning Wyatt that Percy could not figure out. He'd have thought that after meeting his father's fist and being threatened with death in the cabin, the boy would have avoided the place like a den of cottonmouths. Yet Wyatt had introduced the place to Matthew, and it had become the boys' private sanctum during the years of their friendship, as it was now for William Toliver and his friends.

Wyatt had disappeared to the cabin for two days following Matthew's burial. Tonight was colder than the last time Lucy had sent Percy looking for their son, but he found him where he'd suspected he'd be—out on the lake, hunched over a rod in the canoe, much the same way Percy had discovered him then. Like that other time, knowing he was entirely visible in the moonlight, he placed his hands on his hips and waited for Wyatt to notice him. Like then, he was conscious of the lost years between them, as impossible to traverse now as it would be to walk out there to Wyatt on the path made by the moon.

Presently, the silhouette moved, the strong shape

of the hunched back turned in his direction. "Any luck?" Percy called.

"Nah, too cold," Wyatt called back, and wound in his line. Percy heard the soft plop of the bait being tossed into the water. He observed Wyatt methodically stow the rod and reel, take up the paddle, and begin to row to shore.

As he watched, a memory floated to Percy.

Percy?

Here, Lucy.

He was hearing his wife's voice again, the night she had found him in the library and asked him to go find Wyatt after his disappearance. Drawn to the corner where he sat in the moonlight, she had knelt quietly in front of him and placed her hands on his knees. *You've been sitting here like this for two days, Percy. It's night again.*

Again? He had pondered the inaccuracy of her statement. The night had been constant since Matthew had died five days ago. His little boy had been lying in the cold, dark earth for two days and nights.

I feel so truly sorry, Percy. Please believe me.

I believe you, Lucy.

I can't imagine losing a son. I pray to God I never do.

God, or one of His angels, must have pressed a finger to Percy's lips, sealing them, thereby preserving the residue of their marriage. For he was about to say, *I hope you never do, either, Lucy,* and she would have taken him to mean that the loss of his second son would be exclusively her own.

Tonight, as he heard the smooth, unhurried slice of the paddle into the lake, a sadness pierced him to the quick of his soul. How many times had Lucy sent him out to find their son, yet he never had? He'd driven Wyatt away from him right here on this spot, and he had never come back, not in all these years. He would soon turn eighteen. In September, the Nazis had invaded Poland and then France, prompting Great Britain to declare war on Germany. His old friend Jacques Martine, with whom he'd fought in France, predicted in a letter from Paris that America would be at war in less than two years. Two years… two years to find his son.

And what would he be able to give Wyatt if he should find him? Love? Did he love Wyatt? No, he did not love Wyatt, not the way he had loved Matthew, with that heart-stopping, throat-closing rush of feeling that had proclaimed him flesh of his flesh, blood of his blood. He had no understanding why. Wyatt had courage and integrity, loyalty and perseverance. He was not a braggart or a snob, though he had cause to be both. He was strapping and handsome, envied and sought after, but he took no more notice of that than he did of himself as the son of one of the richest men in Texas.

"He wouldn't," responded Sara in a letter when he wrote to her of these observations. "He looks upon all that attention as a result of who you are, not him. Your being rich is a source for *your* pride, not his. I can't believe he's the same boy who was so cruel to Matthew."

It was a thought that had often crossed Percy's mind.

"Give you a hand?" he offered as Wyatt neared where he stood. Wyatt threw him the line, and his father tugged the boat into the small slip, holding it tight until he could jump to the bank.

"Party get dull?" Wyatt asked, taking the rope and winding it competently around the spike.

"No, that's why I came to find you. Your mother and I thought you might enjoy it. You earned it."

"Well, I'm not too much for parties," Wyatt said in his slow drawl. "Rather catch croppy instead. Wish you hadn't disturbed yourself to come out here to get me. You're probably missing a good time."

Percy tried to subdue the throbbing ache within him, a sorrow he hadn't felt so acutely since Matthew had died. Impulsively, he clamped a hand on the boy's shoulder. "Son, how about you and me getting drunk together? It's been a long time since I've gone on a binge, not in years, in fact." The memories were stirring, would not lie still. He felt on the verge of tears.

"When was that, Dad?"

"Oh, it was a long time ago, before your mother and I married."

"What caused you to do it?"

Percy hesitated, unwilling to answer but afraid to break the moment between them. He and Wyatt had never talked of his past. He could not recall a single question his son had ever asked about his youth, the war, life before him. Only Matthew had been interested in his memories. He decided to answer directly. Wyatt was a man now. "It was because of a woman," he said.

"What happened to her?"

"I lost her to another man."

"You must have loved her."

His son was taller, more stalwart of build, than Matthew would have been. His presence was strong in the moonlight. "Yes, I did. Very much. Why else does a man get drunk?" He tried to grin.

Wyatt frowned. "So, for what reason would we be getting drunk tonight?"

Percy found it impossible to answer. The ache within him swelled, shutting off his breath. "I . . . don't know," he managed to get out. "It was a bad idea. Your mother would kill us both. She'll be looking for us, by the way."

Wyatt nodded and snapped closed his jacket. "Then we'd better go," he said.

Chapter Forty-five

After Wyatt's graduation from high school—because of his absolute refusal to go to college—Percy took him off the floor of the lumber mill and gave him a job as assistant to the production manager whose office was in his headquarters building. Wyatt accepted the promotion with his usual taciturnity and listened stolidly at company meetings, taking dutiful notes with a slow hand. For two years, he bore with patience Percy's attempts to fit him into the company as heir apparent and Lucy's ceaseless urging that he comply.

He was rescued in December 1941 when the United States declared war against Japan for the bombing of Pearl Harbor. Within weeks, without consulting his parents, Wyatt had joined the U.S. Marine Corps.

"You must stop him!" a wild-eyed Lucy begged Percy.

"How do you suggest I do that?" her husband asked, equally as distraught. In his sleep now, he heard again the roar of the guns, the cries of pain and death, knew again the sticky sweat of fear, the stench of horror and panic, woke again to the forgotten taste of ashes in his mouth. And in his dreams, in the midst of the swirling smoke, he saw not the combat-fatigued faces of his fallen comrades, but Wyatt's, the blue eyes empty and staring in death, the question *Why?* still in them.

"He's almost twenty, Lucy. A man now. I can't stop him."

"Would you, if you could?" she asked, the question fraught with anguish, not accusation. Such periods of pointless blame-laying were over between them. She knew he'd tried with Wyatt, and for a long time her oblique looks when he spoke of Wyatt told him that she was aware of his growing change toward their son.

"Yes, by God. I'd rather shoot him myself than let him go where he's going," he declared, confounded by his feelings.

"You felt you had to enlist this soon?" he asked Wyatt two weeks later as he packed his duffel bag. It was the beginning of January 1942. Wyatt had been ordered to present himself in three days' time for induction into the United States Marines at Camp Pendleton near San Diego, California, where he would begin the first phase of boot camp. His train was due to leave from Howbutker within the hour.

"No reason why I shouldn't," Wyatt said. "Every able man will be needed as soon as possible to put an end to this mess."

"Maybe you're right," Percy said, remembering his own arguments for signing up. He fell silent as he watched Wyatt stuff tightly rolled pairs of socks into the canvas bag, each spheroid rammed into its mouth bringing him closer to the time he'd pull the drawstring and hoist the bag to his shoulder.

There is no hell, Percy thought. Hell is right here on earth. What greater hellfire than watching the son you never knew go off to war, the uncertainty of his return? There had always been a vacuum in his heart where Wyatt should have been, an empty space where nothing of him had ever caught and hung—no memory of shared laughter, conversation, male confidences. They had never talked about *him*, his dreams, ambitions, ideas, philosophies. The shocking thought came to Percy that, beyond a general impression, he had never paid much attention to the individual details of Wyatt's face. He remembered Matthew's still—the way his eyes had caught variations of light, the position of every cowlick, the small, round reminder above his left eye of his bout with chicken pox. But Wyatt's features had remained as indistinct and undefined as a face underwater, sure to be a struggle to recall almost as soon as he was gone.

"Son..." Percy stepped forward, desperate that

the boy should not go to war without something of himself having found a peg in the void, something he could remember him by.

"Yes, sir?" Wyatt said, continuing his packing.

"Tell me something before you go?"

"Sure. What is it?"

"Why did you suddenly stop hating Matthew DuMont? Why did the two of you become such close friends, almost…like brothers?"

Seconds ticked by. Wyatt appeared unmoved, his thickset profile as expressionless as ever as he cleared the bed one by one of the necessities and belongings that would go with him to war. Shoving the last item into the bag, he said, "Well, because he *was* my brother, wasn't he?"

A roaring silence filled Percy's ears, as if he'd stood too close to a mortar blast again. His hands balled in his pockets. "How…long have you known?"

Wyatt shrugged without looking at him. "I figured it out in the cabin that afternoon you knocked the crap out of me. You almost gave it away yourself, remember?" He threw Percy a wry grin. "You said, 'If you so much as look cross-eyed at your—' But you caught yourself in time. I guessed it then. It was instinct, but I was pretty sure you meant to say 'your brother.' I figured you might knock my teeth out for beating up another man's kid, but you'd only threaten to kill me if I beat up the son you loved."

Percy made a move toward him. "Wyatt—" he

began, but a wave of bereavement overpowered his words.

"It's okay, Dad. I never blamed you for loving Matthew. Hell"—he laughed shortly—"everybody did, even Maw." He stopped his packing to level a gaze at his father that brooked no contradiction. "But nobody loved him more than I did. I want you to know that. I never hated Matthew. I envied him. You were right about that. But I didn't envy him for being what I wasn't, I envied him for having what I wanted... what I thought should have come to me. I punished him for winning your respect and approval when I couldn't—a boy not even your son, was my way of thinking. When I realized who he was..." He set the cylindrical bag upright on the bed. "Well, it explained a lot of things."

Percy itched to halt Wyatt's hands, to stop him from drawing the bag's cord. "And... you never had any doubt at all after that day?"

"No, sir," Wyatt said, cinching the mouth of the bag closed. "Not since I heard you admit to Maw later that night that Matthew was your son. I had come down the hall to apologize and to tell you I'd never hurt him again, when I heard your row."

Percy groped for the bedpost. "You... heard everything?"

"Uh-huh. Everything. That explained a lot of things, too."

Percy swallowed in an ineffectual effort to clear his

ears of the deafening absence of sound. "And that's why...why you and I never...made it."

"Oh, we made it, Dad—in the only way we could. And I don't want to leave you thinking it was Matthew that had anything to do with the way things were between us. If he had never been born, it wouldn't have changed the way you feel or don't feel about me. Matthew just made things worse by comparison, that's all. The way I saw it, by learning the truth that day, I picked up a brother."

And lost a father, Percy cried to himself, paralyzed by a yearning to reach out and grab him for one minute before he could leave, hold him like the little boy he'd never held, never found, until now. *I love you...I love you*, he longed to cry. The feeling was miraculously there, released like a bird from lifelong captivity, but Wyatt would never believe the words came from his heart rather than the emotion of the moment. *Forgive me...*, he wanted to beg, but he feared Wyatt's answer. He could not be left with that memento to hang in the void.

"One other thing," Percy said. He had to know. "Did...did you ever tell Matthew?"

"Nah, and he never guessed. Matthew was never good at figuring out things like that. He took things as they were." Wyatt gestured toward the bureau. "In that bottom drawer are Matthew's jersey and the book he gave me for my birthday. I'd take them for luck, but I don't want anything to happen to them. If I don't come home, they're yours."

Incapable of speech, Percy nodded and watched as Wyatt, with one swift motion, swung the heavy bag over his shoulder. Knowing that any attempt at reconciliation would not only be futile, but appear as currying, he stood in helpless resignation as his son took a last long look around his room. Wyatt had always respected him. He would at least let him go with that.

"Well, I guess this is it," Wyatt said, his glance coming to rest on Percy for a rare time in his life. His eyes, clear as a spring stream, were empty of accusation, guile, or condemnation. "I think it's a good idea that you're not coming to the station with us, Dad. You and Maw would just get in a fight, and I don't want to remember you two that way. She'll go to her card game afterwards. Those biddies she hangs around with will help her get through this." He stuck out his hand, and Percy slowly took it and gripped it hard. To his horror, tears filled his eyes.

"I wish . . . I wish things had been different between us."

Wyatt shook his head. "A man doesn't choose his sons. Things happened the way they did. Matthew was a good boy. I'm glad he's out of this business." They released hands. "Take care of Maw the best way you can—if she'll let you," he said, his mouth quirking in a grin that made his rugged features endearing.

But Percy could not let it go. "When you come home, maybe we can start again."

The head shake again. "It wouldn't change things. I'm me, and you're you. So long, Dad. I'll write."

And he did. Percy devoured his letters, following the course of his platoon in the South Pacific from Corregidor, through Guam, and finally to Iwo Jima. Wyatt distinguished himself as Percy had suspected he would, winning commendation after commendation for bravery on the battlefield. Percy read the letters and newspaper accounts of the jungle warfare, of heinous traps and Japanese atrocities, of the rains, mire, and malaria-carrying mosquitoes, and wondered if somehow, some way, Matthew was calling the plays for his brother from beachhead to beachhead, foxhole to foxhole, keeping him safe, keeping him whole.

And then, at last, it was over and Wyatt was coming home. But not to stay, he had written. He had found his niche. He was staying in the marines. He'd been commissioned on the battlefield and would retain the rank of first lieutenant. Percy and Lucy met him at the station. They hardly recognized him when he stepped down from the train, the left side of his uniform jacket a jaw-dropping testimony of the battles he'd survived. It had been four years since they'd seen him. Percy had passed his fiftieth birthday, and Lucy, already gray, was forty-five.

"Hello," he said simply, his voice that of a stranger,

the eyes foreign to them. Lucy was slow to embrace this man she'd raised. He was powerful in build, taller even than Percy, and awesome in presence. Battle-hardened, combat-fit, his visage was that of a warrior who had found his tribe, his destiny, his peace.

"So, you're not planning on returning to the business?" Percy asked later.

"No, Dad."

He nodded. There would be no starting over again after all. He extended his hand and clamped his other hard over Wyatt's grip. "Then I wish you safe landings always, son," he said.

Lucy blamed him for Wyatt's decision. She knew by now that Wyatt had been aware that Matthew was his brother. "Why *would* he want to come home and work for a father who had preferred his first son?"

"I believe Wyatt has come to terms with that, Lucy," Percy said.

Her eyes glittered with the old pain. Percy knew that she was hurt to the core that she'd been deprived of her son. She'd looked forward to having Wyatt home again, marrying, giving her grandchildren. "Well, maybe, but he hasn't forgiven you for it, Percy," she said. "And he never will. The fact that he's staying in the marines is proof of that."

One morning five months after Wyatt had returned to his regiment, Percy looked up from reading his newspaper at the breakfast table to find Lucy standing by his side. She was dressed in a suit and hat.

A mink stole hung from her shoulders. "Where are you off to this early in the morning?" he asked in surprise. His wife rarely opened an eye before ten.

"Atlanta," Lucy said, pulling on her gloves. "I'm going there to live, Percy. There's nothing for me here anymore, now that Wyatt won't be coming home. I've already leased a town house on Peach Tree, and I've arranged for Hannah Barweise to pack and ship my things." She took a sheet of paper from her handbag and handed it to an astounded Percy. "Here's the address and a list of my expenses. I'll also require a monthly allowance for personal items. The total is there at the bottom. It may look outrageous, but you can well afford it, and I'm sure you'll think it's worth the amount to get me out of your hair."

"I don't want you out of my hair, Lucy. I've never said that."

"You wouldn't. You're too much of a gentleman, but this is best for both of us. Now, for old times' sake, would you like to drive me to the station?"

He did not try to talk her out of it, but at the station, he looked down into her plump, middle-aged face and remembered the girl he'd come to meet here over twenty-six years ago. "A lot of water, Lucy," he said, feeling a pull of his heartstrings.

"Yep," she agreed. "The only trouble was, you and I watched its flow from opposite sides of the bank."

Her hat was a little askew. He straightened it and asked on a pensive note, "Don't you want a divorce, while there's still time to watch its flow on the same bank with someone else?"

"Not on your life!" She laughed sharply. "You can forget about that. My threat still holds. No divorce until I say so, and that won't be while Mary Toliver DuMont is still alive."

They did not embrace when it came time for her departure. Lucy seemed disinclined to put herself into Percy's arms and offered her cheek for a peck instead. She allowed him to take her elbow to help her board, and as she started up the steps, she turned. "Good-bye, Percy," she said softly.

"For a little while," he said, and slid his hand down to her wrist in the old way as the train whistle blew. The gesture took her by surprise, and he heard a short hiss of breath before she jerked her arm free as though burned. After holding his gaze a fraction longer than she seemed to wish, she turned her back to him and disappeared.

Chapter Forty-six

After Lucy's departure, Percy did what he'd always done when a hole opened in his life: He added more hours to his workday and expanded operations. He enlarged the pulp mill and gave the go-ahead to begin construction of an adjoining paper-processing plant on the acres he'd bought from Mary. In addition, he had land cleared nearby and blueprints drawn for a residential development that would offer affordable houses to workers and their families willing to live within smelling distance of the odorous emissions from the pulp mill. The proposed number were snapped up immediately. The sulfurous smell was by no means disagreeable to the soon-to-be home owners. The odor meant consistent paychecks handed out each Friday, health benefits, pensions, raises, and paid vacations.

For companionship, he had the constants of Ollie and Mary and a welcome newcomer to their circle of three, a young lawyer named Amos Hines. Amos had wandered into Howbutker in late 1945 on the heels of William Toliver's departure and was immediately asked to join the law firm of his old friend and family attorney, Charles Waithe. Like his father, William had discovered he was no farmer and had taken off for parts unknown one fall morning, not to be heard from for several years. Once again, Mary was bereft of an heir to Somerset.

With her wry half smile, she summed up their failures to Percy in a single observation. "We're a pair, aren't we?"

"That we are," he agreed.

"You miss Lucy?"

He pursed his lips and reflected. "I feel her absence, but not her loss."

He invested in an oil company and was required to sit in on meetings in Houston with several other partners, whose sole endeavors, passion, and income centered on the petroleum industry. It was during one of these conferences that he met Amelia Bennett, a year after Lucy took up residence in Atlanta. A recent widow, she had come by her partnership as a result of inheritance, but unlike Percy, she knew the industry backward and forward. They clashed immediately in a dispute over the financial prudence of drilling for oil in an area of West Texas known as the Permian Basin. He was for it; she was against it.

"Really, Mr. Warwick," she said, addressing him with a disdainful look down the polished conference room table, "I can't imagine how a *lumberman* would have the faintest idea of where to drill for oil, let alone express an opinion concerning it. Perhaps you should keep quiet and let those who know decide where to set up the company's rigs."

Percy's brow arched. Ah, a challenge. Not since Mary had he encountered a challenge.

"I shall take your well-meaning rebuke under advisement, Mrs. Bennett, but meanwhile I'm casting my vote to drill in the Dollarhide Field of West Texas."

Later, when they found themselves alone in the elevator, she looked his six-foot-three frame up and down and declared, "You are the most impossibly arrogant man I've ever met."

"So it would seem," Percy concurred agreeably.

She favored simple pumps and dark, slim skirts that she wore with silk blouses in pastel colors. Her only jewelry was a gold wedding band and single-pearl earrings to complement the mother-of-pearl buttons of her blouses. After several more meetings, Percy experienced the exquisite pleasure of slipping those buttons through their holes and parting the silk blouse.

"Make no mistake, you are still the most arrogant man I have ever met," Amelia said, her eyes glowing with the lambency of the finest amber.

"I would not dream of disputing it," Percy said.

Their affair proved eminently satisfying to both.

Neither was interested in marriage. A mutual need for intimacy with someone they liked, trusted, and respected was all either wanted from the other. They dated openly, letting the gossipmongers make of it what they would. None did. It was the postwar era, and certain social mores were relaxing. Percy and Amelia were consenting middle-aged adults. They were rich, influential, and powerful, accustomed to doing as they pleased. Who was there to dare criticize publicly a healthy, nubile widow for sharing a bed with a virile tycoon who'd been deserted by his wife?

Wyatt was now stationed at Camp Pendleton. He seldom wrote, called only on Christmas and Percy's birthday, and came home never. Percy corresponded frequently, filling his letters with news of the Sabine plant and housing development, of Mary and Ollie and his new friend, Amos Hines, of local events and happenings that might keep Wyatt in touch with Howbutker by however slim a thread. Once, after reading Sara's final letter to him, he wrote that Miss Thompson had married a high school principal in Andrews, Texas. After long consideration, he decided to risk confiding that he and Miss Thompson had once been very close and that her marriage had left him with a bittersweet feeling. To his surprise, Wyatt responded immediately, mentioning Sara with the simple comment: "She always was my favorite teacher."

Six months before the decade ended, a letter arrived from Wyatt announcing his marriage to Claudia

Howe, a transplanted schoolteacher from Virginia. They were living in the married officers' quarters on base. He was now a captain and a company commander. Lucy had recently paid them a surprise visit when she flew in from Atlanta to meet her new daughter-in-law. Wyatt did not suggest that Percy do the same.

Percy at once picked up the receiver and placed a call to Camp Pendleton. A woman with a pleasant and well-bred voice answered on the first ring. "Good morning," she said. "Captain Warwick's quarters."

"Claudia? This is Percy Warwick, Wyatt's father."

He thought he detected a silence of pleased surprise, confirmed when she said with a lilt in her voice, "Why, how nice to hear from you. Wyatt will be so disappointed to have missed your call. He's on maneuvers."

Stung with disappointment, Percy said, "I'm sorry, too. Bad timing on my part, regrettably."

"I hope you'll try another time."

"I will indeed." He searched for something to say to fill the silent line. "I was delighted to hear of his marriage, and I hope to meet you soon. You must get Wyatt to bring you to Howbutker."

"I will certainly mention that to Wyatt."

Percy noted the avoidance of an invitation to visit them and framed several more polite queries regarding their welfare that Claudia met with gracious but brief answers not conducive to prolonging the conversation. He hung up feeling cheated and depressed.

He sent a large check for a wedding gift that was promptly acknowledged in a note from Claudia with one line added from Wyatt. Percy suspected the short salutation had been his wife's idea. A year later, another letter arrived from his daughter-in-law. She wrote in a fine, distinct hand that he was now a grandfather and that the enclosed photograph was to introduce him to his grandson, Matthew Jeremy Warwick. They called him Matt.

The next day, he was shocked by bold black headlines screaming from the front page of the Sunday *Gazette:* NORTH KOREAN TROOPS CROSS THE THIRTY-EIGHTH PARALLEL IN A SURPRISE ATTACK AGAINST SOUTH KOREA.

Over the next few days, with increasing alarm, Percy followed news stories of North Korea's refusal to comply with the UN Security Council's demand that its government immediately cease hostilities and withdraw its forces to the thirty-eighth parallel. North Korean troops were already on their way to capture Seoul, capital of South Korea, for all intents and purposes to bring down the recognized democratic government and forcibly unify the country under Communist rule. The UN Security Council responded by sending troops to support South Korea, dominated by American forces and commanded by General Douglas MacArthur. One of the general's first orders: "Send me the marines."

That's it! Percy thought, staring at the picture of

his grandson over his breakfast plate. I'm catching the first plane to San Diego. I don't give a damn if Wyatt doesn't want to see me. The First Marine Division is always the first in, and I'm going to see my boy before he leaves.

He sucked in his breath from a fear so intense, it left him weak. South Korea. Who'd ever heard of it, and why the hell was the United States sending men to die for it? He threw his napkin on the table and shoved back his chair. Wyatt would probably think he'd shown up seeking absolution from the son he'd wronged. He'd think it was a ruse to get near his grandson, have another go at a Warwick, so to speak. At best, he'd think it was something a father does when his only child is going off to his second war, when he'd been lucky to survive the first. And he'd be right on every point. What he wouldn't know was that Percy also came out of love for him, a love that seemed to grow stronger each year despite the distance between them.

The plans he'd formed at the breakfast table were altered when his secretary handed him a telegram seconds after his arrival at the office. "From Wyatt," she said. "I signed for it a few minutes ago."

Percy tore open the yellow envelope: DAD STOP ARRIVING BY TRAIN 6:00 TONIGHT STOP BRINGING CLAUDIA AND MATT HOME STOP WYATT.

Percy lifted his stunned gaze to his waiting secretary. "Sally, my son is coming home with his family.

I'd like you to assemble every cleaning lady in town on the double and send them out to Warwick Hall. I'll pay twice their usual fees. Better still, I want you to go to the house and supervise the cleaning of each room from top to bottom. Will you do that?"

"You know I will, Mr. Warwick."

"And call Herman Stolz—"

"The butcher, sir?"

"The butcher. Have him cut three of his finest filet mignons two inches thick. Also, while you're at it, will you kindly call the florist and order flowers for the first floor and the best guest room. I'd like one arrangement of... red and white roses. Have that placed in the front hall."

"Yes, Mr. Warwick."

Percy got on the line to Gabriel, the houseman Lucy had fired and he'd rehired from the DuMonts after her departure. Gabriel was sixty-five and had rarely ventured beyond Houston Avenue since the day he was born in the servants' quarters above the Warwicks' garage. "Gabriel, I'm sending the car. You're to go to Stolz Meat Market and pick up some steaks I've ordered. While you're there, I'd like you to select Mister Wyatt's favorite foods. Got that? Mister Wyatt is coming home tonight with his wife and my grandson."

Percy allowed for several interruptions of "The Lord be praised!" before proceeding with further instructions. "I have a feeling," he said, "that his wife would like béarnaise sauce with her steak. Do you think you could handle that?"

"I'll get my grandson Grady to read the recipe to me. I got a pencil here. How's it spelled?"

Percy sighed and spelled the word, wishing for Amelia.

Those orders completed, he telephoned Mary. She listened and, after promising to send Sassie down to assist Gabriel, said, "He's bringing the baby and his mother home to leave with you while he's in Korea, Percy."

"You really think so?"

"I do. You're getting another chance."

"I hope you're right."

"I think you can count on it. I envy you, Percy."

"Maybe you'll get another chance someday, too, Mary."

Her laugh reminded him of crystal breaking. "And from where would that come?"

It was as Mary had predicted and as Percy hadn't dared hoped. He didn't ask Wyatt what his mother had thought of his decision. It must have hurt and surprised her, but he put aside his empathy for Lucy to indulge his own feelings of elation and gratitude. The baby was beautiful. Percy gazed at him in awe and could hardly believe the miracle of the forehead, nose, and chin that declared him the flesh and blood of a Warwick.

Sally was shooing the cleaning brigade out the

back door as they arrived at Warwick Hall, and
Percy watched Claudia enter his home slowly, eyeing
its worn grandeur and sweeping dimensions. With
the baby in her arms, she paused at the magnificent
arrangement of red and white roses reflected in the
soaring mirror of the hall table. Wyatt didn't seem to
notice them. "How beautiful," she said.

They'd arrived at six o'clock on the dot, and old
Titus, the conductor, had himself offered his arm to
the pert wife of the uniformed U.S. Marines captain
who stepped down behind her. He'd pointed at Percy.
"That's Mr. Percy Warwick over there," Percy had
overheard him say. "As fine a man as ever there was."

She'd approached him carrying the baby, her
husband, tall and commanding, following behind.
"Hello, Dad," she said.

She appeared to his eye rather characterless at first,
with no single feature to arrest attention. Her hair was
neither blond nor brown, her face neither pretty nor
plain, her stature neither tall nor short. It was the dul-
cet sound of her voice that first drew notice and then
the attraction of her eyes—not necessarily their color,
which was an unremarkable hazel, but the intelligence
and integrity found there, the gentle strength and
humor. Percy liked her instantly, filled with pride that
his son had done so well by a wife. "Daughter," he said
softly as he embraced her, the child between them.

"So what do you think of the place?" he asked her
later of Warwick Hall, glistening as a new pin.

"Think of it? Why, who wouldn't think it magnificent? Wyatt never told me."

"But...he must have told you...other things."

"Yes," she said, her expression knowing and gentle.

He let it go at that, taking pleasure that she liked his house, the home his forebears had built. Time enough to discuss "the other things" when Wyatt was gone, if she was so inclined.

He'd been aghast to learn that Wyatt would be shipping out to Korea within weeks and that he'd be returning to Camp Pendleton the next afternoon. "So soon?" Percy had asked, his heart rived with disappointment.

"I'm afraid so."

Late that night, too keyed up to sleep, Percy left his room to go down to the library for a glass of brandy before retiring. Having seen his family settled in the guest room and Mary's borrowed crib set up next to the bed, he'd thought they were all tucked in for the night when he saw a light coming from the open door of his son's old room. He went down to investigate and found Wyatt, still in partial uniform, standing in the middle of the room, his back to him, his shoulders granite hard beneath the starched fabric of his shirt. In silence Percy watched him, wondering what his reflections were, what voices he heard, what echoes from the past. The memorabilia of his boyhood still hung on the walls. A pennant reading HOWBUTKER HIGH SCHOOL 1939 STATE FOOTBALL CHAMPIONS crowned the head of the bed.

Percy cleared his throat. "A man shouldn't have to fight in two wars."

Turning, the expression on the grown man's face as impenetrable as ever, Wyatt said, "Maybe we'll get this one over soon." He ran his finger down the spine of a book he held. It was the treasured *Adventures of Huckleberry Finn.* "I thought I might take Matthew's birthday present along with me this time. Might bring me luck."

"A good idea," Percy said. "A soldier can never have too much of that."

There was so much more he wanted to say, but he could not get the words past the emotion clogging his throat. Wyatt saved them both from the moment's embarrassment by saying, "Dad, I have something to ask of you before I go. A favor."

"Anything, son. Anything at all."

"If…I don't get back, I'd like my son raised here with you. Claudia feels the same way. She's already crazy about you. I knew she would be. She's no snap judge of character, either, believe me." A small grin appeared, a light of pride in his eye that softened the hard contours of his face. "They'd be no trouble, and I'll feel easier knowing that no matter what happens to me, they'll have a home here with you."

Percy struggled to find his voice. "You…want me to help raise Matt if—if—"

"That's right."

Percy stared into the clear blue eyes. They said nothing; they said everything. All Percy could be sure of were the words he'd heard. "They are welcome here for as long as they wish to stay," he said. "I wouldn't want them anywhere else, and I'm deeply honored that you . . . want them to live with me." He swallowed hard. He must not break down. He must not appear less the man than Wyatt had always respected. But he could not resist saying—he *had* to say: "You must come back, Wyatt. You must."

"I'll give it my best shot. Good night, Dad, and thanks." Stepping around Percy, the book clutched under his arm, Wyatt nodded shortly and left the room.

Chapter Forty-seven

The hours flew. It seemed they were back at the station before they'd left, Claudia holding two-month-old Matt swaddled in a blue blanket, Wyatt militarily correct in his impeccable uniform with its rows of campaign ribbons aligned over his left breast. "You got everything?" Percy had asked before they left Warwick Hall. "You get everything packed?"

"Everything's packed," Wyatt had said. "I'm a good one for not leaving anything behind."

Not so, Percy had thought sadly. But after he'd kissed his wife and son good-bye and shaken Percy's hand, it was to him that Wyatt uttered his last words before boarding the train. "Make sure my son knows that I love him, Dad."

"You'll be back to make sure of that yourself, son."

After returning home, Percy left Claudia and Matt in the garden soaking up the early summer sunshine while he went up to the guest room. He looked for

The Adventures of Huckleberry Finn but could not find it. There was nothing left there of the man who had come and gone in less than twenty-four hours. Relieved, he had to believe that Wyatt had packed the book in with his things. Unbeknownst to his son, Percy had clipped a red rose from the arrangement in the hall and slipped it between the pages of the book. He'd thought of writing a short note and taping it to the stem as they did poppies every year in honor of Armistice Day, but he'd thought better of it. Written words were as useless as spoken ones when the reader attributed them to guilt. He was sure that Wyatt wouldn't have the foggiest idea how the rose got there, what it meant, or what he should do about it. Lucy, he was sure, had never apprised him of the legend of the roses, and certainly Percy hadn't. But he could take comfort in the gesture, knowing that it went away with his son to war, a testament of his contrition pressed between the pages of Wyatt's dearest possession.

Once again, Percy found himself following the war from newspapers and radio. New, strange-sounding terms and names of yet another battlefront in a foreign part of the world emerged: Inchon, Chosin Reservoir, Fox Hill, Old Baldy, Kunuri, MiG Alley, the DMZ. Wyatt wrote: "Men cry here and curse and pray in the same way they did in World War II and in your war, Dad. It's all the same—the fear, the boredom, the loneliness, the adrenaline rush, the comradeship, the tension waiting for the next assault, the long nights away from home and family. In this war, it's the God-awful terrain—hills as bare and brown as a bear's butt—and waiting in your foxhole in nights as black as the inside of a tar bucket for the hordes of Chinese Commies to come at you blowing their bugles—burp guns, we call them—raising every hair on your body. But between times I think of Claudia and Matt there, safe with you."

Shortly after he'd gone, Percy had unwrapped an object he'd put away after Wyatt's return from World War II. He unrolled the red-bordered square of white silk before little Matt, awake and gurgling in his crib. "What's this, you ask?" Percy said. "This, my little lad, is called a service flag. I'm hanging it in the front window. The blue star represents a member of the family serving his country in the military in times of war. In this case, it stands for your dad."

In late September 1951, nearly a year and a half after Wyatt had gone, Percy received a telephone call from Claudia at the Courthouse Café as he was having coffee with members of the OBC—Old Boys' Club—asking that he return home. He did not question why. Quietly, he laid money on the counter, and without a word he walked out into the kind of blue-and-gold morning that had dawned the last day of his older son's life. Upon arriving home, he saw an official U.S. Marine Corps staff car parked under the portico. They had sent a team from Houston—a chaplain and two officers—to inform the family that Wyatt Trenton Warwick had been killed in action on a bleak and forbidding battleground known as the "Punch Bowl." Days later, his body was sent home draped with an American flag that was later folded and presented on behalf of a grateful nation to his widow at the grave site. Percy had chosen the burial spot over the mild disapproval of the funeral director, who would have interred Wyatt in the Warwick plot at the feet of Matthew DuMont.

"Not at his feet, by his side," Percy had ordered.

"If you insist," said the funeral director. "After all, they were best friends."

"Not just friends," Percy had said, his voice shaking with emotion. "They were brothers."

"That's how everybody remembers them," the undertaker had said pacifically. "Close as brothers."

The mill hands with whom he'd worked, his former classmates and girlfriends, his old football chums and coaches, all came to attend the memorial service from wherever the news of his death had reached them. Lucy arrived, clad in black, her face pale and drawn behind her veil, and stayed with the family at Warwick Hall. Percy longed to weep with her, to touch in some way the mother of his son, but her cold eyes forced him to keep his distance. In choosing the family flowers that would lie upon the grave, she said, "Please, Percy, no roses...."

Therefore, it was a blanket of red poppies that flut-

tered in the breeze next to the resting place of Matthew DuMont as an honor guard raised their guns
to fire a farewell salute. The roar of the volley filled
Percy's ears and made little Matthew cry in the refuge of his grandfather's arms.

"So," Lucy said later that evening, "Claudia and
Matt will be staying here in Howbutker with you, she
tells me."

"Yes, Lucy."

"It's what Wyatt wanted, she tells me."

"Yes, Lucy."

"There is no justice in this world, Percy Warwick."

"No, Lucy."

Wyatt's personal effects finally made it home. Percy
was at the station to take possession of the medium-
size box that he lifted himself and placed on the bed
of a company pickup. Claudia, apparently sensing his
pain, insisted they go through the items together.

"What is this?" she asked, holding up *The Adventures of Huckleberry Finn*.

It was the item Percy had hoped to find. "Matthew
gave that book to Wyatt for his birthday when they
were boys," he said. "Wyatt took it with him hoping...it would bring him luck."

He took the book from her and rifled the pages,
looking for the red rose, but he found nothing. Had
Wyatt ever found it? Had he thrown it away without realizing its special significance? Had it fallen
out when the buddy put this box together? He would

never know. He'd have to live with the knowledge that his boy had died without knowing that his father had loved him and solicited his forgiveness.

Despite the constant ache that now joined his other sorrows, his life entered a period of domestic tranquillity he'd not known since his mother had overseen Warwick Hall. Matt and Claudia became the center of his universe. His house took on a new glow and order thanks to his daughter-in-law's capable management. Satisfying meals appeared on his table, enjoyed as a family in the dining room and sometimes shared with the DuMonts and Amos Hines and the Charles Waithes, who did not mind a toddler playing in his peas.

He entertained again, feeling free to bring home at a moment's notice the out-of-town visitors who toured the model facilities of the pulp mill and paper-processing plant that sprawled along the Sabine. Amelia, seeing that she was no longer essential to mitigate his lonely hours and hopelessly in love with a man who would never be free, drifted quietly from his life. From time to time, Percy wished that Lucy could share in the daily delight of their grandson. Claudia sent her pictures, and there were exchanges of telephone calls in which Matt, at his mother's direction, prattled greetings to his grandmother in Atlanta, calling her "Gabby." Percy wondered how she spent her days as a woman alone and if she'd taken lovers to fill the empty spaces in her life.

The Korean War ended and, heartsick, Percy read that the nation for which his son and over fifty thousand American servicemen and women had died was still divided, no political issues settled, no human rights improved. He ordered a popular poster to be hung in the reception room of his office, the caption reading: "Someday, someone will give a war and nobody will come." He hugged his grandson close and prayed for that day to arrive before Matt grew up.

It was two years after Wyatt's body was brought home that Sally entered his office and announced with barely concealed curiosity, "Mr. Warwick, there's a U.S. Marine officer at my desk who's asked to see you. Should I send him in?"

"By all means," Percy said, rising and buttoning his suit coat, his pulse pumping.

A Marine Corps major was shown through the door, his uniform hat under one arm, a cumbersome, rectangular package under the other. "Mr. Warwick, I'm Daniel Powel," he introduced himself, propping the package against Percy's desk to shake his hand. "I knew your son in Korea. We were both company commanders in the First Marine Division."

"Is that so?" Percy said, his heartbeat locking, his mind turning questions like a kaleidoscope. Why had this man come so long after Wyatt's death? Was he here to tell him how and where his son had died? Wyatt would never have approved such a visit. Was he mustering out of the marines and coming for a job? He gestured toward a visitor's chair. "Well, then, take a seat, Major, and tell me what I can do for you."

"Not for me, sir—for you. Wyatt said to look you up if anything happened to him. I'm sorry it's taken so long to get here. I was sent to Japan after the war and have just been reassigned stateside."

"How long have you been home?"

The officer glanced at his watch. "Less than forty-eight hours. I came here directly after landing in San Diego."

Percy blinked. "You mean this is your first stop since coming home?"

"Yes, sir. I promised Wyatt I'd get this to you first chance I had." The marine stood and lifted the thickly wrapped parcel. "I've taken care of this ever since Wyatt was killed. We were together when he bought it in Seoul. He said I was to see you got it if he didn't make it home. I wasn't to mail it to you. I was to deliver it personally, no matter how long it took."

Percy inspected the rectangular shape. "Is it for his wife?"

"No, sir. It's for you. He said you'd understand what it meant."

Slowly, his saliva tasting like paste, Percy carried the package to a table beneath a skylight. It was tightly bound, the bands of tape dirty, the paper smeared from wherever the marine had found a place to store it the past two years. He ripped away the tape and tore at the brown wrapping until the contents were revealed. It was a painting, an impressionist's not very good rendering of a smiling boy in knee breeches running toward a picket gate in the foreground. At first Percy could not make out what he held in his arms or what the indistinct expanse surrounding the boy represented. Then, as both became clear, he lifted his head and bellowed a cry toward the skylight and the blue sky beyond. The boy was running through a garden cradling an armful of white roses.

A SOFT ACHE IN HIS chest forced Percy to open his eyes. He brushed at his face and his fingers came away wet, but not because of the heat, he knew. What time was it? His sitting room porch was now in full shadow, and a slight breeze blew that was customary to late afternoon. He swung his feet to the floor and shook his head to clear it. How long had he been out here, calling up old ghosts? Good heavens—it was after five o'clock, he saw by his watch. Mary had been gone four hours...his Mary. He stood up and tried his legs. They were a little shaky and wet along their undersides where he had perspired. Stiffly, feeling the ghosts clamoring behind him, he let himself in through the terrace doors, his eyes going at once to the painting over the mantel. Instantly, the pain in his chest subsided. Memory could be a terrible thing, he thought, an instrument of torture that persists in its work long after a man has suffered his time upon the rack. He poured a glass of water to quench his bone-dry thirst and lifted it to the painting. "In the end, Gypsy, I suppose the best we can hope for is an armful of white roses."

Chapter Forty-eight

In Atlanta, with the aid of her cane, Lucy Gentry Warwick carefully made her way onto the flagstoned walk of her garden. It hadn't much to recommend it during the day, but on a soft summer night it was something to see. The small walled backyard had been planted entirely with white perennials—Shasta daises, lantana, windflowers, vinca minor, snow-in-summer—and in the moonlight their masses of snowy heads glowed with an unearthly, magical beauty. Lucy took a seat on one of the stone benches, unmindful of her garden's charms. Her thoughts were on Mary Toliver DuMont.

The call from her old neighbor and spy, Hannah Barweise, had interrupted her afternoon nap. Hannah still lived next to the Toliver mansion, and she'd called to report that around noon she'd seen an ambulance arrive and the scurrying around of Sassie and Henry and guessed that Mary had come to some kind of grief. Then she'd seen Percy and Matt slam out of a company truck, and within the hour the whole neighborhood was buzzing with the news that Mary had died. Even before putting the obvious questions to Hannah, Lucy had asked, "How did he look?"

"How did who look?"

"Percy."

"Why…'bout the same, Lucy. Aged, not as spry, but…Percy Warwick, if you know what I mean."

She had replied with a shortness of breath, "Yes, I know what you mean. Go on. What was the cause of death?"

The particulars conveyed as Hannah knew them, Lucy had hung up, her whole body trembling. The day she'd anticipated for forty years had finally arrived: Mary Toliver DuMont dead and Percy alone, grieving for her. It was a pain she'd wanted him to suffer and live with until the end of his days, as she'd lived with hers.

Then why didn't she feel the elation she'd expected? Why this sickening pressure building in her diaphragm at the mental picture of Mary lying dead, those green eyes stilled, that face like marble in a sarcophagus? As usual, even from the grave, Mary had managed to rob her of the satisfaction she'd looked forward to and deserved. As God was her witness, she'd had little enough of it in her lifetime.

She shrugged off the feeling. Her disconcertment came merely from knowing that she, too, was eighty-five and susceptible to the shadow that had overtaken

Mary...Mary Toliver DuMont, that old warhorse, caught unaware on a summer day, taking the sun on her verandah. Before that time arrived, however, Lucy would have her little moment of long-awaited triumph and then afterward...let the shadow come.

"Miss Lucy, what you doin' out here this time of the afternoon?"

It was the voice of Betty, her longtime maid. She held open the door to the patio and frowned out into the hot sunshine. Lucy viewed her in irritation. Mother of God! She thought she'd stolen out while she was watching the five o'clock news. Betty was a good girl, but she carried tales. It wouldn't do for her to be within hearing distance when she initiated her planned victory. "Thinking," Lucy answered. "Go back to your news."

"Thinkin'? Out there in this heat? What about? That woman who just died?"

"Never you mind. Now go back to your program."

"How can I, knowin' you sittin' out here in danger of gettin' a heatstroke?"

"I'm too old to get a heatstroke. I'll be in shortly. For the moment I want to enjoy my garden. It's why I planted it."

Betty sighed. "Whatever swells your balloon, Miss Lucy, but I declare, sometimes you do beat all. Do you need anything?"

Lucy considered asking for a glass of brandy to bolster her courage, but Betty would hover by the door until she finished it, then hang around to make sure she was sober enough to let herself back in. "Just peace and quiet, if you please, Betty."

With a shake of her head, Betty pulled the door closed, and Lucy gave her time to return to the TV before making her move. Earlier—to explain why Hannah had insisted she get her up from her nap—she'd told Betty that an old school classmate and neighbor in Howbutker had died. If her maid was to eavesdrop on her short, pointed message in a little while, she might put two and two together and discover the real reason she and Percy had stayed married all these years.

When she'd first come to Atlanta, everyone had thought her the tragic victim of a powerful, despotic husband who refused to release her, a romantic misconception she did nothing to correct. Her new acquaintances were impressed that even though she was separated from him, he continued to house, clothe, and maintain her in the best style money could buy, indulging her every need, whim, and diversion with no questions asked or restrictions imposed. It added an aura of mystery to her social suitability and gained her immediate entrance into the inner circle of Atlanta society. Otherwise, as the cast-off wife of a rich, prominent man whom *she* refused to divorce, she'd have been restricted to its fringes.

Satisfied that Betty was once again engrossed, she opened the door to a small stone cabinet next to the bench and removed a telephone. The number she was about to call had not been changed since it was assigned, and she knew it by heart. It was the private line to her old sitting room. If anybody answered besides Percy, she'd hang up and try again, but she was betting he was sitting right by the phone in a stupor of grief. She hoped Matt wasn't with him. The boy loved her, but his first loyalty and deepest devotion lay with Percy, as their son, Wyatt, had intended, and he would not take kindly to her adding to his grandfather's pain.

Once again, she felt the dredge of her old resentment. She'd forgiven Wyatt for leaving Matt and his wife in Percy's care when he went to Korea, obviously preferring his custody to hers. But entrusting his son and wife to his father didn't mean that he forgave him for rejecting him as a boy. That gave her some comfort. Percy needn't think Matt was Wyatt's form of a white rose.

But the wisdom of time had caused her to retract her grievances against Percy for the early breakup of their marriage. She'd married him believing the words she'd said to Mary at Bellington Hall: *My love for him will blind him.... I* will *be the woman he deserves.* Her love for him had done nothing of the kind. Rather, it had worked the opposite, and to her disbelief and horror—no more able to prevent it than she could stop a roaring train—in the marriage she became more of the woman Mary had believed not right for Percy. She'd told herself many times that if only she'd played it smarter—been able to rise above her bawdy nature—but, no, their marriage could not have been saved, not when she learned of his feelings for Mary. She could have forgiven him his rejection of her—and even of their son, since he came to regret it—but not his love for that marble statue of a woman who would have married him only to rescue her hallowed Toliver name from scandal. Never that.

Her ancient pain now fully revived, she recalled the lines of an Edna St. Vincent Millay poem memorized long ago at Bellington Hall and recited many times since:

> *Love in the open hand, no thing but that,*
> *Ungemmed, unhidden, wishing not to hurt,*
> *As one should bring you cowslips in a hat*
> *Swung from the hand, or apples in her skirt,*
> *I bring you, calling out as children do:*
> *"Look what I have!—And these are all for you."*

Those lines had perfectly described her love for Percy, but he'd slapped the apples from her skirt and set his heart on a woman capable of loving only a cotton farm. That was her great quarrel with Mary. Let Percy and those who remembered think she'd despised her because of her great beauty and style. She'd hated Mary for the simple reason that she'd been undeserving of winning and holding the heart of the man Lucy loved.

She brought the receiver to her ear, mentally practicing her last chance at the script she'd rehearsed thousands of times for the arrival of this day. "Percy," she'd say clearly and crisply, and after allowing a pin dot of silence for him to digest his surprise, she'd hit him with the line she'd waited five decades to deliver: "*Now* you may have your divorce."

Before another minute passed and her nerve failed, she drew up her prodigious breasts, pulled in a chest full of air, and dialed the number. Now that the act was under way, she rather hoped he wouldn't pick up immediately—that she'd have breathing space to prepare for the voice she hadn't heard since the day they buried their son.

He answered on the first ring. "Hello."

Age…and grief…had dealt a blow to the voice she remembered, but she would have recognized it anywhere, anytime. The years dropped away, and she stood once more on the porch of Warwick Hall, gawking at the young driver of a spanking new Pierce-Arrow as it spun to a halt before the steps. The sun flashed off his blond hair, his bronzed skin, his white teeth. "Hello," he said in a timbre as rich as the sunshine, and her heart fell at his feet.

"Hello?" Percy repeated.

Lucy let out her breath, then, holding the sound of his voice close in her ear, gently replaced the receiver.

PART III

Chapter Forty-nine

In Kermit, Texas, Alice Toliver answered Rachel's call.

"Mama, this is Rachel."

"Have we come so far that my only daughter feels it necessary to identify herself to me when she calls me *Mama*, Rachel?"

Rachel felt the usual twist of her heart at her mother's injured tone. "I'm sorry, Mama. It was only out of habit that I identified myself."

"I haven't been a habit to you in a long time, Rachel. What's up?"

Rachel sighed quietly. "I've called to let you know that Aunt Mary is dead. She died a few hours ago of a heart attack. I just received word from Amos."

In the suspended silence, Rachel could clearly hear her mother's thoughts: *So, Rachel, you are now where you've always hoped to be, where your children will be after you are gone, while Jimmy, like his father and his father before him, reaps nothing.* But she spared her daughter her mental reaction and asked, "When's the funeral? I'm sure your daddy would like to go."

"I won't know until I meet with the funeral director tomorrow. I'm having the company plane pick me up in the morning. I…was hoping we could all fly out together."

"Now, Rachel, you know how I felt about your great-aunt Mary, and so did she. It would be the height of hypocrisy for me to show up at her funeral."

I don't want you there for Aunt Mary, Mama, but for me, Rachel wanted to cry, aching to feel her mother's arms around her, comforting her as she did in the old days when they had been close. "Amos asked that I convince at least Jimmy to come with Daddy. He feels Aunt Mary would want them at the reading of the will."

A long pause. "You mean your great-aunt had something to leave them? Cotton prices haven't been good this year."

"I'm assuming that's the reason he'd like them to be there. Amos expressed it as her last regards to them."

"Well, her regards won't make up for what she promised your father, but we'll take what we can get. If that means a trip to Howbutker, then we'll be there."

"You too, Mama?"

"I can't let those two go off alone. They might wear the same underwear twice."

"I'm so glad you're coming. It's been so long since I've seen everybody."

"Well, whose fault is that?"

Rachel reached for another tissue. She tried to stifle the sound of her grief, but Alice must have heard with her maternal ear. Her tone was several degrees warmer when she spoke. "Rachel, I know you're hurting, and I feel terrible that I can't offer you sympathy for your loss. But you know why...."

"Yes, Mama. I know why."

"I'll go wake your father. It's Thursday, you know."

Rachel remembered. Thursday was the day that Zack Mitchell's grocery store, where her father had worked as a butcher for thirty-six years, stayed open late. Since he was required to man the store until nine o'clock, he was allowed a longer lunch break, and he habitually took a nap during the extra thirty minutes.

"Bunny-hop, I'm so sorry," he said when he came on the line, and at the sound of his voice, she broke down completely. Its consoling, reaching-out quality had the same effect as the times he'd held her after an argument with her mother over her strengthening ties to Houston Avenue. He'd never taken sides, and to give her mother her due, she'd not tried to turn him against her. "Bunny-hop" was the name he'd given her when she was learning to walk.

"Are you better now, honey?" he asked after a moment's wait.

"Yes, Daddy, it's ... that I miss you and Mama and Jimmy so much, especially now. Mama may have told you that Amos has asked you and Jimmy to attend the reading of the will. I really would like for us to fly out together in the company plane tomorrow morning. We can pick you up at the Kermit airport."

William Toliver cleared his throat. "Uh, Rachel, honey, there are several problems with that suggestion. First, don't you think it would be a little tense sitting in close quarters with your mother feeling as she does? Secondly..." He seemed to have heard her audible sigh and rushed on before she could protest, "I won't be able to get out of here until day after tomorrow at the earliest. I can't leave Zack holding the bag."

"Why not? Don't you think these circumstances warrant the consideration you've earned from Zack after all these years?"

"Beggars can't make demands, Rachel, and we're going through midyear inventory."

Rachel blew out a breath in aggravation. Her father wouldn't have made demands anyway. He'd never been one to assert his due. "Promise me you won't let Jimmy dig in his heels and refuse to come. I want to see him, Daddy. He'll make us all feel better." She'd especially missed her snaggletoothed, freckle-faced little brother this year. Jimmy had thought of Aunt Mary as what God would look like if He were a woman, and to him she *had* been an omnipresent deity that had hovered on the edge of his family's lives as long as he could remember.

"I'll try, honey, but your brother's twenty-one. I'll let him know you want him to come."

When there was nothing more to be said, Rachel hung up with her father's words *Beggars can't make demands* still echoing in her ear. Maybe that was soon to change and Aunt Mary had left him enough to tell Zack Mitchell what he could do with his inventory. Extra cash had been tight this year. Everybody thought Aunt Mary was rolling in money, and some years she was. But profits depended on weather and markets and costs of labor and expenses, and often in the farming business wealth was determined by the value of land rather than the amount of money in the bank—realities of which her mother was well aware.

Rachel could hear her now in one of the endless arguments she'd overheard between her parents: *You just wait, William. When Aunt Mary kicks the bucket, there'll have been the worst drought in farming history or three months of rain or a cotton surplus or a hike in energy costs—anything to eat up her profits so that there's nothing left for you to inherit—nothing but that blooming land and the Toliver mansion, which she'll leave to Rachel. I'm sorry to say it, but I curse the day you got it into your head to take her a second time to see your great-aunt.*

Privately, Rachel disputed her mother's claim that the trip to Howbutker in 1966 had triggered her passion for all things Toliver. She believed its seed had been planted long before that, even before she was born. She'd simply never been aware of its existence until the day she discovered a tiny shoot growing beside the garbage bin next to the alley behind her house....

RACHEL'S STORY

Chapter Fifty

KERMIT, TEXAS, 1965

She found the sprout in March when the West Texas wind was still heavy with sand and most days looked like the yellow meat of an eggplant. She inspected it squatting on her haunches in the way that had inspired her father's nickname for her. It looked different from the coarse, spiky weeds and nettles and cockleburs that somehow managed to thrive in the Bermuda grass of the backyard. Light green and tender, it captured her awe so that she thought about the exposed little seedling all through supper and the dishes and homework and went out to cover it from the frost before going to bed. The next day, she hurried home from school and made a fence of rocks around it to protect it from the careless garbagemen and her father's deadly lawn mower.

"What you got there, Bunny-hop?"

"I don't know, Daddy, but I'm going to take care of it until it's full grown."

"Wouldn't you . . . rather have a puppy or a kitten?" he asked, and she heard an unfamiliar note in his voice.

"No, Daddy. I like pets that grow from the ground."

It turned out to be a vine that snaked over the rocks and produced a dark-skinned butternut squash. Her father explained that it sprang from a seed that had escaped from the garbage sack and sprouted where it fell. By the time of its fruition, Rachel had heard him say to her mother, "Don't be surprised if we've got ourselves a little farmer."

"As long as it's not the cotton-growing variety," her mother responded.

One Saturday morning shortly after her brother was born, her mother took her to Woolworth's to buy "something special, but within reason," she qualified. Rachel did not hesitate. She knew her heart's desire and searched out the seed rack in the hardware section of the store. When her mother joined her, she had already selected five packets of vegetable seeds whose glossy covers promised perfectly developed produce.

She had thought her mother would be pleased. The entire purchase amounted to fifty cents. But she pursed her lips and frowned. "What are you going to do with those?"

"Plant a garden, Mama."

"You don't know anything about planting a garden."

"I will learn."

When she got home and her father inspected her purchase, her mother said, "Now, William, let Rachel plant her garden by herself. No helping her. If it turns out well, the full credit should go to her." *Or the failure,* Rachel read in the pointed look she gave her father. She could not understand her mother's displeasure. It was the first time in all her growing-up years that she appeared unwilling to support and encourage her endeavors.

But she did not fail. She carefully read the packets' instructions and the dictates of gardening books checked out from the library and followed them to the letter. Working each day after school, she hoed up the Bermuda grass in a ten-by-ten plot at the side of the house and flooded it with pans of boiling water to kill the grubs and nematodes. To enrich the soil, she scooped manure from the neighbor's chicken pen and hauled sand by the bucketful from behind the row of track houses where she lived, to work into the caliche-striated ground. Already she had scoured the garage and dump ground for containers to serve as planters for her seedlings.

"What in the world—?" her mother exclaimed when she saw the mishmash of tin cans and cutoff milk cartons lining the windowsills of her room.

"I'm germinating seeds for my garden," Rachel

explained brightly, to make the unusual frown disappear between her mother's thinly plucked brows. "The sun comes through the window and warms the soil and seeds sprout and they grow into plants."

The frown stayed in place. "When you water them, see that you don't make a mess, Rachel, or that's the end of the project."

She did not make a mess, and that spring, she entered her garden as her science project. "Well, I'll be damned," the awed science teacher said when he surveyed her handiwork at judging time. "Now do you swear that your father's foot didn't help dig this plot? That his hand didn't pull up Bermuda grass, shovel in compost, and erect this chicken-wire fence?"

"No, sir. I did it all myself."

"Well, then, young lady, you well deserve the A you'll be getting. Your folks should be proud of you. They've got a farmer in the making." She was nine years old.

The next spring, her expanded garden was even more successful, producing a bounty for the table that not even the produce from Zack Mitchell's grocery store could equal in taste and quality. It was that success that decided her father to take her for her second visit to Howbutker in the pivotal summer of 1966. Rachel was never to forget the conversation—or, rather, the argument (rare for her parents)—that she overheard concerning his decision. It was mid-June, and she had gone outside after supper to water her plants from a hose attached to a faucet beneath the kitchen window. Because the swamp cooler was on the blink and the kitchen window was open, she heard her mother demand, "Just what do you aim to prove by taking Rachel to Howbutker, William? That she *is* a Toliver of the cotton-growing variety? That her interest in tomato plants and okra stems from something she's *inherited*?"

"And why not?" William argued. "Suppose, just suppose, that Rachel *is* another Mary Toliver. Suppose she has the makings of running Somerset once Aunt Mary is gone. Why, that would mean the plantation could stay in the family. It wouldn't have to be sold."

Rachel heard the ring of a utensil thrown into the galvanized sink. "William Toliver, are you crazy? The money from that farm is going to buy us a better house. It's going to ensure that we have a decent old age. It's going to let us go traveling and buy you that Airstream trailer you've always wanted. It's going to get you out from behind that meat counter so that you don't have to work the rest of your life."

"Alice..." William sighed. "If Rachel does have the Toliver blood, I can't sell her birthright—what's been in the Toliver family for generations."

"And what about Jimmy's, I'd like to know?" Alice's voice quivered. "What about *his* birthright?"

"That'd be up to Aunt Mary." William spoke as if that were the end of the matter. "For goodness' sakes, Alice, it's only a *visit*. This interest of Rachel's might be a passing thing. She's only ten. Next year she's liable to be interested in boys or music or Lord knows what else when she realizes how pretty she's becoming."

"Rachel has never been interested in girly things, and I doubt she will ever understand how pretty she is."

Rachel heard the decisive sound of a chair scraping away from the table. "I'm going to take her, Alice. It's only right. If the girl has the calling, I don't want to keep her from it. She deserves a chance to find out. That's all I'm giving her."

"And your conscience a chance to ease itself, if you ask me. By giving Rachel to your aunt, you can make up for taking yourself away from her all those years ago."

"Aunt Mary has already forgiven me for that," William said, sounding injured to the bone to the little eavesdropper beneath the window.

"If you take Rachel to Howbutker, you'll be making a mistake we'll all regret, William Toliver. Remember I told you."

That June, outfitted exactly like her great-aunt in a pair of khaki slacks, bush jacket, and straw hat from the DuMont Department Store, Rachel did not miss a day accompanying Mary out to the disputed plantation. She had never seen anything as breathtaking as the row after row of green plants stretching to the end of the world. A feeling stirred way down inside. "This is all yours, Aunt Mary?"

"Mine and those who came before me, those who took the land from the trees."

"Who were they?"

"Our Toliver forebears, yours and mine."

"Mine, too?"

"Yes, child. You're a Toliver."

"Does that explain why I like growing things?"

"It would appear so."

Aunt Mary's short answer further shed light on the reason her father had given her beforehand for making the visit. "You're a Toliver, honey, the genuine article. Not like Jimmy or me or my father. We all bear the name, but you and Aunt Mary carry the blood."

"What does that mean?"

"It means that you and Aunt Mary have inherited a certain ancestral force that has characterized the Tolivers since they founded Howbutker and built Somerset."

"Somerset?"

"A cotton plantation. The last of its kind in East Texas...quite a bit larger than your garden at home." Her father had smiled at her. "Your great-aunt has run it since she was a young girl."

The visit occurred within the three weeks that the cotton was in bloom, and Rachel stayed rapt with wonder from the sheer beauty surrounding her as she and Mary rode out among the blossoms on the two gentle mares kept on hand for inspecting the fields. Mary explained that each flower would fall after only three days, turning from creamy white to pink and finally to dark red. She even taught Rachel a little ditty she'd learned in childhood concerning the short life span of the cotton blossom:

First day white, next day red,
Third day from birth, I'm dead.

Mary explained how a cotton plant works...how its miracle unfolds. First buds appear after five to six weeks of the plants coming up, and then these buds become flowers. The flower falls, leaving behind a small seed pod known as the boll. Each boll contains about thirty seeds and up to half a million fibers of cotton. It is the fiber that's important, the white stuff that bursts out of the boll when it matures and splits open. The value of cotton depends on the length of its fibers, the color, the feel, and the amount of trash remaining in the white heads. The longer the fiber, the more valuable the cotton.

Rachel drank thirstily of Aunt Mary's knowledge, which it seemed she took no particular pains to have her great-niece imbibe. Nonetheless, she was clearly impressed that Rachel's interest never wavered, and by the end of her two-week stay, Rachel's skin, already tinted with the lush Toliver cast, attested to her keeping pace with her great-aunt's activities in the cotton fields under the hot, languid sun.

"So your father tells me you're set on being a farmer when you grow up," Aunt Mary commented when they took a lemonade break on the porch of a house referred to as "the Ledbetter place." It was used as her great-aunt's office but looked nice enough to live in. "Why?" she asked. "Farming is the hardest work in the world, oftentimes with very little reward for the effort expended. What's so appealing about getting your hands and clothes dirty?"

Rachel thought of Billy Seton up the street, who, almost from the time he could walk, so everybody said, had not been without a baseball mitt in his hand. It was no wonder, then, that he went on to play for the New York Yankees, making everybody in Kermit proud. "Born to play the game," they said, and that's how she felt about farming. She couldn't imagine not having a garden. There was no place else that made her as happy. She didn't mind getting her hands and clothes dirty. She *loved* the feel of rich, moist dirt, the sky over her shoulder, and the wind in her hair, but most of all she loved the miracle of the first sight of green breaking through the soil. There was no other feeling like it. It even beat the magic of Christmas morning.

"Well, Aunt Mary," she answered, a swagger in her tone akin to the way some men hooked their thumbs under their suspenders when they were proud of themselves, "I reckon I was born to be a farmer."

A smile hovered around Aunt Mary's finely shaped lips. "Is that so?"

When her father came to collect her, she said, "It was wonderful, Daddy," and looked at her great-aunt with hopeful eyes. "Next summer, Aunt Mary? In August—during harvest?"

Mary laughed, exchanging a glance with William. "Next summer, in August," she agreed.

Chapter Fifty-one

In the next few years, she was to overhear many arguments under the kitchen window in regard to her annual two-week visits to Howbutker.

"William, can you *believe* your aunt's letter? How dare that woman ask us to send Rachel to her for the summer! How selfish can she be? I don't see enough of my daughter as it is, and here she's asking that we let her have Rachel for her entire vacation!"

"Not her entire vacation, Alice. Only the month of August. Aunt Mary is nearly seventy years old. Why can't we humor an old woman? She's not going to live forever."

"She'll live long enough to steal my girl from me. She's driving a wedge between us, William. I'm so tired of hearing Aunt Mary this, Aunt Mary that. She never speaks of me in that adoring tone."

Under the window, Rachel listened, her conscience squeezed in contrition. No, she never did, she admitted. She heard the hurt in her mother's voice and vowed she'd show her more love and appreciation. *But, oh, please, Daddy, let me go to Aunt Mary and Uncle Ollie for August.*

The argument ended in a compromise that nonetheless left her mother tight-lipped as the family car pulled away bearing Rachel to Howbutker for the month requested. It was Rachel's fourteenth summer. The agreement, laid out by her mother, was that she could spend this August with her "daddy's kin," but next summer the whole family would go on a trip together with "no Howbutker, no Somerset, and no Aunt Mary."

It was during her fourteenth summer that Rachel first laid eyes upon Matt Warwick. She had often heard of Mister Percy's grandson, but he was always visiting his grandmother in Atlanta during the two weeks she was in town. Matt's mother had died of cancer when he was fourteen, and his father had been killed before that in a war. She remembered feeling sorry for the boy who'd been orphaned but considered him lucky to live in Howbutker and be looked after by such a wonderful old man as Mister Percy.

Her father said that Mister Percy was immensely rich—a lumber magnate—with large timber holdings all over the country and Canada. Matt was learning the family business and taking to it like a sail in an ocean breeze—rather like her, she thought. He was supposed to be handsome and likable and unaffected, and she was eager to see what all the praise was about.

They met at Matt's nineteenth birthday party. Rachel had a new dress for the occasion, selected with Uncle Ollie's unerring eye. It was a dress of white piqué scalloped at the neckline and hem and set off with a green sash belt. Rachel had never owned such a dress. She felt very ladylike and grown up in her first stockings and abbreviated high heels with her hair dressed specially for the party in a cascade of white daisies and green ribbons.

Aunt Mary and Uncle Ollie were waiting at the foot of the stairs when she came down, both gazing at her in pride and affection. Rachel beamed back, tamping down a niggling guilt at the memory of her mother's accusation: *You think you've become too good for us, Rachel.*

No, Mama, that's not so!

Don't tell me you don't prefer being with your rich aunt and uncle in that big mansion of theirs to living with your mother and daddy in our little house—or that you don't favor that snooty little burg of Howbutker over Kermit.

Oh, Mama, you've got it all wrong! I love both places.

She could not convince her mother that her feeling for Uncle Ollie and Aunt Mary in no way lessened the love she had for them. Uncle Ollie was the sweetest man alive and made her feel special, while Aunt Mary understood and appreciated her love for the land in a way that her mother never could. And as for the mansion on Houston Avenue…from the moment she'd seen it, she'd felt she'd returned to a place she'd known before, a place that seemed to have waited for her. The roses and honeysuckle, the fish pond and gazebo, the house with its elegant sweeping staircase and hushed, luxurious rooms…all felt as familiar—as much *hers*—as her home in Kermit and her room next to her six-year-old brother's. And she felt she'd been connected to Howbutker all of her life, though she didn't know why. Howbutker's red-bricked streets, southern-inspired architecture, and mixture of black and white residents were as different from her hometown of Kermit as water from sand. When she'd mentioned this strange phenomenon to her father, he'd said, "You've come home, Rachel. This house and town are the birthplace of your heritage."

I can't help it, she thought as she descended the staircase. This is my home, too, and Aunt Mary and Uncle Ollie are the grandparents I never had. I belong here.

Uncle Ollie extended his arm to her. "It's like looking at you, Mary Lamb, when you were fourteen."

"I can't remember ever being that lovely," Mary said in her soft voice.

"That's because you never noticed," Uncle Ollie said.

The party was held on the grounds of Mister Percy's massive ancestral home, Warwick Hall. It was a huge affair to which everyone who knew and liked Matt was invited: old and young, rich and poor, white and black. When they arrived, they were led across the tented lawn cooled by giant fans to Percy Warwick and Amos Hines standing next to a young man in a white dinner jacket. So that's Matt Warwick, Rachel thought curiously, prepared to be disappointed. Until she had come along, Mister Percy's grandson was the only child in Aunt Mary and Uncle Ollie's lives. It would have been understandable if they had viewed him through rose-colored glasses.

But they had not exaggerated. Matt stood as tall as his grandfather, with the same athletic build, though his similarly handsome face was a little more unevenly put together. He had the same relaxed manner and easy way with a smile as Mister Percy, but there were differences that made her curious as to who should take credit for his clear blue eyes and bumper crop of light brown hair. Not his silver blond, gray-eyed grandfather, that was for sure. She knew nothing of his parents and had never met his grandmother, who lived far away in Atlanta. She knew only that when he took her hand, a shock went through her and something inside burst into being like the sudden unfolding of a cotton blossom to the morning sun.

She hugged Amos first, whom she thought of as

Abraham Lincoln, her favorite president, and then Mister Percy, staring at her oddly. Uncle Ollie cleared his throat and turned her toward Matt in an obvious attempt to draw her away from his grandfather's transfixed attention. "Matt, my boy, this is Mary's great-niece, Rachel Toliver," he announced needlessly. "She's always come to us the two weeks you've been with your grandmother in Atlanta, so you two have come and gone on opposite trains, so to speak."

For some reason, it was an unfortunate remark. Uncle Ollie immediately reddened, and as enraptured with Matt as she was, she couldn't miss the looks traded between Aunt Mary and Mister Percy and the slight loss of color beneath their summer tans. That's when Matt smiled and shook her hand. "Well, in a few years, I'll have to make sure I'm on the right inbound train."

He was simply too smooth for her and she too inadequate to deal with the blitz of his engaging grin and the flash of male appreciation in his blue eyes. She withdrew her hand and lowered her gaze, retreating into fourteen-year-old adolescence, too self-conscious to care whether he thought her gauche and immature, certainly not ready for the figure-flattering dress and high heels.

"Granddad was not exaggerating when he said you're the spitting image of your great-aunt," Matt went on as if he hadn't noticed. "Think you can handle being that pretty?"

"As well as you can handle being as handsome as your grandfather," she rejoined, shocking herself. It sounded smart-alecky, but she'd meant it as a compliment. To her relief, the group laughed and Matt seemed impressed. He touched a fingertip to the dimple in her chin and she felt anointed, as if a prince had laid his blade across her shoulder.

"Touché," he said, "but I'd say you've got a tougher job than I have. Nice to have met you at last, Rachel Toliver. Enjoy yourself." He smiled and left them to join a group of his University of Texas classmates, among them a number of sophisticated coeds, and Rachel felt as if the sun had disappeared from the sky.

They spoke again, briefly, at the punch table. "When are you going home?" he asked.

She blinked. Home? But she was home. "Tomorrow, I'm afraid."

"Why 'afraid'?"

"Because I...don't want to go."

"You're not homesick?" he asked.

"Yes, I am. I miss my family, but I...miss Aunt Mary and Uncle Ollie, too, when I'm not here."

He gave her his easygoing smile and handed her a cup of punch. "Well, don't think of that as being a problem. Think of it as how lucky you are to have two places to call home."

She must remember to express it that way to her mother, she thought, marveling at his wisdom.

On the way to Houston Avenue, Aunt Mary asked casually, "What did you think of Matt Warwick?"

She replied without having to think of her answer. "Sensational," she said. "Simply sensational."

Aunt Mary pressed her lips together and made no comment.

Chapter Fifty-two

The next August, as agreed, Rachel accompanied her parents and Jimmy to Colorado, where they vacationed at a dude ranch high in the Rocky Mountains. The temperature was a welcome change from the 110 degrees usual for the month in Kermit, and the scenery was so awesomely beautiful that attempts to describe it on postcards ended in frustration. Rachel, however, gazed up at the snowcapped mountains, felt the cold lake breezes fanning her face, and thought of the cotton ready for picking at Somerset and sweat standing on her skin. She had turned fifteen.

"You miss it, don't you," her father stated in his quiet manner beside her.

"Yes, sir," she said.

She returned to school feeling an unfamiliar emptiness, as though some sustenance vital to getting through the school year were missing.

"We can't do this to her anymore, Alice," she heard her father say as she turned on the faucet beneath the kitchen window. "It's like...it's like a light has gone out inside her."

"I'll speak to her," her mother said.

Alice chose the next Thursday night when William was working late at the store and Jimmy was down the street at a friend's house. She slipped the drying towel from Rachel's hands and directed her to a kitchen chair. "Sit down, Rachel. I want to talk to you."

Rachel tensed at her mother's serious tone and stiffly obeyed. "Yes, ma'am?"

Her mother drew her hands into her own, still warm from washing dishes. She gazed deeply into her eyes and said, "Rachel, I'm going to ask something of you that will break your heart as well as mine."

Instinctively, she tried to draw her hands away, but her mother held on. "You love us, don't you?" Alice asked. "Especially your daddy?"

"Especially all of you," Rachel said.

"And whatever your decision, I want you to agree to keep this discussion our secret. Your father is never to know what we talked about tonight. Do you promise?"

Pinpoints of stars, like the kind she sometimes saw when she hit her head, swirled alarmingly in her mental vision. "Yes, Mama," she said in a small voice.

Her mother hesitated, and Rachel recognized a look that always betrayed a struggle with her conscience. "Honey," she began, rubbing her hand up and down Rachel's arm, "I'm sure you know that as things are now between you and Aunt Mary, she's pegged you as the heir she thought she lost when her little boy died."

"Heir...?"

"To carry on in her place when she dies—to keep the Toliver tradition going." Alice squinted an eye as if unsure of whether Rachel sincerely did not understand her meaning or was playing dense.

Rachel blinked rapidly. She, Aunt Mary's heir? She'd already decided to go to Texas A&M University to pursue a degree in agriculture, with hope that Aunt Mary would give her a job after graduation, but...take her place when she died? *Inherit* Somerset?

Alice leaned closer. "It's plain as a cow patty on the lawn at a garden party that she intends for you to step into her shoes, Rachel. Why do you think she continues to buy more land?"

Rachel answered promptly. "Because Somerset is played out. After this harvest, she's going to let it lie fallow until next year when she plants it in corn and soybeans."

She spoke with pride. For the first time in its history, Somerset was to be under another crop besides its steadily declining cotton production. Aunt Mary was "branching out" and had Rachel to thank for it. Over her summer visits, her great-aunt had listened with interest when she'd described the cultural requirements of her vegetable garden, and last year Aunt Mary had turned to her land manager and said, "My great-niece has inspired me to change the character of Somerset, a feat no one else has managed. The land is spent for cotton. It's time I recognized that."

But Aunt Mary was still a cotton planter, and she had bought several thousand acres of ranch land near Lubbock and Phoenix, Arizona, to put under cotton, calling her holdings Toliver Farms. The purchases had upset Alice, who declared she was "emptying the coffers so there won't be a plug nickel left."

Eyeing Rachel sternly, her mother said, "That's not the reason. If you hadn't come along, she'd have been satisfied to get what she could out of that plantation of hers, played out or not. But no, now she has a reason to buy more land and equipment at the expense of what should be going to your father when she dies. She'll be what so many ranchers are around here—land rich but cash poor. Are you getting my drift?"

Rachel nodded. Now she understood fully the gist of her parents' arguments over the years. Her mother had expected Aunt Mary to leave the plantation to her father, who would then sell it. She felt a rush of nausea. Fearful of her mother's growing anger, she ventured timidly, "So what if she leaves everything to me? Would that be so bad? I'd share everything the land produces with you and Daddy and Jimmy...."

"Your daddy would *never* let his family live off his daughter," Alice said.

"Why not? Other kids help out their parents."

"Because your daddy doesn't feel *entitled* to anything produced from Toliver land, that's why. He'd never take a cent."

Rachel was thoroughly bewildered. "Why?"

Alice released her hands and sat back. She tapped her fingers on the table in an apparent effort to decide whether she could trust her. Finally she said, "When your father was seventeen, he ran away from Aunt Mary and Uncle Ollie, that's why."

Rachel couldn't believe it. Why would her father run away from two of the most wonderful people in the world?

"You don't believe me, do you." Alice read her doubt. "Well, he did, honey, and I'll tell you why. Your great-aunt tried to make him into a cotton planter—a Toliver like herself—but your daddy didn't take to the family calling. He hated farming. He hated Somerset. He hated what was expected of him, so he ran away to the oilfields in West Texas. That's how he ended up in Kermit."

Rachel's mouth had dropped open. She'd always assumed that after he'd married her mother, he'd remained in Kermit because it was her hometown.

"Your father may be poor, but he's proud," Alice continued. "That's why he's never allowed his aunt to help us. To give Aunt Mary credit, she's offered. He'd feel the same toward handouts from you. Now I'm going to fill you in on a few other family secrets that I'm sure Aunt Mary's not passed along with the Toliver history she's rammed into your head."

Abruptly, as if needing fortification, Alice got up to fill her dinner glass from a pitcher of tea on the counter. She wrenched ice cubes from a tray and popped them loudly into the glass, spooned in sugar, and stirred with a vengeance. Rachel watched in trepidation. Jiminy Crickets, what was she going to tell her?

Her mother sat back down without having tasted the tea and continued. "Long ago when we first took you to Howbutker to meet your great-aunt, she promised your daddy that at her death, her estate would be sold and the proceeds left to him. Her will was all set, she said. You were an infant. She told him to take you home and forget about Somerset—that there was a curse on the land...."

"A curse?" Rachel felt herself grow as cold as her mother's tea glass.

"A curse, Rachel. She never explained to your daddy what she meant by that, but she told him to be glad that you and his future children were free of the plantation. I swear it on my papa's grave that's what she told him."

Rachel wanted to clap her hands over her ears. She couldn't bear to hear her mother talk of Aunt Mary dying or a curse being on Somerset.

"I'm telling you this," Alice went on, "because ever since then, I've been counting on her to keep her promise to your daddy. It's been like a rainbow in the sky."

Rachel asked in confusion, "But...I don't understand. What's the difference between inheriting the proceeds from the land and...and living off its profits?"

Alice looked startled, clearly having not expected the question. She reached for her glass and gulped several noisy swallows of tea. "Well, to explain the difference, I'm going to have to drag out some more family skeletons," she said. "When Aunt Mary's father died, he left everything to his daughter and not so much as a clod of family soil to his son, Miles, your daddy's father. That's why he went to live in France. As a result of your great-granddaddy's unfairness, Miles— and therefore his offspring—were *dismembered* from ever being a part of what Aunt Mary holds so dear. It's possible your daddy might never have run away if his father had been left a stake in Somerset. He would have had a reason to stay because he had a *claim* to the land. Now do you understand why we don't owe a tinker's dam to Somerset and your precious Toliver heritage?"

Rachel listened, stunned and dismayed. Another

story, similar to the one she'd just heard, surfaced from family history. It had to do with the hurt her mother never overcame that her father, a garage owner, willed his business to Alice's brother when he died. There'd been nothing left for her. Alice had contended that her brother should sell the business and split the proceeds with her. With his share, he could open another shop. He had refused. Rachel wondered how much her mother's own feeling of injustice colored her view of her father's.

"Yes, ma'am," she said meekly.

"So the difference, Rachel, is that your father would look upon the proceeds from the sale of Aunt Mary's property as *compensation*. He'd consider it *charity* to share in the profits of what he ran away from. Do you understand that?"

Rachel nodded numbly, feeling her blood about to pump through her temples. She now could guess what her mother was leading up to. Scalding tears shot to the back of her eyes. "What do you want from me, Mama?"

Alice sat forward again and looked her daughter in the eye. "I want you to get out of the way of your father inheriting Aunt Mary's estate. I want you to give up this... improper notion of becoming a farmer. It's only temporary anyway, honey. You'll change your mind about what you want to do with your life half a dozen times before you graduate from high school, but in the meantime, you'll be feeding Aunt Mary's fantasy that you're another Mary Toliver."

"I am another Mary Toliver—"

A slap to the table cut her off. "You are *not* her! Get that out of your head, you hear? You may look like her, act like her, want to *be* her, but you are *you,* a product of me and my family as well as of your daddy and the almighty Tolivers. Do you know how it makes me feel for you and your father to believe—be proud of, in fact—that not a drop of my Finch blood is in you?"

"Oh, Mama, we never meant for you to feel that way...."

"Well, I do, Rachel. How can I not? And then to add salt to that wound, you're usurping your father's just due, a man who's worked his good hand to the bone for us all these years, whose only chance to escape Zack Mitchell and to have a decent old age is the money from the sale of your aunt's holdings."

It was a sure way to rouse her sympathy—mentioning her father's "good" hand. The other was deformed by an oilfield accident before she was born. "I can sell some of the land," she said, "and give the money to Daddy."

"He wouldn't take it. Haven't I made that clear? Somerset must go to him outright, as your aunt Mary promised."

Rachel pressed at her throbbing temples. "When and how do I ... get out of the way?"

Alice drew in close. "You step aside now—before she rewrites her will. You do that by quashing Aunt Mary's hopes. Tell her you've lost interest in farming and you no longer want to get a degree in agriculture."

"You mean..." Her mother's meaning was clear. "Cut out my summer trips to Howbutker? Break off from Aunt Mary and Uncle Ollie? Never see Sassie or Mister Percy or Amos...or Matt again? But they're my family!"

Another hard slap to the table. "*We* are your family, Rachel—your daddy and Jimmy and I. This is your home, not Howbutker. *We* are the people you should consider before Aunt Mary."

Rachel dropped her head. She could hardly breathe. She dug her nails into the legs of her jeans. "I know it's a sacrifice," her mother said, pushing her hair away from her face in a typical gesture after giving her a scolding, "but you'll never regret that you made it, not when you see your daddy enjoying some of the finer things for once in his life. You'll never be sorry you did the right thing."

She lifted her head. "Does this mean I have to give up my garden?"

Alice gave her a pleading look. "You have to, honey. It's the only way to convince your daddy that you've given up your notion of becoming a farmer. He won't believe it otherwise. He'll still insist on taking you to Howbutker."

Her heart felt trapped in her throat. Give up her garden? Remove the wire fence and let the rabbits and other desert creatures have at it? Allow the weeds and Bermuda grass to poke up through the soil she'd made fertile, take over the straight, neat rows, destroy her after-school place? But what was worse—much worse—would be to *lie* to Aunt Mary, make her believe that she didn't care for her and Uncle Ollie anymore...that she didn't care about Somerset and Howbutker and her Toliver roots.

Her mother held her hand and stroked her arm in sympathy. Dumbly, Rachel observed the rhythmic movement and noticed how work-worn her hands had become. For the first time, she realized all those hands did to keep the family fed and healthy, their clothes cleaned and presentable, their little house spotless—all they did to make their poverty less noticeable and without the modern conveniences other mothers enjoyed to make their work easier. Her hands rarely held anything new for herself. Anything purchased beyond the tight budget went to her husband and children.

"I'm not asking for myself, honey," Alice said. "I'm begging for your daddy."

"I know that, Mama." Rachel brought her mother's rough hand to her cheek. It was barely September...a whole school year to live through and then another and another until graduation without a reason to count the days until summer...without a reason to feel alive. She stood while breath was still in her lungs and tried to smile into her mother's hopeful face. "I'll write a letter to Aunt Mary and Uncle Ollie tonight and tell them I've changed my mind about becoming a farmer and that I won't be going to Howbutker anymore."

Chapter Fifty-three

Daddy, what are you doing here?" Rachel looked up at her father in surprise. He had materialized by her table in the county library, where she was filling in the form of her acceptance to Texas Tech University on an electric typewriter a week after her graduation from high school. Under ACADEMIC DEGREE DESIRED, she had typed, "To be decided." It was Thursday and he was usually at home this time of day, having his after-lunch nap.

"Your mother said you were here," William said. He was wearing sandals with socks, rather than the lace-up shoes with the arch support inserts that he wore to stand behind a butcher counter all day. "She didn't think it was necessary for me to stop by, but I couldn't go off without telling you myself...."

"Tell me what? Where are you going?"

"Honey..." William pulled a chair close to hers and took her hand. "It's your uncle Ollie. He died this morning of a heart attack. I'm on my way to

Howbutker now. Zack's letting me take a couple of days of my vacation time to attend the funeral."

Rachel's jaw dropped and tears surged to her eyes. Uncle Ollie—that dear, sweet man—dead? She hadn't seen him in three years—three years in which she could have been storing up memories of him. She asked, "How is Aunt Mary?"

"I'm not sure. It was Amos who called. He said Aunt Mary looked...lost."

She ripped the acceptance form from the typewriter and inserted it into her college folder. "I'm going with you," she said. "It won't take me a minute to pack. We'll take my car. It's more reliable."

Panic flashed across William's face. "I don't think that's a good idea, Bunny-hop. Your mother needs you here—"

"What for?"

William gulped, clearly at a loss for an answer. He shrugged. "Well, why not? I'm sure Aunt Mary would love to have you with her at this time, and"—he held up his deformed hand—"I could use help driving. It's that...your mother never liked to share you with Aunt Mary."

"This time I'm sure she won't mind making an exception." Her mother owed her that, at least. In the three years she'd separated herself from the people and place she longed for, she'd endured, for her mother's sake, the mindless high school activities she judged right for a teenage girl. She'd given up all interest in agriculture, including her membership in the FFA (Future Farmers of America) and her intention to enroll in Texas A&M and major in agronomy.

And she'd faithfully kept her promise not to reveal to her father the reason for her sudden about-face. He'd been puzzled at first, but eventually he came to accept her mother's explanation that she'd discovered she was a girl, and a noticeable one at that. He never suspected that his wife was responsible for the tears he sometimes found her shedding, believing Alice when she said, "Oh, it's only developing hormones."

"This is a huge mistake, Rachel," her mother said as she was packing.

"I won't be gone long, Mama."

"What about our agreement?"

"For heaven's sake. I'm only going to Uncle Ollie's funeral. How is that breaking our agreement?"

"I can think of thousands of acres' worth of reasons."

On the drive, while her father napped in the passenger seat, Rachel wondered what her welcome would be after her long, vaguely explained absence from Houston Avenue. Aunt Mary and Uncle Ollie had stayed in touch by telephone and letters—at first, theirs outnumbering hers two to one. They wrote of the town and plantation and neighborhood, of Sassie and Mister Percy and Amos. Occasionally they mentioned Matt, every word of which she devoured. He'd graduated from Texas University and had been busy learning the ropes of his grandfather's many business enterprises. She imagined that he was handsomer than ever, polished and sophisticated, a far cry from the bumpkin boys who had tried to paw her in high school and given her the title "Ice Queen" when she resisted their advances. They sent packages, too, boxes of clothes for her and Jimmy from Uncle Ollie's gilt-and-crystal department store. But as time went on, the telephone calls became less frequent and correspondence between them dwindled, mainly because she found it impossible to talk or write convincingly of her new interests, and her responses sounded bored and cool. She was sure she'd succeeded in convincing them that she'd outgrown the need for surrogate grandparents and that her enthusiasm for farming, her family name, and Somerset had been only a grade school interest.

Her eyes shimmered as she drove. Nothing could have been further from the truth. She had missed them with an ache that no substitute in her three years of high school could make go away. And now she'd never have a chance to express to Uncle Ollie what he'd meant to her or her gratitude that he'd not forgotten her. It had been his hand that had selected the car she drove as a graduation present and arranged for it to be delivered to her door, a sleek red 1973 Ford Mustang, fresh off the dealership floor.

But in spite of the generous gift, she would not be at all surprised if she received a cool reception. Aunt

Mary might be forgiving of the shabby way she'd treated her affections, but never Uncle Ollie's.

When they arrived before the familiar verandah, her stomach roiled as if she'd swallowed a swarm of moths. Sassie opened the door, her mouth forming a large cavity of surprise. "Why, Miss Rachel, we didn't know you was comin'!" she cried, grabbing her to her bosom in a breath-squeezing hug. "Lawsey me, how you've grown!"

Her boisterous welcome brought familiar footsteps from the library. "Who is it, Sassie?"

"Somebody you goin' to be mighty pleased to see, Miss Mary."

She stepped aside and left Rachel's great-aunt framed in the foyer. She was seventy-three. Her hair had silvered and time had trifled with her face, but she was the svelte, handsome woman Rachel remembered. Coming up behind her were Percy, still commanding at seventy-eight, Matt, now twenty-two, and Amos, looking as mournfully Lincolnesque as ever. They drew alongside her, her family now that Uncle Ollie was gone, but it was to Rachel Mary held out her arms. "Oh, dear child, you've come," she said, tears breaching her red-rimmed eyes. "I'm so glad...so very glad."

Rachel paused only long enough to realize that returning had been a mistake. Never again would she be able to call Kermit home. This was her home—this house, this street, this town, these people. She loved her family, but her place was here beside this woman whose blood ran in her veins, whose life-giving passion she shared. "I'm glad I came, too," she said, and flew past her father into her great-aunt's embrace.

THE RING OF THE TELEPHONE in the outer office shook Rachel loose from the memory of that reunion. After the funeral, her father had gone back to Kermit without her in the company plane. That fall, with Aunt Mary pulling a few strings, she was admitted to Texas A&M University in College Station, two hours' drive from Howbutker, where she returned for weekends and summers to help Aunt Mary introduce vegetable crops to Somerset and to implement the new techniques she'd learned. Four years later, she graduated at the top of her class with a degree in agronomy. Her hope had been to live in Howbutker and run Somerset's vegetable production while her great-aunt managed her expanding cotton interests. But Aunt Mary had other plans for her. While the sun may have set on Somerset's cotton-producing days, it had not on the cotton-producing Tolivers. She sent Rachel to learn the business from one of the plantation's old hands who ran the company's western division in Lubbock, Texas, and eventually—though Rachel's heart remained at Somerset—to take over as manager when he retired.

Her mother did not forgive her for going back on her promise, but Rachel kept the family secrets her mother had divulged, and her father never learned the real reason for their estrangement. He accepted without rancor that it was only right that his daughter, "the one true Toliver," should inherit the family holdings.

She got up from her desk, returned the tissue box to the coffee table, and opened her office door. Danielle, her secretary of many years, leaped up to express her condolences, and the ever faithful Ron placed an arm about her shoulders. She would be leaving Toliver Farms West in competent hands. "I won't be seeing you all for a while," she said. "I'll run the business from Howbutker, but you know where to reach me if you have questions."

"So you won't be coming back after today?" Danielle asked.

"No, Danielle, not unless something unforeseen forces me to return."

Chapter Fifty-four

William Toliver took a glass of iced tea out to his small patio for a few minutes' reprieve from his wife's stony silence before returning to work. The plastic seat of his chair scalded his bottom, but it alleviated the chill creeping over him. The day that he'd dreaded for years had finally arrived, dashing his hope that his wife and daughter would reconcile before Aunt Mary's death. Part of him was happy that Rachel would be stepping into the shoes she was born to fill. As a Toliver, that meant something to him—a lot, in fact—even if the notion drove Alice crazy. He wished she weren't accompanying him and Jimmy to Howbuker. What a scene there would be when Amos read the will and confirmed to her that Rachel had "stolen" her father's one chance for a better life.

He sighed. But a part of him regretted that he'd taken Rachel to Howbutker in the summer of 1966, as Alice had predicted he would. She was entitled now to say "I told you so" because from that summer forward, his family had never been the same. He'd often wondered—even if he hadn't introduced his daughter to her Toliver roots that year—whether her first garden wouldn't have eventually led her to Houston Avenue and Somerset.

Maybe not. God knew the first trip to Howbutker ten years before to introduce his wife and newborn daughter to his aunt and uncle had not been a success. His little family was received graciously, but with the reserve of strangers. William found that understandable. He had not been home since he'd run away at seventeen. He was then twenty-eight, and there had been little contact with Houston Avenue in the years between. He had lived in Kermit for eleven years. At twenty-one, he had married a drugstore waitress he met when he picked up medication prescribed for a hand he'd injured in an oilfield accident, announcing his marriage to the folks in Howbutker by telegram.

William understood well enough that it was out of guilt that he'd neglected them and shame that, as a Toliver, he'd settled for so little when his heritage demanded he desire so much.

"I ran away from all that was expected of me," he explained to Alice. "I'm sure I hurt my aunt terribly. Aunt Mary and Uncle Ollie's son and only child died a few years after I came to live with them, and I . . . left her with no one to carry on the Toliver tradition."

Alice took a different view. Aroused by the protective instincts William loved in her and put off by his "snooty" aunt's reserve, she declared that it was Aunt Mary's own fault that he had run away. It was she who should be asking for forgiveness. "She tried to make you into something you aren't to satisfy her own ambitions. You're no farmer. You're not even a Toliver—if it means being like her."

William had discounted the last remark. Even at fifty-six, Aunt Mary possessed an intimidating beauty, and her elegance and regal manner were not the kind to put at ease a woman who still wore a Betty Grable hairdo and plucked her brows into a thin arch. Furthermore, Alice had a possessive streak in her. William realized his wife feared that Aunt Mary would lure him back to Howbutker by appealing to his sense of obligation. It had unnerved her to see how closely Rachel's features resembled his aunt's. "She's a Toliver all right," Uncle Ollie had declared, beaming his delight as he lifted her from the bassinet.

Immediately, Alice had snatched her infant daughter into the harbor of her own arms, and William had read in her action that to his wife, living in the world of Houston Avenue would result in a constant fight to keep and hold that which was hers. No one could mitigate her sense of feeling hopelessly out of place, not even his sweetly mannered uncle, whom she'd liked at once. Because he had "rescued" her husband, she tolerated Amos Hines, who was now thoroughly entrenched in the way of life he'd chanced into. Percy Warwick, his blond hair silvered, tanned and still fit at sixty-one, literally took her breath away. She pronounced him handsomer than any movie star and thought his wife must be crazy to go off and leave a man like him alone.

Even so, for all the unfailing courtesy shown her, Alice had felt as inappropriate in the elegant company of Houston Avenue as flour sacking among silks and satins.

The evening before they were to return to Kermit, his aunt had asked him to sit with her for a while in the gazebo. "Your wife does not like me," she stated in her direct way when they were seated on the swing. "She isn't comfortable with us here among the pines."

William cared too much for her to deny it. "She's never been out of West Texas," he said.

"The important thing is that she loves you, William, and that she's made you happy."

"You mean that, Aunt?" He regarded her in surprise. This was a different tune from the one he'd expected to hear, certainly a change from the verse she'd sung when he was a boy. Commitment to one's name, to one's heritage, to that which the sacrifices of others had made possible—that was the song he used to hear from Aunt Mary.

"Yes, I do," she said. "If I've learned anything by now, it's that some things are too priceless to sacrifice for a name. You go on back to Kermit and don't worry about anything you may have thought you left behind."

She spoke sincerely, he could tell, but the stoicism with which she told him to forget what had been her life's work tore at his heart. He spoke softly in the darkness. "Aunt Mary, what about the plantation? What's going to happen to it when...you're..."

"Dead and gone or too old to run it anymore? Why, I'll sell it. You'll receive the proceeds as my heir even if Ollie succeeds me. It's already taken care of in the will. The house I may leave to the Conservation Society."

"It's such a shame...." Through a film of tears, William studied his crippled hand. "I'm so sorry, Aunt."

"Don't be." She slipped her hand over his. "Somerset has always cost too much. It's brought a curse to the Tolivers. No use now enlightening you as to that. Be glad your children will grow up free of Somerset. Take Alice and that beautiful little girl home and enjoy your life, though how that's possible in a sand pit, I'll never know." William caught the sliver of a smile in the darkness.

He asked, "Did you find the red rose I left on your pillow the morning I ran away?"

"Yes, William, I found your rose."

That night when he went up to bed, he found a white one lying on his pillow.

Thinking of that time, he felt a pang of conscience. No matter that Aunt Mary had forgiven him, he'd always believed he owed her for running out on her. Maybe Alice had been right about that, too. Deep down, maybe his main reason for taking Rachel to Howbutker in 1966 was to make up for what he'd done—or hadn't done—because he'd known that no matter what Aunt Mary had stated in the gazebo, she could not resist a chance to install another Toliver on the land. Still, that would have been all right, too, if he hadn't shared with Alice the conversation between him and his aunt that night. If it hadn't been for that information and the fact that his great-grandfather had not seen fit to leave his son an acre of family soil, mother and daughter would still be united.

He heard the telephone ring, and in a moment Alice came to the door. "Your lord and master is on the phone asking where in hell you are," she said.

William's mouth pulled to one side. "Now how did he know where I'd be?"

Chapter Fifty-five

Amos was at the Howbutker Municipal Airport when the small Cessna Citation bearing the name TOLIVER FARMS landed at ten o'clock. He knew he looked ghastly, as if he'd spent time in a Tijuana jail. His face, never one to crow about at the best of times, had shocked him when he went to shave this morning, but how could it not? His guts felt twisted into ball bearings, and he'd been unable to sleep, getting up at three o'clock and spending the rest of the night on his terrace listening to the screech of alley cats in heat.

Dear God, help us all, he prayed as the door to the sleek little jet opened and the short flight of steps popped down. A minute later, Rachel appeared, saw him, and waved. Amos experienced a woozy feeling of déjà vu. How like Mary she looked, when he'd first seen her standing at the top of the stairs in Ollie's department store. Rachel was far younger, of course, but so utterly like her in loveliness and—as Mary had appeared then—looking distressed. He waved back and fixed a smile.

Rachel hurried toward him, tanned legs gleaming in white culottes, and threw her arms around his neck. "Dear Amos," she said, her voice tender and warm. "How are you?"

"About the same as you, I expect," he said, hugging her close.

"Then we'll be a mess together." She linked an arm through his and motioned the pilot to follow with her bags to his car, a dark blue Cadillac as conspicuous in size but as unobtrusive as Amos himself. "I wasn't able to convince my family to come with me, as you can see," she said, "but they should arrive by noon tomorrow. My mother's coming, too. Tell me the plans you've made."

She felt as light as a sprite on his arm—a sacrificial maiden unaware of her doom. "The funeral is set for eleven o'clock Monday, with the burial at three. Viewing hours are tentatively set for Saturday morning from ten until twelve and from five to seven, if those times are all right with you."

"They're ideal," Rachel said. "They'll allow time for all of us to catch our breaths. Anything else?"

He cited other details subject to her approval. He'd given the go-ahead for the burial plot next to Ollie's to be prepared since Mary had not wished to be cremated. And to spare Sassie and Henry, themselves terribly bereaved, he'd booked the church parlor for the reception after the funeral. No use having hundreds of people tramping through the house, dropping food everywhere. Let the Women's Auxiliary at the First Methodist Church handle it. There would be plenty of folks paying their respects at Houston Avenue anyway.

"Seems as if you've thought of everything," Rachel said. "What's left for me to do?"

"You'll need to choose a viewing dress for Mary and decide on the coffin and family flowers. I've prepared a folder of my notes and the telephone numbers and names of personnel for you to contact. They're waiting to hear from you. Also, today, you'll have to go over the obituary in case you wish to add anything. Mary wrote it herself and included it with her legal documents. The funeral home requested it by four o'clock."

Rachel stopped in her tracks. "Aunt Mary had already written her obituary? Did she know she was in failing health?"

"Well…as I've said, she never mentioned heart trouble to me. As for the obituary"—he attempted a weak grin—"it's been my professional experience that southern ladies of a certain age, long before the event of their deaths, like to compose their own histories for print rather than leave the task to relatives. In Mary's case, I believe she wanted to keep hers simple and direct. No flowery embellishments."

"How long ago was it written?"

"I'm afraid I can't testify to the date."

"Then I'll leave it as it is, but I'm surprised that Aunt Mary would have even bothered with it."

They had reached the car. The pilot caught up with them and loaded her luggage into his trunk. "Well, Miss Toliver," he said, sticking out his hand when he'd finished, "it's been nice knowing you."

Rachel took the hand as if she didn't quite know what to do with it. "What do you mean, Ben? Where are you going?"

"Why, didn't you know? My contract has been terminated as of this last flight. I was supposed to have flown Mrs. DuMont to Lubbock today, but...I brought you here instead. This is my last run for Toliver Farms."

"Who told you that?"

"Mrs. DuMont."

"Did you and she have a disagreement of some kind?"

"No, ma'am. She simply told me she'd have no more need of my services. Scuttlebutt has it that the plane has been sold."

"Sold?" Rachel turned to Amos. "Did you know anything about this?"

He lifted his shoulders and looked innocent, but he felt the blood sluice from his face. "She never said anything to me about getting rid of the plane."

Rachel swung back to the pilot. "Ben, I don't know what to say, but I'll get to the bottom of this. There must be some mistake."

"Well, in case it is, you have my card and know where to reach me," Ben said.

Rachel stared after the retreating pilot, looking perplexed. "You know," she mused, "this is the second incident that makes me think something's going on in regard to the farms that I'm unaware of. Yesterday a representative from a textile company we've sold to for years informed me that our contract would not be renewed." She turned questioningly to Amos. "Do you think Aunt Mary knew she had a short time to live and was making certain changes prior to her death? Do you suppose that was the reason she was coming out to see me?"

Amos patted his pockets distractedly in a pretense of searching for his keys, feigning relief when he found them. "You know that your great-aunt was not one to share confidences," he hedged. "I'm sure all will come to light soon enough. Which reminds me, Rachel. Do you think that after the burial, you and your family could meet in my office around five o'clock for the reading of the will?"

"I'm sure that will be fine with them. They'll want to get everything over as soon as possible so that they can leave for Kermit the next morning. I'll stay on, of course. I've left my foreman in charge in Lubbock and will run things from Aunt Mary's office for a while. Too bad that Addie Cameron retired when she did. I could have certainly used her help."

"Indeed...," he murmured, keeping his eye steady

on maneuvering the car off the tarmac. It had been another clue he should have picked up on, the recent and unexpected early retirement of Mary's trusty assistant after she had worked twenty years for her as her right hand. She was now living—and no doubt well compensated—near her son's family in Springfield, Colorado. It would be a miracle if Rachel did not learn of the sale of the farms prior to the funeral, and Lord only knew what her reaction would be. This morning, he'd been on the phone to Mary's lawyers in Dallas to inquire how much longer the news of the sale would be held from the business community. Not long, they'd warned, once the media picked up on the fact of Mary's death.

When he pulled up before the Toliver mansion, Henry, wearing a black armband, came out to greet them and carry in Rachel's bags. "I can take it from here, Amos," she said, the folder under her arm. "Go home and get some rest. Forgive my saying so, but you look as if you could use it."

"Yes...yes, I will do that. One word of caution before I leave you, Rachel. I suggest you refuse to speak to reporters until after the funeral...as a matter of propriety. I'm sure it's what Mary would have wished."

"Good advice." She leaned over and kissed his cheek. "Go grab a nap and then come back for dinner. We'll invite Percy and Matt, too. I'm sure they'll want to be with us."

Through his rearview mirror as he put the car in gear, Amos observed her climb the verandah steps, back straight and head held high—as though already feeling the weight of the crown. Sighing deeply, his sorrow twisting like a knife inside him, he prayed again, Dear God, help us all.

As ALWAYS WHEN IT HAD been a while since Rachel had been home, Sassie threw open the front door when she reached the verandah and embraced her in a bear hug, her smooth dark face, endearingly at odds with her cap of wiry gray curls, puckering into tears. "Oh, Miss Rachel, thank the Lord you're here," she cried, her rich, clean smell as much a part of Houston Avenue as the scent of honeysuckle growing over the backyard fence.

"It happened right over there," she said when they'd parted, and pointed to an area where two wide-armed chairs had been thrown back from a table. "She collapsed right over there. I should have never left her, what with her actin' so strange and all. I knew she wasn't herself."

Rachel stepped to the spot. "How was she acting strangely, Sassie?"

"Why, she was *drinkin'*, Miss Rachel, and you know your aunt never drunk nothin' stronger than lemonade, not even at Christmastime when a little eggnog never hurt nobody. But she done come in from town 'bout lunchtime, and she sit right down in the heat where you're standin' and had me bring her out a bottle of champagne."

Rachel frowned. That *was* strange, Aunt Mary drinking liquor, let alone at noon on the verandah during the hottest month of the summer. "Maybe she was celebrating something."

"Well, if she was, I don't know what. Besides, that ain't the way Miss Mary would celebrate nohow. But that's not the only thing. Before that, she had Henry go up to the attic to find Mister Ollie's old army trunk and unlock the lid. That's what she was ravin' about when I found her. 'I got to get to the attic…I got to get to the attic.' I figured it was the liquor talkin', though she seemed sober enough when she cried out your name, Miss Rachel."

"So Amos told me," Rachel said, her eyes smarting. "Did Aunt Mary say what she wanted out of the trunk?"

Sassie fanned herself with the skirt of her apron. "You know Miss Mary was tighter'n a tick on a dog when it come to impartin' her business. No, she didn't tell neither of us nothin'. I asked her if Henry could get it for her, and she 'bout had a fit. Said she was the only one who knew what she was looking for."

Rachel thought a moment. "I believe Aunt Mary was very sick and knew she was dying, Sassie. That's why she disappeared to Dallas without letting any of us know. I think she was seeing a doctor. She had Henry open the trunk in order to get something out of it—a personal item, I suspect—that she didn't want found after her death."

Sassie looked somewhat relieved. "Well, now, in light of everything else that's happened round here, that makes sense."

Rachel took her arm. "Let's go inside and you can tell me the rest over iced tea."

When they were seated at the kitchen table, two frosted glasses of sweetened tea between them, Sassie said, "I shoulda known somethin' was wrong when Miss Mary up and left town for so long without tellin' Mister Percy. Mister Amos, he was hurt, too."

"How long was she gone?"

"Nearly four weeks."

Rachel sipped her tea. "What else has happened around here to support my suspicion?"

Sassie snorted. "Her lettin' Miss Addie go with such short notice. That shoulda told me somethin', and then there was them pearls of hers, the ones she always wore when she dressed up."

"What about them?"

"She left here wearin' 'em, but Henry say she wasn't when she come out of Mister Amos's office."

"She must have left them with him," Rachel suggested. "Did you know that she was flying out to see me today?"

"Yes'm, that I did know, but only barely. She told me just before she left for Mister Amos's office. I found her overnight bag packed when I took her purse up to her room after the ambulance come. I didn't know nothin' 'bout it 'forehand, though."

"No, neither did I."

The doorbell rang. "Oh, Lawsey, here comes the first of the food. Well, we can use it with all the mouths we goin' be feedin'."

The cook ambled out, and Rachel mused over the series of indicators that pointed to the near certainty that Aunt Mary had been aware of her coming death. The champagne itself was a conclusive clue. Aunt Mary had once told her, "Alcohol for me is a passport to places I've no desire to revisit. Someday when I'm old and whiter-haired than I am now...when there's no time left...I may go back."

And the missing pearls was another sign. The pearls were coming to her. It would have been like Aunt Mary to leave them with Amos rather than in the safe—perhaps to give her after the reading of the will as another token of her last regards. But if so, why hadn't he realized that something was amiss?

She got up from the table wearily, too mentally tired to sort it all out. *I'm sure all will come to light soon enough,* Amos had said. Sassie returned, and she informed her of his arrangements and her family's plan to arrive the next day. "I'll go up and select a viewing dress before I unpack. Then I'll start with the calls on Amos's list. He provided the names of a couple to assist you and Henry, Sassie. I'll contact them first."

"Don't worry 'bout me, honey chile. I'd rather be movin' and doin' than restin' and thinkin'."

Upstairs, Rachel found her great-aunt's suite of rooms dark, the shutters sealed and the draperies drawn. No consoling residue of her spirit reached out to her as she pushed open the closed door that reminded her of the locked secrets her great-aunt had taken to the grave. The room impressed a coldness upon her in spite of the personal touches that were so warmly Aunt Mary. A pink satin robe she was in the habit of slipping into for a nap after lunch lay across a chair, and a matching pair of open-toed slippers peeped from beneath the bed like the eyes of a banished puppy. A host of family portraits, among them many of Rachel, reigned from the fireplace mantel, and an ornate and well-worn silver vanity set—a wedding present from Uncle Ollie—gleamed from the dresser. Beside it stood the overnight case Aunt Mary had packed for her last trip to Lubbock.

Rachel had rarely been in this room and then to step no more than a few feet inside. She and Aunt Mary had passed their time together in the library or her office or on the screened back porch. But once, long ago, the door had been left open and a picture among the framed photographs had caught her eye. She'd stolen in and inspected it. The subject was a dark-haired teenage boy—her father, she'd thought at first. But closer study revealed that it wasn't. His Toliver features were too distinct, and there was a certain strength of character in the young jawline that her father did not possess. She'd turned over the portrait. "Matthew at sixteen," Aunt Mary had written in her distinctive script. "July 1937. The love of his father's and my life." A few months later, the boy was dead. Instinctively, she'd known then that Aunt Mary had never been the same afterward. What else would account for that faint nimbus of sadness that seemed always around her?

She looked for the portrait now, but it was missing. Another mystery. Green, she thought, moving toward the mirrored closet doors. *Uncle Ollie would have chosen green.* She selected a dress of the simple lines and luxurious fabric Aunt Mary would have preferred, pausing to push the slippers with their peeping eyes under the bed out of sight before she left the room.

Chapter Fifty-six

After unpacking, Rachel settled glumly behind her great-aunt's desk in her office to start her round of calls using a private line. Outside its closed door, the house telephone rang constantly, Sassie and Henry alternating taking messages. She'd left word that she was not to be disturbed to take inquiries from the press.

She'd gotten through most of the list when Henry poked his head in from the hallway. "Miss Rachel, you'll want to answer this. Line two."

"Who is it, Henry?"

"Matt Warwick."

Rachel picked up the receiver immediately. "Matt Warwick!" she exclaimed, feeling a rush of pleasure. "It's been a while."

"Too long," Matt said. "I wish we didn't have to keep meeting like this. You still have my handkerchief?"

Rachel smiled. So he remembered the last time they'd met. She glanced at the handkerchief she'd brought down to remind herself to return it to him. "I'm looking at it right now," she said. "I'd hoped to give it back to you in person long before now."

"Amazing that we haven't had the opportunity. You'd think there was some divine conspiracy to keep us apart. Why don't we take care of that right now? Granddad's finally fallen asleep after being up most of the night, and I'm at your service. Maybe I could drive you somewhere? Or head off a few casseroles while you rest?"

It was as if an arm had come around her shoulders, strong and comforting, the same arm that had been there for her when Uncle Ollie had died. She had never forgotten. She glanced at the notes she'd made from speaking with the funeral director. "How would you feel about taking me to the mortuary to...see Aunt Mary? Her body has been released from the coroner's and they're waiting for the viewing dress."

"It would be my privilege," he said, his voice softening. "How about some lunch first?"

"I'd like that. Thirty minutes?"

She flipped the intercom button to tell Sassie she'd be leaving the house for a while and not to worry about lunch for her. Then she took out her compact to repair the ravages of a sleepless night and her periodic crying jags, aware of a familiar quiver of anticipation. It had been twelve years since she'd felt this particular flutter. The gloomy drive to Howbutker with her father in June 1973 to attend Uncle Ollie's funeral had held one bright spot for her: She'd see Matt Warwick again. On that occasion, the object of her distant crush had fully met her expectations. He was drop-dead handsome, mature, and confident, as easygoing as she remembered, but disappointingly cool toward her. The reason had not come to light until the reception, when he'd found her crying her heart out in the gazebo while everybody else was eating and drinking inside the house.

"Here," he'd said none too kindly, and thrust out a handkerchief. "Looks like you could use another one of these."

"Thank you," she'd said gratefully, and covered her face, embarrassed that he'd caught her in such a state.

"Sounds to me like a lot more's going on there than your sorrow for your uncle Ollie," he'd remarked.

Her face had shot up from the handkerchief, and she'd stared at him out of sandpapery eyes. How did he know? It was at that time she'd discovered that a big part of grief was guilt, and she was feeling plenty of it that day in the gazebo—guilt for her treatment of Uncle Ollie, guilt for going back on her promise to her mother. That morning, she had broken the news to her that she would be staying in Howbutker.

I don't know that I can forgive you for this, Rachel.

Mama, please try to understand. Aunt Mary is all alone now. She needs me here.

And we both know why, don't we?

It will be all right, Mama.

No, it won't. It's never going to be all right again.

Matt had sat beside her on the swing, his expression unfeeling. "Would all that angst have to do with dropping the DuMonts from your prom card for three years? They lived for your visits in the summer, you know, and you left them high and dry. You broke their hearts, especially Mister Ollie's. He adored you."

She had gasped in shock, the tears streaming again. "Oh, Matt, I had no choice!" And to her complete surprise—because she couldn't bear to have him mad at her, too—she'd sobbed out the whole story. She'd revealed the family secrets that had led to her promise to her mother and described her pain in being separated from Aunt Mary and Uncle Ollie and having to give up her garden and her dream of becoming a farmer. And now, to make it all worse, Uncle Ollie had died without ever knowing how much she had loved him.

And somehow in the blubbering, she'd wound up with her head on his shoulder and his arm around her, the handkerchief soaked along with the lapel of his navy blue blazer.

When finally the tears had subsided to hiccups, he'd said, "Your uncle Ollie was a very wise, understanding man. I'll bet right now he's sitting on the edge of the sweet by-and-by saying to himself, '*Mon Dieu!* I knew it had to be something like that to keep our Rachel from us.'"

She'd gazed at him, raw-eyed. "You think so?"

"I'd bet on it."

"Do you win your bets?"

"Nearly always," he'd said.

"How do you do it?"

"I bet only on what I believe to be a sure thing."

Rachel smiled to herself, remembering, and snapped her compact shut. The next day, he had returned to Oregon, where the company had an office, but he'd left her with a lighter heart and the handkerchief now in her purse. From then on, they had passed each other, as Uncle Ollie had remarked, on in- and out-bound trains. Now that he'd mentioned it, it did seem as if by design their paths had not crossed sometime in all these twelve years.

She wondered if she'd find him as attractive as she remembered—if he'd developed a paunch or was beginning to lose his hair. Her infatuation had faded with time, and another man had come along to make her forget Matt Warwick altogether. As for him, there had been the beauty in California to whom he'd become engaged: "A debutante from San Francisco," Aunt Mary had said. "Very lovely, though she doesn't seem quite right for Matt, in my opinion."

The marriage had not happened, and the man in her life had flown away—literally—so here they were now, both unattached and back at the gazebo, so to speak.

The doorbell rang, and her heart jumped. She grabbed her purse and the viewing dress in its plastic cleaner's bag and hurried to answer it before Sassie could bustle out from the kitchen and talk Matt into staying for lunch. In the hall, she glanced into the mirror and grimaced. She'd not been able to mask the dim shadows under her eyes or do much with hair that showed her hurried departure from Lubbock. She sighed. Well, she would have to do. She opened the door.

Their grins broke simultaneously. "Well, look at you," he said.

"Please don't. I can clean up better—honestly."

"Don't do it for my sake," he said. "I might not be able to take it."

Her grin widened. "You're so much as I remember, Matt Warwick."

"I'll take it that's good?"

"That's splendid," she said.

He laughed and gave her his hand to draw her out onto the porch. "I just spotted a covered-dish brigade headed this way. Should we get out of here before you're waylaid?"

"Please," she said, and they locked hands and flew like conspirators down the steps to a Range Rover marked WARWICK INDUSTRIES on its doors. Once under way, she settled back, sighing audibly, feeling the tension drain out of her.

"Long night, huh?" Matt said.

"One of the longest of my life. How's your grandfather?"

"Hard to tell. He's the toughest man I've ever known—even at ninety—but Mary's death may be his undoing."

"I was afraid of that. They were awfully close friends."

"Oh, they were much more than that," Matt said.

"What do you mean?"

"I'll tell you about it over lunch, and you're staring, by the way. Not fair. I've got to keep my eyes on my driving."

She flushed. She found him actually *more* of what she remembered—completely hewn and polished off, like strong, solid wood, and she liked the hint of premature gray showing at his temples. "I'm curious, Matt—no, amazed—at how you've managed to escape the snares of some wily female for so long."

He chuckled. "*You* go first. I heard there was some-one...an air force pilot."

"There was. He was stationed at Reese Air Force Base near Lubbock. We met on the side of the road when my car ran out of gas."

Matt hiked a brow at her. "Ran out of gas? A sensible girl like you?"

"Somebody siphoned off all but the gas fumes. You can't imagine how good a United States Air Force officer looks to a girl alone on a long, deserted road at ten o'clock at night."

"And what were you doing on a long, deserted road? Better still, what was *he* doing there?"

"I was driving in from the fields. We'd had a long day of harvesting. I never noticed the gas gauge that morning. He was out for a drive. One of his friends in the squadron had been killed that afternoon on a training mission. He took me to a gas station. I bought a five-gallon drum, and he drove me back to my car with it."

"And then he followed you home."

Rachel nodded. "He followed me home." She toyed with the handkerchief. "But it didn't work out. Our careers didn't mesh. I'm a woman of the earth, and he's a man of the air. Now, what about you? I seem to recall a San Francisco belle almost getting you to the altar."

"Another case of irreconcilable differences."

"Oh." His flat tone discouraged further questions, and she wondered if he still carried a torch for the girl he didn't marry. They must have had *some* differences for her to let Matt get away. "By the way, here's your handkerchief," she said.

"Keep it. You may need it before we're through."

They drove to a coffee shop next to a Holiday Inn on the interstate, Matt explaining his choice as the only place where they'd have a chance to eat and talk undisturbed. "Otherwise," he said, "everybody and his second cousin will be stopping by our table to offer condolences."

"The handicap to living in a small community, I guess," Rachel said, "but I confess it's what I like about little towns...the feeling of everybody sharing the same nest. Are you glad to be back?" She'd been told his grandfather had stepped down and he'd taken his position as president of the company.

Matt consulted the menu. "I believe I can say now more than ever."

Rachel felt her cheeks warm with a feeling she'd not known for a long time. "Could we talk awhile before ordering?" she suggested.

Matt promptly laid aside the menu. "Only coffee for now," he said to the waitress.

When she'd moved away, Rachel said, "Okay, give. What makes you say that Aunt Mary and your grandfather were more than friends?"

"This will come as a shock," he said, and commenced to describe Mary's moment of confusion on the courthouse common when she'd mistaken him for his grandfather. "There was something so plaintive in her voice and the way she held out her arms to me," he concluded. "It just about broke my heart."

"And she honestly said, 'Percy, my love'?"

"Her words exactly. And when I told Granddad of the incident, he admitted the same feelings for her and that he'd loved her since the day she was born."

Rachel sat back, stunned. She had never suspected a romantic interest between Aunt Mary and Percy. "Then why in the world didn't they marry?"

Matt lifted his coffee mug to his lips—for time to frame his answer, she thought. After he'd drunk and carefully set down the mug, he said, "Somerset happened, so Granddad said."

A scene unfolded in her head. She was sitting with Aunt Mary in the Ledbetter house, where she had finished pouring out news of her devastating breakup with Steve Scarborough. She was twenty-five. Aunt Mary had listened with unnerving calmness, her green eyes smoky. Finally she spoke: *I think you may be making a mistake you'll regret bitterly someday, Rachel. No attachment is worth giving up the man you love.*

Rachel heard her in disbelief. She'd expected Aunt Mary to applaud her decision. Steve wanted no part of farming. He had grown up the son of a Kansas wheat farmer and knew too well the thankless demands the land imposed. But what did Aunt Mary know? Uncle Ollie had always supported her love of land and family name. She'd never had to choose between her vocation and the man she loved. Her back stiffened. *There are other fish in the sea, Aunt Mary, one who'll understand that I am my attachment—that I am what I do.* She'd smiled slightly. *Maybe I'll get lucky and meet an Ollie DuMont.*

But chances are never another Steve Scarborough.

Matt said, "Rachel?"

Rachel blinked and was back in the present. "Did...your grandfather explain what he meant by that statement?"

"That was all I could get from him, but I'm assuming it had to do with another one of those irreconcilable differences. Somewhere along the way, my grandmother learned of their relationship. I suppose it's the reason they've lived apart all these years and why she hates Mary."

The waitress returned to take their order, pencil poised and eyebrow quirked at Rachel, still sitting mute and blank-eyed. "We'll have the lunch special," Matt ordered for both of them, and when she had gone, he covered Rachel's hand with his. "I know this has come as a surprise, Rachel, but Mary married a good man. None could have loved her more, not even Granddad."

She said slowly, "She always seemed so happy with him."

"She was content. There's a difference. Did you and your mother ever patch things up?"

The question startled her out of her daze. "No, we never did." She said in pleased surprise, "You still remember what I confided to you in the gazebo?"

"Almost every teary word, and I'm sorry nothing's changed. Let's see if I remember how it went. Against your mother's wishes—and her testamentary hopes for your father—you went on to get your degree in...agronomy, wasn't it? Since then you've been learning the cotton business at Mary's knee."

"That says it all," she said, flattered that he had kept up with her through the years. "When it came right down to it, I couldn't abandon what I was meant to do."

"Any regrets?"

"Oh, sure, but I would have had worse regrets if I hadn't followed through."

"You're sure of that?"

"I'm sure."

He said with an admiring shake of his head, "You're very fortunate to be so positive."

"Only about that. Why are you grinning?"

He picked up his coffee cup. "A bit of private humor. I was remembering something somebody said recently about apples."

AT THE FUNERAL HOME, she felt Matt's presence like a bracing wind at her back. A hard moment came when she first looked upon her great-aunt in death. She lay under a sheet, her face a mask of cold, ancient beauty, the dark lashes and widow's peak stark, the Toliver dimple austere in her bloodless flesh. "You...haven't done anything to her yet?" Matt asked the mortician, an arm tight around Rachel's waist.

"We were waiting for the dress," the man replied.

Later, in meetings with the funeral director, florist, and minister, Matt's calm manner and quiet voice steered her over the emotional hurdles of selecting a casket, flowers, and the order of the service. Finally, their appointments completed, he asked, "Where next?" They were seated in the Range Rover in the parking lot of the First Methodist Church. His hand lay on the back of her seat, and she felt his resistance to touch her hair. "You must be awfully tired. I should take you back."

She heard reluctance in his concern. "What time is it?"

He glanced at his wristwatch. "Four o'clock."

"It's early yet," she said.

"So where else may I take you?"

"Would you drive me out to Somerset?"

Chapter Fifty-seven

Back at Warwick Hall, Matt was relieved to find his grandfather in the library, looking rested and immaculately attired in an ivory silk sport shirt and sharply creased slacks. He was mixing a Scotch and water at the bar. "Want one of these?" he asked as Matt strode in.

"I'm already high enough."

Percy gave him a schoolmaster's stare. "Oh, me," he said, and took down another tumbler. "I was afraid this was going to happen. You're smitten with Rachel Toliver. Sassie said you were together when she called to invite us to supper."

"I'm more than smitten, Granddad. I haven't felt like this since...well, never." Not even with Cecile, he thought. He had been gone from Rachel five minutes and already he was missing her. He'd let her out in front of the Toliver mansion, feeling a moment's bereavement when she opened the car door. He'd watched her walk up the steps, his heart tensed as if she might disappear before his eyes, and on the verandah she'd turned and given him a smile. "See you in a little while," she'd mouthed, and he'd thought, out of the blue, For the rest of my life, I hope.

"I can't explain it," he said, dropping into a club chair before the massive fireplace. "I don't understand it myself, but I don't have to. Recognizing it is enough. I feel as if we've known each other all our lives and were just waiting for the right moment to come together."

Percy handed him his drink. "Are you sure this is not infatuation? You knew she'd be beautiful, and in a way you *have* known each other all your lives."

"Don't insult my experience, Granddad. I've been around the block enough times to know the difference between infatuation and the real thing."

"And do you sense she feels the same?"

"Unless I've become rusty at reading signals."

He thought back to an hour ago when they were standing on the porch at the Ledbetter house, looking out over the budding fields of Somerset. There were blossoms on the plants—acorn squash blossoms, she said, the flower that had started it all for her. He saw the fatigue and sorrow on her face give way to a quiet radiance, as if she'd moved from the shadows into light...Eve gazing over Eden. He'd moved behind her to share the sight over her head, and for a surreal moment he'd felt like Adam and they the only two people in the world.

"It's beautiful," he'd said. "I can understand why you love it."

"You can?" She had turned to him with a flash of delighted surprise in her eyes. They were beautiful eyes, reflecting the green of the land she loved. "I'm happy to hear that," she'd said.

Now, seeing his grandfather's skeptical look, he asked, "Why the reservations, Granddad? Is it because you and Mary didn't make it happen?"

Percy lowered himself into a companion chair and said quietly, "Because Rachel's a Toliver, son."

"What exactly does that mean?"

"It means she seems to have a tendency to put the land first, before husband, home, and family."

"Is that what drove you and Mary apart, what you meant by 'Somerset happened'? She put Somerset before you?"

"That's the sum of it. By the time we realized what fools we'd been, it was too late. Don't get me wrong. I think the world of the girl. I'd like nothing better than to see you and Rachel finish what Mary and I started, but she seems headed in the same direction Mary chose."

"And why is that so bad?"

"Because she makes life choices based on her commitment to her Toliver calling."

"You're thinking of that pilot she turned down because she wouldn't give up everything she loved to follow him, aren't you?" Matt could hear his voice hardening in Rachel's defense. "Well, she made the right decision, no matter how much she cared for the guy. Rachel knows she couldn't be happy any-where else but here in Howbutker where her roots are, doing what she does best, just as Cecile and I both knew."

Percy's look remained doubtful. "And you learned all that about Rachel in one afternoon?"

"I've always known that about Rachel."

Percy's brows lifted over the rim of his glass, but he did not press the issue further. "Well, I'm sure that Mary can rest in peace knowing she's left Somerset and the farms under Rachel's supervision. She'll run them competently for William, then inherit the fam-ily business from him when he dies. Mary could not have asked for a more satisfying end to things."

"That's not the way it's going to work, Granddad."

Percy lowered his glass. "What?"

"No. Rachel will be inheriting the family business, not William."

Percy sat upright. "How do you know that?"

Matt was surprised at his sharp tone. "Because that's what Mary has been grooming her for—to take over the reins when she dies. If William inherited, he'd sell everything lock, stock, and barrel. His wife would see to that. She must be a piece of work, that woman." He related the full story that Rachel had told him in the gazebo, growing more exasperated at his grandfather's lowering brow. "Don't you see, Granddad? How could Rachel have made any other choice for her life, regardless of what she promised her mother at fifteen? How could she choose to be anyone—or anything—but who she is?"

"Indeed," Percy murmured.

His frustration mounting, he said, "And when Rachel came along and proved to be a chip off the old block, how could Mary leave the family holdings to William, knowing that wife of his would have them immediately on the auction block?"

"Because that was the *deal*!" Percy snapped, and immediately looked as if he could have bitten his tongue. Matt could see his mental scrambling to get out of the hole he'd dug. Good Lord. What was he not telling him?

"What deal?"

"Simply this. When the people of my generation made a promise, it was considered a deal—binding forever. Mary promised the land to William. I would have expected her to abide by her word."

Matt was convinced that was not the real reason behind his agitation. "Well, no matter how you look at the situation, it's a shame that Rachel's lost her mother over it. In a way, I suppose I can be somewhat sympathetic to how Alice feels. Her father favored her brother over her and left her with nothing when he died, just like Mary's father left his property to Mary and zip to William's dad. Rachel feels that if that hadn't been the case, Alice wouldn't have been so resentful of her perpetuating the family heritage. As it is, she believes the Kermit Tolivers owe the Howbutker branch *nada*.

That's been the crux of their conflict—" He broke off in alarm. His grandfather looked as if a ghost had popped up behind his chair. "Granddad, are you all right? You're as pale as your shirt."

Percy took a quick sip of his Scotch. "I'm all right," he said. He glanced at his watch. "Are you going to sit at Sassie's table like that? We have twenty minutes before we're due."

Matt eased out of his chair. There was something his grandfather wasn't telling him. He heard that rattle in the closet again. "I'm going," he said, "but I'll tell you this, Granddad. Whatever you're withholding to warn me off Rachel, you'd better speak while there's still time or forever hold your peace. You'll be talking about the girl I hope to marry."

Percy lifted his pale face to him. "The way you feel, any warning would be fruitless, but may I advise you to take it slow? You may have known *of* Rachel all her life, but you don't *know* her."

Matt placed his glass on the bar. "Well, neither one of us is going anywhere, so there'll be plenty of time to prove she's the girl for me. And the way I feel is not as sudden as you think. At five years old I saw Rachel in her crib, too, remember? And I also have an indelible memory of a fourteen-year-old girl in a white dress with a green sash."

WHEN MATT HAD BOUNDED UP the stairs, Percy melted back into his chair. Well, that was tit for tat, he thought, limp from his grandson's revelations. So their old deed had not lain quiet and forgotten all these years. Had Mary known its specter had turned up to haunt the William Toliver household? Had she been aware of the real cause of the dissension between Alice and Rachel? If so, how could she have corrected the misassumption without confessing the crime...and his involvement? All this time— according to Amos, who was deeply disturbed by the discord between Rachel and her mother (Mary never discussed it with him)—he'd believed the rift was based on Alice's jealousy that Mary had "stolen" her daughter. It had not occurred to him that Alice thought Rachel was usurping William's inheritance. Had Mary gone back on their agreement? When push came to shove, had she elected to keep the Toliver flag flying? Was William to be cheated once again?

He inhaled deeply to calm his erratic heartbeat. Well, he held one crumb of comfort. When he was gone, there'd be no evidence remaining of what he and Mary had done, only its unfortunate backwash. That cursed plantation cast its shadow still.

Chapter Fifty-eight

From the verandah, Rachel, with Matt beside her, waved good-bye to Percy and Amos making their way to the navy blue Cadillac at the conclusion of the small dinner party. She was worried about Amos. Something was bothering him aside from Aunt Mary's death. She'd sensed it in Lubbock and at the airport, and tonight she was sure of it when she'd caught him lost in deep reflection, miles away from them, his mouth a mournful U-turn. "What is it, Amos?" she'd asked at one point when they had a moment alone. "What is it besides Aunt Mary's loss that has you so concerned? You'd tell me if you were ill, wouldn't you?"

He'd answered in startled surprise, "Of course. Banish that concern, my dear. I'm as sound as a fiddle. I suppose I'm still in a bit of shock."

She hadn't believed him.

Matt turned toward her. He'd refused Amos's offer

of a ride, saying he preferred to walk home. "I must be going, too," he said. "I only wanted to make sure you're all right before I leave you."

"Oh, but I...," she said in protest, and without thought placed a lightly restraining hand on his chest.

He closed his hand around it. "But what?"

"I...thought that since Amos was taking your grandfather home, you'd stay awhile."

"You've been up most of the night, it's been a long day, and you have a longer one tomorrow. It would be selfish of me to stay."

"May I be the judge of that?"

"For your own sake, I'm afraid not," he said, but showed no inclination to release her hand.

They'd tried all evening to ignore what was happening between them. Every time their eyes met or their bodies inadvertently touched, a current of physical tension passed between them. They'd both been aware of it, but it was more than sexual attraction and they knew that, too. It was more as if they recognized they were two halves of a whole who'd found their missing part. But there would be time to fit the pieces together later. Until then, though, her heart needed an answer to a question. She flushed and asked quietly, "The girl you almost married—do you still...care for her?"

He drew back in surprise, then laughed, as if the idea that he could still harbor feelings for the belle from San Francisco was absurd. "I remember her fondly, but good Lord, no," he said.

Relief coursed through her. "Well, that seems certain," she said.

"Trust me, it is. Now, what about your flyboy? Any residue there?"

She hesitated, leaving her hand swallowed in his. "There was...sadness, but no regrets."

"Was?"

She stared into his eyes. "Until now."

He kissed her lightly on her forehead. "Say no more, or I'll have to stay."

She sighed. She *was* tired, and her body ached for bed. "All right, but I'll see you in the morning?" He had agreed to stand with her to receive visitors during the first viewing.

"In the morning," he assured her, and held on to her hand until he was forced to let it slip from his fingers as he descended the steps. She remained on the verandah until his tall figure was swallowed in the deeper shadows of the trees canopying the boulevard. A feeling of deep peace flowed through her. It was nine o'clock. If she added the ten minutes they'd spoken at Matt's birthday party to the hour they'd spent in the gazebo to the time they were together today, that would amount to...around twelve hours, she counted. How was it possible to feel she wanted to spend the rest of her life with a man in whose company she'd spent only half a day?

*   *   *

MATT WALKED SLOWLY, SAVORING HIS newfound feelings. If this wasn't the beginning of love, it would sure as hell do, he thought. A buddy had once told him, "When a woman who's not your mother remains on a porch to watch you leave, you can bet she's got more than a liking for you." He chuckled. He'd felt her eyes on him as he walked away and didn't hear the front door close until he'd disappeared around the curve of the sidewalk. He would have liked to stay, explain about Cecile, how it was they didn't marry. God knew they'd thought themselves right for each other in every way except the one necessary for a lasting and happy marriage. Recognition of the missing element came after they were engaged and almost too late to prevent them from making the biggest mistake of their lives. When they met, he was thirty and working out of San Francisco, enduring the freewheeling singles scene, union battles, clogged traffic, and salty sea air until he could get back home. She was a dyed-in-the-wool San Franciscan, with ties to the first families who had settled the city by the bay. Sun and surf, beach and ocean, were in her blood. He'd known of her deep attachment to the place when he'd asked her to marry him, as she'd been aware that a day would come when he would return to Howbutker to run Warwick Industries. But they could handle their geographic differences, they'd thought. Already she'd met his family. He'd taken her to Atlanta, where spirit and polish met spunk and brass, and then to Howbutker to introduce her to his grandfather and Mary and Amos, Warwick Hall, and the sleepy little East Texas burg she'd eventually call home. The people and place matched her expectations but, unbeknownst to him, not her anticipated acceptance of them.

As the time approached to mail their wedding invitations, he'd sensed a certain withdrawal. "What's the matter, Cecile? Having second thoughts?" he'd asked half-seriously on a night when the moon highlighted the sun streaks in her hair.

"No, Matt," she'd said, her voice wispy with held-back tears. "Not about you. I could never have second thoughts about you and the man you are."

His heart had plunged. "But you're having second thoughts? What about?"

"Us…together in Howbutker." Her face had wrenched in appeal. "Matt, please understand. I mean no disrespect to your home. It's just that…now that the time is getting closer for me to leave my family, my friends, my home, the place I love more than any place on earth, to—to live in Howbutker…well, it's so different from here, so *provincial*! Warwick Hall is so *baronial*! And our children would have such *limited* experiences. I've been thinking…Couldn't you move the headquarters of Warwick Industries here—to San Francisco?"

The proposal had caught him like a punch in the

stomach. "No, Cecile," he'd said, realizing she'd nurtured this hope for some time. "I wouldn't even consider it."

At least they never played the "if you loved me" card when they tried to work out how they'd keep the marriage going with one of them a fish out of water. They both knew love was not the problem. In the end, she'd loved him enough to let him go—"You'd be miserable here, Matt. You might adjust temporarily but never adapt permanently"—and he'd loved her too much to take her away from her doting parents, the brothers and sisters and slew of cousins she adored, the sunny family home overlooking the Pacific, where ocean breezes filled its gauzy curtains like sails at sea.

So they had parted, and no other woman had piqued more than his passing interest until he saw Rachel again. The minute she'd opened the door and he'd looked into that remembered face, he'd felt an immediate and irrefutable connection, a jolt of recognition, as if he'd come across a keepsake he'd put away and forgotten until now. It was an incredible feeling, deeper, surer than what he'd felt for Cecile, and it had only strengthened as the day went on. He'd felt their kindred roots touch, intertwine. They shared the same interests, culture, love of town and people. There would be no conflict of lifestyles, background, and place. She was the woman his soul had waited for.

His grandfather could relax. These were the eighties. Men weren't hung up on their pride like those of his generation. They supported their wives' careers and shared in the responsibilities of home and child rearing. Nobody had to be first. The idea was to be *together*. Rachel might be a Toliver, as committed to her legacy as her great-aunt, but so what? As far as he was concerned, if this feeling between them panned out—and he had no doubt it would—Rachel could grow her cotton and acorn squash and he'd mine timber—a perfect blend.

Chapter Fifty-nine

The next three days broke overcast and oppressive. Friday's bright sunshine that had sparkled on Somerset and off the white columns of the verandah remained behind mausoleum gray clouds that Rachel was to remember as apt harbingers of things to come. Throngs attended the two viewings, not many of whom, in true East Texas fashion, did not press their humidity-damp cheek to hers, threaten to wring off her hand, or crush her in rib-breaking hugs. Except for the clear vision of Matt's strong presence beside her, making the introductions and keeping the line moving, they passed in a mind-numbing blur. By the end of the first viewing, she felt as limp and squeezed out as one of her mother's hand-wrung sheets.

"I'm afraid the evening one will be worse," Matt said on the drive back to Houston Avenue. "This morning's group was from the county. Tonight's herd will come from all over the state, staying in motels from here to Dallas. But hang in there. By Monday, this will all be over, and you can get on with what you're about and...we can get on with us." He brought his arm around her. "That okay with you?" he asked.

"Sounds heavenly," she said.

Her father's early-model Dodge, kept in excellent condition by the automotive skills of his son, was parked in front of the verandah when they arrived. Entering the hall, she heard his West Texas drawl, inflected with the slight French accent he'd never quite lost, drifting from the kitchen. She hurried toward it, but at the swinging door, she stopped to gather her internal forces to meet an awkward reception.

"Will Lucy Warwick be coming to the funeral?" her father was asking. "It'd be nice to see her again. I really liked her as a boy."

"Oh, Lawsey, no!" Sassie exclaimed. "They ain't been no love lost 'tween her and Miss Mary for nigh on forty years. I imagine Miss Lucy feel pretty proud of herself, knowin' she outlive Miss Mary. First thing she ever put over on her."

"Well, I reckon we have to take our triumphs where we can, Sassie," her father said.

Rachel chuckled and pushed open the door. "Hello, everybody," she said.

The members of her family looked up from the table, where they were partaking of the bounty of food contributions lining the counter. For a heartrending moment, Rachel saw that her parents had aged in the months since she'd last seen them at Christmas.

Middle age was showing in her father's grayer hair and the stoop of his shoulders, her mother's thickened waist and the lines around her eyes.

"Well, look who's here," William cried, pushing back from the table. "How's my little Bunny-hop?"

"Better now that you are here," Rachel said, her defenses sufficiently crumbling at his warm welcome, the sight of her whole family together again.

"Well, is that any way to show it—by crying?" her mother asked, but she smiled slightly as she got up to add her arms to William's.

"Make room for me," Jimmy said, his mouth full of a ham sandwich he set aside to complete the family embrace. Thus bound, they huddled in an exchange of hugs and kisses and damp eyes for a few minutes before disengaging and sitting down again at the table. For the next half hour, they might have been back at the kitchen table in Kermit in those long-ago days when Houston Avenue had been merely a street where her father had sent his annual Christmas card. Everybody began talking and chewing at once, sharing gossip and news of Winkler County, passing plates of ham and cheese, and spreading mustard and mayonnaise together. And then, as if a bomb had been thrown into the room and detonated instantly, Alice shattered the family bonhomie.

"Well, Rachel," she said, "how does it feel to know you're going to inherit all of this right out from under your daddy?"

At the counter, Sassie threw a shocked glance over her shoulder, and Henry, who'd come in for a coffee break, pushed away from the pantry door. Jimmy groaned, and William snapped, "Alice, for God's sake!"

Rachel felt the joy of the reunion dissipate like air from a burst balloon. "How could you say such a thing at such a time, Mama?" she asked, her voice soft with offense.

"I'm only asking out of curiosity."

"Alice...," William warned.

"Don't 'Alice' me, William Toliver. I've made no bones about the way I feel, and Rachel knows it."

Rachel stood up. "Henry, have you shown my family their rooms?"

"Yes, Miss Rachel, and their luggage is already stowed." The chimes of the doorbell suddenly reverberated throughout the house, as shrilling as sirens in the charged atmosphere. Quickly, Henry rid himself of his coffee cup. "There's the bell again," he said, sounding eager to get out of the kitchen. "We got more callers. I'll go let 'em in, if that's all right, Miss Rachel."

"Thank you, Henry. Put them in the parlor and tell them I'll be right out." She turned to the members of her family, still sitting at the table, her father and brother looking miserable, her mother guileless and unperturbed. "These are visitors come to pay their respects. Do you want to go to your rooms before you get snagged down here?"

"Why? Are you ashamed of us?" Alice asked.

A groan again from Jimmy and an exasperated sigh from William. Rachel said in as even a tone as her disappointment could manage, "I thought you might like to avoid receiving condolences from strangers on the death of a woman you didn't like."

"Alice, Rachel is right," William said, yanking his napkin from his shirt collar. "We don't want to get stuck down here. Neither of us is dressed to meet these people, and I need a nap before we go to the funeral home."

Jimmy scrambled out of his chair with an air of apology. At twenty-one, he was tall and rangy. His reddish brown hair was a legacy from his mother, but the origin of his Howdy Doody looks had remained a mystery. "I'm sorry about Aunt Mary, sis," he said. "I know you loved her very much and that you'll miss her. She was a nice old lady. I'm sorry she's gone."

Sweet, uncomplicated Jimmy. Since he didn't feel entitled to anything he hadn't earned, he'd never understood the dissension that had separated her from the rest of the family. She rumpled his hair affectionately. "Thanks, Jimmy, I appreciate that. Is there anything you'd like to do while the folks rest?"

"If it's all the same to you, I'd like to have a look at the limo. She's still got it, hasn't she?"

Rachel opened a counter drawer and tossed him a set of keys. "Here you go. Take it for a spin if you like."

The doorbell rang again. "I'm outta here!" Jimmy announced, the keys jingling as he made for the door.

Alice confronted her daughter. "Which stairs are we to use—the servants' or the main staircase?"

Rachel faced her mother. She still wore the clothes, makeup, and hairstyle of the post–World War II era in which she was her prettiest, but little about her now was the same as the happy-go-lucky woman who used to take Rachel to the playground and push her in the swing, arranged vases of wildflowers Rachel had gathered that wilted by the time she got them home, read to her at night, and taught her how to swim. Years of resentment—for which Rachel took full blame—had robbed her of her vivacity. If only Rachel's father would agree to share in the revenues of her inheritance, he could quit his job tomorrow and enjoy a comfortable retirement. That's all her mother wanted. But her father's pride, the only trait he'd inherited from the Toliver line, wouldn't allow it—as her own Toliver blood would not permit her to make the sacrifice required to save her mother's love.

"Whichever one you feel more comfortable taking, Mama," she said, leaving the kitchen to greet the callers in the hall.

Tension prevailed among them throughout the remaining gray, sultry, exhausting days, brightened only by Matt's constant assistance and support. The night before the funeral, he said, "There's a place I'd like to take you where we can have a quiet drink together. Want to go?"

Tired and anxiously awaiting what the next day would bring, she said, "Lead the way."

It was to a cabin deep in the woods. Beyond its screened back porch lay a lake. The large, partitioned room smelled freshly cleaned and cooled by a window air-conditioning unit and ceiling fans. "You were expecting me," she said.

"I'd hoped. What would you like to drink? White wine?"

"That's fine," she said, drawn to an ancient Indian headdress hanging on a wall. "You have eclectic tastes."

"Not mine. This place was built and furnished by our grandfathers and your great-uncle when they were boys. I'm the third generation to use it as a getaway. I've left it pretty much the same. If I'm not mistaken, that headdress belonged to Miles Toliver."

"Really?" Rachel touched it reverently. "I've never seen anything belonging to my grandfather. I suppose because nothing belonged to him." She threw him a look over her shoulder. "Our families are so...interconnected. Are you sure we're not related?"

Matt popped the cork of a bottle of Chenin Blanc.

"I sure as hell hope not. As far as I can tell, you and I are among the few good things that came from the bust-up of my grandfather and your great-aunt."

"Well, thank God for that," she said, taking the glass he offered.

"And Somerset," he said with a wry smile, tapping his Scotch and water to the rim of her glass. "I don't know whether I'm sadder for them or happier for us."

"We can do nothing about the past—only the future," she said. They sat on the couch, their shoulders touching. She glanced toward the curtained bedroom. "The tales this place could tell. Do you... suppose this cabin is where it all began for Aunt Mary and your grandfather?"

"I wouldn't be surprised."

"Is that why you brought me out here tonight?"

"No," he said, putting his arm around her shoulder, "but I'm not above keeping the tradition alive."

She chuckled and nestled against him. "I'm all about tradition when the time is right," she said, and added soberly, "How I wish I could get my mother to understand that."

"Don't worry about your mother," he said, his lips against her hair. "All you have to do to get back on track with her is to give her an offer she can't refuse."

"And what would that be?"

"Grandchildren."

She laughed and snuggled deeper. "Sounds like a plan."

On Monday, the funeral service seemed interminable owing to the many eulogies Aunt Mary would have hated but that Rachel had permitted as a fitting tribute to the woman who had meant so much to the town, county, and state. The grave site rites were mercifully brief, and the crowd dispersed quickly to the reception to get out of the cloying heat. Because of Amos's instructions that refreshments not be replenished once everyone had made a pass at the table, people did not linger, and the Tolivers were freed to leave for his office at the expected time.

He had driven on ahead and stood watching for their arrival from his office window. Rachel spotted him through the slatted blinds, his dark-suited, cadaver-thin figure reminding her of a forbidding bird of omen. Once again, the odd feeling flitted through her that had begun when the textile agent had shown up empty-handed. Percy's Mercedes pulled up shortly, and Matt gave her hand a reassuring squeeze as they all filed into the law office. He said quietly in her ear, "Granddad wonders what in hell he's doing here unless Mary left him Ollie's box seats at Texas Stadium. But who knows? They may stay in the family."

"Who knows?" she said, jabbing him playfully in his ribs.

The air-conditioning had not been on long enough to cool Amos's private office. "Lord, it's hot in here," Alice complained, fanning herself furiously with a funeral program. It was the first time she'd broken her sullen silence since leaving the reception.

"It will be cooler in a moment," Amos apologized, patting his face with a handkerchief. He indicated they were to take chairs arranged in front of his desk, ceiling fan spinning at top speed, and took his position before them.

"Surely we won't be here that long, Amos," Percy remarked, apparently knowing something about the cooling system that the others did not.

"Uh, no...this shouldn't take long at all." Rachel noticed that he studiously avoided their eyes, as if he were a juror coming into the courtroom to deliver a guilty verdict. "First, let me say," he began, joining his hands over a legal folder on his desk, "that Mary Toliver DuMont was of sound mind when she dictated and had duly witnessed as genuine the codicil before me. It is extremely unlikely that any part of it is contestable."

"A codicil?" Rachel repeated, her skin prickling. "You mean she added something to her original will?"

"The codicil *invalidates* the original will," Amos said.

The room went pin-dropping silent.

William coughed dryly into his closed hand. "None of us would want to contest Aunt Mary's wishes, Amos. You can be assured of that."

Percy's look had sharpened. "Perhaps we should get to it," he said. "It's time for my Scotch."

Amos sighed and opened the folder. "Very well, but before we go on, there is a second matter I should mention. Mary brought this codicil to me a few hours before she died. It was a heart attack that claimed her life, but you should know that she was already dying from cancer and had only a few weeks to live."

Another stunned silence filled the room. Percy was the first to speak, his voice sounding like a dried corn husk rattling in the wind. "Why didn't she tell us? Why didn't she tell *me*?"

"She planned to tell you upon her return from Lubbock, Percy... I'm sure to give you a few more days of peace."

Rachel swallowed, her mouth suddenly dry. "Was that why she was coming to see me, Amos—to inform me of her cancer?"

"Well, yes, and to explain the reason for the codicil."

Her fanning halted, Alice said, "What about the codicil, Amos?"

Amos removed a document from the folder. "I will be brief and summarize. There's a copy here of the codicil for each of you to take with you and read in its entirety. You will see that provisions have been made for Sassie and Henry along with several other minor recipients. Now, in regard to you, the main points are these: Mary sold Toliver Farms last month in highly secret transactions. Details of the sale can be learned by contacting Wilson and Clark, the firm in Dallas that handles her real estate ventures. Somerset was not included in the property sold. The total of the sale was..." He glanced at another sheet and stated a sum that drew a breathless exclamation from Alice in the astonished silence. "The proceeds are to be divided equally among the three surviving Tolivers—William, Rachel, and Jimmy."

No one spoke. No one moved. Percy shook out of his shock first. He frowned at the lawyer. "Is this a joke, Amos?"

"No," Amos said, his sigh sounding dredged from his soul. "I'm afraid this is no joke." He rested his sad gaze on Rachel, who stared at him out of eyes blank with disbelief. "Rachel, I am so very, very sorry. I know what a terrible blow this must be to you."

It was as if an explosion had gone off in her head. She could not see, hear, or feel. She blinked rapidly, as if clearing her vision might assist her hearing. She had misheard Amos. She thought he'd said that Aunt Mary had sold the farms, but that was not possible....

"Did we hear you right, Amos?" Alice asked in the awed tone of a lottery winner. "Aunt Mary *sold* her holdings and divided the money among *us*?"

"Er...among her *blood* heirs, Alice. I'm afraid you were not included."

"Well, glory be!" She slapped the desk and turned to her husband, still sitting dumbfounded. "Did you hear that, William? Your aunt did right by us after all. She *sold* her land."

"All except Somerset," William said with a quick glance at his daughter. "I'm assuming, Amos, that Aunt Mary left the original farm to Rachel?"

Amos shook his head regretfully. "No. She left Somerset to Percy."

Jolted from her daze, Rachel cried, "No—no—she couldn't have!" Horrified awareness surged into her numb senses. "There's been some mistake."

"Good God, Amos!" His look furious, William wrapped a protective arm around his daughter's shoulders. "Why the hell would she leave the family plantation to Percy? She must have been insane! How could you let her do that to Rachel?"

"She wasn't insane, William, believe me, and there's a letter here from her doctors to testify to that. She knew exactly what she was doing despite my best efforts to convince her otherwise."

Jimmy leaped from the chair as if ants were crawling up his pants legs. "This isn't fair! Rachel was supposed to get Somerset. Aunt Mary *promised* it to her. Well, she'll just have to buy it back." He rounded on Percy. "What do you say, Mr. Warwick? You'll sell it back to my sister, won't you?"

Percy was staring off into space, still as a figure in a tableau, seemingly oblivious to Jimmy shouting into his ear as if he were deaf. William said, "Son, take your seat and be quiet for now. This is not the time or place to discuss these matters." He turned his attention to Amos. "The house? Who gets the house, Amos?"

Another sigh. The bony ridges of Amos's cheeks reddened. "The Conservation Society of Howbutker," he said, and added in visible embarrassment, "Mary stipulated that Rachel is to have anything in the house she wants—jewelry, paintings, furnishings. The rest that is not historically associated with the mansion will be sold at auction and the proceeds deposited into the estate."

William's grip tightened around Rachel's shoulders. "This is unbelievable."

"Why?" Alice demanded, twisting to look at him, a line of annoyance between her brows. "You don't think your aunt was capable of coming to her senses?"

Still standing, Jimmy cried, "I don't care what you say, Mr. Hines. She was crazy. She had to be, to do this to Rachel. She had no cause to give Somerset to somebody else and leave the house to a bunch of old busybodies."

"Hush, Jimmy." His mother tried to draw him back into his chair. "No use taking that attitude. What's done is done. It can't be helped."

Jimmy shook off her hand and glared at her. "And aren't you happy about *that*?"

"Amos, I don't understand..." Rachel's voice, quavering, cut through the war of words. "Why did she do this?"

"She listened to her conscience for once," Alice answered. "I know you're hurt, Rachel, but she did the right thing. In the eleventh hour she realized it was wrong to go back on her promise to your daddy. And it's not like you weren't remembered, sugar. Why, with your share of the money, you can buy as many farms as you want." She reached to brush away Rachel's hair, but her daughter raised a shoulder to fend off the gesture.

"Oh, Alice, be quiet," William said. "Can't you see that's not what she wants to hear?"

"Did she give you any explanation?" Rachel persisted to the lawyer, tears of disbelief standing in her eyes. "Surely she said something...."

"I begged her to tell me, my dear, but she said...there wasn't time. That's why she was flying out to see you...to explain her reasons. But she assured me that she'd acted only out of her love for you. You must believe that. Her words to me were: 'I know you think I've betrayed her. I haven't, Amos. I've saved her.'"

"Saved me?" She struggled to understand, reaching in her mind for some clue to explain this insanity. "Oh, I see," she said, as if suddenly enlightened. "Her idea was to save me from the mistakes *she* made in the name of Toliver, is that it? How noble of her, but my mistakes are my own business to make and should have been none of hers."

"And there was another thing...," Amos said, his voice feeble. "She mentioned that there was a curse on the land from which she wished to protect you."

"A curse?" Incredulity sparked with growing anger behind the shine of her drying tears. "She never said anything to me about a curse."

"She mentioned it to me once," William cut in, "but she didn't explain what it was."

"And I mentioned it to you, Rachel, remember?" Alice said.

"Didn't I tell you she was crazy?" Jimmy declared. "Only crazy people talk about curses."

"Rachel, please..." Percy spoke as though shaken from a deep sleep. "I know what this is all about. I know Mary's reasons. They're not what you think. They'll take some telling, but you'll understand once you've heard her story."

"I believe I already know them, Percy. My mother is right. Aunt Mary wanted to clear her conscience before she died. This codicil is nothing more than atonement for past sins. She sold the farms to fulfill a promise she made to my father...."

Alice shot her daughter an indignant look. "As well she should have!"

"Alice...," William hissed. "*Shut up!*"

"And she left you Somerset to settle some obligation she believed she owed you, Percy," Rachel continued.

"I now know that the two of you were in love and would have married—*should* have married—if the plantation hadn't come between you. So bequeathing Somerset to you was Aunt Mary's way to say she was sorry and to ask your forgiveness, no matter what the cost to me. Her notion of a red rose, I suppose." Her smile felt cold as death.

Percy shook his head in stern denial. "No, Rachel. I know it seems like that, but you've got it wrong. Mary did this for you, not me. She gave up what she loved the most in the world out of love for *you*."

"Oh, I don't doubt it, however misguided her sacrifice. Jimmy asked you a question a while ago. Will you sell Somerset back to me?"

Despair flooded his handsome old face. "I can't do that, Rachel. That's not what Mary wanted. That's why she left Somerset to me."

"Then we have nothing more to talk about." She rose swiftly and slipped a copy of the codicil under her arm. Alice and William quickly followed suit. Rachel held out her hand to the lawyer. "Good-bye, Amos. I was certain something else was troubling you. I'm relieved that it had nothing to do with your health."

Amos clasped her hand between both of his, his eyes sad and contrite. "I was following Mary's wishes, my dear. I cannot tell you how deeply sorry I am for your loss... for the loss to all of us."

"I know you are." She slipped her hand away and turned to go.

"Rachel, wait—" Percy stepped into her path, still a formidable figure despite his age. "You can't leave like this. You must let me explain."

"What's there to explain? Aunt Mary's property was hers to do with as she chose. I had no claim of my own. I was only hired help and well paid for my services. There is nothing more to be said."

"There is much more to be said. Come with me now to Warwick Hall and let me tell you her story. I guarantee that once you've heard it, you'll understand her reasons for this madness."

"Frankly, I couldn't care less what her reasons were. What's done is done."

"What about Matt?"

"At the moment I'm not sure. I'll need time to come to terms with his grandfather inheriting what I'd had every *reason* to believe would come to me. After that we'll see." She stepped aside, but again Percy blocked her way.

"Don't you see what you're doing?" he cried, gripping her elbows. "You're putting your love for Somerset above your happiness. Mary was trying to save you from that path."

"Then she shouldn't have encouraged it." She removed her elbows from Percy's grasp. "Let's go, everyone."

She marched out, the members of her family behind her, past Matt, lounging with his legs crossed and engrossed in a magazine, unaware of what had transpired in the other room. She did not answer when he called her name—she could not—and by the time he'd recovered from his confusion to pursue her, Jimmy had shot the limousine out of the parking space.

Chapter Sixty

On the return to Houston Avenue, the silence in the car hung as thick as fog. Jimmy drove with his hands tight on the wheel, William in the passenger seat, his heartache for his daughter evident from his sad profile, observable to Rachel sitting rigidly beside her mother in the back. She was conscious of Alice now and then stealing a wary glance at her but wisely saying nothing. For all her mother's attempt to maintain an expressionless face, the slight twitching of her mouth betrayed the thrill of triumph.

When Jimmy had parked the limousine in the garage, the quartet paused on the drive, no one making a move toward the house, the awkward silence of unspoken but clearly discernible thoughts continuing. William cleared his throat. "We've got to decide what to do," he said, directing his comment to Rachel. "Should we stay or hit the road?"

"I want to go home," Jimmy said. "Like right now. I hate it here. I can't breathe. Living in Howbutker is like swimming underwater with your mouth open."

"I want to leave, too," Alice said. "If we stayed, I'd feel like a trespasser."

Beyond feeling, a block of ice wedged in her heart, Rachel said, "If you want to leave for Kermit now, go ahead, but I'm staying."

"Not without you, honey," her father said.

"It will have to be without me, Daddy. There's something I must do here."

"You be sure to take everything you can, Rachel," Alice said. "Every fur, every piece of jewelry, every knickknack you can get in the car. You deserve it."

"The witch! She was a witch, Rachel!"

"Hush, Jimmy." Alice swiped her son's sleeve half-heartedly. "Don't speak ill of the dead."

"That's a whole lot less than *you* would have said if Rachel had got everything."

"*Son!*" William gripped Jimmy close to his collar-bone. "That's enough."

Rachel squeezed her lids shut and pressed her fingertips to her temples. The clamor ceased. When she opened her eyes, they were all watching her in chastised silence. "Let's be clear about one thing," she said. "I don't begrudge you your inheritance. No doubt Aunt Mary believed she was being fair in leaving things as she did."

When Alice made to speak, William clamped a hand around her arm, and she remained silent.

"But you can understand why I'm not full of congratulations at the moment," Rachel went on. "Suit yourselves about leaving. It's getting late to begin the drive back, and I'd advise you to wait until morning, when you've had a night's rest. But you do what you want. I'm staying overnight and will leave for Lubbock tomorrow to...clear out my office." Downcast eyes and a shuffling of feet met this sad intent, but no one protested. "So what is your decision?" Rachel asked.

"We're leaving," Jimmy and Alice said in unison.

William's forlorn gaze begged her to forgive them. "Looks like we're leaving, honey."

A half hour later, they were packed and ready to go. "We'll stop at a motel somewhere along the way and give you a call," her father said. "We won't try to make it in one night."

Relieved by that decision, Rachel steeled herself to endure her mother's customary gesture of farewell, but Alice's hand remained around the shoulder strap of her handbag. "You think I'm happy only about the money, don't you? I admit I'm thrilled that we're going to have a better life—ecstatic, even—but I'm just as happy to know that now I have a chance to get my daughter back."

"You've always had a daughter, Mama."

With a jerk of her head, Alice indicated they step out of earshot of William and Jimmy. Softly, she said, "But you haven't always had a mama—is that what those Toliver eyes are accusing me of? Well, maybe now you have an idea of how I felt when I believed Aunt Mary had gone back on her promise to your father...a promise that you influenced her to break, Rachel. When you find out how hard it is to forgive Aunt Mary for her betrayal, maybe then you'll understand how difficult it's been for me to forgive yours."

Her mother's look dared her to dispute her. Rachel asked after a long moment, "Did you ever...forgive me?"

Her answer appeared in the hard flicker of her eyes. No. Her long-hoped-for dream had been realized, the glimmer told her, but through no design of Rachel's. "It doesn't matter now," Alice said. "What's past is past. All I want is for you to shake off the dust of this place forever and come home so we can be a family again."

"It wouldn't be the same, Mama, and you know it."

"We could try, Rachel. We could try to make it happen again."

"All right," she said, but the look they exchanged carried no conviction.

The trio climbed into the car. Her father started the motor while Jimmy adjusted his Walkman to his ears in the backseat and Alice secured a towel over the passenger window to block the strong setting sun. Her father made one last appeal before he closed his door. "Come with us, honey, at least for a little while.

The sooner you disentangle yourself from this place, the better. What's so important that you have to stay behind?"

"That's what I intend to find out, Daddy."

She kept the Dodge in sight until it had turned the corner, then sought out Sassie in one of the guest rooms, pulling sheets off the bed. "Leave that, Sassie," she said. "You're worn out. Wouldn't you like to take the night off, have Henry drive you to visit your sister? There's nothing that needs your attention around here tonight."

"Are you sure about that, Miss Rachel? Seems to me that *you* could use a little attention." Sassie had obviously deduced from her refusal to take Matt's calls and her family's stamp down the stairs, bags packed, so soon after returning to Houston Avenue that something must have gone haywire in Mister Amos's office. She and Henry were due to meet with him tomorrow to hear of the annuity they'd be receiving for life. They, too, would soon be forced to leave the home they had known all their lives.

Rachel patted her plump shoulder and forced a smile. "I'm okay, just strung out from the past few days. I suppose I need some time to be alone."

Sassie untied her apron. "In that case, I wouldn't mind gettin' outta the house awhile. Neither would Henry. Might do us both good to go see his mama."

"Then by all means go. Tell Henry to take the limo and stay as long as you like."

When she heard the limousine drive away, Rachel locked all the doors to keep Matt from storming in on her when she did not answer the phone. She was of no mind—or heart—to see him right now, and she had a mission to complete before Sassie and Henry got back. Sassie had blamed the champagne for Aunt Mary's frantic ravings to get to the attic in the final moments of her life. Rachel was now convinced that she had actually been fully lucid and aware that she was dying before completing one last and crucial task. She'd had Henry unlock Uncle Ollie's trunk for a reason. It may have been to recover a diary or batch of love letters—probably from Percy—or some other ancient indiscretion she wished to keep out of the hands of the Conservation Society, but Rachel didn't think so. Whatever she'd meant to retrieve had been so important that it had been the last thing on her mind as she was dying—that and the guilt that had caused her to cry Rachel's name.

And she intended to find it.

The telephone shrilled again as she headed down the upstairs hall to a narrow door that opened to the attic stairs. Its insistent ring cut off abruptly, even angrily, by the time she'd climbed the steep flight. Ignoring a twinge of pity for Matt's frantic concern, she creaked open the door and entered cautiously.

It was a cavernous place, hot and airless and filled with the domestic cast-offs of over one hundred years of Toliver occupancy. Good luck to the Conservation

Society pawing through this mass, she thought, a little short of breath from the climb. The stairs, not to mention the lack of air, would have been quite a struggle for an eighty-five-year-old woman in poor health. To make it easier to breathe, she propped open the attic door and levered a rusty andiron under the stuck frame of one of the windows, then looked around to assess where to begin. Her glance passed over an organized arrangement of household items, old books, vintage clothes, musical instruments, and sports equipment, landing on an assortment of trunks, packing cases, hatboxes, and wardrobes. She'd start her search there.

Her guess was rewarded almost immediately. She found the army-issue footlocker behind a tall wardrobe, stacked on top of two other metal trunks. Its lid gaped open, and a pair of keys hung from the lock. Her breath caught. *This is it.*

She peered inside, instantly assaulted by the stale odor of packets of letters long closed away, many of them tied with faded ribbons. A momentary aversion to what she was about to do made her draw back. Rummaging about in the trunk would be like pawing around in somebody's underwear drawer, but every instinct shouted that something was here that it was imperative she find. Intuition conquered her squeamishness, and she glanced back into the trunk. A packet of letters whose handwriting looked familiar grabbed her eye. The top envelopes were a dime-store variety and bore the return address of Kermit, Texas. Her throat closed. Aunt Mary had kept every one of her letters, it appeared—from her grammar school years through college. They had obviously been read many times. She put them back, surprised at her great-aunt's sentimentality. Or was it Uncle Ollie who'd preserved and tied them with the maroon-and-white colors of her alma mater? She picked up another group, skimpy in number, addressed in a childish hand. The thinness of the envelopes suggested they each contained no more than one sheet of paper. The return address listed a boys' camp in Fort Worth and above it the name of the sender: Matthew DuMont. She held the fragile envelopes tenderly. Had these letters from her son been what Aunt Mary had been after? Maybe so. She laid them back carefully and drew out another bundle—two, actually, tied separately and then together. The initials *PW* were written above the lengthy U.S. Army return address of the first group. *Percy Warwick*. There were ten envelopes, postmarked 1918 and 1919, bound with a green ribbon. Or could it have been these she'd wished removed?

The second group, double in volume and post-marked the same years, was secured by a faded blue ribbon. Rachel recognized Uncle Ollie's finely penned characters and wondered if the fact that Percy's had been placed on top had been inadvertent or a deliber-ate ranking of Aunt Mary's affections. Well, what did it matter now? What did she hope to find here that would change by one iota what Aunt Mary had done? And written in whose hand? Matthew DuMont's? Uncle Ollie's? Percy's? Her grandfather's?

Rachel paused. Her grandfather's...

She knew hardly anything about him. Her father barely remembered him, and Aunt Mary had spoken of him only once, when she'd asked why her grandfather had chosen to live in France. "Was it because your daddy did not remember him in his will?" she'd asked.

Aunt Mary had grown stone still. "What makes you think he wasn't remembered?"

"Because my daddy said he wasn't."

"Is...that the reason your mother resents your interest in your Toliver heritage—because he left Somerset and the house to me?"

She'd been embarrassed that Aunt Mary had perceived the truth. "Yes, ma'am," she'd said.

Aunt Mary had looked stricken with some thought she'd appeared on the verge of sharing but had thought better of confiding. "Your grandfather had short roots for the land," she'd wound up saying. "His passion was for ideologies and people, mainly the less fortunate, and he found them in France."

Rachel gazed thoughtfully at the piles of letters. Had Miles corresponded with his sister during those years in France...written of his son's birth...his wife's death? Had he enclosed pictures of himself and his family, especially of his wife, her grandmother?

She knew virtually nothing of Marietta Toliver. Would his letters have reflected his feelings of being left out of his father's will? Could his voice reach out to her even now, generations after his death, and help her deal with a similar pain?

Carefully, she delved into the assortment of brittle keepsakes. If her great-aunt had saved these other letters, she'd have kept her brother's. *What was this?* She removed a large, bulky bundle packaged in thick paper. Upon unwrapping it, she discovered a tight ball of knitted cream strips compacted around a wad of pink satin ribbons. It looked like an aborted attempt at an afghan or shawl, not Aunt Mary's, she didn't think. Aunt Mary had been averse to needles and thread.

She rewrapped and tied the package and—her curiosity now fully off the leash—removed the lid of a long, slender box. *Wow!* Folded in tissue paper was a pair of lovely fawn leather gloves, exquisitely made but evidently never worn. The edge of a note peeked from inside one of the cuffs. She withdrew it and read, "For the hands I hope to hold for the rest of my life. Love, Percy." She slipped the note back and reset the lid, moved in spite of herself. She took out another box from a florist's shop and found inside the desiccated remains of a long-stemmed rose; the petals were brown as tobacco stains, but most certainly had once been white. Beneath the fragments, another note: "To healings. My heart always, Percy."

She had her answer now. These old letters and treasured mementos of an unrequited love must have been what Aunt Mary had wished to remove. Tomorrow, she'd perform one last family duty to her and sack up the whole lot to destroy when she returned to Lubbock. The light was fading. She was hot and tired and at the bottom of her emotional barrel. She wanted out of the attic. Quickly, she returned the items to the trunk, making room for the bundle at its base. Her hand struck something... the metal casings of a box, she thought. She paused. A box....

Her heart beginning to race, she felt farther down and lifted out a dark green leather case. It was locked. She set it on the stack of hatboxes and grabbed the key ring from the lid of the army trunk, inserting the smaller of the two keys into the lock of the case. Despite its age, the top released instantly. She raised it and gazed inside. In the dim light, bold letters jumped out at her: **The Last Will and Testament of Vernon Thomas Toliver**.

Chapter Sixty-one

Dusk in summer was the feature William most remembered about the Piney Woods of East Texas. It seemed to him that when the sun went down, a cast came over the landscape the color and luster of gray pearls and was never ending. Nowhere else did he think the light lasted as long before dying.

As a boy just come from France, he'd been grateful for this aspect of the region, for when his mother died, he became afraid of the dark. His father understood and left a light burning while he slept, but he could remember very clearly, at five or so, being ashamed of his fear. When he came to Howbutker, he sensed at once that he must say nothing of this to the tall, commanding woman to whom his father had sent him. The portly, gentle man he called Uncle Ollie would have understood, but not his aunt. He'd known instinctively that she was not one to tolerate weakness.

Or so he'd believed.

The first night, he'd fallen asleep long before darkness fell and was carried to his room in his uncle's arms. But after that, all through the summer when going to bed, he'd raise the shade his aunt had pulled down and go to sleep by the light of the dusk. When fall came and shorter days, he worried that his aunt would turn off the light by his bed when she came in to say good night. But instead, she surprised him by asking with her small smile, "Shall we leave the light on a little longer?"

"*Oui, Tante, s'il vous plaît.*"

"Well, good night, then. See you in the morning."

Thereafter, it became their routine bedtime exchange, and he'd awake in the mornings to find the lamp still burning. He'd thought she hadn't bothered to return to switch it off, but he was wrong. One winter night several years later, he awoke to see her in the lamplight at the side of his bed. She was wearing a robe and looked like a goddess pictured in his mythology books. Her hand on the light switch, she asked kindly, "Shall we turn it off now?"

And it was then he realized that she'd been aware of his fear of the dark all along. "Yes, Aunt," he'd said, recognizing that his fear was gone and had been for a long time. It had simply disappeared, wandered away with the other dragons of his childhood.

William glanced at his wife, snoring with her mouth open, the towel still up at her window. She'd begun to doze almost immediately after she saw how disinclined he was to talk of their new wealth. "Rachel will get over it, William, believe me," she'd said, reading his worried mind as easily as her romance novels. "And it's not like she's been kicked entirely out of Howbutker. She can marry Matt Warwick and get Somerset back through him when Percy dies. What's the big deal?"

"The big deal, Alice, is that Somerset won't go to Matt Warwick. Percy will have it removed from his estate. That's why Aunt Mary left it to him. She knew he'd make sure Rachel never got her hands on it again."

"Why, for God's sake?"

"That's the sixty-four-thousand-dollar question. I really think Percy's got the right idea. I believe Aunt Mary was trying to save Rachel from that curse she spoke of back in '56."

"And you don't know what it is?"

"No, but Percy does."

He was thankful that once Alice was asleep, Armageddon couldn't wake her. She would not have approved this detour onto a country road through the pine forests he remembered from his boyhood, and Jimmy was plugged into his Walkman with his eyes closed, too lost in the oblivion of his frenzied music to notice he'd turned off the interstate. This little jaunt would make the trip longer, but he might never pass this way again, and he had a hankering to linger in the twilight of the Piney Woods for as long as he could, revisit memories he wouldn't be adding to after today. Close by over there, he recalled, was a creek where he and a buddy used to seine for catfish. God, the water moccasins and cottonmouths they'd draw up with their catch!

And somewhere around here ran a railroad track, the one that had taken him out of Howbutker when he made his escape forty years ago. His plan had been to hide in the bushes by the side of the track until the train started to roll, then jump on and buy his ticket on board. But the conductor had said the train was full and he'd have to wait for the next one. Amos, then a recently discharged army paratrooper on his way to Houston, had gotten off to stretch his legs before reboarding. William still remembered his surprise when he had shoved his ticket into his hand and told him to hop on. Once out in the oilfields of West Texas, he'd thought of the tall, gangly soldier from time to time, wondering what had possessed a stranger passing through town to part with his ticket to a kid he could tell was on the lam. He learned later from Aunt Mary that at fifteen Amos had tried to run away from home but was hauled back by ham-fisted deputies to a father who had punished him by strapping him to a post and whipping him publicly. Amos, unsure to what he'd be condemning him if he was caught, had made the decision to help him. That turned out to be a good thing for the old boy. He had stumbled into a town that had taken him in as one of their own—no mean achievement in Howbutker. Funny how things happen.

The pine-canopied road was quiet and peaceful—no sight or sound of another car—and he had the sensation of driving through a silent green tunnel, a good stretch to think. He kept recalling Aunt Mary's words to him in the gazebo that summer of 1956: *Be glad your children will grow up free of Somerset.* What had she meant by that? He was convinced it was behind her decision to sever his daughter from her Toliver roots. To hell with Alice's theory that she'd done it to keep her promise to him. Aunt Mary was free to change her mind at any time, and they'd both known she owed him nothing. He also couldn't buy that she'd willed Somerset to Percy as an expression of regret. That bit had come as a shock—that they'd been lovers—but not when he thought about it. They had looked made for each other, and he had wondered at one time why Aunt Mary, a goddess, had chosen a cherub over a Greek god. Not that there was ever a better man than Uncle Ollie.

Then why, when she'd primed Rachel to step into her shoes, had Aunt Mary snatched them away?

Somerset has always cost too much, she'd said.

He now had an inkling of what she'd meant by that. Somerset had cost her Percy and God knew what else she had been alluding to that summer. In a way, it had cost her him. He'd have stayed if he hadn't been made to work out at the plantation. God, how he'd hated the place—the chiggers and mosquitoes, the heat and sweat, the sucking mud in the rainy season and the clinging dust in drought, the burrs and constant fear of snakes coiled under the cotton bushes, the never-ending cycle of work, work, work. And someday, so he was made to understand—because he was a Toliver—it was all going to be his.

He shook his head as if a fly had penetrated his ear passage. He could not have abided it. No sirreebobtail. And now Somerset had come between his wife and daughter, and it would cost Rachel that fine Matt Warwick, too. They were another couple that went together like peas and carrots, if ever he saw one, but she could never marry a man whose grandfather possessed the land that she would always believe should have been hers. His aunt had meant well, but she'd blown it. Rachel would never forgive her, as Alice would never get past their daughter throwing in her lot with Aunt Mary.

He blew out a woeful breath. He could understand the costs, but what of the curse? What in blue blazes was the Toliver curse? How did it show itself? Had Aunt Mary saved Rachel from it? How would she know?

The winding, narrow road under its green awning swam before his vision. His senses swelled with a sorrow for the tragic barter of things... those cherishables folks traded away that could never be reclaimed. His eyes and ears and nostrils were so filled that he did not register the urgent blowing of the train whistle in the distance. The car windows were rolled up, his right view blocked by the towel and a hang-up bag in the back. The air conditioner hummed. A faint blare of Jimmy's rock music leaked from the Walkman. When first he heard the cry of the train whistle, it sounded like a natural sound of the region, so much a nostalgic part of his childhood this hour of the day that the car was on the track before he realized that a freight train was bearing down upon them.

Alice and Jimmy never opened their eyes. For an illuminating instant before the train struck, William's mind was fully alert, and he understood with perfect clarity the gist of the Toliver curse.

Chapter Sixty-two

Back in her room, hardly able to draw breath, Rachel climbed up on the bed, opened the green leather box, and carefully lifted out the last will and testament of her great-great-grandfather. It was dated May 17, 1916. She was aware that he had died in June of that year, so the document must have been drafted shortly before. A letter had been inserted between the pages. She unfolded the single sheet and glanced at the closing signature: "Your loving father, Vernon Toliver." A chill grabbed her spine. She felt as if she'd found the key to a locked, forbidden room.

Dearest wife and children, she read.

> *I have never thought of myself as a cowardly man, but I find that I do not have the courage to apprise you of my will's contents while I am still alive. Let me assure you, before its reading, that I love each of you with all my heart and wish, as deeply, that circumstances could have afforded*

*a fairer and more generous distribution of my
property. Darla, my beloved wife, I ask you to
understand why I have done what I've done.
Miles, my son, I cannot expect you to understand,
but someday, perhaps, your heir will be grateful for
the legacy I leave you and entrust you to retain for
the fruit of your loin.*

    *And Mary, I wonder that in remembering you
as I've done, I've not prolonged the curse that has
plagued the Tolivers since the first pine tree was
cleared from Somerset. I am leaving you many and
great responsibilities which I hope will not force
you into a position unfavorable to your happiness.*

    Your loving husband and father

Rachel met her startled gaze in the dressing table
mirror beyond her bed. This was the first written reference to a Toliver curse she'd ever come across. What
did it mean? How was it manifested? And what was
this legacy that Vernon Toliver had left his son? The
chill gripping her backbone spread. With a growing
sense of the unthinkable, she turned the brittle pages
until she found the name *Miles Toliver* listed as sole
beneficiary of a tract of 640 acres and a description of
its location along the Sabine River.

*No! No way! Aunt Mary couldn't have... she wouldn't
have...* She fixed her eyes on the paragraph again,
rereading the words expressed in their legal jargon,
her mind reeling from their implications. But there

was no mistaking their meaning. Contrary to what her family had believed—to what Aunt Mary had *allowed* them to believe—Vernon Toliver had left a section of Somerset land to his son.

Rachel lifted her white face to the mirror. Aunt Mary had lied by omitting the truth of her brother's inheritance. But why? What was the point of the secret? She'd have thought Aunt Mary would have *wanted* her father to know of the land Miles inherited, to encourage his interest and commitment. What happened to those acres? Had Miles Toliver sold them? Had Aunt Mary been ashamed of the sale and not wanted her nephew to know what he'd done?

There were two other envelopes in the box, held together by a rusted paper clip. The faded name above the return address of the top one caused her to lose breath. *Miles Toliver.* It had been mailed from Paris, but the postdate was too faint to read. She unclipped it, setting aside the other envelope without a glance, and carefully withdrew a letter dated May 13, 1935.

Dear Mary,

I am in hospital, having been diagnosed with lung cancer, a result of the phosgene gas I inhaled during the war. The doctors tell me that it's only a matter of time now. I'm not afraid for myself, only for William, my son. He's seven years old and the sweetest little fellow in the world. His mother died two years ago, and it's been only the two of us since.

I'm writing to say that I'm sending him to you and Ollie to take in and raise as your own, perhaps as a younger brother to Matthew. He looks exactly like a Toliver, Mary, and who knows but that someday he may grow up to appreciate and respect the family name with the enthusiasm his father lacked. I'd like you to give him a chance to try. I have made arrangements for him to arrive in New York on the Queen Mary *June fifteenth. Attached is the dock information.*

Also enclosed is the deed to the section along the Sabine that Papa left me in his will. As you can see, I have transferred it to you to hold in trust for William until he is twenty-one, at which time you're to transfer the property to him to do with as he sees fit. I'm hoping by then, for your sake as well as his, he'll be so entrenched in the Toliver tradition that he wouldn't dream of parting with a nugget of his inheritance.

I am at peace knowing that he is going to a good home. Tell Ollie that I still consider him and Percy the finest friends a man ever made. I hope you will all remember me in the memories of the good times we shared.

Your loving brother,
Miles

Rachel stared at the letter in dumb disbelief, unable to grasp its shocking revelations. Irrelevantly, she recalled her father's description of himself arriving in New York Harbor at seven years old, alone and afraid, looking foreign and speaking only French. She'd heard the story many times of how Uncle Ollie, his cherubic face wreathed in a smile, had hailed him from the waiting crowd on the dock and put him at ease immediately, buying him ice cream and sodas and regaling him with boyhood tales of Miles on the long train journey to Howbutker. Uncle Ollie had been sent alone to collect him because it was planting time at Somerset.

Feeling as if every corpuscle were jumping, Rachel picked up the other envelope addressed to Mary DuMont and instinctively, horrifyingly, guessed that the bold black handwriting belonged to Percy Warwick—perhaps because it had been clipped to the clear proof of betrayal and deception by the woman he loved. No return address, stamp, or postdate, which meant it had been hand-delivered. She slipped out the brief message, noting that it was dated July 7, 1935.

Mary,
Though I have misgivings, I believe I can see
my way to agree to your proposal. I have gone to
Ollie's creditor, and he cannot be moved from
his position. Therefore, I will buy the section we
discussed. Let's meet Monday at the courthouse at

three o'clock, and we will take care of the matter.
Bring the deed, and I will bring the check.
    As ever,
    Percy

Rachel drew back her shoulders, inwardly seeing the smokestacks and emissions rising from the site of Warwick Industries' huge pulp mill and paper-processing plant bordering Somerset's eastern boundary. On the other side of the complex lay the Sabine River. She had always thought its juxtaposition next to the Toliver plantation accidental, but now...

Dear God—was it possible? Did Percy's note refer to her grandfather's section along the Sabine, and had Aunt Mary *sold* it to him against Miles's instructions? Were Percy's misgivings based on knowledge that the land wasn't Aunt Mary's to sell? Rachel studied the date: July 7, 1935... two months after her father's arrival in New York Harbor.

Another remote possibility, logical and less shocking, but no less shameful, nudged in. By the time William Toliver had reached twenty-one, Aunt Mary was well aware of her nephew's lack of feeling for the plantation and his heritage. Had she simply incorporated his acres into the rest of Somerset and never mentioned them to him because she was afraid he'd sell his inheritance? If they did *not* abut Somerset and she hadn't sold them to Percy, where along the Sabine were they located? Where was the deed? And what section, then, would she have sold to Percy?

Rachel pressed her cold hands to her hot cheeks. What had she discovered? Evidence of fraud? Or plain deceit and thievery? Was her father the culprit here? Had Aunt Mary transferred the deed as instructed and he'd sold it and the two of them kept his secret all these years?

No, never. He wouldn't have allowed her mother to believe a lie that was at the root of her resentment against the Tolivers. But then—until today— she wouldn't have believed Aunt Mary guilty of her crimes, either, and as for Percy Warwick...he was the most honorable man she knew. She gazed at the note and felt sick to her stomach. *Bring the deed....* Was it conceivable that he would agree to a proposal that would defraud a six-year-old boy of his inheritance?

At least she would get one answer when her father telephoned tonight. She'd tell him of her discovery and question the whereabouts of the deed, but she was certain he'd say he had no idea what she was talking about. He'd never known he was to inherit a section of land that had belonged to his father. And tomorrow, she'd go to the courthouse and check the record of deeds for the location of the land.

Car lights flashed across her bedroom windows, reflected off the closed garage doors. Sassie and Henry were home. She scrambled off the bed to let them in before they rang the bell and she'd have to explain the locked back door. She was halfway down the stairs when the kaleidoscopic play of a squad car's blue and red lights struck the fanlight. She halted in midflight as other tires screeched to a stop before the verandah, followed by the slam of car doors and the urgent pitch of men's voices—among them Matt's and Amos's. *What in the world—?*

The back doorbell buzzed. She barely heard the sound for the frantic beat of her heart as she rushed to answer the imperative summons of the front door chimes. The insistent ring came again as she struggled to wrench the cranky bolt from its antiquated casing and finally throw open the door. A contingent of men stared at her, Amos and Matt in the forefront, the county sheriff and two highway patrolmen behind them, their grimly set faces almost stopping her heart.

"What is it?" she demanded.

"It's your...parents and...Jimmy," Amos croaked, his Adam's apple bouncing like a Ping-Pong ball.

"What about them?"

Matt stepped across the threshold and gripped her hand. "Their car was struck by a train, Rachel. They were killed instantly."

PART IV

Chapter Sixty-three

Rachel stood by the front door of her childhood home—car keys in hand, a packed bag at her feet—and took a last look around. She was leaving no visible trace of the lives lived here since before she was born. The scrapes and marks and stains left behind by her family members were under coats of eggshell white paint she'd applied herself, unwilling to trust strangers with the obliteration of their memories. It had taken her six weeks to clear and clean the place for the new occupants, whoever they would be. She had made an agreement with the Realtor that the house was not to be shown or the FOR SALE sign to go up until she was ready to leave.

Her next-door neighbor, a woman she had known all her life and her mother's best friend, had asked, "Why do you have to sell the house so soon, Rachel?

Why can't you give yourself time to come home awhile?"

She'd shaken her head mutely, her voice still lost in the well of her grief. She didn't deserve to live in this place she'd loved and betrayed. It would be a sacrilege.

"Rachel, will you stay in Lubbock?" Danielle had asked when she went to pack her things from her office. Someone was already occupying her desk, a young Japanese man who had neatly boxed her personal belongings and stacked them in a corner. Ron Kimball, whose father was one of the survivors of the death march to Bataan, had already quit and found a job at another cotton farm a county over. No way would he work for a Jap, he told Danielle. She, too, had given notice.

"And do what?" Rachel had asked with a mirthless smile. "Watch Toliver cotton grow under somebody else's management?"

She'd put the town house up for sale as well and boxed her belongings, realizing as she arranged for their storage that with the house on Houston Avenue gone and the one in Kermit soon to be on the market, she had nowhere to send them. She was virtually homeless... for a while.

Rachel took a final glance around the living room, picked up her bag, and let herself out. She'd already visited her old garden plot, now a neatly clipped part of the Bermuda-grass yard that showed only faint evidence of the bounty once grown there.

"I suspect this is where it all began for you," Amos had remarked after the funeral when she'd found him gazing at the grass-covered depressions beside the house, where he'd gone to escape from those paying their respects inside.

"Yes, this is where it all began," she'd said, remembering the late afternoons she'd tended her garden, the conversations overheard beneath the kitchen window.

"He wanted to come, you know."

She had made no comment.

"Percy and I convinced Matt that... now would not be a good time. He's terribly worried about you, Rachel. He can't understand why you refuse to see him, or at least to take his calls. Frankly, my dear... neither can I," he said, his face seamed with concern. "None of this is Matt's fault, you know. Percy says that if you'll just come back to Howbutker to hear Mary's story, you'll understand why she left things as she did and all for the love of you."

"Really?" Rachel felt her lip curl. "I might have been convinced of that once, but not now."

"Now? What's happened now?"

"You'll know soon enough. Excuse me. I have to get back to the others."

Poor Amos, caught in the middle, she thought as she turned the ignition of her BMW. And Matt, too....

For the past two months, she'd tried not to think

of him and how they'd parted. Everything was hazy after she'd answered the door and backed up before the troop of men filling the foyer. Matt had tried to take her into his arms, but she'd turned instead to Amos. Somehow she'd managed to call Carrie Sutherland, her best friend and roommate at Texas A&M, who must have flown over the highway from Dallas to arrive two hours later. She remembered the hurt in Matt's eyes as he watched her and Amos go up the stairs to her room to await Carrie's arrival, leaving him below. And later...through the fog of her pain, she remembered running downstairs when she heard Carrie in the hall and going into her arms rather than the ones Matt looked longing to hold out to her.

"It's best that you leave now, Matt," she'd said finally.

He'd got hold of her at last, taking her by the shoulders and angling his head down to look into her empty eyes. "Rachel, Granddad told me about the will...about Somerset going to him. On top of everything else, I can't begin to imagine how hurt...how shocked you must be. I'm hurt and shocked for you, but I'm not the enemy here. You need me. We can get through this together."

Her voice had come dull as a sleepwalker's. "There are things you don't know. You will become the enemy. You won't have a choice."

He'd looked as if she'd slapped him. "What?"

"Good-bye, Matt."

Over the following weeks, the rest of that unimaginable time came back in cloudy bits and pieces, illuminated now and then by a streak of clarity. The dialogue between her and Carrie on the drive back from identifying the bodies the next day was one of those. In the sick silence, Carrie had asked, "Are you up to telling me why you slammed the door in the face of that gorgeous hunk of man on the verandah last night?"

"I didn't slam it. And no, I'm not up to it. If you're interested, be my guest."

She'd let out a whoop. "Well, that's really sweet of you, lamb chop, but he doesn't impress me as a man who's any woman's to offer. He's crazy about you, Rachel. Why are you shutting him out?"

"I have to. If I don't, it will only make things much worse later."

"Later?"

"When I take back what's mine."

Tears stung her eyes as she took her last glimpse of the house and street where she'd grown up. She would leave the house keys with the Realtor on her way out of town. She was headed to Dallas to bunk with Carrie for a while, but her main reason for going there was to meet with Carrie's father. Taylor Sutherland was an eminent commercial trial lawyer specializing in real estate fraud. She had an appointment with him to evaluate the contents of the green leather box.

*   *   *

MATT PULLED INTO THE DRIVEWAY of Rachel's house, finding its address easily from Amos's directions. He parked the rental van and got out, assaulted at once by the dry heat and gritty wind that blew constantly in West Texas. His heart beat like a bongo drummer gone berserk. Finally, he'd have Rachel in his sights again. If she didn't admit him, he'd force his way in. They had to talk. She had to tell him face-to-face why she wanted nothing more to do with him. There had to be more to it than his grandfather inheriting Somerset. Her last words to him the night of the accident kept running through his head: *There are things you don't know. You will become the enemy. You won't have a choice.*

"What did she mean by that, Granddad?" he'd asked when he reported those words to him. "What is it that I don't know?"

"I have no idea."

Especially disturbing was Rachel's cryptic remark to Amos when he attended the funeral. At one time, she'd told him, she may have been willing to believe Mary had acted out of love for her, but not now, and when Amos asked her what had happened to cause her to say that, she'd said, "You'll know soon enough."

"Why *now,* Granddad? That implies she's discovered further reason to condemn Mary—maybe even us."

A shrug. "I don't know, son."

He had not been totally convinced of his grandfather's ignorance. In the past two months, he'd been aware of rattling skeletons again—those family secrets he wasn't telling.

The yard had been recently mowed. Its baked, dusty smell drifted up to him, reminding him of Amos's observation: *What a godforsaken place! How does anything but rattlesnakes survive out there?* Matt shared his view. On the drive from the airport, surrounded by a desert of scrub brush that had all the beauty of a moon crater, he had wondered how this hardscrabble land had inspired Rachel's passion for farming. It had to be blood, not locale.

He approached the steps to the front porch uncertainly, disturbed by the unoccupied air of the place. The green shutters looked newly painted, as did the closed garage door. There were no curtains on the windows, and the glass sparkled from recent cleaning. *No, don't tell me. . . .* He groaned and made a scope of his hands to peer through the small squares of glass in the door. The front room was empty, deserted as a bird's nest in winter, not a stick of furniture in it. In chagrin and disbelief, he tromped around the sides of the house, gazing in windows, finding each room bare of everything but starkly painted walls.

"May I help you?"

He whirled from a window in the backyard to find an obese woman in a tropical-patterned muu-muu staring at him, hands on hips.

"Well, I—yes, you can," Matt stammered. "The

woman who lives here. Rachel Toliver. She appears to have moved. Can you tell me where she's gone?"

"Who's asking?"

"I'm Matt Warwick." Matt brushed the window dust off his hands and held one out. "A friend of the family from Howbutker, Texas." He guessed her to be a neighbor and perhaps familiar with the names.

Slowly, the woman removed a hand from her hip and allowed it to be shaken. "I've heard of the Warwicks from Howbutker. My name's Bertie Walton, a friend and neighbor. I live next door." She nodded in the direction of her house. "What do you want with Rachel?"

Matt hesitated, then came right out with it. "I've come to check on her and maybe take her home. She needs to be with those who care about her."

The woman seemed to relax. "I couldn't agree more." She looked him up and down and, as if deciding something, said, "Well, I'm sorry to tell you, but you've missed her by little over an hour. I think she may be gone for good. She must have left when I was at the grocery store, and I didn't get a chance to say good-bye." Her tone indicated deep hurt.

"Did she say where she was going?"

"'Fraid not. Told me yesterday she'd be in touch, but...the state she was in, I'm not holding my breath."

Matt's hope for a reunion plummeted. "You know anybody who'd know where she's going?"

"Not a soul. Rachel wasn't close to nobody in Kermit anymore, 'cept me. I was her mother's best friend. The house is going up for sale. I'd try the Realtors in town, if I was you. There are only two. She's bound to have left a contact number with one of 'em."

Matt patted his coat pocket for a pen and notepad. "Could you give me their names and directions?"

"I can do better than that. Come on over and I'll draw you a little map. You won't find them otherwise."

She waddled in the direction of her house, and Matt followed. Minutes later, he was seated at her kitchen table, watching her pour sun-brewed tea into glasses she'd taken from a special cupboard. "Mrs. Walton, why would Rachel move? I'd think that...under the circumstances...she'd want to stay here, where she's known."

"It's Bertie," she said, setting down the glasses of iced tea, a yellow legal pad and a ballpoint pen clamped under her fleshy arm. She wedged into one of the captain's chairs and slapped the pad onto the table. "I can't say I'm surprised that she left. Rachel's been gone from Kermit a long time. There's nothing here for her anymore, if there ever was. I would've thought she'd stay simply because she had nowhere else to go, but she couldn't get outta here fast enough."

"You said...the state she was in when she left. How did she look?"

Bertie had begun sketching streets and landmarks on the yellow pad. "When'd you last see her?"

"Two months ago, when she came for her great-aunt's funeral."

"Deduct about twenty pounds from that pretty figure of hers and add a thin, drawn face and berry brown skin, and you got it. She don't look like the same girl who was here over Christmas."

"She's not the same girl," Matt said softly. "How'd she get the berry brown skin?"

"From all that fixing up of the outside of the house—the roof, the shutters, the yard. Wouldn't let nobody else touch 'em. But that's not to say she wasn't...*together. Something* was keeping her from falling apart. You could tell by the way she hammered those nails."

Matt frowned. "She never hinted at what it was? Anything you can tell me would be a big help."

Bertie reflected a moment. "It looked like some kind of *inner force* driving her, but...not exactly *grit*, if you know what I mean. Not the kind of gumption that makes you keep going whether you want to or not. It wasn't that. No, it was more like she had a *purpose,* an *objective* in mind for when she finished up here." She clicked off the ballpoint pen and ripped the sheet from the pad. "I can't tell it no better than that."

"You've told it very well, Bertie. Thanks for your help." He finished the iced tea and stood up. "Write down your telephone number and if I find out anything, I'll let you know."

Bertie squinted up at him as if she had more to say before she saw him to the door. "You're the boy Rachel first told me about years ago when she came back from Howbutker, aren't you? She was about ten years old then, and mercy! She wasn't the kind to wax on about anybody, but she did you. A while ago you said you were here to take her back to those who care about her. Are you one of those?"

"I'm at the top of the list."

"I can see that. Well, you go find her, young man, and make her understand that...despite all her losses...she's still got everything."

"I plan to do just that, Bertie," Matt said, a break in his voice. He folded the sheet of paper and slipped it into his pocket, then laid a hand on her shoulder. "Stay seated. I can let myself out, and you have my word, one way or the other, you'll hear from me."

"I hope it's a wedding invitation," she said.

He threw her a smile. "If I can help it."

He hit pay dirt with the second realty company but was unable to cash in. The Realtor handling the Toliver house was on her way to put up the FOR SALE sign when Matt walked into the two-desk office. He'd guessed it would be against company policy to give out a seller's out-of-town telephone number and address, but he'd use his considerable charm to worm the information out of somebody. He smiled at the woman and explained that he was friends with Bertie Walton, and she'd told him the house was for sale.

Could she contact the owner at once? He was interested in making an offer before he left town.

Chagrin flashed across the Realtor's face. Wouldn't you just know it? she said. Less than two hours ago, he could have spoken with the owner right here. Now she was on her way out of town—where, she didn't say. It was really very strange. She'd left no telephone number where she could be reached, saying that she'd be in touch when she got situated. However . . . if he'd like to make an offer, she could draw up the contract and present it the minute the owner called.

Did she have any idea when that would be? Matt asked.

The Realtor's face lengthened. Unfortunately, no.

He smiled his regrets, saying that wouldn't be convenient for him, but he'd take her card.

Outside the Realtor's office, he sucked in a long, frustrated breath of bone-dry air. He was fairly certain Rachel was headed to her friend in Dallas, the zany blonde in jodhpurs and boots who'd driven in the night of the accident. Carla or Cassie, or something like that. Her name had not registered in the emotional turmoil. Amos might remember. Once he had the friend's name, the rest would be easy. He'd go through the operator for her address, get a flight plan cleared to Dallas, and be in there tonight.

In the van, he dialed his home phone number on the portable phone he'd brought along. When his grandfather answered, he asked for Amos, knowing he'd be at Warwick Hall. Without delay, Percy handed the receiver to Amos. "What can I do for you, Matt?" he asked when he came on the line.

"Rachel has put her house up for sale and left town without telling anyone where she was headed, but you may be able to help me find her, Amos. Do you remember the name of Rachel's roommate at Texas A and M—that female dynamo we met the night of the accident? I think Rachel's gone to stay with her in Dallas."

Matt could hear his urge to kick himself. "I'm sorry, Matt, but I'm afraid I didn't catch her name either."

Matt struck the steering wheel with his palm and hissed a silent curse, but he said as if it didn't matter, "Don't fret about it, Amos. Maybe Sassie or Henry can tell me."

But Henry did not recall the name either. "Miss Carrie is all I know," Henry said. "Last names of strangers don't stick with me. Maybe Aunt Sassie remembers. She's staying at my mama's. Want to call her?"

"Give me the number, Henry."

But he hit a dead end there, too. Sassie had been so overcome with the events of those awful days she hadn't known whether she was pitching or catching, she told Matt.

A detective, then, he decided, putting the van into reverse. They'd contact a detective agency to track her down. He punched in the numbers of his office in Howbutker, picturing Rachel up on the roof of her house, attacking the nails with a vengeance. Was that her purpose, the driving force keeping her together— vengeance? Against whom? And why? In his heart, he believed he knew. He had the chilling feeling his grandfather was the target.

"Nancy," he said when his secretary answered, "put everything else aside and find me the name and number of a reliable detective agency in Dallas, then call me back with the information. I'm heading home."

Chapter Sixty-four

DALLAS, TEXAS, SATURDAY

Rachel awoke the next morning to find with a start that the enameled clock on the bedside table read nine o'clock. She propped herself up on an elbow in the cold, all-white room, looking about her in confusion until she realized she was in the guest room of Carrie Sutherland's starkly modern town house. She contemplated getting up, nudged by the farmer's inherent guilt about lying abed while the day was wasting. Not since Saturday mornings in grade school had she slept so late. After a moment, though, she lowered herself back down. There were no fields to tend anymore.

As usual when she awoke, a blanket of depression settled over her. She'd learned that if she lay still and emptied her mind, a ray of rational thought would eventually make its way through the gloom. This morning, the thought centered on why she'd decided to drive to Dallas a day early when she'd known that

Carrie would be out of town until midafternoon Sunday, the time of Rachel's planned arrival. But—as with everything else she'd set her furious energies to these past two months—she'd gotten her parents' house ready for sale ahead of schedule and come on because she had nowhere else to go. Now she wondered what she could do to fill her time and endure her solitude in this igloo of a house without losing the rest of her sanity.

The telephone rang down the hall, and Rachel let it ring once before the simple need to hear a human voice prompted her to throw back the covers to answer it. She cleared her morning throat. "Hello. Carrie Sutherland's residence."

There was a surprised silence, then a familiar male voice that always reminded her of suspenders and flannel shirts said her name with delight: "Rachel? That you?"

She grimaced, regretting she'd answered the phone. Taylor Sutherland, Carrie's father, obviously did not know that his daughter was out of town, enjoying the hedonistic delights of the MGM Grand Hotel and Casino in Las Vegas with her latest boyfriend. A strait-laced Southern Baptist, he would not have approved.

"Good morning, Taylor," she said. "I came in early, but I'm afraid Carrie's not here at the moment. Some...early morning appointment, I gather."

"Uh-huh. She's flown off somewhere for the weekend and left you to fend for herself, hasn't she?"

"My fault. I wasn't to have arrived until tomorrow afternoon."

"Well, I won't put you on the spot and ask where she is or with whom. Will you be all right there by yourself in that icebox? Set the thermostat to your liking. Pay no attention to that hands-off warning she's posted. It's ridiculous how cold she keeps that place just to preserve those modern canvases of hers."

Rachel smiled. There was no fooling Taylor Sutherland when it came to his daughter. He was referring to the PLEASE DO NOT ADJUST chrome plate affixed next to the thermostat. Carrie was a serious collector of valuable oil paintings, and her town house was thermostatically controlled to protect them from variations in room temperatures. He asked now in a voice of fatherly concern, "So what are you going to do with yourself all day?"

"Tell you the truth, I don't know."

"Well, she doesn't keep a damn thing worth reading, and I'm sure there's nothing to eat in the refrigerator. Why don't you come to the office? I'm here today doing some paperwork, and you and I can talk over whatever you planned to discuss Monday. We'll have a couple of gin and tonics and then hit a hamburger joint. What do you say?"

Rachel sighed with relief. "I say that sounds great."

"Then I'll see you about eleven." He gave her the address and easiest route to get to his office and advised before hanging up, "Come cool. They turn off the air-conditioning in this place over the weekend."

Rachel had great respect for Taylor Sutherland. He maintained a country-boy-come-to-town persona— but behind the hayseed act was a brilliant legal mind that had led many a gullible opponent to his peril. He was a widower and Carrie his only child. Knowing him to be a stickler for punctuality, she had five minutes to spare before he bustled out in the warm Saturday quiet of his luxurious reception room at eleven o'clock. "Rachel, my girl! I won't ask how you are because I believe I damn well know, but you look pretty good for a girl knocked off her feet as you've been."

"You speak from kindness," she said, returning his bear hug. "I wish my mirror were so kind."

"You're too critical. Come on in and I'll put together a couple of G and T's to cool us off."

Taylor talked indulgently of Carrie's "wild and woolly ways" while he mixed the gin and tonics, Rachel getting the impression the preliminaries were to avoid getting down to the reason for their meeting. Carrie had made the appointment for her, filling in her father on the dispensations of Aunt Mary's will and explaining that Rachel had found incriminating papers that might be grounds for a lawsuit against Percy Warwick. She had a feeling he knew Percy.

Finally, the drinks served, he leaned back in his chair and threaded his hands across the tight midriff of his short-sleeved plaid shirt. "So Carrie tells me that apparently, without your knowledge, your great-aunt sold Toliver Farms right out from under your nose and left the family plantation that you'd expected to inherit to Percy Warwick."

Her optimism dived at the familiarity with which he spoke the name. "So you are acquainted with Percy Warwick."

"I am."

"Will that constitute a conflict of interest if— should I have a case—you decide to take it?"

"It's too early to tell. Let's put that aside for the moment and have you tell me why you're here."

"Before we get to that, Taylor, I'd like to know whether client-attorney confidentiality will apply to what I tell you, regardless of whether I have a case and become your client."

He smiled benignly. "Of course it will, because I'm going to charge you a consultation fee that will automatically establish privilege—lunch on you at the Burger Den."

"Fair enough," she said, chuckling, then added seriously, "Because this has to do with Percy Warwick. How well do you know him? Are you friends?"

"Not exactly friends. Pathway-crossing acquaintances." His tone grew serious as well. "And for my part, an admirer. He's done more for the conservation of forestlands and prudent disposal of industrial wastes than any other man in the industry. What has this to do with Percy?"

Rachel took a bracing sip of the gin and tonic.

"I believe he knowingly bought land from my great-aunt that wasn't hers to sell. It belonged to my father, William Toliver. I have every reason to believe he died in ignorance of the fact."

Taylor sat in noncommittal silence for a few seconds, looking like a man who's heard a language he couldn't identify. "What evidence do you have to substantiate your suspicions, and how did you come by it?"

Rachel succinctly related the events that had led to the discovery of the green leather box and described its contents.

"You have these materials with you?"

Rachel opened her purse and withdrew copies of Vernon Toliver's will and the two letters. Taylor donned reading glasses, and she sipped quietly while he read. "Well?" she queried when he laid aside the papers.

There was a plush squeak of leather as he stood to return to the bar, pointing to her glass to ask if she wished a refill. She shook her head and observed the excessive time he took on the finer points of replenishing his own gin and tonic. She remembered that he fussed inordinately long over sweetening his iced tea, but now she suspected the act was a deliberate stall. "Come on, Taylor," she said. "Do I have a case, or am I wasting your time and mine?"

"Well, I don't know about yours, but certainly not mine," he said with a fatherly twinkle that deepened his crow's-feet. "I have a few questions first. One, did you find the deed?"

"No, it wasn't in the box."

"And in that green box of yours—did you find your grandfather's death certificate?"

Rachel shook her head.

"What about your great-aunt's guardianship papers?"

Surprised that she had never thought to wonder about them, she said, "No, I did not."

"Your father was her ward?"

A crease formed between Rachel's brows. "He always assumed so."

"I ask because—as your father's guardian—your great-aunt may have believed that selling the land was in his best interests. Of course, she would have had to secure court approval to do so. The problem I have with that, though, are these dates." Rachel drew closer to the desk to peer at the dates he pointed out with the tip of a pen. "Your grandfather's letter reads May 13, 1935; Percy's, July 6. We can assume the title was transferred shortly afterwards. Even if Miles had died within days of having mailed this letter to his sister, she would not have been officially notified of his death until weeks later. The wheels of bureaucracy ground even slower in 1935 than they do now, especially since he died abroad in France."

Rachel felt her eyes take over her face. "You're saying that even if Aunt Mary were my father's guardian, she wasn't at the time the deed was transferred to Percy Warwick?"

"That's right."

"If my aunt were appointed guardian *after* the land sale, would that make the transaction legal?"

"No. The court order would not be retroactive. The transfer of the title would still be fraudulent."

Rachel reached for her now watery gin and tonic and took a sip to relieve her parched throat. Setting the glass back on the desk, she asked, "Does this mean I have a case for fraud?"

Taylor picked up her grandfather's letter. "First, do you have another signature of Miles Toliver that would corroborate the one on this letter?"

Rachel thought of the ledger books signed by her grandfather back in the study on Houston Avenue. "I know where I can get corroborating samples of his handwriting," she said. "That takes care of that problem. What's the next?"

Taylor hesitated, and Rachel wondered if he was struggling with an unwillingness to bring legal action against Percy Warwick. "You'll need to make certain the deed *was* transferred, and if so, that the land described on it is the section Percy bought. You do that by going to the Howbutker County Courthouse and checking the deed index records for a land transaction between your great-aunt and Percy Warwick around the date on his note. Then we'll talk some more."

"But if I do find that such a transaction did take place, will I have enough evidence to prove fraud?"

Again, Taylor took his time answering. "Even though Mary DuMont's name is on the deed, her brother clearly instructed that she was to hold it in trust for his son until he reached the age of twenty-one. If Mary DuMont sold the land as her own, without the formalities of court approval, then that's fraud."

"Is there a statute of limitations on fraud?" she asked, and held her breath.

"Yes, but the statute would commence from the time of the discovery of the fraudulent transaction. Where is this land along the Sabine? Is there anything on it?"

She exhaled slowly. "My guess is that Warwick Industries built a huge pulp mill and paper-processing plant on it as well as a large office complex. There's also a housing development nearby." She expected Taylor to show surprise, but his only reaction was to rotate his glass on its damp napkin. "What exactly would I be entitled to if fraud is proven?" she asked.

With an eye now slightly narrowed, Taylor replied, "If the title was improperly conveyed, as your father's heir, you would be entitled not only to the land, but to all existing improvements and buildings on it. The housing development might be an exception."

Rachel closed her eyes and clenched her hands. *Yes!* It was more than she could have hoped. For the first time in a long while, she felt a reason to live. She raised her lids to gaze directly at the lawyer. "How would you feel personally if I sued Percy Warwick for what is mine?"

Taylor frowned. "You...don't literally mean the land, do you?"

"Oh, but I do. I'm not interested in a monetary settlement."

The lawyer studied her for a long moment, then rocked back in his chair and linked fingers again over the bulge of his stomach. "Remember you asked," he warned, "so here it is. Despite your justification, I'd be very disappointed in you, Rachel. Your legal action could seriously damage the most efficiently run and economically essential operation in that part of the state, not to mention impair the final years of one of the truly great men of Texas." He paused to give her time to rebut, but when she remained calmly silent, he continued. "I know of the money you'll be inheriting, Rachel, first due to the generosity of your great-aunt and then"—he wagged his head sadly—"through the awful, untimely deaths of your father and little brother. I don't know, of course, why Percy Warwick entered into such a contract with Mary DuMont in 1935—if, in fact, he did—but I suspect he had good reason. Those were very difficult times, and it could have been that the sale of that land prevented financial disaster for your great-aunt and subsequently for her heirs, of which you are one." He picked up his glass, his eyes no longer warm and fatherly over its rim. "I believe that should answer your question. You're off the hook for lunch, by the way."

Rachel returned an undaunted stare. "We'll see," she said. "Thanks for your honesty. It satisfies me that I've come to the right man to handle my suit, if I have a case."

Taylor lowered the glass. "Say what?"

"I don't want to hurt Percy Warwick or take from his grandson *his* birthright. What would I do with a pulp mill and paper-processing plant? I want to effect a trade—my family's plantation of Somerset for Percy's industrial complex along the Sabine."

Taylor regarded her silently, then his face broke into a smile. "Ah," he said, "now *that* I believe I can stomach."

She glanced at her watch. "Which reminds me. It's past twelve. I imagine you're ready for that hamburger—on me."

He rose hastily. "Not only a hamburger, but French fries, onion rings, a malt, and a double chocolate brownie à la mode for dessert."

Rachel slung her purse over her shoulder. "And you worry about Carrie's eating habits."

Chapter Sixty-five

Rachel followed the arrow signs pointing to the county clerk's office in the Howbutker County Courthouse. It was midafternoon of the Monday following her meeting with Taylor Sutherland. She had chosen the time as the best part of the day to slip in and out of Howbutker unnoticed. It was October, but the enervating heat still hung, and few townspeople were about. Most were napping, sleeping off their lunch, or behind their shop counters, trying to keep cool. She had booked a room for the night at a motel in the next county in case she felt too tired after her mission to make the return trip to Dallas, three hours by the time she was back at Carrie's door.

Rachel had never laid eyes on the county clerk, but she was certain the clerk would recognize her. If the woman hadn't passed in one of the receiving lines during the days of the funeral, she had only to glance behind her at the hanging portrait of her great-aunt at the 1914 dedication of the courthouse to guess her identity. She wished for anonymity. Matt would come looking for her when he heard she was in town, the reason she'd exchanged her green BMW, familiar to Amos, for Carrie's black Suburban and reserved a motel room outside the county. She couldn't risk what seeing him would do to her resolve. If her suspicions proved correct, there was no hope for them anyway. She'd never feel the same for Percy, and Matt would never forgive her if she dragged his grandfather into court and exposed his complicity in committing fraud. She was sure it wouldn't come to that, but the threat alone would destroy what they'd had. She must get her business over before he or his grandfather or Amos should happen to wander in.

The middle-aged woman in a summer dress behind the counter observed her with curiosity as she approached, clearly struggling to place her gaunt face and figure. "May I help you?" she inquired, checking her left hand as she placed it on the worn pine surface.

"I'm sure you can," Rachel said. "I'd like to see the record of a warranty deed transferred to Percy Warwick from Mary Toliver DuMont in 1935. The date would be around July eighth."

The clerk's eyes brightened in recognition. She patted Rachel's hand. "Miss Toliver, on behalf of

Howbutker, please accept our deepest condolences for *all* your losses," she said, the stressed *all* plainly including her expectation of inheriting Somerset.

"Thank you. You are very kind," Rachel replied in the monotone she'd adopted to discourage further commiserations.

"Just a moment, and I'll check the grantor/grantee index for that period." In a short while, during which Rachel kept checking the entrance, she returned with a heavy-bound volume. "Page 306," she said. "If you need any help..."

"Thank you, I can manage. Page 306."

She took the volume to a table away from the clerk's prying eyes and found the answer to her search immediately. Page 306 revealed that on July 14, 1935, Mary Toliver DuMont had transferred by deed a section of land to Percy Matthew Warwick. The legal description designating the location of the land corresponded with that from Vernon Toliver's will. The attached plat map defined the layout of the section along the Sabine. It abutted the boundary of a property that Rachel recognized as Somerset.

She looked up from the book, a sour taste in her mouth, possessed by a rage that shook her in her seat. Percy...and Aunt Mary, robbers and deceivers...staying silent while the lie ate up her mother, wrecked the family peace, made it impossible for her ever to go home again. How different it all could have been if only her father had known the truth. Her parents and little brother might still be alive....

She took the open volume back to the counter and pointed to the map. "Is there a record that would show what, if anything, is built on this parcel of land?"

The clerk lifted her glasses a fraction to scrutinize the plat map through her bifocals. "The tax records would reflect that information, but I don't have to check. That's the site of a pulp mill and paper-processing plant belonging to Warwick Industries."

"You're sure?"

"I'm sure. Our house is...about there." With her finger, the clerk pointed to a spot on the map. "It's in a housing development Warwick Industries built for the workers. My husband's a foreman out there."

"Really?"

Rachel's tone provoked a sharp look. The woman withdrew her finger, clearly wondering why she was interested in her husband's place of employment with its job security, benefits, and pension plan. Was she about to tinker with all that because she no longer had a place here? "May I ask why you're interested?"

"I may have a vested interest in the place," Rachel answered, her voice sounding like ice cracking. "Would you please pull the most recent tax records on this property, and while you're at it, check the record of the date Mary Toliver DuMont became the guardian of William Toliver? She'd have applied in 1935."

"That will be in the basement, in the archives, and it will take a while."

"I'll wait."

The county clerk pulled away from the counter with a perplexed, uneasy look and disappeared behind a door. Rachel felt a spear of alarm. Just her luck that her husband would be Matt's foreman. Suppose the woman, already suspicious, relayed her inquiries to him and he notified Matt? If he was at the plant, it would take at least a half hour to drive into town. She'd give the woman twenty minutes before she hotfooted it to the Suburban.

She was on the point of leaving when the clerk reappeared. "Here's a copy of the 1984 tax statement," she said, slapping it on the counter, "and one of a court order granting your aunt's application for guardianship. Anything else?" She flicked a pointed glance at the clock over the water fountain. "It's past my break time."

Rachel cast a quick look at the date her father officially became Aunt Mary's ward: August 7, 1935. "I'm afraid I have one more request," she said. "I'd like a copy of page 306 as well as one of the plat map."

The clerk pressed her lips together. "There will be a charge," she said.

Rachel unzipped her purse. "Name it."

A tense few minutes later, the photocopies stowed safely in her purse, she made her escape, but at the exit, she glanced back. As she'd expected, the clerk had the phone receiver pressed to her ear and was reading to her listener from the deed record.

MATT, THIS IS CURT. I don't know if this is important or not, but my wife just called from the courthouse. She said that Rachel Toliver was in there a few minutes ago."

The receiver to his ear, Matt swung his chair around from the window through which he'd been staring listlessly for the better part of an hour. "What? Rachel Toliver is in town?"

"That's right. Marie said she was asking about a warranty deed."

"Is she still there?"

"Just left, according to Marie."

"Did she say where she was going?"

"No, Chief." Curt's sigh made it clear that he wondered why he'd bothered to call if Matt was interested only in Rachel Toliver. "Marie didn't find her particularly friendly. I thought you'd like to know what she was poking about in."

Matt pushed the speaker button on the phone and hung up the receiver as he rose. "I do, Curt. What was it?" He threw open a closet door and whipped his sports jacket off a hanger.

"She was in the courthouse asking about a land deed her great-aunt transferred to your grandfather way back in July of 1935," Curt said. "Seems Miss Mary sold Mister Percy a section of land around then."

Matt paused, one sleeve hanging empty. His grandfather had never mentioned buying a section from Mary. And why would that interest Rachel? "Are you sure Marie got her facts right?"

"Sure as I'm sittin' down to meatloaf tonight. It's Monday, ain't it? Marie says the girl don't look so good. Awful thin. We saw her at Miss Mary's funeral, you know. A real knockout. Marie says she don't look like the same girl."

"So I've heard," Matt said, finishing jerking on his jacket. "Did Marie say what land she was checking out?"

"Yes, she did. It's the land right here where I'm standin.'"

Matt stared unseeing out the window. "The plant site?"

"That's it. Marie was disturbed by her inquiries. Said the girl seemed...angry."

"Yes...I'm sure she is," Matt said. Good, he thought. Anger could keep you afloat. Grief would sink you—but anger against whom?

"And here's the kicker, Chief. When Marie asked why she was interested in the plant land, she said that she may have a *vested* interest in it. Now what in hell could she mean by that?"

Matt recalled Bertie Walton's terms: *inner force...objective.* And Rachel's statement to Amos: *You'll know soon enough.* "I don't know, Curt, but I'm on my way to find out."

"One other thing, Matt," Curt said. "The Toliver girl had Marie check the date the court appointed Miss Mary guardian of her dad, William Toliver. Now doesn't all that sniffing around sound ominous to you?"

Matt had his office door open, car keys in hand. "It gives you pause. Thanks, Curt, and...the less said about this the better—to anyone, understand?"

"I sure do, Chief. I've learned never to say nothing to a woman you don't want discussed on every porch swing in the county."

"Good man," Matt said.

He raced out of his office to his car, punching in Amos's office number as he sped out of the parking lot. "Susan? This is Matt Warwick. Put me through to Amos, will you?"

Amos had been pulled out of a deposition. "What's the trouble, Matt?" he asked, his voice sharp with alarm. "Is it Percy?"

"No, Amos. Sorry to scare you. It's Rachel. I was just informed she's in town. What kind of car does she drive?"

"Why, a BMW, last time I saw her. Dark green. You mean she's in town and didn't let us know?" His voice vibrated with hurt. "How did you learn she was in Howbutker?"

"Tell you later. Right now I'm on the way into town to find her."

"Matt—"

"Later, Amos," he said, cutting him off to make another call. If Dallas was her home base, it could be that Rachel had already started back. He consulted an index on his console and dialed a number. "I need to speak to Dan," he said to the dispatcher, and within seconds the sheriff of Howbutker County was on the line. Matt stated his request.

"A dark green BMW," the sheriff repeated. "I'll send some boys along I-20 to see if we can spot her and get back to you."

"If they find her, tell them to go easy with her when they pull her over," Matt instructed.

"What will be the charge?"

"I'm sure they'll think of something, but make sure they're nice about it."

Matt considered his next move. It was almost four o'clock. He hoped to high heaven that Rachel realized she was in no condition to make the drive back to Dallas this late in the day. That would put her in the middle of rush-hour traffic, the craziest in Texas, except for Houston. He dialed his office. "Nancy, call the Fairfax Hotel, the Holiday Inn, and Best Western and ask if Rachel Toliver has registered. If you come up empty, leave them my number and tell them that as soon as she registers, I want to be notified. Then let me know what you find out."

A thirty-minute zip around town turned up no sight of a dark green BMW, and his secretary called to say that the Toliver girl was not registered at any of the three numbers she'd called. At a loss what to do next and worried—why would Rachel think she had a vested interest in the plant?—Matt turned the Range Rover toward Houston Avenue to question his grandfather.

Chapter Sixty-six

Matt ran up the stairs to the upstairs study, where his grandfather seemed to spend more and more time of late. Since Mary's death and the tragic events following, he'd lost his pep. His appetite had fallen off, and he'd given up his routine exercises at the country club. He made few appearances at the office, had not toured the company's lumber sites in two months, and no longer attended the "Old Boys' Club" kaffee-klatsches every Tuesday morning at the Courthouse Café.

His state of mind and health had become a matter of anxious concern for Matt and Amos, who daily exchanged impressions of his attitude and behavior.

Percy's brows lifted in ironic surprise when his grandson strode into his study an unprecedented several hours earlier than usual, wearing what Percy dubbed his "don't mess with me" look.

"To what do I owe the pleasure?" he drawled, stretched out in his recliner before the fireplace with his feet still in house slippers. Matt saw that a luncheon tray had been brought up, the bowl of chicken noodle soup—his grandfather's favorite—congealing alongside a half-eaten ham sandwich.

He helped himself to the sandwich, realizing he'd skipped lunch. "Rachel Toliver is—was—in town," he said.

Percy lifted his head. "How do you know?"

"Curt's wife called him from the courthouse, and he passed the word on to me. I've been out looking for her car but didn't find it." The sandwich gone in two bites, Matt washed it down with Percy's glass of melted iced tea, wiped his mouth, and pulled up a chair to face him. "Marie said that Rachel was checking on a warranty deed to land that Mary DuMont sold you in 1935. Marie said she had a bee up her skirt about it."

If he'd needed reason to justify his unease, he had it now. Matt watched the color drain from his grandfather's face. "I never knew the Sabine site was built on land purchased from Mary," he said. "Now I'm wondering how Rachel knew and what's her interest in it."

Percy sighed and dropped his head against the high back of his chair. "Oh, Matt..."

"What is it, Granddad? What's going on?"

"I think we may be in trouble. I believe Rachel found the papers that Mary meant to destroy the day she died."

The knot in Matt's midsection tightened. "What papers?"

"The papers that were in the trunk Mary sent Henry to open. Remember Sassie telling us that her last words were that she had to get to the attic? Sassie must have told Rachel, too, and she figured out that something important was up there and went after it. Amos said that when he took Rachel to her room the night of the accident, he saw papers scattered on her bed...papers that had been in a green leather box that I remember belonging to Mary...."

"What was in them that would have sent Rachel to the courthouse?"

Percy held up a hand to say not to rush him. "Amos recognized one of them as the will of Vernon Toliver. In that will, Vernon left one section of land along the Sabine to his son, Miles...."

Matt scowled in confusion. "Wait a minute. You said that nothing went to Miles—that Mary inherited everything."

"I never said any such thing. Mary and I *allowed* that to be the assumption. Not that there's much distinction between the two."

Matt pulled within closer conversing distance. "So...let me get this straight. William never knew his father had inherited that section?"

"That's true."

"The information was deliberately kept from him?"

"That's true."

"By Mary?"

"Yes."

Matt felt the return of the ham sandwich. "And Rachel now knows the truth about the lie that helped to tear her family apart?"

"It appears so."

"And our plant is located on the section that Miles inherited?"

"Yes."

"How'd Mary get hold of it to sell to you?"

Percy wiped a liver-spotted hand across his face, looking his ninety years. "Well, I'm afraid the other papers in the box explain that. Amos said that he saw two letters...one in my handwriting and another he couldn't make out before Rachel whisked everything back into the box, but I can guess who it was from...."

Matt felt his stomach heave as his grandfather reached shakily for a glass of water. After a couple of long swallows, he said, "It was a letter from Miles instructing Mary to hold that land in trust for William until he reached twenty-one."

"Good God—" Matt drew back, aghast. "Are you saying that Mary went against her brother's wishes and sold the land anyway?"

Percy nodded. "That's right," he said quietly.

"She must not have shown you the letter."

"Of course she did. That's how I know its contents."

Matt stared at him, speechless. His neck grew hot.

"Granddad, you and Miss Mary *knowingly* committed *fraud*?"

"It looks like that on the surface," Percy said,
"but it was the only way out for all concerned—
Ollie, William, me, the town, and…Matthew. The
DuMonts were in dire financial straits, and Ollie
was about to lose his stores. The sweet bastard would
never have borrowed money from me, and Mary was
broke. I was in the market for waterfront property
to build the pulp mill on, so she deeded Miles's land
over to me. It appeared to be a perfectly legal transaction. Mary's name was on the deed as the new owner.
But for Miles's letter, she was entitled to do anything
with it she chose. The nefarious part comes in by the
boy never knowing he'd inherited from his father."

Matt stood up, too appalled to remain seated. Now
he knew what had been eating his grandfather alive
these past months. He'd figured out Rachel's discovery and had been waiting for the boom to go off. "Do
you have any idea what withholding that information
did to Rachel's relationship with her mother—how it
affected her family?"

"Not until you mentioned it a few months ago,
and I regret it deeply. I'm sure Mary did, too, but she
was powerless to correct the misperception after it
became a problem. By the time Alice saw Rachel as a
threat to William's inheritance, I'd built the nucleus
of Warwick Industries on that section, and Mary
had more to consider than the truth to her nephew,

especially when she considered the type of woman he married."

Mortified, Matt asked, "Why couldn't Mary have sold her precious Somerset to save Ollie's store?"

"Mary couldn't have given Somerset away in those days. Land wasn't worth a plug nickel, and I would have done anything to help Ollie. Besides being the best man I've ever known, he saved my life in France. He pushed me out of the way of a grenade. That's what cost him his leg."

Matt raked a hand through his hair and fell into his chair again. God, the things he didn't know about his family. "What did *your* letter say?"

"I wrote Mary that I agreed to the sale, but of course after fifty years, I can't remember exactly how I phrased it. But the only way Rachel could have learned the approximate date of the deed's transfer and that I was the buyer had to come from my note. By the time you'd arrived the night of the accident, she'd read the papers and put two and two together. It explains her attitude to you and further paints Mary and me as a couple of shits."

Matt hunched forward. "You mean Rachel now has letters in her possession that put the Sabine site in jeopardy? Granddad, how could you build a lumber operation now worth one hundred million dollars on land that did not have a clear title?"

Percy waved a feeble hand. "Oh, Matt, for all intents and purposes, that section was Mary's to sell and mine to buy free and clear. No muss, no fuss. How could we know the legality of the sale would be challenged? If only Mary hadn't kept those letters..."

"Why did she?" Matt demanded.

"Probably because she could not bear to part with her brother's last letter, and maybe she kept mine for... the comfort of knowing she had not acted alone in a breach of trust."

Matt felt as if his blood had pooled in his feet. "Or maybe to blackmail you later."

Percy looked at him, appalled. "Of course not! How can you think Mary capable of such a thing?"

"Why did Mary show you the letter from her brother?" Matt countered. "Why didn't she keep it to herself, rather than involve you in her deceit?"

"Because she wasn't that kind of woman!" Percy retorted, his cheekbones aflame with indignation. "She didn't want me to go into anything without my knowing what I was getting into."

"Well, wasn't that decent of her!" Matt said, matching his fury. "That way she didn't have to carry the burden of her duplicity alone."

Percy slammed down the footrest. "Hold your tongue, boy! Don't judge until you know what you're talking about. Mary showed me that letter in order to give me a chance to say no. I agreed because I didn't see I had much choice. William would have reached twenty-one with nothing left to inherit but a section of waterlogged land. He was seven at the time.

As it was, the store survived, Somerset flourished, the county enjoyed jobs that I'd have had to take elsewhere, and, as Mary promised, William became her heir." He paused to take another hasty swallow of water. "I'm not saying what we did wasn't *wrong*, but at the time doing *right* didn't seem the answer either."

Matt digested all this in shocked silence. Finally, he said, "So you and Mary struck a deal, and that's why she promised William that he'd be her heir. Then why in hell did she lead Rachel on?"

Percy let out a soulful sigh. "Because at the time of her promise to William, she didn't expect Rachel."

Matt shook his head in disbelief. "Damn, Granddad," he said softly. "Did Ollie know about Miles's letter?"

Percy glared at him. "Of course not. He'd never have gone along with the sale."

Matt said dryly, "That sounds like the man I knew. Okay, let's calm down and discuss what we think might be Rachel's intentions. If those letters do prove fraud, do you think she'll sue to get her father's land back?"

"Oh, no," Percy said quickly. "This isn't about greed. She wants returned what she believes belongs to her, and she's determined to get it, just like her great-aunt would have been. Rachel will want to trade. The Sabine site for Somerset. That's what Mary would have done."

"Well then," Matt said, drawing a relieved breath, "that solves the problem. Simply give the place back to her."

A look filtered into his eyes, and Matt—recognizing it—recoiled as if he'd caught a whiff of body odor. He bent forward. "Under *these* circumstances, you *will* give it back, won't you?"

Percy made a sound in his throat. "It won't ever come to that question when Rachel hears what I have to say. I'm convinced of it, Matthew. That's why it's important that you find her. She *must* hear the full story."

Matthew. He never called him by his namesake. A strange pain moved under his solar plexus. "Well, just for the record, if it does come to that and you refuse to meet Rachel's terms, what will you do if she decides to go after the plant?"

"That depends on whether her case is strong enough to win."

"Suppose it is?"

Percy adjusted one hip and then another in the recliner. "Don't box me in, Matt. I will do what I believe to be right, that's all I can tell you."

"I'm sure you will." Hurt seared his throat. "But I wouldn't count on Rachel forgiving and forgetting when she hears this tale of yours, Granddad. I don't believe I'd be able to forgive my birthright given away to someone else. And I could never forgive the shafting of my father—no matter what story was behind it."

The threat rang in the air between them. "I see," Percy said, raking his tongue over dry lips.

Matt felt the need to give his feelings room. He turned for the door but remembered something and swung around. "I see that Amos has released Mary's house to the Conservation Society."

"Not to my knowledge."

"He must have. A black Suburban was parked by the garage a while ago, the hatch was open, and Henry was bringing some things out."

"Oh, son, that's Rachel down there!" Percy cried. "Amos wouldn't release the house until she has a chance to take what she wants."

But he addressed an empty doorway. Matt had sprinted for the stairs.

Chapter Sixty-seven

How long has she been gone, Henry?" Matt asked.

"Maybe about thirty minutes, Mister Matt," Henry said. "She didn't let us know she was comin'. She'd have been gone long before now if Aunt Sassie hadn't stopped by. She's stayin' at my mama's right now, you know."

Matt nodded. "And she didn't give you a hint where she was going?"

"No, sir. She was pretty closemouthed about herself. Looked like she wanted to get out of Howbutker soon's possible. Can't say I blame her."

Matt expelled a sigh of consternation and dialed the number of the sheriff's department. He now had the description of the Suburban, and Henry had even thought to notice the unusual personalized license plate: SKY BEE. Smart girl, Rachel. She had thrown him off by exchanging cars with her roommate. The license plate identification should give the detective something to work with. After giving the sheriff the new information, he hung up and asked, "And you say that the only items she came by to get were the things in Mister Ollie's army trunk?"

"Yessir. Them things and some old accountin' books that have been around for the Lord knows how long. They belonged to Miss Mary's brother. She didn't want nothin' else."

Fodder to use against them in a court of law, Matt surmised. He said, "Maybe he told your aunt Sassie something?"

Henry shook his head. "She didn't tell her nothin' that I didn't hear, except...Miss Rachel told her she ain't drivin' back tonight to wherever she's goin'. Aunt Sassie was worried about that since she looked kinda tired and it was gettin' late, and we all know what happened to her folks when they tried that. But she told Aunt Sassie not to worry. She had reservations somewhere in a motel on the way back."

Matt considered. "Where's your phone book, Henry?" He'd take a stab that Rachel would stay overnight in Marshall, a town located an hour away. The phone book produced, he ran down the listings of area motels in the yellow pages and started dialing. His second attempt proved successful. A desk clerk at the Goodnight Inn in Marshall told him that, yes, they had a guest by the name of Rachel Toliver registered for the night. Matt thanked Henry and ran to his car.

*   *   *

THE EVENING CLERK AT THE Goodnight Inn in
Marshall, a retiree working to supplement his pension,
listened to Matt's request with visible discomfort. Matt
had expected Rachel to be here by now since she'd had
a half hour's start, but a knock on the door of her room
number had gone unanswered, and the sheriff's deputies had caught no sight of her, either. Matt knew that
what he was asking the man to do was against motel
policy. The company could be sued, and him personally, but he owed the Warwicks big time, and he knew
it. Years ago, Percy Warwick had saved his rebellious
teenage son from a life of crime by offering him a job
while he served out his probation. The boy went on
to college, earned a business degree, married, and was
now living the American dream in Atlanta, Georgia.
Matt could see in the man's eyes that he remembered
what he owed Percy Warwick.

Nonetheless, rules were rules, and he detected
that it went against the man's grain to break them.
He really didn't know Percy Warwick's grandson all
that well, and the motel owed some obligation to the
guest. Matt could sympathize with his dilemma, but
he was desperate.

"Mr. Colter," he said, "I wouldn't put you in this spot
if it weren't crucial that I surprise Rachel Toliver."

"Can't you do that in the lobby?"

"That would ruin the surprise. She'd know what I
was up to."

"Which is?"

Matt grinned. "Not what you think, I assure you. You have my word. I simply want to talk to her in a place that's private."

Mr. Colter looked even more uncomfortable. "And that can't be done here...in the lobby?"

"No," Matt answered emphatically.

"Well...since you've given me your word as a *Warwick*"—he emphasized the word with a pointed stare at Matt through his bifocals—"I suppose I can bend the rules this once." He handed over a key. "Room 106. It's on the ground floor to the right."

"Much obliged," Matt said.

ARRIVING A HALF HOUR LATER, Rachel had the feeling that the clerk had been on the lookout for her. He greeted her warily, and she caught him sneaking looks out of the corner of his eye as she filled in the registration form. "If you need anything—anything at all," he said, handing her the room key, "simply run outside and holler as loud as you can, and I'll come running."

Rachel listened in bewilderment. What was he expecting her to find? Scorpions in the bathtub?

She drove around to her unit, realizing how tired she was. The drive out to Somerset had sapped her strength, but it had accomplished what she'd hoped. The sight of the plantation again—and the insolent rise of the pulp mill's smokestacks above the cypress trees—had steeled her determination to get Somerset back. Earlier, she'd asked herself, Why bother with the fight? Why return to Howbutker to live? In spite of its civic pride and history, its serenity and order, the infusion of new blood and money, Howbutker was still an insular, class-conscious town. White-man rule arguably still reigned. She was a rich woman now, young and modern and progressive. Why not take the money and go, start the Toliver tradition all over again like her South Carolina forebears?

Because she *belonged* here, she answered herself. And the even rows of lush fall crops stretching to the horizon convinced her she could never abandon the land of her family's blood and sweat and toil and...sacrifices. She could never relinquish her own children's legacy. To do so would be the biggest betrayal of all, making her own betrayal worthless—all for nothing. The fields looked healthy and well tended. Henry had said that Aunt Mary's land manager was still in charge. "But after this year...who knows what's in store for the plantation?"

Staring off across the fields in the late afternoon sun, she'd smiled ruthlessly. She knew.

The key turned smoothly, and she opened the door to a room filled with dusk, the air conditioner unit humming. Before she could grope for the light, a familiar voice spoke from a corner. "Hello, Rachel."

Chapter Sixty-eight

Percy sat by the phone in his study, pondering. The hurt he'd heard in Matt's voice when he'd called to say that he was in a motel room in Marshall waiting for Rachel to check in still lingered in his ear. He should never have left the boy in doubt as to who would come first if he was backed against a wall. He had simply believed he would not be forced to make an either/or decision. With typical confidence—or arrogance—he'd been certain that once Rachel heard him out, he'd be able to honor Mary's trust in him and keep Rachel's birthright from her while not sacrificing Matt's.

Now, though, he had cause to wonder what that revelation might cost him. Matt's threat—*I could never forgive the shafting of my father, no matter what story was behind it*—ricocheted like a gunshot in his mind. Was the risk of Matt's love and respect—his forgiveness—worth the salvation of Rachel's feeling for Mary? He couldn't relate Mary's story without confessing his own, and what would he have accomplished if this new discovery of Rachel's made it impossible for her to forgive Mary, anyway? What if—no matter what his story—there was no hope for her and the grandson of the man who'd defrauded her father? Would baring the consequences he and Mary had brought about—the people they'd hurt, the lives they'd altered, and all because of Somerset—do anything but damage him further in his grandson's eyes? Did he have the courage to take that chance? He looked up at the painting over the mantel. *Would you want me to leave this earth with your son's image of me in shambles?*

He rubbed his hands over his days-old beard. *Oh, God, Mary, what a pickle you've placed us in.* If Matt succeeded in bringing Rachel here tonight, what would he tell her, after all?

MATT ROSE FROM HIS CHAIR slowly, his expression briefly betraying his shock at her changed appearance. Unconsciously, Rachel pulled down one leg of her khaki walking shorts. "How did you get in here?" she demanded.

Matt held up the object responsible. "With a key."

Her lip rose in disgust. "Oh, I see. The desk clerk."

"I called in a Warwick favor. I'm not proud of myself, but I'm a driven man."

She set down her bag and held the door against the

wall while she shoved a doorstop under it with her foot, her heart in her throat. He looked wonderful, as dear as she remembered. She must give herself an escape route from this man who could throw her off course. "How did you know where to find me?"

"I let my fingers do the walking. Henry told me you'd made overnight reservations somewhere on the way back. I figured you'd be headed to Dallas and that a logical stopping point would be a motel in Marshall."

"Clever you."

"Cleverer you," Matt said. "Reserving a room out of the county and exchanging vehicles were smart moves. They threw me off."

"I want you to leave."

"I'll be more than happy to, if you'll come with me. Granddad's dying—literally—to talk to you."

She'd been afraid of that. Despite her bitterness, she felt a deep lance of concern. "I'm sorry, Matt, I really am, but I'm not going anywhere with you."

"Well, then, let's talk, Rachel...like we used to." He gestured toward the chair, inviting her to sit down.

"You make it sound as if we've had a long association."

"We have, and you know it. Too long and special to throw away. Don't you agree that what we had together is at least worth a little conversation?"

Rachel hesitated, swallowing at the dryness in her

throat, feeling light-headed from the rapid pump of her blood. She set her purse on the table between them and reluctantly pulled out a chair. Perhaps this meeting was a good idea. She'd show Matt her hand so that he could advise his grandfather of the cards she held. They might come to an agreement this very night. "Talk can't save us, Matt," she said. "I'm assuming the county clerk called your foreman, and you know where I've been—the records I found."

Matt took his chair again, drew open his sport jacket, and crossed his legs in a way that suggested he'd won a small victory. "I've been so informed. Don't you want to close the door? We're losing our air-conditioning."

Rachel glanced at the wide-open door, remembering the offer of assistance from the little gray-haired man at the registration desk. What a joke if he thought he was a match for Matt Warwick. She'd have preferred scorpions in the shower. Ignoring his request, she unzipped her purse and removed copies of the letters found in the green box. "I found these among Aunt Mary's personal papers, along with her father's will," she said, slipping them across the table. "It seems that he *did* leave a section of Somerset to his son, Miles. Since you're aware of my findings at the courthouse, you'll recognize their implications. Read the longer letter first."

She watched for signs of shocked dismay as he read, but he maintained a poker face, a trick she attributed to years of negotiating contracts for Warwick Industries. But he didn't fool her. She caught the small jump of muscle along his jawline. "You know, of course, that the section to which your grandfather refers is the one on which he built his pulp mill—the section he and Aunt Mary *stole* from my father."

Matt refolded the letters thoughtfully. "It would certainly seem that way, wouldn't it? That's why it's important that you come hear what Granddad has to say. He can explain why at the time they thought their action justified—"

"*Justified?*" Rachel clutched her throat as if the word were choking her. "You *know* what that deception did to my family, Matt, the years I lost with them...."

"Yes, but Granddad didn't until I told him two months ago. That knowledge, along with the animosity he knew you must be feeling toward him and Mary, has been tearing him apart."

"Well, so be it," she said, refusing to be moved. "Wait a minute—" An astonishing notion occurred to her. "You talk as if your grandfather *knows* of this evidence."

Matt's face betrayed the first glimmer of despair. "When Granddad learned from Amos that he'd seen Vernon Toliver's will on your bed and two letters, one of them written in his handwriting, he figured out, as you did, that they were the reason Mary was babbling to get to the attic when she was dying. He remembered the note he'd written and guessed that the other letter belonged to Miles."

"So he *was* aware of what Miles's letter contained?"

Matt toyed with the edges of the paper, obviously reluctant to answer for fear of implicating his grandfather further.

"I'll take that as a *yes*," she said. She dropped back against the chair. "There's no doubt, then. He *knew* he was committing fraud by buying that land."

Matt set his elbows on his knees and bent forward. "Rachel, a depression was on in 1935. Granddad says that if he hadn't bought those acres, the DuMonts would have probably lost everything, including Somerset. The sale was contingent on Mary naming your father as her heir—"

"To make up for the swindle," Rachel interrupted.

Matt looked uncomfortable. "Well, maybe…but he assures me that once you hear the full story from him, you'll understand everything."

"So I can fall victim to his charming spin as you apparently have?" she said. "Your grandfather's reason for buying those acres may have been noble, but it was self-serving, too. He needed a site to establish a pulp mill. They were convenient and cheap. If you knew anything about the history of the founders of Howbutker, you'd know that the families *never* borrowed from each other. If Uncle Ollie had been in trouble, no way would he have allowed your grandfather to bail him out."

"He didn't know those acres weren't Aunt Mary's to sell."

"But he had to have known the money came from somewhere. Who else but his wealthy friend?"

She read defeat in Matt's stumped silence, the dull frustration in his eyes. "Okay," he said. "What do you want?"

"An even trade. He keeps the pulp mill, and I get Somerset. The originals of these letters get destroyed. If he doesn't accept those terms, then I'm going after my father's land. I've already contacted a lawyer specializing in fraud litigation. Taylor Sutherland. You may have heard of him."

A range of emotions—anger, despair, disbelief—swept Matt's face. "You would take my grandfather to court at his age, risk endangering his health, destroy his good name?"

"That will be up to him. I sincerely hope it doesn't come to that."

"And you'd throw away any chance for us?"

"My great-aunt and your grandfather threw away any chance for us, Matt." She pushed the letters toward him and stood, signaling their meeting was over. "I'm sure when he reads those, he'll want to do the right thing for all concerned."

"Why?" Matt asked quietly, remaining seated, a frown of incomprehension drawing his brows together.

"Why what?"

"Why is Somerset so important to you that you'd

destroy what we could have—what may never come again for either of us—certainly not to me."

She heard the heartbreak in his voice, an echo of her own, but she forced herself to confront the hurt in his gaze. "Because it's my duty to keep it in Toliver hands. I will not see it slip away at the expense of salvaging a dead woman's conscience."

"It was hers to leave to whom she wished, Rachel."

"No, it was hers to keep and hold for the next generation of Tolivers. Your grandfather stands to lose nothing—only to keep what he has and the reason to call Howbutker home. I want the same for me, since..." Her voice faltered and her chin trembled. "I have nowhere else to go, no other place to call home."

"Rachel, honey..."

He was out of his chair before she could move, his arms suddenly around her, holding her fast against his thundering chest. "I can give you a home," he said gruffly. "I can be the reason you call Howbutker home."

She set her jaw against the urge to cry and gave herself a moment before she wriggled her head free from beneath his chin. "You know that's not possible, Matt. Not now. Can you imagine how I would feel seeing the plant puffing away on land your grandfather stole from my dad? The irony is"—she stared into his eyes like one seeing the last of the supply ships pull away—"if Aunt Mary had left things as they were—if she hadn't interfered—we could have been together."

"Rachel...my love." His embrace tightened. "Don't do this to us. Somerset is only a piece of land."

"It's the family *farm*, Matt, the legacy of generations of Tolivers. It's the soil of our history. To lose it...to see it in the hands of anyone not of my blood...I couldn't bear it. How can you ask me not to fight for the only connection I have now to my family?"

He dropped his arms. "So that's the way it is."

She turned toward the table and wrote a number on the motel notepad. "This is my number in Dallas. Your grandfather can reach me there, if I don't hear from him tonight. Tell him he has until the end of the week to agree to my terms. Otherwise, Monday morning I give Taylor Sutherland the go-ahead to file suit."

"You realize you'll be forcing Granddad to betray Mary's trust. How can he ever live with that?"

"The same way he's learned to live with the betrayal of mine."

"Answer me this, Rachel," Matt said, taking the note. "If Mary had remembered you as you'd expected, would you still regret reneging on your promise to your mother—and sacrificing all the years you could have had with your family?"

The question rocked her. She had not thought to ask it of herself, perhaps never would have. He deserved the truth. It would make it easier for him to forget her. "No," she said.

He inserted the notepaper and letters into the breast pocket of his jacket. "Well, I guess that makes you a Toliver after all. We'll be in touch," he said, and strode through the open door without looking back.

Chapter Sixty-nine

In the kitchen of his bachelor domicile—an elegant six-room apartment set atop a row of shops that faced the town circle—Amos studied the contents of his pantry for something effortless to prepare for supper. He was hungry, but too dispirited to go to the trouble of making a meal, and if he went out, he might miss a call from Matt or Percy or—dared he hope?—Rachel. All afternoon, he'd waited to hear from one of them, hoping to learn what she was doing in Howbutker. There was certainly nothing here for her anymore except, of course, those who loved her, but it looked as if she wanted nothing to do with them.

Bran flakes, he decided, taking down a bowl. Lord, he was depressed! Not since Claudia, Matt's mother, had died had he felt this low. He could guess what *she* would have thought of this mess. As he'd predicted, the fallout from that damn codicil had been ruinous for everyone concerned—Rachel most of all, of course, but his main worry was Percy. He'd never seen a man go down so fast. Always faultlessly groomed, confident, energetic—he now looked like a patient on bed rest and chicken broth. He had expected him to grow old, but not *shrivel*—not Percy Warwick, business magnate, prince among men, his hero.

The buzz of the apartment's intercom cut sharply into his gray thoughts. His heart jumped. *Rachel!* He set down the milk carton and hurried to speak hopefully into the grid. "Yes?"

"Amos, it's me. Matt."

"Matt!" Thank God *somebody* was checking in. He pushed the button to unlock the street-level door. "Come on up."

He stepped out onto the landing expecting to see Rachel behind Matt's broad shoulders, but that hope dived like a rent kite as Matt alone stepped through the security door, his look auguring nothing good. "You didn't find her," he said as Matt started up.

"Oh, I found her all right."

"She spat in your face."

"Might as well have. Got a beer?"

"An unlimited supply. Come on in."

Amos led his guest into a small living room with French doors opening to a terrace that overlooked the trim acres of the city park. It was his favorite spot. "If you don't think it's too warm for the terrace, I'll bring a couple out there," he said.

He heard the French doors open as he went into

the kitchen, returned the milk to the refrigerator, and tore two cans out of their paper packaging. An ominous chill rippled along his skin. He sniffed bad news like the threat of a storm.

"Where did you find her?" he asked as he joined Matt and handed him a can of beer inserted into a foam holder. Matt had not sat down. Amos could almost feel the heat of suppressed emotion keeping him on his feet, but also a cold control, reminding him somehow of Matt's rugged Marine Corps father, whom he'd known only through Claudia.

"At a motel in Marshall. She knew I'd find her if she booked a room in Howbutker. It was just by luck that I learned her whereabouts from Henry. She'll be leaving for Dallas in the morning. Don't take it personally that she didn't contact you, Amos. She wasn't here on a social call."

"What, then?" he asked, choosing to sit down.

Matt took a strong pull of the beer, set it down, and removed his jacket. He draped it over the back of a fat striped lounger and took two letters from his pocket. "Are you familiar with the name Miles Toliver?"

Amos nodded. "Mary's brother. William's father. He died in France when William was about six, leaving the boy orphaned. That's why he became Mary's ward."

"You know your Toliver history well. I wish I had before today, but let me tell you a tale I'll bet you don't know."

Amos listened in silence, his jaw slack, the beer turning to sour mash in his stomach. When Matt had finished and he'd read the copies of Miles's and Percy's correspondence, all he could manage to say was, "What arrogance, what *conceit,* to believe I've ever known anything about the Tolivers, Warwicks, and DuMonts of Howbutker, Texas. What does Rachel intend to do with this information?"

"Sue Granddad for land fraud, if he doesn't meet her terms."

Amos whipped off his glasses. "You can't be serious. And her terms are...?"

"She wants Granddad to trade Somerset for the land he *stole* from her—her word."

"Oh, dear." Amos closed his eyes and massaged the depressions in his nose where his glasses had sat. In light of the child's appalling discoveries, how could she do anything else? "Will Percy be willing to do that?" he asked.

"I...don't know. He said he'd do the right thing, whatever that is. I'm here to ask if we're in trouble—if Rachel's boat has a chance of floating."

Amos handed back the letters. "If it doesn't entail returning Somerset, your grandfather may not have the choice of doing the right thing. Those letters pose a credible threat to the property in question. So, yes, I'd say that you're in trouble and up against more like a frigate with a full sail."

Matt reached for his jacket. "Let's go see Granddad, Amos. He needs to hear that from the only man who can convince him."

But will he listen? Amos wondered, getting to his feet despite the heaviness of his doubts.

IN THE LIBRARY, WHERE HE'D been waiting for Matt and Rachel, Percy returned the receiver to its cradle, crestfallen. "Rachel won't be coming, Granddad," Matt had telephoned to inform him. "She has her own interpretation of the facts, and no amount of artful persuasion will budge her from it. She wants Somerset back, and she may have the leverage to get it. Amos and I are on the way now to discuss options with you."

"How...is she?" he'd asked.

"Feeling betrayed, deceived, lied to, kicked in the gut, definitely not kindly disposed to the Warwicks— or the memory of her great-aunt."

"What a terrible injustice to Mary," Percy had murmured.

"You'll have to convince me of that, Granddad."

"I intend to."

Sighing, Percy worked himself out of his chair on trembling legs, his earlier hopes evaporated. He did not feel well. A thin film of perspiration stood on his forehead, and his loafers felt as if there were weights in them, not a good sign. He shuffled to the intercom and pushed the ON button. "Savannah, there's been a change of plans," he rasped into the speaker. "I'm afraid we won't be entertaining our special guest after all, but your good meal won't go to waste. Matt and Amos are on the way, and they'll make short shrift of your efforts. Leave everything warming and we'll serve ourselves."

"The appetizers, too?"

"Send them upstairs. The boys'll need sustenance. And a bucket of ice and a bottle of my best Scotch," he added.

"Mister Percy, you don't sound so good."

"I'm not good. Put Grady on. I have one further request."

In the hallway, he bypassed the staircase, which at the moment looked an Everest beyond his strength, and took the elevator, which he rarely used, but tonight he must conserve himself for what he had to do. At his age, and feeling as he did, tomorrow might be too late. If Rachel refused to hear his story in person, he'd set the record straight another way—and in the presence of Amos and his grandson, who—no matter what it cost him—were entitled to the truth.

MATT, WITH AMOS FOLLOWING IN his car, arrived ten minutes later. He smelled something delicious drifting from the kitchen and saw the flowers and prettily set table and felt sick to his soul. The feast was laid, but Rachel would not partake. What a tragic and unnecessary waste. He'd feebly believed that, given time, he'd get over her, but even now that she'd shown him where her heart lay, he knew he wouldn't. She was a string of the girl he remembered, brown as river rock, all angles and sharp edges, but she had taken his breath away when she'd stepped into that motel room, and he'd have given everything he possessed in that moment to sweep her up and carry her away to some...bower to love all the hurt and pain away. His grandfather had warned him, and he wished he'd listened, but there it was. She was the woman he wanted in his life for the rest of his days. After her, there would be no one else. A wife, maybe, but no other woman.

He entered the sitting room to find his grandfather returned to his old impeccable form, but his sick pallor shook Matt to the center of his being. "Granddad, how are you feeling?"

"Up to what I've got planned for the evening. Take a seat, fellows. Amos, will you do the honors?" He gestured toward the bottle of Scotch set beside a sterling silver ice bucket on the bar.

"Gladly," Amos said, sharing a look of grieving concern with Matt.

Matt sank in his usual wingback. The ghosts from the past were galloping this evening. He suddenly longed for his mother, for the father he never knew. He had never felt so lonely in all his life. The seat of his chair was frayed, he noticed, provoking even more acutely the memory of his gentle, soft-spoken mother. She had decorated this room. The blues and creams and greens, the occasional bright burgundies, all faded now, had been her choices. He could remember a discussion at the breakfast table about wallpaper, his grandfather saying, "I'll like whatever you decide upon, Claudia. You could not possibly disappoint me."

Apparently, she had not. Not even a lamp shade had been changed in twenty-five years. Only the painting over the mantel had not been her selection. It was his father's, brought by a marine buddy from overseas after his death.

"Isn't it time this room was redone, Granddad?" he asked. "It's beginning to look a little threadbare."

"So is the time I have left," Percy said, declining a drink with a motion of his finger. "I'll leave it to you to do something about."

"Start with that," Amos said wryly, nodding toward the painting.

Percy gave him a twisted smile. "Can you not make out the subject, Amos?"

"Frankly, no. If you'll forgive my saying so, its quality has not inspired a close look."

"Well, give it a close look, and tell me what you see."

Amos unwound himself from the wingback and drew close to examine the artist's attempt at an impressionistic setting. Matt, too, craned his neck around. What was his grandfather getting at? The painting had hung there so many years, it had become invisible to him. Other than the sentiment attached, it held no artistic value to him whatsoever.

"Why, I see a small boy running toward a garden gate...," Amos mused.

"What's in his arms?"

"It looks as if they're...flowers."

"What kind?"

Amos turned to Percy, his face brightening in surprised recognition. "Why...they're white roses."

"My son Wyatt had that painting delivered to me posthumously. Not a very good one, I grant you, but its message means the world to me."

Matt knew something was coming. He caught the emotion in his grandfather's voice, the soft shine of tears in his eyes. A pit opened in his stomach. "What message, Granddad?"

"A message of forgiveness. Did you ever know about the legend of the roses, son?"

"If I did, I've forgotten."

"Tell him, Amos."

Amos explained, his Adam's apple bobbing, its tendency when he was feeling deep emotion, Matt was aware. The history lesson completed, he said, "So my dad was saying he forgave you. For what?"

"For not loving him."

Matt slowly straightened in his chair. "What are you talking about? You were crazy about my father."

"Yes, yes, I was," Percy said, "but that was many years after he came into the world—and past the time when it mattered. You see, I had two sons. One I loved from the beginning. The other—your father—I did not."

Both men gaped at him, their glasses held motionless. "*Two* sons?" Amos croaked. "What happened to the first?"

"He died at age sixteen of influenza. Wyatt lies beside him now. There's a picture of him on my bedside table. Mary mailed it to me the day she died."

"But—but—that's Matthew DuMont," Matt sputtered.

"Yes, son. Your namesake. Matthew was Mary's and my child."

Shocked silence met this calm revelation, broken by Grady's tentative knock and Percy's, "Come in." He tiptoed in as if entering a sickroom and set down a tray wafting a savory smell. On it was a plate of appetizers and a tape recorder. When he had departed, Percy turned to his still thunderstruck audience, Matt looking as if hell had opened up, Amos as if the heavens had parted. "Better eat up, fellows, before Savannah's cheese puffs get cold," he said. "It's going to be a long night."

"Granddad," Matt said finally, "I think it's time we heard your story."

"And I think it's time I told it," Percy said, and punched on the tape recorder.

Chapter Seventy

Up the street from Warwick Hall, next to the Toliver mansion, Hannah Barweise sat rocking on her verandah, in the grip of a quandary. Percy Warwick was failing, and now the question was whether she should inform Lucy to be prepared for the worst. Her friend would never admit it, but it was plain as the freckles on Doris Day's face that she was still in love with her husband.

Should she tell Lucy of the latest developments that may have sent Percy over the edge? The first began around noon when she'd spotted the Toliver girl go into Mary's house. She'd stayed long enough for Henry to carry some boxes out to her car, then left. She hadn't been gone any time before Matt had come careening up the street like a madman, screeching into Mary's drive. Not long afterward, he'd come tearing out as if he had a plane to catch.

As a past president of the Conservation Society,

she'd considered it her duty to question Henry in regard to Rachel Toliver's visit. The society had received no instruction from her concerning what to do with Mary's possessions. Without Sassie around to curb his tongue, he'd told her plenty. First, Rachel had taken only a few antiquated ledgers and the items from a trunk in the attic. She'd wanted nothing else of Mary's. That told Hannah what the girl now thought of her great-aunt, and who could blame her, considering the bomb she'd tossed in her lap?

Next, she'd gotten out of him that Matt had taken off after Rachel on a hunch that she was holed up in a motel outside Howbutker. How she'd have liked to be a mouse under the bed for *that* reunion. It was no secret around town that before everything blew up in Rachel's face, she and Matt had been a hot item. She was guessing he'd found her and she was the special guest expected for dinner, based on a conversation she'd listened in on between her housekeeper and Savannah, the Warwicks' cook, a little while ago.

Savannah had called to wail that after all her hard work, the girl wasn't coming and that Percy was terribly disappointed. Hannah would bet two to one that he'd hoped to redeem himself with Rachel and salvage a chance for her and his grandson to get back together. Matt and Amos were down there now, Amos looking longer in the face than usual and Matt not much better. According to Savannah, they were all three closeted in Percy's study drinking Scotch while the chicken Florentine dried out in the oven.

It was Savannah's contention that Percy couldn't take much more and that it was only a matter of time before he succumbed to the inevitable. It would break Lucy's heart to hear it, but Hannah had promised to inform her of news that affected her family. If worse came to worst, she would want to be there for Matt. On that note, Hannah left her rocker and went inside to make the call.

LUCY HUNG UP THE PHONE and rang for Betty.

"Yes, ma'am?"

"Forget the dessert and coffee tonight, Betty. Bring the brandy."

"Somethin' wrong?"

"There most certainly is. My husband is dying."

"Oh, Miss Lucy!"

"How *could* he?" Lucy thumped the floor with her cane. "How *could* he?" Thump. Thump. Thump.

"But, Miss Lucy!" Betty stared at her mistress in astonishment. "Maybe he don't have no say about it."

"Yes, he does! He doesn't have to give up the will to live because of that woman."

"What woman?"

Lucy caught herself. She pulled up her shoulders, neutralized the cane. "The brandy, Betty. Immediately."

"Comin' right up."

Lucy dragged in a deep breath. Her heart was thrashing like a caged wild bird, but Lord, when had it not when it came to Percy? She was beginning to dread these calls from Hannah, but at the same time she was grateful for the information. Hannah hadn't a clue how to put the pieces together, thank God, but Lucy did. Hannah relayed, and she assembled. From the tidbits she'd sent on through the years, assisted by the unwitting Savannah and the information she could pump from Matt, Lucy had had a clear picture of the happenings at Warwick Hall.

And what was happening now was that Percy was allowing Mary to rob him from the grave of the life he had left. That damn plantation would be the ruin of the Warwicks yet! How *dared* that woman leave Somerset to Percy and transfer its curse along with it? Because that's what it was—an evil that destroyed anyone who possessed it. What *was* Mary thinking to put Percy in such a spot? Hadn't she realized the split it would cause? That was the grief cratering Percy. He'd hoped to see Matt and Rachel married, picking up where he and Mary had left off, making good on what they had let slip through their fingers. The only way that could happen now was for him to restore Somerset to Rachel, which had as much chance of transpiring as worms sprouting legs.

And, of course, Mary had counted on him to abide by her trust, God send her soul to hell.

But Lucy was puzzled. Mary may have been bull-headed, but she was never irrational. Why not sell the plantation along with her other farms? Why burden Percy with it? Why sell her holdings at all and leave the house to the Conservation Society? Why would she *disenfranchise* the heir she'd primed to carry on the legacy she'd sacrificed so much to preserve?

Betty placed a snifter of brandy beside her. "Miss Lucy, you starin' like you seein' the second comin'," she said.

"Almost, Betty…almost," Lucy whispered, awe-struck. An amazing notion had shot into her head, as if straight from the mouth of God, and before she'd had a sip of brandy, too. *Why, Mary Toliver, you sly old bitch, you. Now I know why you did it. You saved Rachel from becoming you. You saw where she was headed and deprived her of the means to get there. For once in your life, you loved someone more than that bloodsucking plantation. Well, I'll be a horse's patootie.*

But, as usual, Mary had shown up too late with too little, typical of her eleventh-hour timing through-out her life. Matt had said she'd died within hours of delivering the codicil to Amos's office, apparently before she had an opportunity to clear her skirts with Rachel. Now her good intentions had blown up in everybody's face like a misdirected bomb. Rachel now loathed her, she and Matt had split, and Percy was slowly expiring from the rock and a hard place where Mary had left him. Once again, she'd stuck it to him, and now her clone—unless somebody shook some sense into her—was sticking it to Matt, too.

Lucy picked up the snifter, her fury smoldering. Damn if she hadn't seen this coming, ever since Hannah reported the first summer visit of Mary's greatniece to Howbutker. Hannah, who had known Mary all her life, described the child as having the same "witch black hair, shade of foreign-looking eyes, gypsy complexion, and hole in the middle of her chin" as her nemesis.

"In other words, she's beautiful, isn't she?" Lucy had asked.

"I'm afraid so," Hannah had admitted, "and looking so much like Mary at her age that I had to pinch myself to make sure we weren't back in elementary school."

It was then that Lucy had considered the irony of Matt and Rachel one day enacting the Mary Toliver–Percy Warwick saga all over again. She'd held her breath and crossed her fingers. For how could she be happy for Matt in love with an heir to the throne who suffered the same dysfunctional attachment to it as its present owner? How could she embrace a granddaughter-in-law cast in the same mold as the woman she detested?

She'd breathed easier when their first reported meeting—at Ollie's funeral—didn't take, but when years passed and neither married, she'd had a terrible feeling that it was only a matter of time before the inevitable happened. And it did. Within days of Rachel returning to attend Mary's funeral, Matt had called to say that he'd met the girl he hoped to marry.

"You're sure of that?"

"I'm sure of it, Gabby. I've never been as sure of anything in my whole life as I am of her and me. I've never been this happy. Hell, I don't think I've ever *been* happy, not if it feels like this. I know you and Mary had your differences, but you're going to like *this* Toliver."

So she'd sucked in her breath and said, "Well, then, get the ring on her finger, Matt, before your grandfather and I become too old to chase babies."

A week later, it was over. As her great-aunt had Percy, Rachel had dumped Matt over that miserable plantation. She'd spared him the sops grandmothers usually give to grandchildren who are casualties of love. She hadn't told him he'd get over Rachel, that time would heal, and that there were other girls in the chorus line. Like his grandfather, he'd found—and lost—his one and only love.

But God save the boy from the rebound mistake Percy had made in his marriage.

The brandy was warming her bloodstream, softening her rage to sadness. Never before had she felt so completely separated from her former home and those she loved. If only she could meet with the girl, she'd set her down and give her an earful of the truth about her great-aunt and that plantation ... truth that would set her free to love and marry Matt. But what could *she* do from her golden cage here in her self-imposed exile?

Chapter Seventy-one

*You came into our lives when our stories were done…
and we were living with their consequences,* Mary had
said, and Amos now understood her meaning. Percy's
story was over. A heavy silence hung at its conclusion,
breached by the mellow tone of the clock on the mantel announcing the time as nine o'clock. Two hours
had passed. The ice bucket stood sweating on the bar
with the bottle of single-malt Scotch beside it still full
except for the two drinks poured earlier, the tray of
appetizers, long grown cold, barely touched.

Percy had related his and Mary's pasts in the calm,
flat voice of a prisoner in the dock, apparently leaving
out no event, consequence, or effect resulting from
the day that had started it all—the day that Mary,
at sixteen, had inherited Somerset. Amos saw Matt's
face reflect the gamut of his own profound feelings
during the narration, the greatest drop of his heart
coming with the unthinkable implication of Ollie's
war injury. Matt's appeared to have occurred when

he heard of the beating in the woods. If nothing else came of the story, now they knew that Matthew was more than a name on a time-bleached headstone, Lucy more than a harridan who had left her husband in a fit of menopause, Wyatt more than the rebellious son who had turned his back on his father's hopes and expectations. Now they knew why Mary had bequeathed Somerset to Percy.

Percy pushed off the tape recorder, its sharp click like THE END at the conclusion of a long novel. Amos unkinked his legs. "So that's the story Mary meant to relate to Rachel?"

"That's the story." Percy glanced across at his grandson, who sat with closed eyes, templed fingers pressed to his lips, a silver streak down each side of his face. "What's going on in that head—rather, that heart of yours, Matt?" he asked huskily.

"Too much to express," he said.

"Are you going to be all right?"

"I'll be all right, Granddad. I'm just...sad. My father was quite a man, wasn't he."

"Yes, he was. The best."

"Are you going to divorce Gabby?"

"Of course not."

"She still loves you, you know."

"I know."

Matt cleared his throat, wiped his eyes, and gave his grandfather a little salute—all he could manage for the moment, Amos thought, and Percy turned to him. "And you, old friend, what are your thoughts?"

He roused himself. He removed his glasses, flapped a handkerchief from his suit pocket, and began to polish them assiduously. "Oh, Lord, where to start?" He'd been thinking of Mary—sensuous, beautiful Mary—and her life after Percy. How had she endured her celibacy? How had she borne her faithfulness to Ollie, exemplary man that he was? How had she lived with the knowledge that Matthew died without ever knowing Percy was his father? "I suppose," he said, restoring his glasses, "that I'm thinking foremost of the curse Mary mentioned in my office the last day of her life. I thought she'd lost her mind because"—his brief smile mocked himself—"as the *absolute* authority on the founding families, I had never heard of a Toliver curse. The answer to the mystery was there all along in *Roses*—revealed in the genealogy chart. I didn't connect the paucity of offspring to the inability of the reigning Toliver to procreate."

Percy maneuvered out of his chair and collected their glasses. Regardless of his future fate, he seemed reenergized to Amos, like an old fire engine with its pipes cleaned. "Not only to procreate, but to keep the children alive," Percy said. "Mary pooh-poohed the curse until her own experience made a believer out of her."

Amos rubbed a hand over his face at the wonder of

it. "And Mary convinced herself that the only way to save Rachel from her childless fate was to sell and give away everything remotely connected with the Toliver legacy."

"I'm convinced of it."

Matt reached inside his coat pocket. "Well, I'm afraid Mary's plan may not have succeeded. I believe you know what these are, Granddad." He handed Rachel's copies to Percy as he took his drink. "As you guessed, Rachel's not interested in restitution of her father's property. She wants to trade it for Somerset. You have a week to give her your decision, then she plans to file suit against you for fraud."

"I'm sure Mary never dreamed your letter would come back to haunt you, Percy," Amos said as kindly as his view of Mary's foolishness would permit.

Percy took the letters to his seat and perused them quickly. "I'm afraid she did. That's why she wanted to destroy it along with the others. How damaging are they, Amos?"

Amos pulled a sorrowful face. "I'll have to study the situation more deeply, but for the moment, they appear very damaging."

Percy directed his next question to Matt. "And you believe there's no chance of Rachel sitting down with me and listening to the story I've just told?"

"I'm afraid so, sir. She's convinced of her version of the story and wants Somerset too badly to hear yours."

"Even though she cares for you?"

"She cares more for Somerset."

Percy's "Ah..." carried a world of understanding. He turned his attention to Amos again. "Cannot the simple truth be the best defense against these?" He tapped the letters. "Records will show that the sale of that land secured William's financial future." As Amos made to reply, Percy held up a finger to say he had one more point. "Also...let's not forget that William elected to run away at an early age from his responsibilities to his family's business and never returned. As a result of my purchase, he inherited a fortune, as did Rachel. So I ask, Where are the damages? I'd think a court would be hard-pressed to award any to Rachel based on Mary's disregard of her brother's wishes."

Amos stirred uncomfortably in his seat, wondering if Percy had forgotten the damages done to the Kermit Tolivers resulting from the belief that William's father was left out of Vernon Toliver's will. If Rachel's lawyers brought that up—and they would—that particular argument would be dead in the water. Percy had made some valid points, but they could be challenged.

"What you've said makes for a good defense, Percy," he said, his tone holding a large "however." "What strengthens it is that the court could look upon Rachel going after her father's land as greedy, given the generous dispensation of her great-aunt's estate...."

"But?" queried Matt.

"But her lawyers will argue that at the time of the sale, Mary was acting solely on behalf of her husband, not William. She was ensuring the present, not the future. That William later inherited the fruits your beneficence made possible will be argued as irrelevant to the issue. It will have no bearing on the way they'll present the sale. Mary knowingly sold property not hers to sell, and you knowingly bought it...a simple case of fraud. They'll explain away Mary's generous remembrance of William in her will as compensation for stealing his property. The fact that it came so late in his life—when he and his family were living in extremely modest circumstances and did not live to enjoy it—will not help your case either. That's the kind of fact trial lawyers like to milk for every drop of emotional appeal."

Matt coughed and looked pained. "Let me stick one more pin into your defense, Granddad. Your point that William ran away from his obligations can be offset by the fact that his daughter did return and assume her responsibilities as Mary's likely heir."

Amos nodded his approval of this observation and further pricked Percy's balloon. "And there would be the question of why you simply didn't *give* the money to Mary and Ollie rather than enter into an illicit transaction."

"Well, that's simple," Percy said with a confident wave of his hand. "I'll explain the rule the three families lived by. You know it, Amos. Ollie would have let his creditor take the store before he'd take a cent from me."

"Which the court will view as no less ignominious than taking money from the illegal sale of a seven-year-old boy's property."

"Ollie didn't know it was an illegal transaction."

"But you and Mary did."

Percy's shoulders sagged slightly. "Are you saying we're cooked in the squat, Amos?"

"There is little leavening power in your arguments, I'm sorry to say." Amos pushed a hand over his bald scalp in frustration. "What are you hoping for, Percy? What do you want?"

Percy settled back, his fine old chiseled features warmed by the depth of his feeling. "I want to hold on to Somerset without forfeiting the Sabine property. I want Rachel to give up her battle, come home, and marry Matt. I want her to grow trees instead of cotton and be happy doing it. I want her to understand Mary's intentions and forgive her. That's what I want, and I believe there's a chance of getting it."

"You're dreaming, Granddad."

"Maybe so," Percy murmured, sipping his drink.

Amos peered at Percy over the rim of his spectacles. "Rachel has engaged Taylor Sutherland to represent her. You know him?"

"By reputation, mainly. A superb attorney."

"Rachel will have the best in her corner."

"But I'll have the truth and you in mine, Amos."

When Percy saw his friend's horror at the expectation of mounting his defense alone, he added, "And whomever else you wish to bring in. That is, if we go to trial."

"I hope you won't even consider it, Percy," Amos said. "We can present a worthy defense, but it's not likely to influence the outcome, and the publicity will be horrendous. The media will tear your honored name and all you've built to shreds, never mind what they'll do to Mary's memory. Do you really think the fight is worth it? Mary wouldn't want you to finish out your days embroiled in a court battle against Rachel—to bear the brunt of what is admittedly Mary's fault. She would beg you to give Somerset back, to let the chips fall where they may in regard to Rachel's future. And think of Matt, the cloud you'll be leaving him under."

Percy glanced across at his grandson. "Is that how you feel, Matt?"

"I don't want you hurt, Granddad. You're my only concern. Forget about the fallout on me. You've always said that the only true judge of a man's integrity is himself. If he believes he's done nothing wrong, it doesn't matter what anybody else thinks. But I do care what people think about you, how you'll be remembered, and I'm afraid of what a court trial would do to you."

"Giving Somerset back might do worse to me, son."

"How can it?" His tone vibrated with consternation. "Rachel wins the plant and we're stuck with a plantation. There's no win for either of us. I agree with Amos. I say give the fucking place back to her and to hell with her. Let it eat her up like all the Tolivers before her."

Percy raised his brows. "You've lost feeling for her?"

"I've lost hope for her."

"What a tragedy." He pushed down his footrest. "I hear your stomach growling, Amos, and you must be starving, Matt. I'm hungry, too, and that's a good sign. It's late, but we'll all be up most of the night anyway. Let's go downstairs and warm up Savannah's chicken Florentine and wash it down with a couple of bottles of Pinot Grigio. I have until Monday to give my decision, right, Matt?"

"Right," Matt said, exchanging a disconcerted look with Amos that demanded, *Why a week?* Matt stood but remained at his chair as the others filed to the door.

"You coming, Matt?" Percy asked.

"Give me a few minutes."

MATT GAZED UP AT THE painting after the door closed. So much now was clear to him. He had the answers to questions he'd asked himself all his life. Why did his grandmother remain in Atlanta when it was clear that she'd prefer to live here with him and his grandfather? Why had they both been unable to move beyond the sadness of his father's death and recall him in loving, easy terms like the family next door, who had also lost a son in the war? Instead, his grandparents—and even his mother—had talked around his memory as if they might disturb him in the ground. All he'd known of his Marine Corps dad had been learned from the scrapbook of newspaper clippings describing his war exploits and the shadow box of medals and ribbons hanging in the library. Only once had he felt close to him in memory. His grandfather had presented him with a leather photograph holder containing a picture of him as an infant and one of his young and smiling mother. "Your dad was carrying that when he was killed," he'd said. "He'd want you to have it. And something else, too. His final words the last time your mother and I saw him were, 'Tell my son I love him.' Now I want you never to forget those words and keep them here." And he had touched his heart.

The lump in his throat mushroomed, cutting off his air, smarting his eyes. My God. All the wasted lives and years, the tragedies and regrets, the unimaginable grief and guilt…all leading back to that stretch of Toliver land. And now Rachel was continuing its legacy of destruction.

He picked up the recorder. It had been a good idea…his grandfather taping his story. Whatever might befall him now, God forbid, there would be a record of the truth. He'd made mistakes—what man didn't?—but they were forgivable, and God knew he'd paid for them in full measure. Matt supposed he could send a copy to Rachel, but she'd refuse to play it, and even if she did, he doubted that it would change her mind...give her pause, maybe, but not sway her. She might even use it against his grandfather in court as an admission of his guilt.

He removed the cassette and pocketed it. But there was someone else who must hear it—someone for whom it might make all the difference.

Chapter Seventy-two

The next morning—bored, frustrated, and hungry—Rachel hung around in her motel room until nine o'clock before deciding that Percy was not going to call. On the off chance he might, she took time for breakfast at the coffee shop, stopping by the registration desk on her way back to ask if there had been a message for her. The fresh-eyed day clerk informed her there was not. Chagrined, she returned to her room, threw her things into the car, and headed for Dallas.

The silence from Warwick Hall did not bode well. It sent the message that after reading the evidence against him last night, Percy had not caved. But he would, she told herself. It had been foolish of her to have expected a response so soon. Percy Warwick was not an easy man to make cave, even with the odds stacked against him. He'd need time for Amos and a team of the best lawyers he could hire to convince him of the folly of refusing her demands.

Once clear of Marshall, she dialed Taylor's office on the car phone. "On the face of it, you've got a viable case, Rachel," he told her when she'd reported her courthouse findings. "Did you speak with Percy?"

"No, his grandson. I stated my proposition and gave him copies of the letters. When his grandfather reads them, he won't want to go to trial."

"You're convinced of that?"

"I am." Rachel decided not to mention that she'd expected to have Percy's verbal capitulation before she left Marshall. "I told Matt I'd give his grandfather a week to make his decision. If I haven't heard from him by next Monday morning, I'm going to file suit."

"Did his grandson think he'd be amenable to making the trade?"

She considered her answer. " 'Amenable' is not the word he'd choose. Matt's afraid of the effect that giving Somerset back will have on him."

"And how do you feel about that?"

He knew which buttons to push, Taylor did. She said with more asperity than she felt, "I feel the consequences of the alternative would be inestimably worse. I'm sure he'll not choose that."

Taylor's silence led her to believe that he did not share her assurance. "I'm assuming, then, that you and the grandson did not part on cordial terms?"

Once again she selected her words carefully. "He's…very hurt. We were friends once."

"Friends make the worst enemies, Rachel."

She caught her lip between her teeth. "Uh, Taylor, it's like the Indy 500 out here. I'd better hang up."

"I simply want you to be aware of what you're giving up for what you'll be getting," he said, calmly ignoring her evasion. "Carrie's impression from meeting Matt Warwick was that you were much more than friends."

"Is this conversation necessary to my case, Taylor?"

"And also of what you're letting yourself in for if you go through with this," Taylor went on, undeterred. "The Warwicks could make living in Howbutker very difficult for you."

Rachel forced a bitter laugh. "Well, that's nothing new to the ancestry of the Tolivers and Warwicks. We come from warring houses."

"I beg your pardon?"

"I'll tell you about it sometime. Meanwhile, I'll be in Dallas around noon."

"Well, we might as well get started. Don't come to the office. I'll meet you at Carrie's."

He rang the bell of the town house within minutes of her arrival. He entered wearing a rumpled suit and loosened tie and carried two white delicatessen sacks. His immediate objective was the thermostat.

"My daughter thinks she's a polar bear," he grumbled, adjusting the temperature to a higher setting. He held up the sacks. "Lunch. I'll make some hot tea to settle down the goose bumps. What's in those boxes I saw in the SUV?"

Following him into the kitchen, she said, "Ledgers in my grandfather's handwriting. Also private letters and memorabilia of my great-aunt's. I thought they might be helpful, and I... didn't want outsiders pawing through them." At Taylor's raised brow, she added defensively, "It's the least and last thing I'll ever do on her behalf."

"If you say so. Bringing those things was a good idea. We might find something useful." He took off his suit coat, rolled up his sleeves, and stuck the teakettle under the spout. "Hungry?"

"No, but I'll try. I've got to get back into shape." She rubbed her arms. "Not only to face off with the Warwicks, but for body heat."

Taylor gazed around the clinically clean kitchen, whose all-white decor was prevalent throughout the house. "This igloo can't be very cozy for a farmer."

"The company makes up for it, but I won't be here long—only until Monday."

"That so?" He turned up a flame under the teakettle. "Then what?"

"I'll go to Howbutker and move into the Ledbetter house on the plantation. I'm sure Percy won't object. It's used as the manager's office now, but I plan to renovate it for my residence. I've always wanted to live on Somerset."

Taylor opened a cabinet to take out cups and saucers. "You're pretty sure Percy will go along with the trade, aren't you."

"Aren't you? What defense could the Warwicks possibly have against my claim?"

Taylor seemed not to hear her. He set out their plastic container lunches from the paper sacks. "Boiled shrimp salad for you, a fried shrimp po'boy for me."

"Why aren't you answering my question?" she asked as he added boiling water to the teapot.

"Because you don't want to hear that this is not a slam dunk," he said, "and I don't want to ruin your appetite. Let's talk about it on a full stomach."

After clearing the table, Taylor said, "Now, let's get down to business," and asked to see her photocopies of the court records. "Did Matt Warwick say why Percy, knowing he was committing fraud, bought your father's land?"

"Yes, it was as you'd guessed. Times were hard." Briefly she related Matt's explanation, adding that Ollie DuMont had not known the sale was fraudulent.

"Why didn't he simply accept a loan from Percy if he was so desperate?" Taylor asked.

Rachel explained the families' "neither a borrower nor a lender be" policy. "Percy told Matt that Ollie would have lost the store rather than take a cent from him."

Taylor gave her a curious look. "Why don't you believe him?"

She frowned crossly. "What difference does it make whether I do or don't? I have no doubt that Percy wanted to help Uncle Ollie out, but his primary consideration was for the Warwick Lumber Company. That section was a perfect location for his pulp mill, and he saw Uncle Ollie's predicament as a way to get it."

"That doesn't sound like the Percy Warwick I know."

Angrily, Rachel pushed back her chair. "Whose side are you on, anyway, Taylor?" She grabbed the teakettle and thrust it under the full stream from the faucet. "I get the distinct impression that you're riding with the hounds but your heart is with the fox."

"I'm on your side, Rachel," Taylor said, his glance unperturbed, "but it's my job to play devil's advocate. I must point out the weaknesses in our case so that we can prepare for them—because I can assure you, the defense will. They will present the extenuating circumstances as a favorable motive for Percy acting as he did and point out that it was not surprising for a man of his caliber..."

She set the kettle back on the stove and turned to him, a hand on her hip. "And you will present the *extenuating* circumstances as having no bearing on the crime, right?"

Flames were shooting up around the base of the kettle. "Right," he said, leaving his chair to lower the gas. He patted her shoulder. "I'm going outside to bring in those two boxes. Don't burn the house down before I get back."

They sorted through the contents of the boxes together, drinking cups of scalding tea. Taylor declared the ledgers ample corroboration of Miles's signature and rummaged carefully through the other box to look for anything that might further force Percy to return Somerset. His letters and notes to Mary were such items. They proved their affair and the undying affection that had influenced Mary to bequeath the plantation to him rather than to her expected heir. "Sympathy value for our side," he said. "The judge will instruct the jury not to be swayed by sentiment, but they're human. The fact that you were bypassed in favor of Percy will be irrelevant to the case, but it will explain why you want *something* that once belonged to your family." He unwrapped the collection of knitted strips and pink satin ribbons. "What is this?"

"I'm not sure," Rachel said. "It looks as if somebody had an afghan in mind but never got around to completing the project. I know it wasn't Aunt Mary. She was forced to learn needlepoint in finishing school and avoided needles and thread like sandburs."

Taylor fingered the cream strips. "These must have been knitted by someone she cared about for her to have kept them. Her mother, perhaps?"

"I don't know. I never heard Aunt Mary mention her mother, but in any event, she wouldn't have chosen pink ribbons for her daughter's blanket."

"Why not?"

She wondered how best to explain. "Well, because

in our families—the Tolivers and Warwicks and DuMonts—pink represents unforgiveness. You won't find the word in the dictionary, but that's what it is. Red to ask forgiveness, white to say forgiveness granted, pink to say forgiveness withheld. That's why this must be the work of someone outside the family."

Taylor gazed at her, clearly fascinated but uncomprehending. "So what do you folks do? Fly those colors from your housetops to express your sentiments?"

Rachel laughed. "No. We give roses." She reached into the box and withdrew a book. "You can read about it in here. It will explain what I'm talking about better than I ever could and why the Toliver name and Somerset mean so much to me."

Taylor read the title aloud. "*Roses.* I'm intrigued, Rachel. I'll start it tonight." He pulled out a kitchen chair. "Now park yourself. You're going to make two columns headed *A* and *B*," he instructed, and took a legal pad and a pencil from his briefcase. "*A* will represent the defendant's side, *B* the plaintiff's. If this case goes to trial, the jury will hear, determine, and interpret the *facts* in the case. We must make sure they're favorable to our side. To do that, we have to anticipate and prepare for every fact the opposition plans to use in their defense. You say that Percy wanted to meet with you to explain why your great-aunt left him the plantation. You should have met with him, Rachel—"

"No! He has nothing to say that I want to hear."

"Even if it strengthens his case?"

"How could it? If our case hinges on whether or not the sale was legal, I'd like to see his side beat mine."

Taylor slid over the legal pad and pencil. "That's what your two columns will help decide. Write Percy's name next to *A* and yours by *B*."

Rachel wrote. "I think I know where this is going," she said. "What do you want me to write under Percy's?"

"If you have to ask, that's why we're doing this. Percy Warwick is a respected and beloved business tycoon, a man who's played by the rules all his life. His reputation is spotless."

"Until now." Under *A*, Rachel wrote, "Spotless reputation." "Now, what about *B*?"

"You tell me."

She gave him an injured look. "Well, I may not be as beloved or well-known, but I'm honest."

"No doubt," Taylor said, "but the defense will present you as a woman from a poor home in West Texas that her rich great-aunt took to her heart when she was a little girl. She clothed you, educated you, employed you, loved you, and left you an inheritance worth the value of a small country. What more could she have done for you? And now, on top of all her generosity, you want the land she sold to Percy Warwick in the Depression that provided jobs for hundreds of Howbutker County residents and saved the livelihoods of the two people entrusted to care for your father."

"All right, I see your point," she said. "I don't have sympathy on my side—only the hard, cold facts. But I'm not after his property. I'm after Somerset. That's what I've hired you to do, Taylor—convince Percy and his lawyers that the facts don't give him a chance of winning in court."

The lawyer carefully set his cup in the saucer. "When we get through with this list, you'll see that I may not be able to convince them of that. They'd have good reason to take their chances. The only convincing I can do is to make sure they understand that you *will* sue if Percy is not willing to trade. But remember, Rachel, that win or lose your suit, Somerset is lost to you anyway. The court cannot force Percy to return it to you."

"Won't that work to our advantage?" she asked. "I have nothing to lose. Isn't that a powerful spot to be in?"

"It is if you're sure you have nothing to lose."

Rachel regarded him in exasperation. If she couldn't convince her own lawyer that she meant business, how would he convince Percy's? "All I need to know, Taylor—list or no list—is whether I have a good chance of winning if we go to court."

Taylor met her irritated gaze with a benign smile. "Not to appear immodest, but considering that I'm representing you, I'd say that, yes, you have a good chance of winning—*if* you want to call it that. You could end up with a huge award for damages or be awarded the return of your father's property along with most everything it supports."

Rachel relaxed with a sigh of relief. "Then that should be persuasion enough for Percy Warwick. I know he looks good on paper, Taylor, but the fact is he and my great-aunt defrauded my father."

"So what?" he asked idly, and looked ready to duck if Rachel threw the teapot at him.

"*So what?*" She appeared ready to grab the handle. "So Aunt Mary and Percy's deception cost me my mother, that's *so what*!"

"Ah," Taylor said, "now we're getting somewhere." He drew the pad toward him and picked up the pencil. "Tell me about that, Rachel. Tell me what the court should hear from your side."

Chapter Seventy-three

The week dragged by. No word came from Percy. Rachel grew to detest the cold ambience of the town house, spending most of her time on the sun-warmed patio waiting for the phone to ring. The day after her return from Marshall, Taylor had telephoned Amos to introduce himself and leave his private number. Amos had wedged a stick in their spokes when he said that Percy would contact Rachel personally with his decision—a move that had rendered her a virtual prisoner in the house since she was then obliged to hang by the phone. She angrily told Taylor that it was a maneuver calculated to give Percy a last chance to justify himself, but if he tried, she'd refer him to Taylor's office and hang up.

But so far, Percy had not allowed her that opportunity.

Her anxiety and loneliness had deepened by the day. At first it had seemed a good idea, while she was still so shaky, to live with a friend who could provide emotional support and comfort in the uncertain days ahead. Now, in less than a week, Rachel had come to regret accepting Carrie's invitation to move into the extra bedroom. The all-white surroundings reminded her of a medical lab, and Carrie was rarely around to offer the companionship she'd expected. She was gone all day—first to her demanding job at the public relations firm where she was in charge of new accounts—and in the evenings as well, either working late or meeting clients for dinner.

"Lamb chop, I'm so *sorry!*" Carrie had wailed Thursday night when she came home late to find Rachel washing the pan used to make herself another omelet. "I had no idea when I asked you to move in that I'd be so busy. But I'll tell you what. We're going to a party tomorrow night, then out shopping Saturday and meeting some friends of mine for dinner. Percy can leave his message on the answering machine. No buts about it, now. I insist. You're starting to grow algae!"

That night—or rather, in the wee hours of Friday morning—Rachel had said to herself that if she could only get through the next three days, come Monday, she was out of here and out of Carrie's and her father's hair. Percy would have called by then, agreeing to her terms, and she'd discontinue Taylor's services and move to the Ledbetter house.

Somehow she'd managed the party at somebody's penthouse, Carrie's shopping spree on Saturday, and dinner that night with her friends at Old Warsaw. Both nights they'd returned to messages left only for Carrie.

Today was Sunday, and she'd awakened with the sensation that ants were crawling under her skin. She'd shivered her way into the kitchen to make coffee and found a note from Carrie. Brunch at the Mansion on Turtle Creek was off. She'd been summoned back to the office to meet a looming Monday deadline. Good! Rachel thought. Feeling as she did, she would have been miserable company over champagne and eggs Benedict.

The day inched along. She could not sit still. With metronomic regularity, she was in and out through the sliding door of the patio. She drank endless cups of hot tea to soothe her nerves and warm her raised flesh. The phone, hanging in pristine white from the white kitchen wall, became her most dreaded enemy, her dearest friend. What was taking Percy so long? What was there to think over? He had only one choice, and he knew it. Steadfastly, she refused to consider the unbelievable—that he would reject her offer.

Back sitting on the patio for a countless time, she heard a neighborhood church bell begin its Sunday toll. Eleven times the chimes rang out, sending an ominous chill through her. Percy would wait until the eleventh hour to inform her of his decision, she was now convinced. Simply to keep her on pins and needles, he'd keep his hand off the receiver until tomorrow morning shortly before her lawyer's office opened, then telephone. She should not expect a call before then. That's when the phone would ring.

Vexed, she picked up the ancient tome of the unpublished history of the Tolivers she'd brought out to pass the time. Odd that Aunt Mary had never mentioned the history or shown it to her... perhaps because it contained nothing she didn't already know of Toliver lore. To the sound of the church bells dying away and the buzz of the last of Indian summer's bees in the queen's crown, she opened the aged cover and began to read.

PERCY LISTENED TO THE OVERHEAD toll calling the congregation to the First Methodist Church of Howbutker, where he'd presented himself a willing worshipper nearly every Sunday of his life, except for the interruptions of his war service and business trips. He'd lost track of the names and faces who had filled the pulpit. Most stayed as long as the bishop allowed, for the church coffers were full, the needs of the flock few, and life in Howbutker simple and undemanding. Not one of them had said much of anything to inspire or instruct him for many years. He came for the peace, the music, and a kind of solace he received nowhere else.

This morning, he was in special need of solace. All week, he'd heard arguments debating his case. He'd sat in a smoke of them for five days, listening to Amos and the crackerjack team of lawyers called in, and once everything was considered—even the strong possibility that Rachel could wind up with nothing but lost time and lawyers' bills—the consensus was that he should return Somerset. As a matter of fact, the out-of-towners could hardly refrain from scratching their heads over what the delay was all about. Why would Percy even remotely consider any other decision but giving back the plantation to spare his company the expense and disruption of a lawsuit and himself the stench of scandal?

And still he could not say the words they wanted to hear, including Matt. Matt was in Atlanta now, springing a surprise visit on Lucy. He'd informed his grandfather Friday after the conclave broke up for the weekend that he would take the plane to see his grandmother and not be back until Sunday afternoon. Percy had nodded in understanding. Matt saw Lucy in a different light now and needed to make up for the years of his misassumptions. Percy had been sorry to see him go at such a time, but he was happy for Lucy. They'd become closer now, and that was good. When he was gone, Lucy would be all Matt had left.

He closed his eyes. That would be soon, he believed. Mornings now he was surprised to find himself awakening. He was tired, weary of living. A man out of dreams was out of life, and his were spent. Not one had come true, not the important ones, anyhow—

those of a happy marriage, a loving family, a house filled with children and grandchildren. Ironic how— even in death—his Mary had robbed him of the last dream he really hadn't known he'd nurtured—Matt and Rachel falling in love, marrying, uniting their empires, living happily ever after under one roof, the war of the roses over at last. But Mary had killed that dream when she left him Somerset.

The organ prelude began, quieting the murmurs among the congregants. Never came this moment of a Sunday morning but that he did not look across the aisle up two rows and remember Ollie and Matthew and Wyatt. There were Sundays when he could all but see them sitting there in spit-and-polish order, Ollie's pate gleaming and the boys' hair still damp and showing the coercive rake of comb and brush. The backs of their heads, their profiles, were indelibly imprinted upon his memory. Sometimes he closed his eyes as if in prayer, as he was doing now, and he could see them lined along the pew, Ollie's plump shoulders trimmed by the masterful cut of his suit, Wyatt's hunched typically forward, Matthew's squared against the seat. How he missed them.

The service began. As he rose with the congregation to sing the first hymn, he sensed Amos's pointed concern and frustration from six rows back. Percy sympathized. There was no one more maddening than an old fart who couldn't decide what direction to take, though his way was as clear as a West Texas highway. He knew what he must do, but still he was here today in his own Gethsemane, asking that this cup pass from him...that he be spared the anguish he must face tomorrow. Perhaps somewhere in the sermon was a nugget of divine wisdom that would direct him to another path.

The reading of the Word commenced. Percy's mind wandered, waiting for the message. He thought of Mary. He couldn't remember when his prayers had finally been answered and the sexual fires for her had died—the fire, but not the flame. It had been such a blessing, the final banking of the embers. What a relief to feel simply love and nothing else. Right now, it was as if she were inside his head pacing back and forth...back and forth...with those long strides of hers, slender hands wringing. *Percy, Percy, what are we going to do?*

Damned if I know! he answered, and looked about him to see if he'd spoken aloud. No one was paying any attention to him, but the minister had him locked in his gaze. He had raised a forefinger, not in admonition, but as if in emphasis of some point directed solely at Percy. His ears pricked. Here it comes! he thought.

"Hearken to me, you who pursue deliverance, you who seek the Lord..." The minister was quoting from the Old Testament, but Percy had missed the book, chapter, and verse. "Look to the rock from which you were hewn, and to the quarry from which you were dug."

The minister's eye roved on, and Percy grappled to understand the application of the words. *Now what in hell am I to do with that?* No answer for him *there*. He'd never put much stock in the rock from which he'd been hewn or the quarry from which he was dug. That was Mary's pitch, the song and dance that had caused all their woe.

The service came to an end with "Rock of Ages" sung as the closing hymn. Percy rose to his feet slowly, thoughtfully, hymnal in hand. The sermon had been about rock. *You who pursue deliverance, look to the rock from which you were hewn, and to the quarry from which you were dug....*

Percy gripped the back of the seat, the hymnal nearly falling from his hand. Joy lit his face like sunlight breaking through clouds. Of course! Look to the rock! That's it! he exulted. By damn, he had his answer.

Lucy sat in the late morning sunlight of her parlor, the room mellow with the Sunday peal of the carillon from the church tower on the corner. Its golden cadence struck terror in her heart. The sound was a pitiless reminder that time was running out for Percy and Matt—even for that little chip off the old block waiting by her phone in Dallas, though she didn't know it. By this time tomorrow, Percy would have answered her ultimatum, and another generation of lives would be skewed off course by one Toliver's bulldogged obsession with Somerset.

It was as she'd guessed. Mary had detached her great-niece from that cursed body of land to protect her from the consequences she'd suffered at its hands. And holy Mother of God, what consequences!

She was still numb from hearing Percy's replay of them on the tape Matt had spun for her Friday night. He'd arrived unannounced, and at first when Betty told her he was in the living room, she'd thought he'd come to report that his grandfather had died. She'd popped up from her chair in such a fright that the blood had whooshed from her head, and she'd had to grab hold of her dressing table to keep from hitting the floor. Matt had found her there, swaying, and rushed to catch her before she fell.

"*Gabby!* It's not what you think. Granddad's all right!" he'd cried, and snatched her to him as if she were a child he'd saved from certain death. She'd begun to cry—from relief, regret, or the surprise and intensity of Matt's feeling, only the saints knew.

"Then what brings you here?" she'd asked, looking up through her flooded eyes from the massive environs of his chest and shoulders.

"I've brought something you need to hear. You have a tape recorder?"

They'd gone outside in the growing dusk to hear the tape while the moon rose and highlighted her lunar garden. Neither said anything during the playing. She'd listened, still as the stone on which she sat, now and then reaching for another tissue from the box Betty had thoughtfully provided. When the tape was over and the recorder clicked off, she'd snatched another Kleenex and plugged it to her raw nose.

"Now we know," she'd said.

He'd nodded. "Now we know."

"Lots of blame to go around."

"And to forgive, Gabby."

"And to forgive." Percy's voice was inside her, touching all the still raw places, making her ashamed of her nastiness, though taking its cause upon himself, never blaming her... not once in his story. She had wiped her puffy eyes and added the tissue to the wadded pile at her feet. "I hope you'll believe that I never would have revealed that Matthew was Percy and Mary's son. That was an idle threat and base of me, but I never would have told even if your grandfather had filed for divorce. I hope you'll believe me."

"Of course I do. And Granddad does, too. It wasn't your threat that kept him from divorcing you."

"Why, then?"

"Because he knows you still love him." His voice had come to her gruffly in the moonlight, reminding her of Wyatt's.

She'd reddened and hoped that in the darkness he couldn't see. "Still... I held the threat over him until the day of Mary's death—a shameful thing to do. I... just couldn't bear to let him go. But now... you tell him to go ahead and file for divorce. I won't stand in his way."

He'd reached for her hand. "Granddad's not going to divorce you, Gabby."

"How do you know?"

"Because he told me so."

She'd given in to a spell of crying again and, when she was down to sniffles, had said, "Your father did a wonderful thing sending him that painting. I'm glad he forgave him. Of course, I never knew about the red rose Percy slipped into the book he took to Korea. Imagine Wyatt familiar with the legend of the roses. . . . So what now? What do you think Rachel will do?"

It had broken her heart to see the grief in his eyes. "Repeat her great-aunt's mistake."

Damn the little witch, Lucy had thought.

And now Matt was gone, and here she sat, helpless to save the men she loved. Twenty minutes ago, as he was leaving, he'd asked, "Will you be all right, Gabby?" the blue eyes he'd inherited from her saying she had only to utter the word and he wouldn't go. Another unprecedented first.

"I'll be all right, Matt. Go see to your grandfather."

He'd left the tape, one of several copies, he'd said. It sat on the coffee table, a five-by-seven cassette holding the misdirected journeys of two lifetimes. What a tragedy that Rachel would never hear it. It could save the day and all the tomorrows to come.

"Mopin's not going to help," Betty said from the doorway. "Maybe you shouldn't have canceled your bridge party today."

"I couldn't have concentrated. What's that?"

Betty held out a slip of paper. "I don't know if Mister Matt intended to throw this away or not. I found it on the floor next to the trash basket in his room."

Lucy examined it. It was a sheet of notepaper bearing the name of a motel in Marshall, Texas. Scribbled across it was a telephone number preceded by a Dallas area code. A light popped on in Lucy's head. Matt had said he'd tracked Rachel to a motel in Marshall where they'd had their last confab. She was staying with a friend in Dallas, the daughter of her lawyer. This must be a contact number where Matt could reach her. An idea started to form.

"Bring me the phone, Betty," she said.

"Uh-oh. I know that look. What are you up to now?"

"I'll tell you later."

She dialed directory assistance, and an operator gave her the name and address of the number on the notepaper. Carrie Sutherland. Lucy then dialed the number of a wealthy friend who'd long shared her companionship. "Of course," he said when he heard her request. "You'll find my plane and pilot waiting for you, and I'll arrange for a car and driver to meet you at your destination. Have a good flight."

Lucy rang for Betty. "I'm going on a mission out of town," she announced. "A very important one. I'll need a taxi to take me to the airport."

"How long you goin' to be gone?"

"As long as it takes. I should be back tonight, but pack my overnight case anyway. Now scoot, dear girl. Time's of the essence."

Lucy picked up the tape on her way out of the room. A stroke of luck had opened her cage door, and she was ready to fly.

Chapter Seventy-four

Rachel looked up from the final page of the family history and took her dumbstruck gaze to the pink explosion of queen's crown, busy with pollination, draped along the wrought-iron fence. Fertilization in action, she thought numbly, an accomplishment that seemed to have eluded the Somerset Tolivers. The buzz mocked the facts she'd never known or realized. None who had possessed the plantation had been prolific sires or bearers of children, and only one child in each generation had lived to inherit. Thomas and Vernon had been the sole heirs in theirs, and Aunt Mary's only child had died in hers, leaving, with her father's death, only Rachel as the remaining Toliver. She stared at the antiquated volume. Did she hold here the explanation of the Toliver curse?

It wasn't possible. There was no such thing as a curse. But her great-grandfather had believed in it, and so had Aunt Mary. She'd told Amos that she had saved her from it. Dear God...had Aunt Mary feared that by leaving her Somerset, she was sentencing her to the barren state she'd known? She recalled the picture of Matthew DuMont displayed on Aunt Mary's dressing room table, the heartache in the words written on the back. Her father had described him as a wonderful fellow—kind and patient, teaching him English and allowing him to participate in the big-boy games he and Wyatt Warwick had played on their front lawns. Aunt Mary and Uncle Ollie had been devastated when he died, he'd said. They had gone on with their lives, but life was gone. There had been no other children. . . .

Had Aunt Mary hoped to spare her the tragedy she'd suffered?

The kitchen phone shrilled, sending the bees into a frenzy. She jumped. A flash of intuition told her the name of the caller. She laid the book on the patio table through a second ring, then got up with robotic stiffness to slide back the door and enter the all-white kitchen. She removed the white receiver from the wall. "Hello."

"Good afternoon, Rachel. This is Percy Warwick."

She listened emotionless as he briefly informed her of his decision, wished her well, and hung up. Slowly, she returned to the patio and sat an hour in the sun, reflecting to the hum of bees in the queen's crown. Afterward, her own decision made, she dialed Taylor Sutherland.

A half hour later, the doorbell rang. Rachel surmised

that Carrie had forgotten her house keys again or Taylor had come around to hold her hand. A squint through the peephole proved both guesses wrong. A mound of snow white hair as fluffy as cotton candy met her eye. She moved her gaze downward to encounter a pair of oddly familiar blue eyes fixed unflinchingly on the glass eye in the door. She opened it inquiringly. The woman had arrived in a black limousine, its liveried driver propped against the hood, snapping a lighter to a cigarette. Her visitor—short and round, in her mid-eighties, and wearing a suit the color of her eyes—reminded Rachel of a cupcake. "May I help you?" she said.

The woman blinked. "Hannah was right," she said. "You're the mirror image of Mary, only less…" She peered at Rachel more closely. "Intense."

"Excuse me?"

"I'm Matt's grandmother," the woman announced. "Lucy Warwick. May I come in?"

THE TIME WAS SIX O'CLOCK. The thermostat had been adjusted, and the town house was at a comfortable temperature. To hell with Carrie's posted monition. The telephone had rung twice and gone unanswered. Rachel had not moved from her chair once Matt's grandmother clicked on the tape recorder. Through the living room window, at some level of awareness, she registered the driver pacing by the limousine, cigarette smoke streaming like dragon fire from his nostrils. The man was probably hot and thirsty and needed to use the facilities, but she could not have stirred from her chair to offer water and a bathroom if her life had depended on it.

There had been no exchange of pleasantries, no time to offer coffee or tea. Wielding her cane, Lucy Warwick had thumped straight into the living room, sat down, and unsnapped her purse. "You're going to listen to this, girl, whether you want to or not," she'd said, extracting a tape recorder and plunking it on the table. "There are things you don't know about you Tolivers and a hell of a lot you don't know about the man you seem bent on sending to an early death. So sit down and listen and then I'll be gone, and you can do what you have to do."

So she had listened, her pity for Percy and Aunt Mary starting as a trickle and then building to a full stream as the tape unreeled the hidden years of their tragic lives. Overlaying it, she recognized her own short history, like the superimposed reflection of her face over the young Mary Toliver's in the glass of the photographer's portrait hanging in the library. She'd often thought, standing before it, that if a picture of her in the same pose hung beside it, their faces would line up feature for feature, plane for plane...as her life so far had repeated Aunt Mary's.

"There now, that's done," Lucy said, whisking the tape back into her purse. She snapped it shut and planted the cane to rise. "I hope that tomorrow you'll take into account what you've heard here today."

"You came too late, Mrs. Warwick," Rachel said. "Percy called earlier to tell me his decision, and I've contacted my lawyer with mine. By now he's informed Amos Hines."

Lucy's plump face whitened, then fell. "Oh, I see...."

"No, I don't think you do. Please don't go, and I'll explain."

"I'm in no mood for whitewash, young lady."

"How about the unvarnished truth?"

Chapter Seventy-five

ATLANTA, GEORGIA, A WEEK LATER

Crossing the hall to the parlor where her mistress was hosting two tables of bridge, Betty glanced through the screen of the decorative outer door to see a chauffeured black Lincoln Town Car drive up before the town house. The chauffeur hopped out immediately, and Betty nearly dropped the plate of sandwiches she'd been on her way to serve when he opened the door to the passenger in the backseat.

"Oh, my goodness," she said aloud, setting the plate on the foyer table and smoothing her apron. "Oh, my goodness."

She'd never met him or seen him except for newspaper shots when he was younger, but she knew who he was. She watched him climb out, elderly as you might expect, but matching the image she'd had of him in her mind all these years. She'd pictured a tall, distinguished man, wearing fine clothes and carrying himself in a way that communicated power without shouting it... a true *massa*. Her awe turned to dismay when the chauffeur handed him a vase containing a single red rose. Miss Lucy hated roses.

Betty hurriedly closed the pocket doors of the parlor, muffling the between-hands chatter, and stationed herself before the screen. The chauffeur, resettled behind the wheel of the limousine, had laid his head back and tipped his hat forward, as if anticipating time for a snooze.

"Good afternoon," she said through the screen as Percy reached the porch. "Mister Percy Warwick, I'm thinkin'."

He acknowledged her assumption with a nod of his silver head. "Betty," he returned as familiarly as if he'd known her for years. "Is my wife at home?"

"She is, sir." Betty unlocked the door and held it open for him. "She's playin' bridge with her lady friends in the parlor."

"Her Sunday gathering, I presume?"

"Yessir. Would you mind waitin' in the foyer while I tell her? I... don't believe she's expectin' you."

"No, she isn't," Percy said, "but I'm sure she won't mind the interruption." He held out the vase. "And will you please give her this?"

"Oh, sir—" Betty's face screwed up. "She don't like roses."

He smiled. "She will this one."

The plate of sandwiches forgotten, Betty slid open

one of the pocket doors and closed it behind her, holding the vase at arm's length as if it were a dripping diaper. "Miss Lucy, you have a visitor."

Lucy eyed the rose balefully. "Why are you whispering? And what in God's name is that?"

"It's a rose, Lucy," one of the bridge ladies enlightened her.

Lucy snapped a look at her. "I can see that, Sarah Jo. Where did it come from?"

"Your husband," Betty said. "He's in the foyer."

All heads in hues denoting ages over seventy turned in concert to Lucy, who shot up from the bridge table, sloshing coffee into saucers. "What? Percy is here?"

"Yes'm. Outside in the foyer."

"But he can't be...."

The parlor doors slid open. "But I am," Percy said, entering. "Hello, Lucy."

Now all gawping mouths and dilated eyes turned to the dark-suited figure of legend and speculation. He nodded and smiled. "Ladies, would you mind excusing us? I have something urgent to discuss with my wife."

Immediately, the ladies rolled back their chairs and hastily collected handbags and canes. The more audacious among them shook hands with Percy as they filed past and murmured that it was nice to have met Lucy's husband at last. Lucy stood as if flash frozen and Betty as if uncertain whether to go with the group or stay with the rose. "Uh, Miss Lucy, what do you want me to do with this?"

Lucy snapped to. "Take it to the kitchen and add water to it," she said. "I'll call you if we need anything." Left alone with her husband, she said, "What are you doing here, Percy?"

"After what you did for us, surely you know?"

"Rachel had already spoken with her lawyer by the time I saw her. I could have saved myself a trip. What good did I do?" The backs of her wobbly legs had found her chair, and she managed to lower herself into it with a semblance of grace.

"You confirmed to her that she'd made the right decision. Because of you, she and Matt now have a chance."

"I don't know that I did him any favor."

Percy chuckled and rolled out another bridge chair, seating himself with the ease of the master of the house. "We'll have to wait and see, but my bet's on the two of them living happily ever after. He's gone after her. She took off to San Angelo to help a laid-up A and M classmate run his cotton farm until he's back on his feet."

Short of breath, she fought the urge to fan herself. "Tell me, what made you call Rachel's bluff? Weren't you taking an awful gamble with our grandson's birthright?"

"Maybe, but I looked to the rock and the quarry, you see."

"The rock and quarry?"

"From the scriptures. Isaiah 51, verse 1."

Lucy looked at him in exasperation. "You're not going to be more specific than that?"

"I gambled she'd do the right thing—like her great-aunt."

Lucy dropped her gaze to wipe at a spill on the bridge table lest she appear to be absorbing his features. Age had done its work, but not unkindly. His looks could still break her heart. "What's the rose for?"

"Oh, just a general asking forgiveness for the way things turned out—to say I'm sorry they couldn't have been better for you."

An ache ballooned in her throat, and she clamped her jaw tight, daring herself to show tears. It was a moment before she trusted herself to speak. "They weren't any better for you, Percy, due to me. And I wronged Mary terribly. If only I'd known from the beginning how you felt about each other, I'd have had…other expectations. I'd have made do with your friendship. It would have been enough."

"You deserved more, Lucy."

She gave a short "*Humph*" and said, "Didn't we all? Matt tells me you're not going to divorce me. Is that true?"

"It's true."

"Well, that's…nice of you." She made a racket in her throat in her attempt to unclog it. "What are you going to do with Somerset?"

"I'll bestow it on Texas A and M, Rachel's alma

mater, as an agricultural experimental center. The Ledbetter place will become a museum in commemoration of the contributions the generations of Tolivers have made to Texas cotton."

She felt her face flare with admiration. "Well, call you King Solomon. I'm sure Rachel will be very pleased." His presence, as always, warmed the room...like sunlight on a winter's day. "Do you think she'll be able to forgive you and Mary for denying her father knowledge of his inheritance?"

"Only time will tell." He said it with a small smile that suggested the reality they both shared—neither had a lot left. "But speaking of that," he said, "one of the reasons I came was to ask you to consider coming home if things work out between Matt and Rachel. As you recall, there's plenty of room for you to have your own space, and I'm sure they'd want their children to have a great-grandmother around."

Her eyes were now thoroughly stinging and her throat incapable of swallowing. Urgent, he'd said to the girls. She brushed at some cake crumbs caught by her bosom. "I'll...certainly give it some thought. Anything else?"

"No...I don't think so," he said, and to her dismay he got to his feet, a little creakily, but still in the slow way he used to draw to his full height and square his shoulders—always a turn-on for her. "I only wanted to bring you the rose and to express my gratitude for coming to our rescue."

She forced herself to rise as well and her lip not to tremble. It seemed only yesterday they'd faced each other in this way. "Good-bye, Percy," she said, repeating her words from the train station forty years ago.

She saw the same memory float into his eyes, but unlike then, this time he placed his hand around her shoulders and smiled. "For a little while, Lucy," he said, and she closed her eyes to better remember the brief touch of his lips upon her cheek.

Betty, with her uncanny sense of timing, arrived to show him out. Lucy remained glued to the spot until she heard the front door close and Betty return. "Well, well, well!" Betty said.

Lucy smiled softly. "I'd say so," she said.

MATT STOOD A MOMENT BY the Range Rover, taking in his surroundings. He was parked before a sprawling white clapboard farmhouse bordered on both sides and beyond by fields of burgeoning cotton. A couple of mechanical cotton pickers were lined up along a service road, and in the distance a lone figure—a man, not Rachel—worked on a stretch of irrigation pipe, but otherwise there was no other sight or sound of human activity to break the snoozing quiet of the early Sunday afternoon. No pickups or other vehicles were about. He'd expected to find Rachel's BMW parked in the yard, confirming that he'd come to the right place. The peace increased his apprehension. Against such a tranquil backdrop, how could he bear the shattering news that Rachel wanted nothing more to do with him?

He'd been ready to refuel the plane and go to her the minute he landed back in Howbutker and heard the great news, but his grandfather had admonished him to wait. "Give her space, son—time to deal with the issues she still has to work out."

He had agreed, though he'd worried that every day that passed might give Rachel—the woman he loved now more than ever—greater reason to tell him to go to hell. It had occurred to him that there might be something going on between her and the classmate she'd gone to help. Carrie had described him as an old A and M buddy—a cotton farmer like herself—when he'd called to get her address. "Married?" he couldn't resist asking, and she'd said archly, "Well, now, that's for me to know and you to find out, big boy."

He heard a clump, clump, clump in answer to his ring, and his heart fell a fraction when a boyishly handsome man opened the door, as tall as himself and big enough, even on crutches with his leg in a hip cast, to make him think twice about muscling his way in. "Afternoon. What can I do for you?" he asked.

"Excuse the interruption. I'm looking for a friend of mine—Rachel Toliver."

"That so?" he said. "And who might you be?"

"Matt Warwick."

"Ah, so." He held him in an appraising gaze for a few seconds, then shouted over his shoulder, *"Honey!"*

Matt's heart sank lower until a pretty blonde appeared with two small children trailing behind and a third on the way, judging from the bulge of her apron over her dress. "We've got company asking for Rachel."

The young woman smiled. "Well, get out of the way, Luke, so we can let him in. Kids, go wash your hands and get ready to eat. Hi," she said to Matt, "I'm Leslie, and this big lug is my husband, Luke Riley. You must be Matt Warwick. Come on in. Rachel's been expecting you."

"She has?" Matt said in astonishment.

Her husband had apparently held off his grin until then. It broke across his face, big and sappy, as he stuck out his hand. "Now, honey, I don't think you were supposed to tell him that," he said with a wink at Matt. "Howdy, Matt."

"Well, knowing Rachel, she might not get the point across. You're just in time for Sunday dinner, Matt. I hope you like fried chicken."

His head whirling, his heart about to race out of him, Matt said he was crazy about fried chicken and followed Leslie, Luke thumping behind him, into a large kitchen sparkling with sunshine and redolent with the aroma of the chicken sizzling on the stove. Rachel glanced up from her task of setting the table, the most beautiful sight he had ever seen. "Hello, Rachel," he said.

She nodded, color mounting in her cheeks. "Matt."

In the silence, Leslie glanced from one to the other and said, "Just a thought, but maybe you guys would like to take a walk before we sit down. The chicken won't be ready for a while."

"A good idea," Rachel said. She removed her apron from over an elegant sleeveless sheath and without a word led Matt out, Luke giving him the thumbs-up behind her back.

They walked without speaking down a path to a white-fenced paddock, Matt conscious of the smooth length of her brown arm and the way a couple of tendrils of her hair, swept on top of her head, curled alluringly at her neckline. He guessed she and Leslie must have attended church services earlier, and he wondered how anybody sitting a pew behind her had been able to concentrate on the sermon. At the fence, he set his foot on the bottom rail and draped his arms over the top, his attention on a fine chestnut stallion munching grass. "I understand you were expecting me," he said.

"I knew Carrie couldn't keep a secret."

"Did you want her to?"

"I was counting on her loose lips."

He let out a silent breath of relief. "Granddad said your lawyer called Amos with your decision to drop the lawsuit even before you heard the tape. You never intended to go through with it, did you?"

The chestnut discovered them and whinnied, the greeting obviously for Rachel. She stuck her hand through the railing and twiddled her fingers, and he sauntered over. "My intent was to convince your grandfather and Amos that I would."

"Why didn't you go through with it? You had us, Rachel."

"Somerset had already caused too much pain. And what would I want with a paper-making plant?"

"To exact vengeance, maybe?"

She shook her head. "Not my style."

His eyes watered. Was there ever such a woman? "Well, I'm very grateful to you."

"Is that why you came—to thank me?"

"Among other reasons." They were talking side to side, like men do when they are discussing the weather or other innocuous subjects.

"Such as?" She stroked the white markings on the stallion's forehead.

"Well, for starters, Amos sent you something from Mary that she asked him to hold for you on the day she died. She told him that he'd know the best time to give them to you."

"Them?"

"Her pearls."

She stopped her stroking. "Oh," she said, and out of the corner of his eye he caught the movement of a hard swallow down her throat and the rapid flutter of her lashes. "I'd say the timing is perfect. What else?"

"I thought you'd like to know Granddad's plans for Somerset."

He detected a loss of breath. "Tell me," she said, placing both hands on the railing. By the time he'd finished explaining, she'd brought one of them to the neck of her dress. "How...thoughtful and sensitive of him," she said in a voice of quiet awe. "I'm so pleased. Aunt Mary would be, too."

"I also came to ask what *your* plans are," he said, dropping his arms from the paddock fence, his vocal cords losing a little power. "I suppose you'll...stake out another Somerset somewhere and grow cotton and acorn squash."

They were addressing one another side to side again. "Oh, I'll stay in some aspect of the agricultural business," she said, "but cotton and acorn squash have lost their savor for me."

"You'll grow other crops, you mean."

"No. I mean I have no desire to farm anymore—not on anybody else's land."

"Buy your own."

"It wouldn't be the same thing."

He took his arms from the fence and turned to face her. "I don't understand, Rachel. I thought farming was your passion, your calling in life—all you ever wanted to do. Do you mean to give it up?"

The horse whinnied, annoyed at being ignored, and she gave him her hand to nuzzle. "Did you ever hear of a baseball player named Billy Seton?" she asked.

Matt nodded, puzzled. "He played first base for the New York Yankees in the early seventies."

She gave the stallion a final pat and walked over to a hydrant to rinse her hands. "He was from my hometown. When they traded him, he left the game. He's coaching it now. He discovered that his passion for playing baseball and his dream of playing for the New York Yankees were one and the same—inextricably interwoven—and when one part was missing, the other didn't work. Once the Yankees let him go, he had no desire to play for another team. Now do you understand?"

He did—completely. The blood rushed to his ears. He whipped out his handkerchief and handed it to her. "In other words, farming any land but a Toliver's gives you no cause to be a farmer at all."

"I couldn't have stated it better myself."

He watched her dry her hands, resisting the desire to take her face between his hands and kiss her eyes, her mouth, her throat, to draw her deep into himself and hold her there forevermore. The horse had followed them and tossed his head over the fence. *What are you waiting for, boy?*

"Well, in that case," he said, forcing his voice steady, "you might be interested in my proposition."

She handed him his handkerchief. "Try me."

"I'm looking for a partner to help me run a stretch of land along the Sabine. You might say it's Toliver land. I believe you once said you had a vested interest in it, as a matter of fact."

"I know nothing about growing trees."

"Well, actually, it's not much different from cultivating acorn squash or cotton plants. You put a little seedling into the ground and watch it grow."

Her eyes were growing moist. She reached again for his handkerchief. "I suppose that's not too far afield from what I'm accustomed to. May I have some time to think about it?"

He looked at his watch. "Sure. That chicken's not ready yet."

She smiled. "Aren't you taking a chance on me as a partner?"

"Not at all," he said, drawing her into his arms, where she belonged.

"Why not?" she asked, lifting her face.

"Don't you remember? I always bet on what I believe is a sure thing."